# The Unicorn Conspiracy

QUENTIN COPE

THE UNICORN CONSPIRACY

COPYRIGHT & DISCLAIMER

The moral right of Quentin P Cope to be identified as the author of this work has been assessed in accordance with the Copyright, Design and Patents Act, 1988.

This book is a work of fiction. However, some real events may have been referred to or been described and unless otherwise noted, the author and the publisher make no explicit guarantees as to the accuracy of the information contained in this book and in some cases, names of people and places have been altered to protect their privacy. Any other resemblance to actual persons, living or dead, events or locales is entirely coincidental.

No part of this book may be reproduced, stored in a retrieval system, or transmitted by any means without the written permission of the author.

Copyright © 2012 Quentin P Cope

All rights reserved.

ISBN-10:1478136766
ISBN-13:978-1478136767

MINIMUM RRP IN PRINT

USD: 17.99. GBP: 13.99. EURO: 15.99.

Available in Kindle from Amazon

# DEDICATION

To Geoffrey who encouraged me to do it.
To Jackie who allowed me to do it.
To Poppy who interrupted me whilst doing it
To you, the reader, for whom I did it in the first place.

THE UNICORN CONSPIRACY

# ACKNOWLEDGMENTS

With grateful thanks to the Marine Corps Staff College for producing such a detailed and relatively unbiased account of the happenings in what became known as the Jebel Akhdar war in the Oman from 1954 to 1959.

THE UNICORN CONSPIRACY

# PROLOGUE

During the September of 1973 world politics are changing rapidly. Only two years previously, President Nixon had ended the 'Bretton Woods' agreement which effectively cut the link of the value of gold to the US Dollar, known as the Gold Standard. The US economy is falling in to rapid decline, being dragged down by an unwinnable war in Vietnam that has been rumbling along for close to eighteen years. The world Stock Markets have crashed in relative terms since the beginning of the year with US GDP falling from 7.2% to zero and still heading south. US Banks are being bailed out left, right and centre with the Stock Exchange losing over 70% of its value since the beginning of the year. Relations between the US and Russia have declined since Nixon visited China in February 1972, at a time when Sino-Soviet relations were at an all time low and border incidents were increasing in intensity. Despite an accord between the US and Soviets signed on June 22$^{nd}$ 1973, packaged as an agreement to prevent Nuclear War, the cold war actually continued unabated.

Since enacting the disastrous Nixon-Kissinger plan that turned in to operation 'Giant Lance' in 1969, where the Americans attempted to goad the Soviets in to starting a nuclear war, Brezhnev considered Nixon a complete egotistical megalomaniac and his word, or signature on any document relating to détente to be completely worthless. Within a couple of months, with the word 'Watergate' lingering on almost everyone's lips, to the disgrace of a fumbling US Government, Brezhnev would be proven correct.

On January 1st a severely worried Europe signed up to an enlargement of the 1957 European Communities charter to include the UK. This group was now to become a powerful political and trading entity consisting of Belgium, France, Germany, Italy, Luxembourg, Netherlands, Denmark, Ireland, UK, Greece, Portugal & Spain. The US is increasingly worried that a united Europe would not be in America's best interests and begins to strategically retreat politically and militarily from NATO commitments in Europe. By July 1973, the dollar has plunged on the international exchange markets from a 1962 benchmark of $1.0 to $0.67 with inflation doubling from the previous year to 6.6%. The UK has ended its political and military support for the Persian Gulf Sheikdoms, known as the Trucial States, on December 1st 1971 and now the newly formed, uneasy alliance known as the United Arab Emirates, with its membership of OPEC, (Organisation of Oil Exporting Countries), becomes an important element of the largest oil producing block in the world. By joining forces with Saudi Arabia, Iran, Kuwait and Iraq, they become a disturbing world economic voice controlling more than 30% of the worlds known oil reserves.

As a result of the US termination of the Bretton Woods agreement, OPEC will now only accept payment for oil in gold as the dollar begins to freefall. This factor alone in the long hot European summer of 1973 has a massive impact on the world's major, but increasingly shaky economies, with worse to come. Ahmed Hassan al-Bakr, now President of Iraq guided by a power hungry Saddam Hussein, moves very close to the Soviets having signed a full political, economic and military treaty with them in 1972. Egypt and Syria are following closely behind leaving a defiant Israel surrounded on all sides by a Soviet supported, oil rich, discontented Moslem block. But holding a stockpile of nuclear weapons and having received the very latest military technology from the United States, the Zionists led by the iron lady, Golda Meir, stand their ground. Israel is a state under siege both politically and militarily.

This is a time before mobile phones, laptops, tablets and the Internet. The fastest means of legal and secure electronic communications in 1973 is the Telex system, short for TELegraph EXchange. The terminal machinery is cumbersome and in some parts of the world, unreliable making it necessary for any high level intelligence to be exchanged face to face. The world political situation is tense; inter-governmental communications are poor and against this troubling background, a conspiracy, hatched by a group of extremely wealthy and powerful Middle Eastern individuals is being formed. A conspiracy that would in one way or another, affect the lives of every man woman and child on the planet!

# The Beginning

*January 25th 1959 – Jebel Akhdar – The Oman Interior.*

It was dark and very, very cold sitting on a damp, dusted mud floor within the confines of the half destroyed mud walled hut on the edge of Bani Habib village. This was Jebel Akhdar, a high plateau reaching to 10,000 feet on the edge of Oman's Al Hajar mountain range. The temperature was three degrees centigrade and that was low enough for the thirty one year old Englishman sitting huddled in the corner of the dilapidated hut wearing a British Army greatcoat bearing the blackened shoulder pips of a Captain. Sitting on the other side of the hut, clutching Martini rifles in one hand and putting together the required items to light a fire in the other, were the Imam of Awabi, Sulayman bin Abdulla and his brother, Tammam bin Abdulla. They were both 'forty something' with Tammam being a few years younger than his brother. Sulayman had a birth date somewhere in between 1908 and 1912, depending upon which calendar you preferred to consult, but however old they both really were, they were fit, hard mountain fighters and they looked the part. Along with their military ally, Aasif bin Hashem, they were all wanted men. In fact they were wanted dead or alive and had been on the Sultan of Oman's list for over four years.

The natural fortress of Jebel Akhdar had protected and kept them relatively safe for all those years, but the chill wind blowing relentlessly across the top of the Jebel that night, would bring with it betrayal, death and a disaster that would have repercussions for the Arab Gulf States for decades to come. The blackness of the night was invaded by the first sparks of a fire in the middle of the hut floor, now moving to a flame as Tammam bin Abdulla carefully placed small, dried kindling sticks over the smouldering sun burnt grass. Within minutes, a fire was roaring fed by two men who had entered the hut with armfuls of dried acacia branches. After twenty minutes, nearly a dozen fires were blazing away all round the hut with several tribal fighters gathered around each, mostly chatting loudly or smoking small copper lined pipes as they drank up the welcome warmth, leaning on their long barrelled Martini-Henry rifles, the weapon of choice in the Oman peninsular.

Small arms fire could be heard in the distance along with the odd flat, low register, vibrating sound of 81mm mortars. There was much activity in the north, as there had been for most of the day. The British 'A' Squadron SAS was pushing hard in to the Imam's defences at Hajar and Aqabat al Dhafar. It was decision time. One of the donkey men loyal to the Imam and his cause had been at the British briefing the day before. Something serious was about to happen, but not the way the briefing Army Major had explained it. The Sultan of Oman and his British friends were determined to remove the Imam one way or another to end his rightful claim to being the religious and political leader of the Oman interior. This was not about political power, it was about money and that money was ripe to rise up out of the ground in the form of oil; a black sticky currency desperately needed by a still colonial minded Britain that sent mercenaries and the finest of British Special Forces to solve what was essentially a problem of history and tribal rights. The British were expert at supporting despotic regimes' in third world countries. Their leaders were usually quite ruthless, had little or no social conscience and were sometimes proven to be completely mad, but the main thing was to make sure they were compliant. The Sultan of Oman filled all of these requirements admirably. The Imam spoke first.

'Well Maxwell my friend' what is your advice now?'

'I have a feeling that we are somewhere in between 'a rock and a hard place'...as our American cousins would put it.'

Captain Maxwell Armstrong, British military advisor, was seconded as a negotiator between the Imam, the Sultans representatives and the Commander of the British SAS forces in the Oman. He had been with the Imam and his tribal army for over a year now and had got to know the man well. He had used his time on the Jebel to learn Arabic and was now proficient. He had been summoned by the Sultan and should have been off

Jebel Akhdar two days ago. He knew nothing of what was to shortly happen on the plateau. He was not party to military briefings, but he did know by the change of tactics over the past three days, that something was about to happen and tonight was probably the night. The aerial campaign by British Lancaster bombers and Venom jets had suddenly stopped and now there were literally hourly probes by the SAS in the north. The Imam had around fifteen hundred brave mountain fighters loyal to him on the Jebel and it would be up to him to decide whether or not these valuable lives should be sacrificed or spared in any ensuing battle. Tammam, the Imams younger brother spoke.

'We should stand and fight…..look at the damage we have done to the stupid Nasrani already. If we attack now in the north, we stand a chance of defeating them.'

'Chai' arrived and the men in the hut took a glass each of the over sugared black tea and began to drink. There was silence for a minute or two. The Imam, although tired, looked equally relaxed as he looked toward his English friend for a response. Maxwell simply shook his head. The Imam finally spoke.

'My brothers…..my heart is heavy and sad but I must consider the lives of all our brave followers who will get little or no mercy from the devilish agents of the Sultan. We will finish our tea and then move to Sharqiyah, where we have friends who will look after us and our brave fighters can disperse toward the Gulf coast, God willing.'

Everyone in the hut remained silent; if this was the will of the Imam, then there was no question that this was the correct path to take. Tammam was about to say something, but held back as he got up from his cross legged position on the mud floor and moved outside to organise the body guard of over eighty hardened fighters.

'Will you be coming with us Maxwell' the Imam asked in a low, slightly emotional voice.

'No my old friend, that is not possible. I fear that something will be happening here tonight and I think you should leave as quickly as possible. I will stay here and if all is well in the morning, I will move north to meet up with the Trucial Oman Scouts at their Rustaq camp.'

The Imam raised himself as did the English Captain. They hugged together for a long moment, a sign of great affection between two men from such differing backgrounds and cultures. Both men picked up their rifles and ammunition bandoliers and left the hut. A great shout went up from the assembled tribesmen as they shot the blackened clouds with endless rounds of ammunition. Finally all was silent. The Imam raised his arms, turned to look back at Maxwell and then disappeared out of the ring of light provided by the still burning fires and in to the misty shadows of the night, followed silently by his shabby looking band of rebel fighters.

\*\*\*\*\*\*

The commander of 'D' Squadron SAS was facing a dilemma in his attempt to lead his troops on what would be a most difficult ten thousand foot climb up to the top of Jebel Akhdar in broad daylight. It was not broad daylight. It was three o'clock in the morning and his troops were fading fast as they reached the operationally coded 'Causeway'...... a mountain crest about one third of the way up to the top of the Jebel itself. He had to do something or his troops would not reach the plateau by daylight. Each soldier was carrying a Bergen rucksack weighing nearly ninety pounds. He made the decision and ordered his men to remove the ammunition and grenades and then stash the rucksack on the ridge. If they survived the night, they could come back later for clothes, canteens and food rations. If they didn't, then they wouldn't need them. The part trek and part climb continued with no rest.

When daylight finally came, 'D' Squadron and 'A' Squadron SAS were on the plateau. They were exhausted. There was no expected resistance, in fact the only sign of what could be called 'the enemy' was a small band of about twenty Bani Riyam tribesmen who were quite happy to 'surrender' if that was what the white, Christian soldiers .... the 'Nasrani'... wanted. There was no sign of the Imam Sulayman bin Abdulla or his brother Tammam bin Abdulla. There was also no sign of Aasif bin Hashem the leader of over two thousand 'rebel' fighters .... or in fact the very fighters themselves. The so called 'rebellion' was over. After four long years, Jebel Akhdar had been taken. The London Times described the operation undertaken by the SAS on that dark day January 25th, 1959 as 'a brilliant example of the economy in the use of force'. Maxwell Armstrong knew better.

# Chapter One

*January 6th 1973 – Poltava – Northern Ukraine - USSR*

It was an exceptionally cold winter in northern Ukraine. The early January air temperature was minus ten and the wind chill factor was driving it down even further on that bleak, seemingly lifeless Saturday night. Captain Maksym Borsuk checked his black faced, Poljot stainless steel military watch. It was twenty three hundred hours and four minutes. Any time now. The snow was still falling on the arrow straight road between Poltava and Stasi, as it had been for the past three days, narrowing the navigable width down to one single track with ice banks piled up to over a meter on either side. Captain Borsuk, with three of his troop, was manning a simple red and black striped, single pole timber barrier, placed across the road some four miles from the Soviet Military Air Base at Poltava. It was unusual for a Captain of the Spetsnaz GRU Tenth Separate Brigade to be manning barricades in the middle of the night. But this was an unusual situation. The barricade had been in place for only ten minutes. He and his troop of eight men were waiting for one particular vehicle to appear from the near white-out in front of him. It would be coming from the direction of Stasi. The barrier guards wore the uniforms of standard Russian Airborne Troops beneath dark grey greatcoats and heads covered ineffectively by light blue VDV berets. The four men at the barrier all carried powerful, heavy, rubberized, steel cased torches and AKMS automatic assault rifles. The remaining five members of the troop were hidden from view some meters north of the barrier, dug in behind the ice banks. Straining eyes picked up the glimmer of a headlight through the continuous snow flurries, then two, then three. The middle one would be a motorcycle escort and the other two would be the ten ton truck. There could be an escort of some kind behind the truck, Maksym mused, either a four wheel drive of some sort... or maybe another motorcycle. The Captain spoke into a hand held VHF radio.

'This is the one!' No reply was required.

The noise of steel tire studs crunching into the compacted ice became louder and the stabs of light brighter as the small convoy approached. Whatever it consisted of, the plan hadn't changed. It was a simple one, as all good plans were. Kill everyone and take the truck. The motorcycle crawled up to the barrier made visible by the beams of torches moving casually back and forth across the striped pole supported on two, rusting steel tripods. He stopped, as did the KAZ-717 semi trailer behind. The rider dismounted ready to approach the great-coated officer at the barrier, but as he did so, barely heard through the considerable wind noise, a shot was fired. He instinctively turned his head to look back past the truck where he thought the disturbing noise had come from. Straining eyes revealed the morphing shapes of two shadowy figures approaching either side of the truck from the rear.

"What the hell was going on?"

It was, in fact, a final thought as his head was pulled back sharply, twisted violently to the left and a stiletto shaft of case hardened, blue metal driven upward beneath his rib cage. With neck broken and heart ripped apart, the lifeless body of the motorcycle rider was allowed to fall to the icy roadway. At exactly the same moment, two nine millimeter bullets, efficiently delivered by military issue Makarov pistols ended the promising careers of Junior Sergeant Demichev and Private Ogienko, the bodies of which were roughly pulled out of the truck cab and dumped behind the steadily growing ice banks. The bodies of two motorcycle escorts and their warm mechanical mounts would follow suit as the Captain dropped the tailboard and jumped in to the canvas topped rear of the truck in order to examine its cargo. Four or five pairs of eager hands ripped the canvas cover back behind him. There were, as expected, two sturdy, well manufactured timber ply boxes on the flat bed of the truck. He released the dozen or so snap catches that secured the lid of one box to check its contents. Inside, held by tailored anti-vibration brackets and mounts was a black missile shaped object about three meters long and a meter in diameter. Captain Borsuk pulled his torch downward, to quickly read the light grey, Cyrillic scripted code, stenciled on the casing of the missile. He grunted in satisfaction. One of his men opened up the other box. The contents were the same. This, so far silent, group of highly trained, highly intelligent military specialists were now the proud owners of two Russian manufactured RDS-4, 30 Kiloton nuclear devices. The Captain spoke to the man nearest to him as he vaulted athletically from the back of the truck.

'You…drive the truck. Tell the others to get in under the canvas cover at the back'

'OK Maksym' the soldier replied. First names were always used in Borsuk's unit, regardless of rank.

'Help me with the barrier'

In the yellow glow of the truck's poor quality headlights, the two men threw the pole and two tripods over the snow layered ice banks and with a quick look back to ensure all the men were aboard and out of sight beneath the stiffened, tailored canvas cover, they clambered in to the cab, pulling the ill fitting doors as tightly closed as possible. The Captain spoke again.

'Right… you know where to go. First stop Kremenchuk' The driver pulled up the heater lever to its highest level, coerced the stubborn floor mounted gear lever in to first, accompanied by some level of protest from the non-synchromesh gearbox and they were on their way.

\*\*\*\*\*\*

The normal twenty minute drive to the large lock-up store in Kremenchuk took nearly an hour. They were now behind time. Using a loading ramp and A-frame chain hoist, the nine men transferred the two timber crates weighing around 4,000 Kilo's each from the Kaz and in to two smaller Kolhida five ton panel trucks. Fully fuelled and eager to get away from the area as quickly as possible, the two trucks edged out of the lock-up into the murky night. The bad weather was a godsend. There would be no police out on a night like this and any military roadblocks between Kremenchuk and the coastal town of Berdyansk would be passed easily with one simple flash of a Spetsnaz GRU identity card. No one in the military, with even half a brain, would want to take them on. The team, tightly packed inside the two trucks with their sensitive cargo, would need to make up some time on the 330 Kilometer trip to Berdyansk, but Captain Borsuk was confident they would make it without blowing themselves and the southern half of the Ukraine to shit.

******

The deadline was midday on Sunday, January 7th. They made it to the outskirts of the town with half an hour to spare. Here, the two trucks parted company; one heading east to a lock-up store on Dyumyna Street and the other, containing Captain Borsuk, three men and one crate, toward Yuvleina Street and the gated entrance to the small commercial port. The dilapidated looking tramp steamer was waiting for them at the quayside. The Sea of Azov led into the Black Sea and on through to the Aegean. Borsuk did not know the final destination of the cargo that had so far cost four lives and didn't need to. A forklift appeared from nowhere and headed straight for the drab grey vehicle parked on the quay side next to the rusting coastal vessel. Captain Borsuk walked purposely over to the port office and made a thirty second phone call. As he put the handset down, he was smiling. On the short walk back to the truck, he raised a hand to his expectant comrades. Within minutes, the timber crate was off and carefully ensconced in cargo hold number three. The boat was carrying nothing else commercially and was in ballast. As soon as the one box was loaded, she was to be away. With doors tightly shut and the three members of his team on board, Borsuk gave the word and the matt grey painted panel truck headed for the port gates without fuss. The whole operation had taken literally minutes with little or no attention being paid to the transfer of the 30 Kiloton nuclear bomb by passers-by and port staff. Now, a reward was due…two point seven million US Dollars in used notes. It was where it should be. Maksym had checked. That was why he was still smiling; one in the bag and one as a deadly insurance policy. This had been a good day's work.

# Chapter Two

*September 22nd 1973 – Nakosongola – Uganda – East Africa*

The pale blue Mazda pickup pulled to a halt a few yards in front of a dilapidated looking red and white banded security barrier blocking the entrance to Nakasongola airstrip. The drive north from Kampala had been long and tiresome along an ill-maintained and pothole ridden excuse for a road that only a few years previously had been a main trunk route to Uganda's thriving agricultural community and gateway to the massive shallow lake at Kyoga. But now nobody cared. Deteriorating roads were left un-repaired; subsidies to farmers left unpaid and since the advent of the 'economic war', seized properties and estates were often left to rot with their European or Asian owners forced to leave the country. Since a takeover of the government in a military coup on January 25th, 1971 by Idi Amin, the country was heading for total bankruptcy and law and order had been reduced to disorganized chaos. With bands of tribal thugs and army deserters freely roaming the bush border areas, scavenging for food and looting village settlements, a lone traveler in Uganda often took the risk of finding himself on the wrong end of an AK-47. Travelling by day was a risky business but any movement at all by night was not recommended.

Maxwell Armstrong fiddled in his shirt pockets for all the necessary documents; a British passport describing him as English by birth and an economic adviser by profession, a current Civil Aviation Authority pilot's license and a pink multi-stamped security pass issued by the Food and Agriculture Organization in Rome. He replaced the checked papers in the top right hand breast pocket of his khaki, open necked bush shirt and looked impatiently in the direction of the crumbling, ramshackle guard hut. No sign of life. Maxwell hit the car horn a couple of times and in response a shabbily dressed African guard appeared from behind the hut, buttoning his trouser fly with one hand whilst attempting to hang on to an ill maintained Kalashnikov rifle with the other. The battered weapon dropped to the ground as the guard finally accepted he would need two hands to tackle the last button on his World War Two surplus jungle combat denims.

Maxwell continued to view the annoyingly comic scene for a further half a minute and in sheer frustration bore down heavily on the horn with the palm of his hand. The surprised guard looked up. He was annoyed and glared angrily at the blue pickup with government license plates. He paused for a moment and then casually picked up the rifle, pulled back the sliding bolt, and with indefinite aim let go a burst of three shots. One missed the vehicle completely, one shattered a nearside headlamp and the final shot ripped through a front wheel rim and carried on to completely destroy the surrounding tire. Maxwell got the message; let go of the horn, closed his eyes, and counted slowly and carefully to ten before opening them again. The mute soldier sauntered over to the Mazda, noting the FAO badge crudely painted on the cab door and the expression of the European driver, who had so far made no attempt to leave his seat. He poked the hot muzzle of the battered AK-47 through the open cab window and stood back, finger still on the trigger. A wide idiotic grin crept over his black, dirt encrusted face, exposing uneven yellow teeth, badly stained with lavender betel juice, the nut of which he was nervously chewing as he spoke.

'So white masa, what de hell hurry you honkin de horn like dat? Now you got broken wheel to mend and blockin de entrance. Better be pretty damn quick'.

Maxwell turned his head to face the undernourished Lango tribesman. The two men locked eyes for a long second. He reached for the door latch as the guard stepped away a few paces, holding the rifle at waist level. Maxwell opened the cab door, slid out of the seat with calm, deliberate movement and stood in front of the African. He was tall but at six feet two inches Maxwell topped him by nearly an inch or more. The guard stared up at the tall, lean European with dull, listless dark eyes, waiting for a move, preferably one that would give him a cast iron excuse to pull the trigger once again. Maxwell walked round to the back of the truck and still simmering, pulled out a jack and well worn spare. Without a single word he began to change the shattered front wheel to the great delight of the guard who wandered away giggling childishly and spitting purple flecks of half chewed nut from the side of his smirking mouth. It took no more than five minutes to finish changing the wheel and stow the jack beneath the driver's seat where it was normally kept. Maxwell was still very pissed off, but exercising the maximum of self control as he walked over to the check point in an attempt to persuade the irksome and semi-literate guard to let him into the airstrip. The whole process took up another valuable ten minutes, during which time Maxwell was forced to absorb many more verbal insults mostly related to his parenthood and nationality.

Finally the great event happened as the guard reluctantly lifted the barrier and waved him through with a meaningful gesture of his rifle. Maxwell breathed a quiet sigh of relief as he maneuvered the little pickup around some old and decaying wooden buildings, evidence of better and busier days at Nakasongola, until his aero plane finally came into view. He checked his watch, ten thirty am. If he could get away quickly he could be in Kenya and home within a matter of a couple of hours. He pulled up ten yards from the Piper Cherokee, jumped out and lifted a large canvas bag from the rear of the pickup. A gently swirling dust trail emerged in the distance viewed over the bonnet of the Mazda and leading it, an army Jeep travelling at speed down the soil caked runway. Two shots were fired, seemingly in the air, as the Jeep approached.

'Oh shit!' Maxwell exclaimed as he threw the bag into the truck; and feeling for the aircraft keys in a trouser pocket, he quickly bent down and threw them under the driver's seat, covering them with the jack.

The olive green jeep careered to a halt alongside the Mazda and two well equipped soldiers dressed in jungle fatigues jumped out, covering Maxwell with mean looking Uzi machine pistols. From the rear of the Jeep emerged a smartly dressed Colonel wearing the shoulder flashes of the Ugandan State Research Bureau, swagger stick in one hand and Colt pistol in the other. He spoke with a refined and very British accent as he indicated with his stick that the Englishman was to be searched. One of the soldiers began to carry out the instruction, thoroughly and expertly.

'Mr. Armstrong,' said the Colonel, 'my name is Agali, Colonel Agali of the SRB. I believe you're planning to make a little trip out of our lovely country without telling us' He paused to inspect his brass mounted stick. 'If this is the case I must inform you I am quite dismayed. I would like to think that we have done everything possible to make the stay of yourself and your FAO colleagues in our fine country, as comfortable and as pleasant as possible, and if you wish to leave for any reason it would be most impolite of you not to go through the normal exit permit procedures.'

Maxwell eyed the short, squat officer suspiciously as the searching soldier tipped the contents of the kit bag onto the ground at Maxwell's feet and started to rummage through them. The Englishman stood before the smiling Colonel in a relaxed pose, an imposing, lean, muscular and suntanned figure, towering above all three men before him. He ran a hand through a shock of blonde, sun bleached hair before moving down to thoughtfully caress pale stubble covering a broad square set chin. The expansive blue grey eyes flashed as he rapidly evaluated the situation, his possible response and the odds. He spoke assuredly.

'I haven't applied for an exit permit Colonel, because at present I don't require one. I have a pipeline survey to complete for the final phase of the Lake Kyoga district water project and I have just come from Kampala with signed permission from the Minister of Natural Resources to carry out the survey.'

He pulled a white document covered with grandiose stamps from his back pocket and handed it to the amused looking staff officer.

'Now, I am on my way back to Kenya to put the relevant funds in place for the survey to be completed'.

Colonel Agali took the paper and without looking at it ripped it up and threw the remnants to the ground.

'This permission has been rescinded as the signature is no longer valid Mr. Armstrong and therefore….. you will not be needing your aircraft today' he took on a determined, stony expression. The eyes had lost any hint of friendliness

'Perhaps you would be good enough to let me have the keys.'

Maxwell continued to rub his chin, noting that the search of his personal belongings had been completed; crumpled shirts, dusty underwear and two pairs of leather sand boots, laying in a careless pile at his feet. Patience was beginning to desert him as he spoke again, firmly.

'May I ask why a Minister of State has apparently no authority to sign an official government document; or at this moment in time would that be considered a little naive?'

The Colonel's face tightened and the expression became grim.

'There is a very simple reason,' he replied bitterly.

'The minister in question is no longer with us, in fact he is extremely dead. You will therefore appreciate that we cannot allow you to fly off in your little aero plane on the word of a dead man, and until the circumstances of his demise are fully investigated, I'm afraid that you will have to stay with us a little longer'.

Maxwell considered for a moment if it was 'flight or fight' time.

'Where are the *keys* Mr. Armstrong, I shall not ask again?'

Maxwell calculated the odds of taking out all three men without resorting to gun fire. They were not very good. The two soldiers accompanying the officer appeared well trained and alert and their eyes never left the big man they were covering with the lethal stub barreled automatics. At short range one burst could cut a man in two and everyone in the present company, including Maxwell, was well aware of the fact. He dropped his hands to his side and made a loose shrugging gesture.

'There you've got me Colonel. I have only one set of keys and when I arrived I left them with the duty mechanic who was supposed to refuel the aircraft and change one of the batteries. I've been away for five days now and there seems to be no sign of anyone who knows anything about them.'

The Colonel made another move with his swagger stick and one of the soldiers stepped over to the Cherokee to check the doors and hatches. They were locked. Agali clicked his tongue in a gesture of frustration.

'Well then Armstrong, if you say you don't have the keys ….. we shall have to try and find them for you. In the meantime I suggest that you go back to the Nakasongola guest house and rest awhile until we contact you again' He paused

'….. and one of my men will be more than happy to keep you company. We will no doubt meet again later when the full report concerning the sudden and unexpected death of our brave and sorely missed minister reaches me'.

He began to walk away, stopped and turned.

'This short pause in our relationship will also give you time to put your story together concerning your activities during the past twenty-four hours, as by now you may have guessed that perhaps you were privileged to be possibly the last person to have seen the minister alive.'

With that the Colonel turned on his heel and clambered aboard the jeep in company with one soldier, the other opening the passenger door of the Mazda to escort Maxwell away from the airfield and on to Nakasongola town.

\*\*\*\*\*\*

The twelve room guest house was nearly deserted and the single, surly staff member had little difficulty in finding a room for Maxwell. The desk clerk cum cook cum steward threw a key across the peeling varnish of a cheaply veneered reception counter and shuffled away out of sight through a door marked 'office.' The silent but observant soldier by Maxwell's side held his hand out for the room key and the ignition keys to the pickup. Maxwell noted the time displayed on a nearly accurate wall clock above the counter and without checking his watch calculated it was now well past eleven. The guard nudged his charge with the barrel of his pistol. It was an indication that movement was required and he followed the European out through the empty reception area to the bedroom wing consisting of one single long corridor off which led twelve doors, some marked with numbers, some not. The one Maxwell was searching for should have been marked with a five and luckily was. He turned and looked inquiringly at the alert, expressionless soldier who handed him the key. For a few brief seconds the African's gaze was averted as Maxwell fiddled the key in the lock. It was time to make his move. He stooped slightly, seemingly to give the lock a little more attention and then sprang back from the door, rising up and turning at the same time as his left arm streaked out and caught the African a searing blow across the throat. One hand left the Uzi as the guard gasped for breath and began to double over, the other raised the machine pistol at an awkward angle, index finger tightening on the trigger. Maxwell continued his turn, pivoting on his left foot and raising his right in a low sweeping arc. The heel of his right boot caught the soldier levelly in the solar plexus and as he completed the one hundred and eighty degree turn, he whipped back and crashed down on the back of the falling man's neck with both hands linked together in a stunning blow. As the soldier hit the scuffed brown linoleum floor covering of the corridor, Maxwell pounced on his victim, pinning the lightly built African to the floor. With arms outstretched and hands still linked he delivered two more blows to the back of the guard's neck between the second vertebrae and the mastoid bone. He felt something snap, as the spinal column of the body beneath him gave way and the head suddenly rolled back at an acute angle. Maxwell gasped with nervous effort as he quickly opened the door to room number five and hauled the lifeless body inside. The whole operation had taken less than thirty seconds and had been relatively noiseless.

Maxwell methodically searched for his keys to the pickup and when found, carefully removed the Uzi pistol and a spare ammunition clip from the African and left the room, locking the door behind him. He didn't know if the guard was supposed to report in to the Colonel or one of his staff when it was confirmed that Maxwell was under lock and key, but he calculated that time would be short. He checked his stainless steel Seiko chronometer now; eleven twenty. He cautiously made his way along the corridor, through the deserted reception and out to the little blue pickup. No one seemed to notice the pale blue FAO Mazda moving hurriedly through what remained of the once proud portals of Nakasongola guest house. The carved stone lintel across the entrance had collapsed years ago and broken into several pieces, one of which still lay where it had fallen, half blocking the entrance and causing Maxwell to swerve the Mazda determinedly as he made good his escape. The hardy Japanese pickup bounced bravely onto the rutted and potholed track leading to the main road and with rear wheels spinning into a murky red dust cloud, set off in the direction of the airstrip.

Maxwell drove off the road about a mile from the main gate where he hoped the guard who had offered him such a sincere and friendly welcome a few hours earlier would still be on duty. He pushed the truck as far as it would go into the scrub bush at the side of the road, grabbed the aircraft keys from their resting place beneath the driver's seat, and checked the Uzi. The attached nine inch ammunition clip was full, the spare one he pushed into his trouser belt and set off on foot toward the main gate. Maxwell knew it would have been easier simply to negotiate the rusting barbed wire and iron posted perimeter fence only a hundred yards away on his right but he needed to know if the airfield guard contingent were aware of his present difficulties with the SRB and how many of them were on duty that day, feeling sure that his grinning, betel chewing friend in the guard house would be able to tell him. Maxwell approached the ramshackle hut from a windowless rear. From inside could be heard the dull rhythm and tuneless chords of electronic African high life music. The area around the gate seemed to be clear and whoever was on guard duty would more than likely be in the hut. Releasing the safety catch on the Uzi, Maxwell crouched down and negotiated a path to the roadside of the guard house, stopping beneath a half opened window. The music was now louder. He bobbed his head up for a quick view inside the room and noted to his satisfaction that only one person was visible and it looked like just the one he wanted. Maxwell took two rapid steps around the left of the hut and paused, scanning the area carefully for any other signs of life or activity. Everything appeared clear; he took one more step, kicked the half rotting wooden door to the hut open with a well placed blow from a swinging right foot and two seconds later had the barrel of the machine pistol firmly jammed in the flaring nostril of a surprised, shocked and now quivering guard. The pressure from the pistol barrel restricted the African's head movement but he rolled wide jaundiced eyes up as far as he could to get a good look at his attacker, at the same time continuing with a natural movement, raising his hands in the air to full stretch. Maxwell growled an instruction to the trembling Lango who quickly did as he was told and undid the buckle to his uncared for leather army belt and let it out a notch. He then pushed the guard's hands through the belt by his hips and swapping the pistol to his left hand Maxwell pulled hard on the belt and slipped the buckle; both hands were now both firmly pinned to his sides.

The hut stank of marijuana smoke and a crudely rolled cigarette was still burning on the edge of a cane table, next to the seated African. There was no other furniture in the room. A radio blared in the corner of the small dirty, un-crowded space and next to it, carelessly propped against a peeling plaster wall, stood the AK-47. Maxwell asked the first question concerning the guard's knowledge, and preferably the whereabouts of a certain Colonel Agali. The African remained mute and shook his head in terrified response, now staring wide eyed at the unwavering pistol barrel only inches from his sweating top lip, perspiration breaking out all over the man like a hot shower. The reply was not too reassuring and Maxwell did not have time to mess around so he deliberately rammed the black steel barrel down into the guard's decaying teeth. One cracked and then gave way completely as the terror stricken guard gave out a sharp high pitched whine of pain. The end of the pistol barrel was now covered in bright red blood which Maxwell studiously wiped clean on the faded shoulder flashes of his victim's ragged and hardly recognizable uniform. He asked the question again and this time received a burbling, blood spitting reply in the negative. The next one was easier to answer and Maxwell discovered that there were three other guards on duty at the strip, one on the south perimeter check point and two others in the control tower and flight building. Tears of fright and now panic were streaming down the African's cheeks. He was still spitting blood and had begun to cough nervously and uncontrollably. Maxwell walked over to the automatic rifle standing in the corner and removed the sliding breech. The rifle was now useless. He moved back to the blood spattered guard and reminded him of the events of their earlier meeting to which the African responded with violent nodding agreement. Maxwell also reminded him that this was no way for a well trained and disciplined soldier to behave, to which once again the guard nodded frantically in vehement comprehension. Maxwell left the hut with the guard lying on the floor; one of his holed and stinking socks rammed firmly in his mouth and boot laces biting into swollen ankles, securing bare and bleeding feet. Maxwell felt satisfyingly sure that the punishment he had inflicted upon the guard's feet with the butt of the now useless rifle during the last thirty seconds would be nothing to the treatment he would receive from Colonel Agali when he caught up with him. Maxwell moved off at a measured trot towards the east side of the airstrip where hopefully his aero plane was still parked.

Managing to gain ground to some deserted nissen huts he checked the area around him until satisfied that he still remained undetected. He crept around the last of the lifeless buildings and spied the Cherokee about three hundred yards away, just as he had left it. Racing across the empty space between the deserted hut and the parking bay, he threw away the breech to the guard's rifle he had been carrying and dropped flat to the ground beneath the starboard wing of the Piper. The aircraft had not been tied down and the only wheels chocked were the nose and starboard oleo leg. He pulled the chock ropes in one sharp powerful movement and clambered onto the wing walkway, keys in hand. Once inside the cockpit he clambered over to the left hand seat, slamming the door shut with one hand and pumping the fuel primer with the other. Ignition on, gyros winding up, he hit the starter and the single propeller in front of him began a juddering spasmodic rotation. Suddenly the engine fired and roared up to a thousand revs. Maxwell fastened his seat belt, set the flaps for a short take off and noted thankfully that both fuel tanks were registering some fuel below half, but how much he would simply have to guess. Half a mile away he noticed some shadowy movement on the balcony of the two storey control tower. They were now only curious but within minutes the other guards would know that Mr. Armstrong was making an illegal take off and would no doubt be trying to stop him. He set the revs at eight hundred and let go of the brakes. The sturdy aluminum frame leapt forward as Maxwell taxied at high speed for a hundred and fifty yards before pulling back the power and bearing down on the starboard rudder bar to bring the little aircraft round into a tight right hand turn. He was now parallel with the patched and pitted concrete strip that served as a runway but running on a track which kept him a further fifty yards out from the control tower. His radio was off so he had no way of knowing what was happening up there but as he opened up the engine in preparation for his take off run, a red flare appeared above the tower informing the pilot of the taxiing aircraft that permission to take off had not been given.

'Bollocks to you," smiled Maxwell to himself,

'I never asked for your *fucking* permission in the first place!' he shouted out loud, partly in the tension of the moment and partly in relief. They would not catch him now.!!

With brakes off and throttle wide open the ageing but tough little Cherokee rolled forward, picking up speed with every yard. Within seconds the shuddering airframe was level with the tower from which two unhealthy looking individuals were spraying the area in front of them with automatic fire from AK-47s held at waist level. Maxwell quickly calculated that the only way a drunken militia handling badly maintained weaponry and firing at such a distance could possibly cause any damage to such a swiftly moving target would be with a lucky shot; a very lucky shot. He turned back to the job in hand and concentrated on his take off run. The airspeed indicator nudged up to sixty knots allowing Maxwell to pull back gently on the control column. The nose lifted fractionally, then at a more acute angle. Next minute the rumbling and drumming of the low pressure tires over the poorly compacted ground surface ceased and Piper Cherokee, registration Golf Papa Golf Hotel, was well and truly in the air.

Maxwell pulled the aircraft round in a tight climbing left hand turn and spiraled his way upward through a low level cloud layer and headed east, leaving wild gunfire far behind him. He was on his way home. Pulling a less than pristine handkerchief from his trouser pocket, Maxwell wiped a perspiring brow and glanced back toward the rear storage locker, noting that his battered old leather suitcase was still on board. Arriving back at Archers Post without at least half the luggage he had left with would cause the odd eyebrow to be raised and prompt a torrent of questions from Helga. It had been over three months since they had last been together and that was three months too long. After a worrying forty minutes skirting the Ugandan border, he set course for Samburu.

# Chapter Three

*September 23rd 1973 – Archers Post – Kenya – East Africa*

The flight to the little airstrip, on the Weismuller property, three kilometers from Archers Post, was completed without event and was one that Maxwell had undertaken from the west many times during the past few years. Admittedly he had never before had to 'escape' from anywhere in the long time he had been rolling around this vast continent and was unsure of the reception he might receive when reporting in to Samburu control. However, there was little love lost between Ugandan and Kenyan authorities and if Nairobi were aware of the circumstances of his hurried exit from Nakasongola, they gave no indication of the fact as they cleared his flight directly to Samburu, terminating a few miles away at the private airstrip belonging to the Weismuller farm.

As soon as he was in range Maxwell called up the airfield on the VHF radio and a friendly Australian voice answered. Harry Jordan was the nomadic, wayfaring, crop sprayer cum aircraft mechanic who used the farm strip as his base and over the years had become more than part of the family. Maxwell checked his fuel level as he began the descent into the Weismuller estate. Both tanks were on reserve. There was no time to mess about. As he touched the brakes, Maxwell could see Harry standing in front of the corrugated steel construction at the edge of the strip which served as hanger and maintenance workshop for the Cherokee and Harry's Piper monoplane crop sprayer. He knew Helga would also be there waiting for him and as he taxied the PA28 off the strip and up to the hanger, he noticed her favorite form of transport tucked in behind the generator house. As the smiling pilot clambered out, the stone faced mechanic stood moodily by the leading edge of the port wing, tut-tutting in one breath and swearing quietly to himself in the other.

'Evening Harry,' shouted Maxwell, 'where's Helga? I see her old Nissan truck parked out back ....'

He was cut short in mid sentence. Carried by the stirrings of the gentle early evening breeze came a voice, a voice he had not heard but longed to hear for over three months.

'I'm over here, waiting for you......as always.' The tone was admonishing and not the words of welcome Maxwell had expected. Helga leant casually against the half open hanger door dressed in tight, faded blue jeans and a brown gingham short sleeved shirt. The jeans were pressed into a narrow waistline by a wide calf leather belt, matching the flare topped Texan high step boots.

She looked gorgeous, five feet nine of perfectly formed female; a near impeccable hour glass figure, not normally popular in these days of dieting and breast-less matchstick models looming from every page of Vogue, but one that suited

Maxwell. Her finely chiseled and tanned features served as a jeweler's setting for a pair of widely set, remarkably hypnotic, emerald green eyes that could cut a man in half with one flashing glance; the whole faultless being crowned with a natural jewelry that no amount of money could buy; shimmering waist length red brown hair. Maxwell slapped Harry on the back, quietly passing him the superfluous Uzi at the same time. Helga began to move away from the background of the wind worn and paint flaked hanger toward the tired looking aero plane as Maxwell threw his flight bag to the floor and ran to greet her. Their bodies met in a bone crushing, lip swelling embrace and it was nearly a minute before they finally broke free.

'Where the hell have you been? She paused studying a blank expression.

'I've not even had an *effing* letter. Surely you could have at least written?'

An angry flush invaded her face now as she brushed the talcum powder like red grey dust from a glowing, suffused cheek, fighting hard to hold back a flood of tears. Maxwell looked down tenderly at his woman, his mind racing. There was so much he should tell her, so much that she should know. A long pause followed before he replied.

'Darling this is not the time or place. Let's get home and then we can have a long talk and I promise you .... ' He was cut off in his explanation as Helga broke free and stalked off toward the Nissan. He stood there helplessly for a few seconds but in that short time he knew his mind to be finally made up. He sighed inwardly and followed her quickly, managing to jump in the passenger seat and rapidly slam the door as Helga turned the ignition key, wrenched the gear lever forward and shot off over the rippled bush track at an incredible rate, liquid eyes staring straight ahead. Her lips moved.

'You asshole'

Maxwell turned in his seat to face Helga. One hand was firmly gripping the steering wheel as the other brushed away tangled chestnut tresses being grabbed momentarily by the turbulent slipstream forcing its way through the open window. She spoke again.

'If you think I'm going to take this shit from you for *very much* longer, then you're mistaken'.

A pear shaped tear fell. Maxwell knew there were special words to say at this particular time and he was struggling to find them. She glanced in his direction.

'…. and another thing. Whilst you are *buggering* about doing whatever the *hell* it is that you do, father and I have a fifty thousand acre farm to try and run and with the state of his health I'm finding it nearly impossible. Don't you think it's about time you gave me some form of commitment other than, "See you when I get back"? Every time you leave here I haven't a clue where you're going, what you're doing, when you'll be back or even if you will be back.'

Maxwell bit hard into his lip as the truck swerved violently off the track and onto a graded road leading up to the farm entrance. With a crunch of gears, Helga persuaded the Nissan into two wheel drive and picked up speed again. Within minutes, they were stationary in front of the Weismuller house; an impressive white painted, brick built colonial style house that was the main residence of the enormous farm property. Max waited for the dust to settle and before the driver's door was fully opened Ralph came rushing down the steps, waving eagerly and shouting greetings in English, German and Swahili. Combined with his excellent command of a further three more European languages, his ability to cook to perfection, control a staff of six house servants, drive just about anything with wheels and always come up with an engaging smile on a black, wizened old face, no matter what the problem, one could say that Ralph was a minor jewel. In fact that was how Helga described him; her shining jewel in this fading silver crown called Africa. With Ralph leading the way, all three began to climb the eight short steps leading to the front veranda of the house. Helga gripped Max's hand tightly and spoke to nobody in particular.

'Maxwell's luggage is still in the plane and Harry will probably bring it along later.' Ralph replied with a

'Yes Miss. Nice to see you back again Mister Max, Miss Helga missed you bad these past few months.'

'Yes Ralph,' said Maxwell ruefully, 'Miss Helga has already explained her feelings on that subject.' Max and Helga passed through the massive hand carved timber front door.

'Where's father, Ralph?' Helga asked casually.

'Mr. Kurt is up on the north lot and is not expected back until about nine o'clock, Miss,' came the fading reply as Ralph headed for the drawing room and Helga turned Max in the direction of the magnificent polished African teak staircase which led the way to the first floor bedroom wing.

'I'll wake you both before nine, Miss,' said Ralph, not turning his head and unfaltering in his movement towards the substantial ground floor entertaining area where long cool citrus drinks that had been laid out earlier, were getting warm and would now obviously go to waste.

Over an hour had passed in quiet slumber before Maxwell with half opened eyes reached out in the near total darkness to the pale cream china table lamp. He registered the time; 20:30 hours. Helga's eyelids moved suddenly and sharply, exposing emerald lenses refracting and amplifying every joule of light in the room.

'There was a man looking for you here last week,' she said in a voice that had taken on a sort of soft glow that would not have been noticeable an hour earlier. Maxwell was now restrainedly alert, alarm bells ringing.

'He didn't say what he wanted but was insistent that I tell him when you would be back.' Max remained silent; there was obviously more to come.

'I had a strange feeling that I had seen him before somewhere, actually' Helga said, her voice becoming more awake with each syllable, the words flowing a little faster. Max sat further up and asked casually,

'Well, did he leave a name or anything'?'

'No, but he promised to call tomorrow morning to see if you were back from wherever it is you've been.' There followed a short pause.

'He seemed very nice, in fact he was extremely well dressed and quite handsome…..sort of Arabic looking.'

'Well, we'll see what he wants tomorrow, then!' The shower water began to steam as it rushed towards the pale blue Italian tiled floor displaying a slightly disconcerting brown color which reminded Max to check the well filters later.

'The only bloody thing you appreciate when you haven't got it' he muttered to himself, thinking back over the past few weeks when dreaming of this same activity had overtaken his normal passion for fantasizing over Helga. In the relaxing atmosphere of the shower Maxwell carefully scanned a series of names that could conceivably be attached to the presence of the enquiring visitor. But the continuous pounding action of the massager began to dull all mental processes and a General feeling of repose and contentment blotted out all busy thoughts for the next ten minutes. Through the swirling grey steam that completely filled the bathroom appeared Helga. She joined him determinedly in the shower but before their two drenched bodies could move together again a loud knock was heard coming from the direction of the bedroom and a distant, intruding voice informed them,

'It's nine o'clock Miss Helga, Mister Maxwell.' Helga swore loudly in German and Max laughed quietly to himself.

The two lovers dried and dressed quickly, both now feeling more than a little hungry. Making their way downstairs Helga turned slowly to Max and smiled one of her special, feline 'thank you' smiles. In response, Max squeezed her hand lightly as they reached the bottom of the classic timber staircase and turned towards the drawing room.

Helga slumped down in to the Grande deep cushioned Spanish sofa which provided a perfect background to a superbly proportioned body. She picked up a prepared cup and began drinking her tea, long slim legs drawn together and leaning slightly to one side, indicating to Maxwell that he should now sit. He sank on to the cushion on her left, leaning back into the sofa.

'Father will be back shortly. I talked to you about the subject matter on the way here from the airstrip. Something has to be sorted out this time. He simply can't go on running the farm for much longer without help and you well know what kind of help I mean.'

He knew accurately the situation and had given it some dedicated thought lately. Helga carried on.

'You don't have to work for that bloody FAO, you know. This whole farm could be yours for the asking, and, to get down to real basics, I really simply need to know what is happening to the two of us'

Maxwell sat silent, his expression showing little emotion.

' How long are we going to go on like this?...... you rushing off all over the damn place, me not being able to contact you or see you for months on end. I can't handle it anymore.'

Maxwell rose from his warming, comfortable place on the sofa and walked over to the impressive picture window which looked out on to a splendid view of the house gardens that had been tirelessly planned, laid down, nurtured and nourished by three generations of Weismullers. This was the Weismuller's total life. Maxwell's last few years under his official cover with the Food and Agriculture Organization had been, in fact, enjoyable despite the lack of funds and constant political battling involved to get even the remotest thing done.

Helga was right, of course, and he knew it. Something would have to be done this time to try and bring some sense and organization to his life. He was about to reply when in the distance the horizon line was violently disturbed by a darkening mushroom shaped dust cloud that could only signal the hurried approach of Kurt's zebra striped Land Rover.

'It looks like Kurt's on his way in,' Max said, moving back into the shadowed interior of the drawing room, planting a quick but affectionate kiss on Helga's forehead.

'So, let's leave all this until after dinner. I make you a promise that I really will sort something out' he paused '….. and from then on we can make some positive and definite plans.'

Kurt strode through the already opened-front door some minutes later with purposeful steps, shaking the ever present grey brown coating from thinning, graying hair that refused to be released from a lined and sweating forehead, tanned deep brown and permanently etched from the years of consistent exposure to a giant, larger than life, Kenyan sun. He was an impressive man by anyone's measure and stood an inch above Maxwell in the scuffed brown, calf length riding boots that he consistently wore when working around the farm. The big framed German moved easily and athletically across the hall with one hand extended in preparation of greeting to Maxwell. The deep, short, clipped words reverberated first in German as signs of greeting to Helga and then in English for Maxwell, who grasped the proffered hand and embraced the broad shoulders of his friend and mentor of many years standing.

'Well, you made it then, at long last, you young devil,' joked Kurt, looking down slightly at Maxwell as he freed himself from the powerful and sincere grasp of friendship. An infectious smile of greeting, that also somehow betrayed a sense of relief, crossed Helga's face as she kissed her father gently on each cheek, her hands caringly brushing even more clinging soil from his shirt lapels and breast pockets. Her father was home and her lover was by her side once again. Ralph, as always, was hovering silently by the half open kitchen door

'Tea will be with you in just a moment, Mr. Kurt,' said Ralph as he retreated back in to the kitchen.

The three moved towards the drawing room, amidst much bantering conversation between Kurt and Maxwell. Since they had last met the lines had grown a little deeper, the hair a little greyer, forearms a little thinner and the once dazzling grey eyes a little duller. Kurt looked up and caught Maxwell's searching gaze.

'I've been up to my ankles in bloody mud all afternoon near by the north river crossing. The poachers have been at it again. Two elephants killed today and one of them lying half in the river.'

There was a short, strained silence.

'I'll go up there tomorrow morning with a couple of the boys,' said Maxwell, '…and see if we can pick up some tracks.' Kurt sighed despondently.

'If I get my hands on the bastards, I'll shoot their balls off,' he said despairingly, leaning back again into the sofa, suddenly looking extremely worn and tired.

Over dinner, Helga listened intently, as always to the never ending banter between her two favorite men and Kurt eagerly looked for the flashing laughter in her eyes, a laughter he dearly missed at the dinner table when Max was not present. Kurt felt considerably relaxed and managed to put to the back of his mind the constant waves of pain invading the left side of his body, so that nothing would spoil his palpable contentment and restrained relief at seeing Maxwell home again, with Helga laughing as she was now, as her mother had done for so many years before. Kurt had been aware for some time there was more to Max than him being purely and simply a technical officer, albeit an apparently senior one in the FAO and although he had never questioned the man on the subject he somehow sensed there was a new and hopeful air of decision about Max today

'I think father wishes to speak to you, Max.'

The timbre of Helga's voice was firm and caused a simultaneous pause in a conversation that up until then had been flowing freely. Kurt knew that that this was not yet the right time and countered her remark with,

'Not now, darling, Maxwell and I will have a little chat after dinner in the library over a glass of superb Taylor's vintage that I've been hiding from him.'

A broad grin passed over Maxwell's face in support of the statement but a determined Helga carried on,

'I'm sorry father, but I really feel we should discuss this now.' She looked determined.

Max and Kurt fell into thoughtful silence and took up eating again. Finally, Kurt steeled himself for the fray, mentally raising the pain threshold a little further and then spoke.

'Well, Max, you know the General situation and we've discussed certain items concerning the farm and its future in detail many times before. By now you are aware I'm not a well man and I have to make a decision very shortly about the place. If you are unable to give me some kind of commitment to come and live here permanently and take over the day to day operations completely then I've simply no choice but to employ a manager and some more European staff; this then becomes a business, not a home. Helga's mother didn't want that and neither do I.'

There ensued a tense silence.

'I completely understand where you are coming from, Kurt,' said Maxwell gently, now looking up from his plate and directly across at Helga.

'There is no need to say any more, and as I am officially on a month's leave from the FAO, I shall write my resignation out tomorrow and use this leave as my notice period which will mean that I don't officially have to go down to Nairobi to finalize handover details until next month.'

The words tumbled out quickly and to their recipients, somewhat unexpectedly. Kurt smiled deeply with a genuine look of heartfelt gratitude shining through misted grey eyes. Helga jumped up from the dinner table, rushed round to where Max was sitting, and gave him a long affectionate hug, terminating in an exaggeratedly prudish kiss. His cover as Senior Project Development Officer in the FAO during the past few years had been his last reserve position and after the end of this month the contract with his overall masters would be legally finished. He had made the decision and gave out a stunted sigh of relief that was hopefully not noticeable in the course of the continuing conversation. Perhaps he would now be able to settle in one place and try to lead a near normal life although what the definition of 'normal' was, in these deeply troubled times, he could not really tell.

By the time Ralph arrived with the coffee the General air of well being in the room was unmistakable.

'Has Harry Jordan arrived yet from the airstrip?' inquired Maxwell, glancing at his watch. It was past midnight and Harry had normally left the airfield workshop by ten o'clock at the latest.

'No Mister Max. In fact, I took the liberty of sending one of the boys out to the strip about half an hour ago to see if there was any problem.'

'Thanks Ralph. I'll wait up until he gets back.' Maxwell must have looked somewhat concerned.

'Don't you worry, Mister Max,' said a reassuring Ralph, 'I'll make sure everything is all right. You've had a long day and I believe you'll be up early in the morning too. You go to bed and get some sleep and I'll wake you at five thirty.'

'OK Ralph, but first thing tomorrow make sure the boys have topped the Land Rover up with fuel and water and checked all the tire pressures. I don't particularly want to have any transport problems up on the Samburu; that can be pretty inhospitable country.'

With Ralph's assurances that all would be looked after and supervised personally by himself, Helga stood up and moved across to kiss her father goodnight, once on the forehead and once tenderly on his cheek.

'Good night darling,' he said quietly, his relaxed countenance reflecting her obvious happiness. 'I'll see you at breakfast.

Maxwell raised himself from an encompassing Chesterfield, finishing his port with a final sip, and following Helga in the direction of the hall to climb the inviting staircase with her at his side, as they would do for so many nights together in the future; or so he thought.

# Chapter Four

*September 24th 1973 – Archers Post – Kenya – East Africa*

The morning came quickly and Maxwell was unprepared for it. In the depths of a reposing unconsciousness intruded a hollow tapping sound and echoing words spoken in a deep, clipped edge timbre that seemed very, very far away. There was a pause. It happened again but much more audibly and a slowly awakening brain was now taking control, directing suitable murmurs of reply to Ralph's repeated information that it was five thirty and time to be up and about. Max disentangled himself from a profoundly slumbering Helga who turned over and snuggled closer into her pillow without waking. Early morning light was stealing through the bedroom window, giving Maxwell the energy to force himself in the direction of the bathroom and stand motionless beneath a tepid shower for three minutes. With wet hair clinging to the back of his neck, he completed his morning routine of simple isometric exercises that had kept his stomach muscles firm and discoid over the recent years. He cleaned teeth with practiced rapidity and dried his body completely on one of the voluminous tufted cream bath towels. Maxwell rooted through the dressing room to quickly re-establish the whereabouts of his clothes since his last visit and finally reached for a light green cotton safari suit to wear on his imminent trip up country. He tied a dark brown sweat neckerchief around his neck, pulled on rubberized combat boots and exited the bedroom, quietly closing the door behind him.

The first hurried sip of steaming black coffee burnt his lips. A watchful Ralph reached for the crystal glass jug of iced water resting on the kitchen work top and poured a glass to hand to the wounded breakfaster.

'Thanks Ralph,' Max murmured, putting a testing finger to his burning lips.

'Is the Land Rover ready and kitted out? ...... and by the way, I think I'd better take the magnum with me this morning, just in case?

'The rifle is already in the rear seat fixing, Mister Max' said Ralph, as Maxwell finished his coffee, raised himself from the kitchen stool and walked to the outside kitchen door.

'Right, I'm off then, see you about lunch time if not a little before? The green brown jungle camouflaged Land Rover was waiting in the forecourt area running parallel to the rear of the stables buildings. Two farm boys were sitting on the bonnet with shotguns in hand and waiting impatiently to go.

'Jambo, jambo, fanya haraka!' shouted Maxwell. The boys got the message and jumped off the bonnet with Jonas heading for the driver's side door and Peter clambering over the tailboard to take his seat in the rear of the vehicle.

'Jambo, bwana, jambo bwana.' The words came back with some excitement as Jonas started the engine. Max climbed in and pointed to the left track leading from the compound. Jonas released the clutch with a jerk and in a cloud of rising red dust, the little expedition was off towards the east territory and the banks of the river Ewaso Nyiro. By six thirty they would be on the edge of the small Samburu game reserve and there Max planned to stop at the south warden's post to see if any of the rangers had picked up the trail of the poachers or had any fresh news since Kurt's visit the previous day.

Jonas drove well and extremely quickly in the heavy Land Rover. He had been working on the farm since he was a small boy and knew the area better than anyone within five hundred miles and especially the better tracks to navigate in any season, enabling men and vehicles to cross the bush and arrive at their intended destination all in one piece. Maxwell was first to notice the peeling hand painted signs giving warning that they were now in the reserve area of Buffalo Springs and he nodded to Jonas as a signal to change direction towards the northeast which would bring them to the compound of the south area warden's base camp. The khaki clad guard on the compound gate gave a wave as they cruised by and turned in the direction of the warden's office situated in the middle of a cluster of wood and barasti constructions on the east side of the isolated bush settlement. The Land Rover pulled to a halt in front of the office steps and Joe Mogamba, the head warden, appeared with a welcoming smile on his face and a huge mug of tea in each hand.

'Habari za ashubhi, Mister Max,' he said, giving Maxwell the politest good morning he had heard in a long while.

'Jambo, Joe,' was his reply as he took the simmering mug of tea gingerly in both hands, remembering the earlier experience with his liquid breakfast.

'Ralph called on the radio and said you'd be here about now so I thought I'd better put the kettle on and break out the Teachers. Maxwell sampled his tea carefully whilst Joe ran over the events of the past few weeks. As they both sat on the wooden planked steps leading up to the warden's office, Joe described some of the various cases of slaughter that had recently taken place in and around the reserve in vivid detail, the latest having been discovered only two days previously.

'This is not the work of simple ivory poachers, Mister Max; we've had a whole family of leopard wiped out and even bushbuck killed and left lying where they fell in their tracks. The only thing we know for sure is that whoever is doing this is part of a team of experienced hunters and they are seemingly well equipped. There are very few deep tire tracks around the kills, or by the water holes, indicating they are using low ground pressure vehicles. They are also probably fitted out with accommodation, as the only signs we can find of their camps are dusted out fires; no tent pole marks or remains of temporary shelter, simply nothing.'

Maxwell mused silently on the subject for a while, knowing as Joe did that this was not the work of hungry local natives, or over ambitious European hunters and army poaching groups that did, unfortunately, stray into the area, often from nearby Uganda.

'What kind of weapons are they using, Joe?' he asked, whilst assimilating the information relayed by the most experienced game warden in the area. Joe plunged his hand into the leg of his smartly pressed khaki combat trousers and produced the remains of what was instantly recognizable as a fifty caliber high velocity magnum range bullet. This indeed, was professional stuff and as the bullet was being weighed in his right hand, Max asked if there had been any tracking since Kurt had been up on the south range of the farm yesterday.

'The Patrol that I sent out at first light will not be back until around ten o'clock but we've had no more reports since Mister Kurt and Jonas radioed in yesterday morning' replied Joe with a pained and frustrated look on his face.

'OK, my friend,' said Max. 'We'll go up to the north river bank on the reserve and follow it down to the farm property and hopefully meet your patrol somewhere on the way and compare notes. If I find anything new I'll give you a shout on the short wave when I get back to the house. Kwaheri, Joe'.

'Kwaheri, Mister Max, good hunting'.

Max jumped into the Land Rover after handing Joe the half empty tea mug. Jonas fired up the muddied vehicle, slammed it into gear and they were off once more in the direction of the river.

The expedition skirted the small tourist encampment area and by eight o'clock, they were at the banks of the muddy, lazy, Ewaso Nyiro river. Following the course of the north river bank the Land Rover carefully picked its way amongst sparse bush and broken tree trunks, rubbed clean of bark by the permanently itching elephant. Suddenly, Peter shouted and banged the roof of the cab to indicate that something was afoot either ahead or behind. Jonas switched off the engine and the vehicle coasted to a halt. There was no need to enquire about Peter's excitement, as the obvious reason lay clearly marked in a dark grey, brown, bloodied mess about a hundred and fifty yards away from the river and off to their left.

The three men cautiously descended from the Land Rover and spread out in a fan about twenty yards apart. Maxwell cocked the magnum, slamming one bullet in the breech and at the same time releasing the safety catch. There were trails leading up to and away from the massacred elephant which Peter carefully avoided and marked regularly with broken twigs during their heedful movements towards the blood soaked animal. The valuable ivory had been crudely cut out and one of the ears was missing from the unfortunate beast. The area was damp with fresh blood indicating that the surgery had taken place whilst the animal was still alive and probably no earlier than two hours previously.

Maxwell painstakingly checked the area for signs of an encampment but there were none and some visible tire marks were so slight that, even as they searched, the indentations were being covered by settling dust raised in the first stirrings of the early morning ground winds. Jonas had now joined Peter and they were talking excitedly, pointing to the ground, with Peter waving one arm towards Maxwell shouting,

'Bwana fanya, fanya, ni muhimu.' Max knew that any find would be important so, marking his present spot with a pile of dried grass, he ran over to the boys to investigate the discovery. A discovery it surely was, for there, clearly visible in a patch of loose soil, moistened by blood that had now dried over to leave a crisp clear impression, was the most unusual footprint that any of them had ever seen. Maxwell ran back to the Land Rover to fetch a Polaroid camera and close up lens attachment that Jonas had packed with the gear that morning.

By the time he arrived back, the boys had spread out and were searching away from the site of the footprint that was now marked with a small cairn of loose stones. He took eight photographs of the print, moving in a circle around it. The footprint itself, was of a size eight or nine male shoe with a deep heel impression showing the man to be about a hundred and eighty pounds. The really unusual point about the print though, was the design on the heel that appeared surprisingly clear and distinct, suggesting that the footwear was probably brand new. The area was covered by a pattern depicting the head of a unicorn, bent forward in classic pose with the single horn pointing towards the toe of the shoe sole. The unusual design was encircled by seven stars and surmounted by a crescent moon.

'There are not too many of those rattling around in bloody Africa,' Maxwell thought despairingly as he checked each Polaroid picture for clarity in the final phase of development. The boys arrived back having found nothing new, with Peter explaining that the tire tracks were so faint there was hardly anything to see and there were no other significant marks or footprints around.

The vultures were now casting grey, sweeping shadows on the ground as they circled high above the carcass of the dead elephant, so the three man investigative party moved back to the Land Rover to continue their search and leave nature to clear up the mess of this senseless murder and mutilation. They continued south west following the course of the river bank and after about half an hour came across the morning rangers patrol that Joe had sent out at first light. After exchanging information and discovering the patrol had seen nothing of significance, Max gave the head ranger two of the photographs to take back to Joe and asked the patrol to cover the area north east of their present position, reporting back to the farm by radio if any new evidence was discovered. They waved goodbye to the patrol at about ten o'clock. They would be back by twelve thirty, just about as planned.

\*\*\*\*\*\*

Helga watched patiently from her bedroom window, waiting for the tell tale dust cloud to appear on the horizon, signaling the return of Maxwell from his morning expedition. At twelve thirty five the misty merging of land and sky to the west was broken by a rising shadow of grey that prompted her to move away from the window towards the oval dressing table mirror. By the time Helga reached the bottom of the stairs, Ralph was opening the door and Maxwell was walking up the veranda steps. He spied her through the interior gloom, extending his arms to hug her tightly for a second or two as she rushed towards him. He asked about Kurt and whether he would be in for lunch.

'I'm sorry, Mister Max, he won't be back at the house until about three o'clock. He went off at ten thirty to the Buffalo Springs Ranch to have a look at some horses that Mister Geoffrey wants him to buy.'

'OK Ralph, not to worry, I'll see him at dinner this evening,' Maxwell replied, moving towards the drawing room with Helga close by his side. They both sat on the sofa discussing the morning's gloomy events although Max omitted to mention the discovery of the strange footprint found by the south boundary. Lunch would be ready in about half an hour, so Max excused himself to make a phone call to Nairobi to confirm his arrangements with the FAO regarding his terminal leave.

Maxwell entered a small ground floor room agreed by all to be his study and closed the door firmly behind him. He wrote down on a slip of paper a memorized UK London number then proceeded to write underneath a reversal from right to left of the first three numbers and then the second three numbers. After dialing the London code he dialed the new number written on the paper and a female voice answered after exactly four rings. He had a brief conversation with the voice and then rang the FAO Nairobi number, waiting for about twenty seconds until the call was answered. Eventually he was put through to the station chief, Johnothan Rainbird, who greeted the news of his resignation with little surprise and asked Maxwell to fill in all the relevant paper work in the Nairobi office, next time he was through. Johnothan knew nothing of his real work except that one day he suddenly appeared on the payroll and his project work was coordinated directly from headquarters in Rome. However, the past few years had nurtured a genuine friendship and so he sincerely thanked Maxwell for all his efforts over the past years and promised to be in attendance at the wedding when the final date was decided. Max put down the phone. All appeared to be going well, so far, but at the back of his mind lurked a niggling suspicion that perhaps things were, in effect, going *too* well.

He wandered over to the window again, pulled an ashtray across the sill and took a folder of waterproof matches from his left hand breast pocket. He waited until the small slip of paper he was holding was completely burnt in the ashtray and then powdered the remains with his right index finger. Leaving the study, he carefully closed the door behind him and made his way upstairs to wash away clinging trail dust before preparing to eat Lunch.

Helga greeted the news that his resignation had been accepted by the FAO with unconcealed delight, but there was still something sifting restlessly through the back of his mind, something he couldn't pinpoint, but he was forming the sneaking sensation that the day was far from over and it would more than likely end up being another long one. He was about to be proved right. During continuing conversation, neither noticed the approaching mushroom dust trail emanating from the Archers Post track in the far distance. Ralph appeared on the veranda and caught Helga in the act of giving away the final remnants of her bread roll to a noisily pleading peacock. He spoke quietly,

'There are two cars coming up the drive, Miss Helga, and the gate boy has rung up to say that none of the occupants care to give their names but he has let them through as they say you are expecting them'. Maxwell and Helga exchanged a long wordless but conversational look. Helga's message was

'This must be the last time!' and Maxwell's message was

'I will deal with it and deal with it quickly'.

# Chapter Five

*September 24th 1973 – Archers Post – Kenya – East Africa*

Max turned his head in the direction of the driveway and he felt his pulse rate increase. The imposing outline of two perfectly preserved Mercedes 600 Pullman saloons materialized through the agitated trail of surface dust which chased them to the edge of the tended grounds. The cars were jet black and sparkling in the reflected light of several layers of clear paint lacquer. Side windows obscured the occupants with the use of one way reflecting glass, reproducing a distorted picture image of veranda railings and creeping bougainvillea. Maxwell guessed by the way both cars were sitting on their air suspensions they were either loaded down with occupants, or armor plated, and when the driver's door of the first vehicle opened with the accompanying faint hiss of compressed air, he voted for the later.

An African driver, in pristine whites, emerged from behind the wheel of the first car and casually opened the rear door in anticipation of an exodus. There was no movement at all from the car behind. It just sat there menacingly with engine running and the occupants, if any, totally invisible from distant scrutiny. A stocky well dressed gentleman emerged from the first Mercedes wearing a mixed grey mohair suit that had obviously not been cut within a thousand miles of Nairobi. His skin was dark Latino but he bore definite Arabic features, crowned by a great shock of jet black hair, combed straight back from the forehead with no parting, making him look possibly a little taller than he really was. Max estimated the visitor to be about five feet nine or ten as he walked around the car to approach the veranda steps. He possessed a bulky figure but moved with uncommonly athletic ease. As he stood patiently at the bottom of the steps, the two men locked eyes warily. Maxwell's brain was working overtime; searching all recalled mission files, scanning distant memories of many past briefings or remembered newspaper cuttings; something was up and he felt mildly disturbed. The smile was easy, the outstretched hand beautifully manicured, the white silk shirt cuffs exactly half an inch below jacket sleeves, the refined tones and pronunciations of an Eton and Oxford education were overlaid with the authoritative quality of one that was used to being obeyed. The Arab looking gentleman spoke first of all to Helga. There was still no discernible movement from the second car.

'My dear Miss Weismuller, what a great pleasure to meet you once again. He looked at Maxwell but directed his conversation towards Helga. Ralph stood in front of the main door, respectfully but firmly, barring entrance to any unwanted visitors.

'I really must apologize for my rudeness in not offering you my name yesterday and in fact for all this silly cloak and dagger stuff, but I'm afraid until I have been able to have a private word with Mister Armstrong, I can offer you little more than my assurances that I normally prefer to act in a more gentlemanly manner in the company of ladies, especially a lady as beautiful and elegant as yourself.'

The stranger was now on the top step and grasping Helga's hand in a practiced and polite handshake but maintaining his gaze in Maxwell's direction. Suddenly, the long awaited mental bell rang and a file broke open to offer up the information required. Whether it was good news or bad news, Max now took comfort in knowing who the bringer of the news was and it prompted him to relax noticeably, followed by a confident step forward to introduce himself to the mysterious afternoon visitor.

'I'm Maxwell Armstrong. I know you have already met my fiancée, Helga Weismuller, so perhaps, if you could now tell us who you are, we could all sit down and enjoy some early afternoon tea. The stranger beamed a very rehearsed but nevertheless, engaging smile and swung his outstretched hand in Maxwell's direction.

'I am so pleased to meet you, Mister Armstrong, and there is nothing I would like better than to join you in some tea, for which you are so famous, not only in your country but also in my country.'

Ralph moved away from the door at a signal from Max and pulled up a chair for their guest. Upon seeing him seated, Ralph retreated indoors to prepare tea. The stranger spoke again.

'Simply to establish my General credentials, without just yet revealing my identity, I can offer you this piece of information which is basic in content but will hopefully confirm the sincerity of my intentions in wishing to speak with you today.'

He removed a gold Dunhill pen from his left inside pocket and looked back towards the driver of the first car who immediately mounted the veranda steps carrying a leather bound, loose leaf, notepad from which he removed one sheet and handed it to the waiting Eastern scribe. Helga sat watching the proceedings with a casual but nevertheless interested smile on her face, as she had done since the beginning of their lunchtime interruption. By now, she was used to all sorts of strange people arriving at the farm looking for Maxwell with requests for meetings at all strange hours. They were never discussed afterward and conducted mostly in the privacy of his small but adequate study. This was probably nothing different. Normally, the incumbents were emissaries, future ministers, present ministers or ex-ministers of various African and third world governments who were in turn hoping to run away with the till, wanted information about which till they could reasonably run away with, or had just run away with the till and needed to know how they stood in the eyes of that part of the world which had put the money in the till in the first place. Maxwell, with a history of having to deal directly with ministers of such countries, often on behalf of international agencies, coupled with his notoriety for independence and his official connections within the United Nations, was often an early port of call. Helga raised herself from the lounging chair on the veranda and diplomatically excused herself whilst the 'gentlemen' carried on their business. Just one warning word was spoken in the final parlance.

'We will be going to meet my father in the paddocks at four thirty, so I hope your discussions will be over by then.'

The visitor held out his hand yet again and purred quietly,

'I'm sure we will have come to a complete understanding within the next half an hour, Miss Weissmuller, and then I shall leave you in peace.'

He immediately raised himself and half bowed, somewhat awkwardly as she left and then settled himself in a chair next to Maxwell at the lunch table. The slip of paper was neatly folded in half and handed over to the host who accepted it, got up from his chair and moved toward the veranda railings. He opened the paper message and was initially surprised, for written there was simply two series of numbers, one on top of the other. The lower set was the reverse of the first and second series of three and Maxwell immediately understood the connotation. He deliberated for a long moment and was frankly puzzled but managed not to show it. He held no positive position of advantage and therefore decided to say nothing.

'I see the information on the paper I have given you has some meaning, Mister Armstrong,' said the visitor with the cut glass accent.

'Yes, it does, Mohammed al Shukri,' replied Maxwell, now turning to look his Arab visitor straight in the eye.

'Well, now you know who I am, it will save time relaying to you the details of my position as an emissary of the lower Arabian Gulf countries and allow me to discuss the purpose of my visit, after which you will be able to make your four thirty meeting'

The delivery was sharp with a touch of irritation and perhaps slight impatience in his voice as Mohammed al Shukri signaled to his driver once again. This time he appeared with a black leather briefcase which was quickly transported to the table and laid before the Arab Gulf Co-operation Council Roving Ambassador, or Minister Without Portfolio, for that was what Maxwell assumed he was. He was known to his host by reputation only, which did little to impress; in fact he felt unnaturally wary of the man and slightly ill at ease. The briefcase was opened promptly and Mohammed removed a grey manila file with no title or heading and simply decorated with a crimson slash across the top right hand corner. Maxwell returned to his seat, calm but now curious with one eye on the visitor in front of him and the other regularly checking the second darkened vehicle from which there was still no movement. Mohammed al Shukri opened the file and began his obviously rehearsed speech.

'I have here a complete file dossier of your background and personal history to date' He paused for effect '…. and I really do mean complete. This information has been released to me by the British Secret Intelligence Service and the properly informed officials within that service are aware of this meeting and the reason for it'. His words were clipped and controlled.

'Although this file contains a detailed listing of your movements before joining and whilst working with the SIS, it does not contain any information concerning your direct activities in countries outside of the United Kingdom or the names of any of your associates in those countries. I bring this file only to convince you that my mission has the full but covert support of your government. Also I am aware of the contract conditions attached to your cover in the FAO and that your official contract with them terminates at the end of this month.'

Maxwell stared long and hard at the man who had just spoken and decided that for some reason he didn't actually dislike him but on the same level, he couldn't pinpoint anything he could say he specifically liked either. It was a strange situation. His finely honed instincts dictated that he remain extremely wary. Mohammed spoke again,

'I have only brought this file with me as simple proof of my credentials and for your viewing, after which it will be immediately destroyed and I can assure you that there are no other copies in my possession'

'Let me have a look at the file,' said Maxwell, without emotion and little movement of the eye to betray the speed at which his well trained mind was now working, searching for all the right questions in an effort to take control of the present situation by coming up with the right answers. He opened the cover, took out the first page and held it up to the light. The water mark showed up clearly, proving that the information contained in the file was at least typed on departmental paper; Maxwell commenced to read:

*Name: Maxwell Armstrong. Operative Number: 1134.*
*Nationality: British. Country of Birth: United Kingdom.*
*Date of Birth: October 30th, 1928.*
*Place of Birth: Lee Meadows, Soningdale, Berkshire.*
*Last Update: June 1973.*

It was strange reading about oneself in such matter of fact terms, and although Maxwell had never read his own personal file and therefore didn't really know what was listed in it, one thing he did know was that it was the sort of information that should definitely not be revealed about him to anyone outside of, 'the company' He carried on reading.

*Father: John Anthony Armstrong. Surgeon General, British Army, Medical Corps. Surgeon and Medical Advisor to British Special Air Service in sixties and seventies. Knighted in 1956 for extraordinary services to Her Majesty's Government and appointed Special Medical*

*Liaison Officer with the American military in the early sixties. Died of lung cancer, February 1968.*

*Mother: Sybil Dorothy Lee-Smith, only daughter of Lord and Lady Lee-Smith. Leading member and fund raiser of the World Wildlife Fund. Worked for six years during the early fifties full time for the Swiss managed WWII Refugee Children fund and in the late fifties was appointed a main board negotiator for the International Red Cross. Died of natural causes: June 1969.*

*Brothers and Sisters: None.*
*Other close family connections: None known.*

*Current Pensionable Military Rank: Lt Colonel.*

'Well,' thought Maxwell, pensively, 'everything seems to be all right so far.' There was a high level of detail that he thought would be missing, especially his father's unusual involvement with the military and the SIS, but that was to be expected in a file that had received official release sanction to a third party. He skipped the paragraph on his early childhood and education and moved on to when he left university and joined the army.

*Maxwell Armstrong. Left Leeds University at age twenty two with a First Class Honours degree in mechanical engineering and joined the Royal Mechanical Engineers on a short service commission.*

*He undertook an intensive Special Equipment and Weapons Course at Malvern followed by Counter Intelligence Training at Henley. MA considered highly adaptive to debriefing agents on complex engineering subjects and translating technical intelligence data received from class three reliability sources.*

*Attachments: Attached in 1956 to the Special Air Services Regiment as a Technical Advisor and Counter intelligence Specialist with the rank of First Lieutenant.*

*Service: Served one year in Northern Ireland mid 1956 to mid 1957 under cover involving Operation Harvest.*

*Transfers: Transferred to the Rosemarkie SIS establishment for advanced counter intelligence and electronic warfare training.*

There appeared to be little sensitive detail exposed in Maxwell's history as he read it. He began to feel considerably more relaxed. In fact, this was a very brief dossier indeed and was obviously one that had been carefully edited, as expected, to offer the reader a General picture of an individual and background without any definitive analysis. More importantly there was no exposure or scrutiny of operations undertaken in the past. As he continued to read, some poignant memories came filtering back and his temperature rose by half a degree until he was perspiring slightly. Without looking up, Maxwell turned the page and slowly but deliberately pulled the brown cloth from around his neck and wiped his forehead with it. He carried on reading.

*Activities since joining Special Intelligence Service are classified but the following confirmation of overseas activity will indicate the level at which subject has been able to operate effectively.*

'Well, well, well…….' Max remarked out loud.

Mohammed, sitting patiently, looked up and smiled condescendingly, not wishing to accept this particular invitation to further conversation.

*'Officially accepted engagements on behalf of SIS overseas from 1958 to present date:*
*1958/59. Location: Awabi, Sultanate of Oman.*
*Official Capacity: Military Advisor. Rank: Captain*
*1959/63. Location: Abu Dhabi, Trucial States.*
*Official Capacity: Commercial Attaché.*
*1963/64. Location: Nairobi, Kenya*
*Official Capacity: Commercial Attaché.*
*1964/67. Location: Salisbury, Rhodesia.*
*Listed Capacity, Covert Operations, Classified.*
*1967/68. Location: Port Harcourt, Biafra.*
*Listed Capacity, Covert Operations, Classified.*
*1968. Official transfer to the Food and Agricultural Organization, United Nations. MA has UN Staff member privileges with the addition of British Diplomatic status.*
*Base: Nairobi, Kenya.*

Maxwell carefully put the file down across his knees, reached to pour himself another glass of wine and turned his gaze toward his Arabic visitor who was still seated at the table and had not moved during the five or six minutes that Maxwell had so far taken to read and re-read the file. It remained open in front of him whilst he refreshed his glass with the now tepid wine. He turned back to the file, scanning the remaining information that mainly concerned notations and Generalities. He closed the file deliberately and returned it to the table. Just at that moment, the front door opened and Harry Jordan stood framed in the half light beckoning anxiously to Maxwell. Mohammed noticed the interruption but made no comment. He simply sat looking at his host in a slightly disinterested fashion, as he had done throughout the reading of the file.

Max excused himself politely and walked over to Harry who looked uncharacteristically perturbed, directing regular glances in the direction of Mohammed and then at the driver waiting motionless by the front door of the big black Mercedes.

'What's the problem, Harry? I told Helga that our visitor and myself were not to be disturbed'. He hadn't in fact, but felt sure that Helga would have conveyed that message to anyone planning to join him on the veranda that afternoon.

'You know I wouldn't disturb you, if it wasn't important mate' said Harry, glancing nervously over Maxwell's shoulder at the Arab visitor.

'I've been out with Kurt this morning, exercising the horses and as you know I'm not normally in contact with the airstrip on me days off, unless there is a flight planned for the area and I'm needed to man the control room or provide a beacon service for crop sprayers. Well, I left in a bit of a rush last night and I still had me portable UHF radio in me bag when I went out with Kurt this morning. I received a strange call from one of my boys out at the strip about an hour ago and thought I ought to see to it and tell ya straight away. A bloody great Learjet 24D has landed at the strip without any flight plan filed in Nairobi and it's sitting on the end of the runway with the crew refusing to leave the aircraft. It's running on the air power unit turbine and the crew will only communicate by radio. The pilot sounds English but the aircraft is registered in Oman. The really queer bit is, I've checked on the short wave with Nairobi and although they can't give me a flight plan they say that the aero plane has full clearance to enter and leave Kenyan airspace, filing flight information by radio once airborne and not below ten thousand feet. All other private flying in the whole of the bloody region has been suspended until the aircraft leaves Kenyan airspace. Now get this. The bloody pilot says he will receive his next instructions from the Weissmuller farm and will be contacting us every hour, on the hour, local time from 1600 hours by UHF.'

Several expletives crossed Maxwell's mind at that moment but he took control of himself and calmly asked Harry to go back into the house, stand by the radio, and acknowledge any transmissions from the Learjet and pass on any messages. Returning to his chair and re-seating himself at the table, Max asked what now seemed to be the only obvious question.

'OK, fuck all the intrigue, what the hell is going on here ….. and let me assure you the story had better be good or else you're going to leave this property the hard way.'

The Arab looked up and slightly past Maxwell's right shoulder, seemingly focusing on something in the distance. Other people, who knew Mohammed well, would have laid an unpleasant interpretation on such action but after a second the dark, glacial eyes re-focused upon Maxwell and the engaging smile returned but perhaps a little more forced than when first viewed less than half an hour ago.

'Well, Mister Armstrong, now you know who I am and hopefully I have convinced you I know who you are. You also appear to know there is an aircraft belonging to my government awaiting the result of this conversation before moving from the estate airstrip only a few miles from here. You may by now appreciate that this visit is in pursuit of a matter of some importance both to myself and to the parties I represent.'

As he spoke, Mohammed reached out for the file and placing it in the briefcase, changed one number in each combination set.

'This briefcase contains an acid spray system that is guaranteed to destroy all contents within forty five seconds of activation. The case is lined with a special neoprene preparation and will be safe to open in less than a minute'.

He checked his watch and placing the case flat on the veranda boarding, he cautiously opened it, taking care to avoid the rising vapour cloud that escaped when the seal was initially broken. The file had gone. Even the red silk lining had disappeared, leaving a dull black rubber finish that appeared totally unmarked.

Maxwell chuckled quietly to himself at this dramatic and slightly 'James Bondish' way of proving a point. Mohammed was not so amused at Maxwell's obvious and inconsiderate response. He decided to carry on the conversation.

'As you are no doubt aware, the world at present is not the well oiled machine our politicians would like us to think it is and quite frankly, is not running too well for most people's liking'. He paused to gather his thoughts and carefully choose his words.

'Since the removal of the gold standard, the dollar has nose dived, European currencies are in substantial decline and the two super powers are as close to starting world war three as they have ever been'. Maxwell remained impassive as his visitor continued.

'As members of OPEC, the UAE have agreed to accept payment for oil in US Dollars, but in effect, we are now earning substantially less for our oil than we were two years ago. There is much unrest in the Arab oil producing countries and I can advise you now that we are considering accepting only *gold* in payment for oil deliveries to western countries. By the Americans dropping the US dollar gold standard, they have effectively created a new one; oil Mister Armstrong....*Oil!*' Maxwell was now paying attention.

'There is also a movement, a quite powerful movement, among all oil producing countries within OAPEC, to increase the price of a barrel of crude oil substantially. By substantially, I mean... *double*'.

Maxwell leaned back a little deeper into the slip covered cane chair in anticipation of a possibly longer conversation than first expected. The Arab Diplomat studied Maxwell's expression for second of two, searching for some kind of reaction. There was none. Mohammed continued in cultured monotone.

'I would like to take you back to your time in the Oman, at Awabi in fact, where you were the main negotiator and facilitator in the effective exile of Imam Sulayman bin Abdulla and his younger brother Tammam to Saudi Arabia'.

Maxwell's brain was immediately locked in to scan mode in an attempt to recall the events of that particular time.

'The Imam had broken the Treaty of Seeb,... *twice.* He knew it, so did the British. After the bloody events at Jebel Akhdar, he simply had to go ..... but I made sure it was of his *own* accord .... and not that of others.' The Arab visitor spoke again.

'You are aware of course of the Imam's tireless activity at the United Nations to have his exile made illegal and his position is supported by many

Gulf States, Iraq and Saudi Arabia. He is now the religious leader of the world's Ibadi Moslems, believed by many to be an off shoot of one of the earliest 'Khawanji' schools, a form of Islam very distinct from the Sunni and Shia denominations'

'I am very much aware of that Mohammed. I spent an awful lot of time with the man on Jebel Akhdar itself and during his residence in Saudi Arabia as part of several attempts by the British Government to mend fences with the Imam. This was all part of an effort to persuade him to give up on his crusade to have Britain reprimanded within the hallowed halls of the UN. I have not had contact with him for nearly two years now. However, I know of his sincerity and I know of his rightful place, which is back in Awabi ruling the interior of the Oman.'

He paused for a second, realization beginning to dawn.

'I, as a reluctant conduit for British Government thinking from 1958 to 1960, also know more than most and in substantial detail, about the betrayal of this great man by the British Government and the unacceptably colonial manner in which his exile was engineered'.

A meaningful smile emerged on the smooth, beardless face of olive skin.

'Now you are beginning to see the reason for my visit with you today. The Imam Sulayman is no longer in Saudi. He is in fact in Iraq. His brother is in Qatar. The Imam is in Iraq at the personal invitation of the President, Ahmed al-Bakr and Deputy President, Saddam Hussein. The Imam is not a well man, but he has a following that is increasing daily throughout the Middle East. He is a bitter man I'm afraid; his health is fading fast and his brother Tammam, is publicly pushing for a religious awakening in the West that some have described as a form of Jihad. Tammam appears to have accumulated some powerful political contacts over the past few years and certain events now taking place in Iraq are worrying the Gulf States'.

Mohammed paused again to extract a Dunhill filter cigarette from a slim, beautifully engraved, gold case which he replaced in an inside jacket pocket. His discreetly hovering, but mute attendant leapt forward with a light which Mohammed acknowledged with a slight nod of the head. He now appeared to be inviting some comment from the listener, but none came.

'The leaders of Iraq, President Sadat of Egypt and Hafez al-Assad of Syria are hanging on the Imams every word. As the west tighten the screw and are intransient in accepting oil price increases in real terms, the Arab block sit patiently and wait for European and US investment in our countries that is now essential to keep our economies growing'.

Mohammed leant forward to add emphasis to his words.

'Mr. Armstrong, this is a bubbling pot of religious fervor mixed with economic desperation and political polarization....and it is about to boil over. There is only one man that can keep the lid on the whole situation, to give the more enlightened among us more time to find an acceptable diplomatic and political solution. That man is Imam Sulayman bin Abdulla!'

Mohammed leant back in his seat, slapping the table with both hands. Max leant forward and finished his glass of unpalatably warm wine and reached for the bottle protruding from a waterlogged ice bucket. He glanced down at his watch and spoke.

'Much as I accept the truth of what you're saying, I really don't see what this can now possibly have to do with me. As you can see, I am settled on a completely self supporting farm here and I will see to it that it stays that way. I have, quite frankly, had enough of the world of intrigue, crooked politics and religious fanatics and I now intend to devote my whole time to looking after this family, the farm and its workforce and, if necessary, the whole of this part of *fucking* Kenya.'

Mohammed appeared visibly disturbed at the use of such a profanity but composed himself quickly as he carefully stubbed the half smoked cigarette out in a rose shaped crystal ashtray that he pulled towards him from behind the ice bucket. He suddenly took on the appearance of someone fatigued, a curtain drawn over a tight expression that dropped down at this very moment; he carried on talking, seemingly ignoring Maxwell's comments and managing to expertly conceal his extreme irritation.

'Perhaps you have not been aware in detail of the massive build up of Russian military support and political influence in Iraq since the takeover by al-Bakr; one point four billion dollars in the past year and similar figures in Egypt. This is all modern technology, not world war two leftovers. The Gulf States are nervous, Iran is nervous, the EEC is very nervous and the Yanks appear unwilling to apply pressure on the Iraqis individually, or the Egyptians and Syrians collectively, all of whom are demanding more of a western economy that is on the point of collapse.' He leant forward once more and spoke in a much lower tone.

'Israel is the trigger Mister Armstrong. Rumor has it that the Zionists have some form of nuclear weapon ...... and the means to deliver it. Now, where do you think they got those from?' His face delivered a smile as he leant back but his eyes did not.

'Let me come directly to the point, so that we may terminate this meeting as quickly as possible and I may report back to my masters'.

Maxwell remained silently studying his glass, deep in thought, as Mohammed raised himself from his chair and leaned with knuckled hands on the veranda table. He spoke directly and firmly, phrasing his words with a certain amount of control and composure.

'I am here to ask for your help in averting a major political crisis in the Arab world. Since the Imam moved to Iraq two years ago, he has become increasingly reticent to communicate with anyone other than his close advisors, some of whom are now unbelievably.... Russian. He feels there is a major Islamic struggle to be undertaken and that he has been chosen to lead it. This is a message that grows in volume every single day as it is being echoed at Friday payers in just about every mosque throughout the Middle East. He trusts no-one and all efforts by senior Arab and European delegations to obtain an audience with him in the last twelve months have failed completely'

Maxwell interrupted.

'Look, my friend, I really do see why you feel you should be here, but what the hell do you expect me to be able to do that could have any effect on a situation that looks to me to be going down-hill at a rate of knots.?'

Mohammed bent a little lower.

'Go and see him ….. you are the only person now who could possibly get near him. He remembers the work you did on his behalf in Oman before his exile. He often talks about you. Whether you like it or not, a bond was established between the two of you back in Awabi and on Jebel Akhdar and although this was frowned upon by the British Government at the time, it was very much welcomed by the tribal leaders of the Gulf States. If you were to go to Iraq we are sure he would talk with you. It is imperative that we know what truly is in his mind and at this time, I am authorized by the governing members of the Arab Gulf Co-operation Council, to offer you all and any assistance that is required, plus any sum of money you may ask for'.

Maxwell was left deep in thought and genuinely taken by surprise as the Arab visitor finished speaking and returned to sit in the chair which he was now noisily pulling back up to the table. His mind was racing; his resignation from the FAO, the basic all-clear for retirement from the clutches of the SIS and most importantly the promise made to Helga and Kurt.

'How long would this little visit take, removing all the bullshit and speaking with words that I would need to be *convinced*...... conveyed the solid hard truth?' he asked archly, now more wary than ever of the man sitting in front of him; a man he suspected had rarely uttered a word of real unadulterated truth in his life.

'A little over a week, we estimate; maybe ten days at the outside. If you wish, your friends in the SIS will also confirm this and offer you their unqualified assistance.'

Maxwell gritted his teeth hard and informed the Minister or Ambassador, or whatever he was… that SIS promises were firstly, not worth a shit and secondly, the last time they had 'offered their assistance' as he called it, six good men were left for dead in an oily bog in Nigeria and he had been lucky to escape with only a leg broken in two places. The whole murky, underhand plan was now becoming clear.

'If I were to agree, what time would we plan to leave Kenya?' he said with remnants of undisguised anger and frustration showing in his voice.

'Latest tomorrow morning, but preferably tonight,' Mohammed said resolutely, studying the man before him in depth, searching intently for a sign indicating acceptance of the assignment thereby avoiding the otherwise inevitable use of his final means of persuasion.

Maxwell rose from the table, walked over to the west railing of the veranda and silently scanned the lovingly manicured lawns and gardens soaking up for one long moment the inimitable smell of fresh cut grass. He glanced again at his watch and then one more time at the immobile Mercedes. It was nearly four. Although he was seemingly being given a choice, he somehow felt that there wasn't one. He turned his head to look back at Mohammed, this man who had rudely interrupted his life at a time when everything was beginning to fall properly into place. He did not trust the situation. Although the Arab sitting a few paces away from where he was standing had not said anything really untoward, there was something very sinister in his manner. His thoughtful gaze was attracted once again to the second black Mercedes, sitting squat on deflated air suspension in front of the veranda. It's very presence was menacing and the fact that no movement had been made from within, even more so. Mohammed followed Maxwell's eye movement but said nothing; the trump card was there, available and ready to be played if required, but the Arab visitor felt that now it would not be necessary.

Something had changed in Maxwell's expression, a decision had been made. Maxwell excused himself from his visitor's company for a moment and walked quickly past Ralph, who was hovering in the hallway. He was heading for his study. He made the single phone call to his control officer in London confirming the basic credentials of the envoy now waiting patiently on the veranda and in guarded phrases, the contents of the past half hour's conversation. As it was an open line the discourse was slightly cryptic and the total communication necessarily short.

He replaced the receiver and sat pensively for a moment, wondering how to tell Helga he would be going away again. This would definitely not be easy and he would have to steel himself. Maxwell moved through the lounge and back into the main entrance hallway. As he closed the lounge door he turned and caught a flash of green from a pair of eyes that were welling with tears, moist and shining even in the fading afternoon light. It was too late. Helga turned quickly away before the tears finally came and ran towards the kitchen and out through the rear door, searching for a suitable refuge. Max knew it was useless to try and follow. Instead he elected to reappear on the veranda to advise Mohammed he would make available the maximum of ten days of his time. They would leave that night and he would be at the airstrip by nine o'clock. There was no shaking of hands, no effused thanks; simply exchanged nods of agreement and understanding as the Arab envoy returned to his car.

'Just one small thing before you go Mohammed. Who is in the second car?' The Arab turned to face Maxwell as his head dipped to enter the rear of the leading limousine, his lips curled in a cynical smile, a smile that nearly became laughter.

'My mother Mr. Armstrong….my mother!' and with that the visitor…..and his 'mother' left the property, followed by fresh clouds of billowing red dust as the two ungainly looking Mercedes and their occupants disappeared down the drive.

# Chapter Six

*September 23rd 1973 – Bowater House – London
– UK*

Hamish McWilliam stepped awkwardly out of the underground train to join the seething mass of trailing rush hour workers as the train door slid open to the accompaniment of hissing compressed air. The station clock clicked forward one minute to indicate six fifteen; he was late. He joined the battling throng for the race to the escalator and managed to steal a step on the bottom riser. He stood patiently on the step, wedged between swinging briefcases and plastic shopping bags, as the rumbling, ascending stairway hauled him past graffiti decorated advertising posters, intermingled with the inevitable, accusing, no smoking signs. He had not had a cigarette between Heathrow and Knightsbridge and, after passing through the electronic ticket barrier, he headed with mild desperation towards the north side exit and freedom, his gloved hands already feeling for the gold packet of Benson and Hedges and silver Mappin & Web lighter, buried deep in the left outside pocket of his military cut dark navy overcoat. A blast of unexpectedly cold, chilling, early evening air stopped him short at the bottom of the subway steps as he fumbled with the packet and finally took a long inhaling draw from the half lit cigarette. He hated London, summer and winter, especially winter when he seemed to have permanently damp feet, wet hair and the beginnings of a constantly irritating head cold. Winter had crept up early to autumn this year and by today's weather it could well have been December. Christ, he really did hate London, with its 'don't do this, don't do that' signs everywhere, its lousy bloody weather and even worse, its arrogant, inhospitable people. Hamish had spent the past ten years in much warmer climes, in the company of much friendlier people and, although he was now permanently back in the UK, he was thankful he didn't have to work in the sprawling metropolis of England's capital city. Modern, quickly evolving, high speed data communications systems such as Microwave, Telex and a new thing called 'Facsimile' were now making it unnecessary to have a headquarters in London, even if you were in the banking business, as Hamish very much was. As the present director of the British Clearing Banks Association he did need to travel to 'town' fairly regularly but this was more than compensated for by the return to his main headquarters and home, in a beautifully restored Georgian mansion, set in the rolling Oxfordshire countryside. He was aggravated and out of sorts; aggravated by Lord Fotheringale's phone call telling him to return from New York immediately and out of sorts from the long and tedious flight across the Atlantic, made even more tiresome by the fact that he could not get a booking on British Airways and had to fly TWA, whose ground handling staff had decided to hold an unplanned protest strike just as he was boarding the aircraft. He'd had to leave his luggage at the airport but hoped by now it would be securely ensconced in the boot of his official car which his driver, with any luck, would be aiming along the M4 motorway, through the dense evening traffic to meet up with him at Bowater House. He pulled back his coat sleeve to look at his watch and hoped that whatever this bloody meeting was about, it wouldn't take long.

Hamish waited for the traffic lights to clear his way across the road leading beneath the Bowater Arch and on to Hyde Park. The little green man above his head started flashing as a crowded black taxi curved its way through the crossing on protesting tires, prompting angrily breathed swear words from a chilled and exhausted pedestrian. In the ground floor lobby of Bowater House, Hamish was questioned reverently by a military suited commissionaire who, on discovering the identity of the auspicious visitor, lightly fingered the patent leather peak of his cap in a mild sign of deference and led him to the bank of lifts hidden from direct view when standing at the dimly lit reception desk. He exited on the eighteenth floor as instructed and found himself facing a pair of smoked glass doors, displaying the sign, Research and Development Finance Corporation Ltd. He'd never heard of it, but pushed his way firmly through the doors to be greeted by a very smartly dressed, dyed blonde receptionist to whom he made another enquiry. In reply the pert young lady escorted Hamish along a well lit paneled corridor and ushered him through a single door in the panel work, closing it gently behind him. The room was not over large and fitted out in the same light ash veneer as the corridor. The major piece of furniture appeared to be a medium sized boardroom table, with seating for about fifteen people. Six pairs of eyes locked onto him as he entered the room and made his way towards the semi royal personage of Lord Peter Fotheringale. He accepted an outstretched hand as Fotheringale welcomed him and absorbed his muttered apologies for being late, at the same time directing him towards a chair at the conference table. Lord Fotheringale now spoke to the small assembly.

'Firstly gentlemen, let me thank you all for managing to be here at such short notice and probably some measure of inconvenience.'

To this, Hamish silently agreed.

'Secondly, I have to inform you that I am instructed that this meeting is to be held in the strictest of confidence and not one word uttered in this room is to be repeated or discussed with anyone, and I really do mean, anyone.' Fotheringale sat down at the head of the table, flanked by three men on either side, all of whom wore a serious and businesslike expression.

'Some of you already know certain gentlemen present here today, but let me start by briefly introducing you all. On my immediate left Herr Heinrich Smitt, managing director of Deutsch Bank and a leading authority on Russian financial affairs. On his left is Mr. Willard P. Morgan,

President of the United States Chemical Bank and director of the American Bankers Union. At the far end, we have Mr. Hamish McWilliam, an ex-director of the Saudi Arabian Development Fund, considered in my opinion to be the world's leading expert on Arabian finances and presently director of the British Clearing Banks Association.'

Hamish had briefly met both men on his right before at various International gatherings and financial conferences and he exchanged nods of greeting. Fotheringale half turned to his right to complete the introductions.

'On my right, sits Sir Charles Hawthorn, director of operations for the British Secret Intelligence Service, followed by Mr. Joe Starkley, head of CIA Operations in Middle East and Africa. Finally, General Sir James Bryce, a senior representative of the International Institute of Strategic Studies. For those of you who have not met me before, and I think that there is only one at this meeting today, I am Lord Peter Fotheringale, present chairman of Findlays International Bank and President of the European Bankers Union.'

In the pause that followed there were a few more nods around the table and the restrained shuffling of papers as Sir Charles Hawthorn arose from his chair and placed a thin, loose leaf file in front of each man. Hamish's hopes faded. This looked like being a long one and with the sinister overtones of sworn secrecy he felt it would be fairly superfluous to ask if he could ring his wife to say he would be late. Other parties at the table might be used to cloak and dagger meetings, carried on through the early hours of the morning but he was not and felt distinctly ill at ease. To confirm his suspicions the SIS man made what was meant to be a reassuring announcement.

'This could take some time, gentlemen, so I have arranged for coffee and sandwiches to be brought up in about half an hour and all of you with drivers waiting, please be assured they are being well catered for and will be available to drive you home when we have finished .'

'Oh, by the way, Hamish ….,' Fotheringale said, 'you will be pleased to hear that your luggage has been found and your driver will be here with it in half an hour.'

The meeting was now handed over to Sir Charles Hawthorn, who began speaking in slow, deliberate and monotonous tones, giving the impression that he had spent half his life in these types of meetings. In the irregular light of that West London conference room, Sir Charles would have passed for slightly over seventy, but was, in fact, only coming up to his sixty fifth birthday and had devoted over forty years of his life to the SIS. He had been brought up in the traditions of the 'old guard ,' the intelligence careerists left over from the World War Two Special Operations Executive. Despite the increasing supremacy of modern electronic surveillance, spy satellites and the high flying U2, he was still a great believer in the man in the field. As such, he now controlled all SIS field agents personally through a small team of control officers, three of which were sitting only three floors below, busy in their secret, but often boringly routine, private world. The speaker sported a short close cropped ginger moustache, which he irritatingly stroked now and again with the back of a long, bony, pale forefinger, as he attempted to educate the participants of the meeting in the importance of the confidentiality of the discussions now taking place, coupled with a few dramatic phrases such as 'National Security', enlarged into probable world financial security and finally the piece de resistance,

'Gentlemen, I must impress upon you that the results of our discussions here today may avert the possible beginnings of World War Three!'

There followed a brief pause as he scanned around the table to ensure he had gained everyone's attention. After the last statement, he definitely had and even a disbelieving and naturally cynical Hamish was now intrigued. Sir Charles looked back down to handwritten notes scrawled on yellow legal paper that covered the pink file in front of him.

'We now live in extremely dangerous and difficult times and as you bankers amongst us will be aware, there is presently tremendous pressure on the value of all free world major currencies to an extent where gold reserves in Great Britain, France, Germany, Italy, Canada and Australia are at very critical levels. As of today, if called upon, such reserves would not be sufficient to cover forward trading in any of those countries' currencies by October first, this year. You will hear the American point of view from my friend

Mr. Starkley in a moment, but I am free to tell you that the American Government has informed the President of the European Economic Community that as of October fifth, they will revoke all agreements for support of the European Monetary Exchange System and draw up a new gold standard, basically isolating themselves from western Europe's monetary control machinery. In other words, gentlemen, Europe will be on its own and as a trading block, probably fall into quasi bankruptcy.'

There were disbelieving looks from Hamish's side of the table and all three men attempted to talk at once.

'That's rubbish,' he shouted, somewhat louder than the others, 'I have just returned from a meeting of the M5 Policy Committee in New York and new support agreements have been signed for another twelve months. How the hell could anyone do that if the American representatives knew that the whole bloody thing was going to be revoked in less than two weeks? Christ, even the damned ink won't be dry by then.'

Willard P. Morgan also backed this point of view, stating that the US Treasury could not take that kind of decision without consulting the Bankers' Union. Heinrich Smitt restrained himself from adding to the verbal protestations and sat in silence, accompanied by an intensely worried look shadowing his lean, angular Germanic features. Sir Charles raised his hands in a plea for silence which he lowered progressively to the table as the protests faded away. He continued.

'Let me assure all of you that the American decision is fact, but this information is far less disturbing than the intelligence analysis that I am about to relate to you which has mostly led to the White House agreeing to such a drastic change in foreign policy.'

Herr Smitt now spoke and politely asked if any members of his own Government were aware of this change in policy and was told that short of the EEC President, only five other people outside of the room knew about the American decision; the American President himself and four senior aids. Sir Charles carried on to express that the reason for such secrecy was entirely obvious, but also a second factor exists in that the actioning of such a decision could be delayed, postponed or even cancelled altogether, depending upon a sequence of events which may take place during the next few days. If word got out to the General public that such a move was even being considered, there would be world-wide panic, a run on all the banks and probably uncontrollable civil strife in Europe.

'The EEC President, Senor Bantellas, has given us forty eight hours to review the situation and report back, at which point he will decide when, where and how to inform the leaders of individual European countries but only, and I stress *only*, after final confirmation that the American decision will be enacted on the planned date. The reasons for this will become clear shortly.

This was definitely heart attack material, Hamish decided. Although there were more than modest whispers circulating that the Yanks had been quietly reducing their commitment to NATO, thereby Europe as a whole over the past few years, it was felt in senior financial and military circles that this was altogether not a bad thing. Europe was now militarily stronger than it had ever been with dramatic increases in sophisticated conventional and nuclear weaponry. Nearly all of Europe was now right of centre politically. Most of the Communist and Trotskyite, ultra-left wing union leaders were fighting to generate unrest within a Generally hard working public, and often finding it difficult to generate the support required to make an impact after the revolution that was itself the whole of the nineteen sixties. However, they were very active and still very much alive. Edward Heath, British Prime Minister had his hands full with the miners and the Irish and Richard Nixon, US President, was in total overload in an attempt to contend with losing three hundred men a week in Vietnam and twenty two billion dollars a month slipping out the back door. However, Britain, in particular, had begun to surge ahead in high technology development and push through drastic reforms in the archaic social security system.

Achieving all this wondrous advancement unfortunately consumed a large amount of money and the massive government borrowings that had taken place during the late 1960s created an inflationary spiral which had now run completely out of control. UK inflation sat at a very manageable 2% in 1963 and was now an unhealthy 9.2%. Forecasts were rife amongst economists that unless this could be contained quickly, the rate could double within the following twelve months. To add some more fuel to the fire, indebted South American countries had actually reneged or were about to renege on all of their World Bank loans, closely followed by a majority of the so called non aligned countries, led by a much more economically independent India. The world was in a very confused state as a result and now consisted of half a dozen power blocks, combined with what appeared on the surface as a mish mash of political ideologies. The United States led what was known as the North American block, encompassing Canada, South Africa and Japan. Britain and Germany led the EEC and Russia, of course, led the Comecon block which had moved ahead in leaps and bounds under the calm and calculating hands of Brezhnev. The non aligned block, led by India, was in effect, bankrupt. Australia and New Zealand, Singapore and most of the other South East Asian States had grouped together loosely on the basis of anti-nuclear everything, probably hoping that when World War Three started, they would be left alone to take over the world in three hundred years hence when the lowest levels of radiation in London and Washington had calculatedly reached half life. The last and financially most powerful block consisted of the so called Moslem movement led by Saudi Arabia and a loosely entitled Arab Gulf Co-Operation Council (AGCC), still not fully engaged as a single political entity encompassing Iran, Iraq, Pakistan,

Syria, Jordan, the Emirates, the Yemen and Egypt. This block was the biggest single worry to most governments in Europe, as it appeared to control just about everything needed to feed an industrially hungry western world. The Gulf Arabs had given it sixty five per cent of the world's known oil reserves. Pakistan was working hard to give it nuclear energy whilst Syria, Jordan and Egypt had given it more or less food self sufficiency. Militarily, the block was fitted out with the latest weaponry, courtesy of an increasingly influential Soviet Union. The strongest bond in this block was definitely the one of religion bolstered by Sharia law and a collective conservatism overriding all sensibly thought out political considerations. China, forced to sit quietly on the sidelines having retreated back into itself over the past few years, diplomatically courted all parties in the non-fathomable ways of Confucius. Reflecting for a moment on all of this, Hamish had to agree with Charles that they were indeed living in dangerous and difficult times.

There was a light tap at the conference room door and Sir Charles reached for a switch or button of some sort beneath the table. With a short buzz and a click, the door was open and in staggered the blonde receptionist with a large overloaded salver of sandwiches, coffee and tea. There were polite nods of thanks from seven gloomy faces and with a noticeably exaggerated movement of the hips she swayed out of the room, presumably to return to other less domestic duties. Hamish looked at his watch to discover that it was nearly eight o'clock. After the noise of clattering coffee cups and murmured pleasantries concerning sugar, milk and cheese and tomato or ham had died down, Sir Charles continued speaking.

'As you are all aware, the American economic block has isolated itself more and more from Europe during the past few years and we appreciate better than most that the attitude of the EEC towards the American States, as of late, has not been conducive to very close ties of a political nature, but let me say we have always been in agreement on financial matters and although it is appreciated that we do not need one another to actually survive, we do need one another to grow, and joined together, we are probably the most powerful economic bloc in the world.'

Most expressed some kind of agreement, except Herr Smitt, who remained stubbornly silent, leaning on his elbows with his head in his hands, gazing sightlessly at his pink folder.

'Now, Gentlemen, please open the folders in front of you and I will hand you over to Mr. Starkley of the CIA for the next part of this briefing'.

Joe Starkley stood up, thought better of it, and sat down again. He was a balding man of average height and build, in his late fifties and looked completely nondescript. He had a face one probably wouldn't remember easily, which was presumably an advantage in his profession, mused Hamish. On his left wrist he wore the inevitable gold Rolex Oyster watch, exposed by jacket sleeves that were an inch too short and in combination with the rest of his attire, indicated that he shopped exclusively within thirty miles of Langley, Virginia.

'Well, fellas, I suppose I'm in a sort of awkward situation here.'

'You better believe it,' echoed Willard Morgan, as he studied the first page of his pink file. Joe, playing uneasily with his left ear lobe and refusing to establish eye contact with anyone in particular, carried on.

'The executive White House decision, of which you've been informed, was taken against a background of extremely disturbing intelligence information that has been analyzed, not only by our own direct sources within the United States but also outside agencies such as the Soviet Studies Department of Glasgow University, here in Great Britain. Most of the detail is contained within the files in front of you, but to put it in simple terms, we believe that the Soviets and the Moslem block are joining forces to take over Europe, militarily, under the guise of a Moslem Jihad and possibly led by the intractable President of Iraq, al-Bakr'.

Joe Starkley's statement was greeted in stunned silence, broken after a few moments by the refined and dulcet tones of General Bryce, who spoke out for the first time.

'Mr. Starkley, I can assure you that my Institute, the ISS, has not been involved in any analysis of the type you mention and we are supposed to be regarded as the leading independent analytical intelligence source serving NATO'.

'That is correct, General,' muttered Joe, '…..and that is because we regard your organization as insecure.'

The old man's face nearly exploded, as he turned sharply towards Sir Charles, seeking some sort of explanation.

'That is correct, James, I'm sorry.'

'Then why,' the General asked, 'am I present at this meeting today?'

'Because, James,' soothed Hawthorn, 'you as an individual are trusted completely but the offices of the International Institute for Strategic Studies are not. Today, we require the benefit of your personal experience and input, not that of the Institute. Also your personal study and corresponding advice on the overall military situation that will hopefully be revealed in the course of the next few days is regarded as invaluable, not only by myself and the President of the EEC but also our,' and here he paused to catch Joe's eye, '…friends in the CIA and the White House.'

The General reached for the insulated coffee jug and with unsteady hand, poured himself another cup-full. His blood pressure was returning to normal and after a brief, near under-breath, apology for the interruption, asked the man from the CIA to continue. Joe turned a few pages of his file and addressed the gathering once more, at the same time pulling his tie down a little and loosening his collar.

'There is evidence in the files in front of you of a ….. shall we say, unholy alliance between forces inside the Kremlin and a secret group within the hierarchy of the Arab AGCC. The present situation is unclear. Our knowledge of this secret group is limited to its name, Unicorn, and its probable membership of at least seven, theoretically well placed persons. The objectives of this group or society have, however, become increasingly clearer during the past week. Joe stopped to shuffle one or two papers in his file and Heinrich Smitt took advantage of the pause to voice a basic question and one that proved at the moment to be on everyone's mind.

'Tell me, Mr. Starkley, how can it possibly be conceived that there would ever be any kind of political union between the Soviets and the Arabs, each with such historically opposing cultures and religious views? The persecution of religion and particularly Moslems within Soviet Russia has been documented fact for over half a century and you now expect us to believe that these two diverse political ideologies could link together in some kind of religious war against Europe! The whole thing seems to me to be more a figment of a paranoid American imagination than something which would force us all to embark upon the beginnings of World War Three'.

One or two heads nodded vigorously in agreement, to which Starkley countered by handing the meeting back to Charles Hawthorn without comment. Charles took up the reins.

'Gentleman, may I suggest that you all take ten minutes or so to digest the content of the files we have given you whilst I order some more coffee; then we will be able to discuss the matter in some detail'. Lord Fotheringale, who had been non-forthcoming up to the present adjournment, sat in deep and muted thought as, between sips of fresh coffee, he studied each loose document in his file with care. Willard attempted to strike up some sort of conversation twice during the break, attempts which Fotheringale brushed aside with a disinterested wave of the hand. Willard P. Morgan still held British Royalty, down to the rank of Lord or Lady in a certain amount of awe and took Fotheringale's rudeness as a sign of regal eccentricity, forgiving him immediately and turning his attentions towards Heinrich, who was equally absorbed in the contents of his file and only replied to Willard's questions in polite monosyllables. Fotheringale played a strange and often misunderstood role within world financial circles, in his dual capacity as chairman of Findlays and President of the European Banking Union. Strange, in the fact that Findlays Bank, although originally a British banking operation in Europe and the colonies, had no High Street outlets in the UK. The strength of Findlays had been its unchallenged position as the leading banking institution in third world countries, especially Asia and Africa; operating over three thousand branches worldwide and handling more than twenty per cent of the world's foreign exchange transactions on a movement by movement basis. Today that figure was nearer twenty five per cent. It had therefore inadvertently ended up as the banking link between most of the world's power and economic blocks and as a result wielded tremendous influence in all financial circles. During the past ten years, certain dark forces had tried to do away with the name of Findlays and it's rather unconventional chairman but this was not to be, due mainly to the enormous amount of respect and personal influence held by Fotheringale with the bank's prime customers and heads of countries within which Findlays operated. He was a man of few words, but when he spoke it was Generally considered that whatever he had to say was worth listening to.

Lord Peter Fotheringale had decided to speak. He tapped the table lightly with a gold, engraved Waterman ballpoint to attract the attention of the assembled group of bankers, spies and military strategists. All heads turned in his direction. Hamish studied this impressive man distantly as well groomed hands pulled one sheet of paper from the file and placed it on top of the others. Fotheringale, when standing, was an imposing six feet or more in his stockinged feet, complimented by a lean athletic frame and at the age of sixty two, weighing in at a trim 182 pounds. He was dressed immaculately in an obviously Saville Row, dark blue pinstripe suit with matching waistcoat, across which hung the gold chain of an antique half hunter. He was famous for producing this beautifully engraved watch at meetings with government ministers and crowned heads alike, to indicate the termination of one and time to move on to another. Amazingly, for such a widely travelled man, he admitted to being only conversant with the English language, of which he was a master. He ran a long fingered, pink hand through a full head of silvering hair and began.

'Gentlemen, from the information gleaned as a result of the conversation to date and a short study of the contents of the file now before me, I would estimate that the only way the Moslem block could legitimately convince its populace to engage in any form of Jihad is if they are given a suitable reason. I would suspect that 'suitable reason' would be money, or to be more correct, the withholding of money, namely a major share of current Arab investments in the United States and Europe.' Hamish began scribbling notes on the back of one of the foolscap sheets taken from his files.

'You are correct, Peter, and one of the tasks of the banker's representatives here today is to come up with as much information as possible during the next seventy two hours, concerning where those investments lay and what they consist of.' Fotheringale glanced in Hamish's direction and said,

'I think Mister McWilliam is already working on that but a quick estimate from myself would be from between two and a half to three and a half *trillion* US dollars and if even one third of that amount were to be withdrawn from the western banking system in a short period of time, there would be created a liquidity crisis of catastrophic proportions.' He paused and looked purposefully round the room.

'Therefore……..you are trying to convince me that there will be a move to make such a withdrawal this month and that when we all say no, our Arab friends will call some sort of 'Jihad' and millions of them will start marching on Europe to take by force what they regard as rightfully theirs'.

Joe Starkley breathed the words, rather than spoke them.

'That's about it, in a nutshell, and let me assure you that we are sitting on a time bomb which is at this moment ticking away....loudly! We have to take action, now! '

Fotheringale tapped his ballpoint again a few times on the table, which Hamish took to mean that he had finished speaking. As a quick figure, he had calculated nearer the top end of the amount Lord Fotheringale had mentioned, excluding gold stocks held in Switzerland that were untouchable in this particular scenario and guarded by stiff-necked members of the Zurich financial mafia. The meeting indicated that it would now welcome input from Hamish as to where the Arab money was and, if possible, how much, country by country. It took the best part of three quarters of an hour to go through a fairly extensive list from memory, with the conclusions that, other than Saudi Arabia, the second largest deposits by far, belonged to Kuwait. During the sometimes heated discussions that followed Hamish's revelations and evaluating the wealth of intelligence information expounded by the British and American spy masters, most agreed that the target for the Iraqi President's financial manipulations would probably be Kuwait. Saudi was regarded as too conservative to join in such a plan, and the United Arab Emirates too wary of the immediate repercussions to its industrial base to be a leader in such a scheme. The other Gulf states didn't really have enough financial muscle to make a big enough dent in the overall world economy to hurt significantly and Iran, although in close contact with the Soviets, would probably remain on the fence, if such a thing was possible of course. Information from Iraq and of late, even Kuwait, was scarce, but pieces of the puzzle had started to come together. The activities of the deposed Imam, Sulayman bin Abdulla, now a permanent fixture in Iraq, were having a distinctly unifying effect in welding together religious opinion across the Islamic world. Major political leaders throughout the Middle East were echoing the thoughts and preaching's of the Imam and that was where the all important religious connection was being made. Only one fairly major hole in this complex religious and political tapestry was left to be filled. What was the real Russian connection?

That question now sat with the man from the SIS as he proceeded to put forth a theory. Not everyone was comforted by the fact that it was only a theory, but as it turned out, it certainly was an absorbing one. Sir Charles pressed another of his under-table buttons and a large projection screen majestically dropped from the ceiling near a wall at the far end of the room. There was a familiar buzz and a click from the conference room door and the expressionless blonde reappeared, pushing a trolley affair covered with numerous buttons, levers and glowing LED lights. The non cloak and dagger members of the audience were suitably impressed as the screen lit up and various maps of several countries flashed by. Sir Charles pressed one of the buttons and a broad scale map of the Middle East appeared reaching from Cairo in the west to Kabul in the east, covering the Arabian Peninsula to the south and the middle part of Turkey to the north. He began speaking,

'You are all aware of the fairly dramatic change in what we today know as the USSR since the beginning of the Brezhnev era, especially in the arena of human rights. What you may or may not know is that of the total number of dissidents held at the beginning of 1970, only an estimated fifteen per cent were being held on political grounds; the rest were in detention because of religious beliefs and again, of that total, over eighty per cent were Moslem. The figure, gentlemen, runs into thousands. Where did they come from? Look at the map again, which I will now expand to cover an area north to the Baltic Sea and overlay with an outline of countries which form the Union of the Soviet Socialist Republics'.

Sir Charles pulled at one of the little levers on the console and continued in a flat schoolmasterly tone,

'In the make-up of the USSR, if we exclude the Russian Soviet Federal Socialist Republics, we are left with fourteen individual republics. Since the days of the great Mongol Empire most of these areas have been strongly Moslem in the east. The countries that are of particular interest to this discussion are Georgia, Armenia, Azerbaijan, Turkmen, Uzbek, Tadzhik, Kirghiz and Kazakh, which have mostly resisted all efforts to date to break the strength of a fervent Islamic religious following and one that is canvassing openly and gaining more converts by the day.' He paused, looking round the room at the silent, expressionless faces

'Over three thousand Moslem leaders from these countries were under detention by their Soviet masters in one form or another and during the past two years nearly all have been released, spreading the word that Brezhnev is a new enlightened leader who actually understands the complexity of their religion; in some cases the preaching only just falls short of calling him a convert to the Holy Koran. Although the Moslems from these areas are mainly bound by the laws of the Sunni sect, they are, nevertheless, Moslems and full time professional Soviet soldiery is now probably thirty per cent Moslem.'

Charles pressed another button and the screen blanked out. The assemblage remained un-amused as each man in the room digested this new information, with Hamish continuing to scribble hurried notes on the rear of further documents drawn from his file.

Fotheringale broke the silence.

'We must now then assume that as much as it is out of vogue to be anti-nuclear in Europe, it is now similarly out of vogue to be anti-Moslem in Russia, would that assumption be correct?'

'It certainly would' broke in Joe Starkley, 'and the most concerning factor to us is the tacit support that the Kremlin seems to be giving to the growing popularity of one Sulayman bin Abdulla as the new revolutionary Moslem leader. I think you now begin to see the 'Russian connection' and probably will accept that this situation has not happened overnight. It has, in fact, been manipulated and planned over several years and so cleverly that we have all been totally fooled; until now. Unfortunately, we can only regard 'now' as the eleventh hour. There are some very sinister forces at work, not the least of which is the brotherhood or whatever you wish to call it, of the Unicorn. They are the real motivating power behind some sort of unfathomable plan, a plan that we confidently predict will be enacted and become stark reality before this year is out.' General Bryce looked towards Sir Charles questioningly.

'What do we actually know of this Unicorn movement, other than what you've been able to tell us so far, I mean about its aims, its purpose, what does it have to gain?' The director of the SIS admitted that the likely theory was an obvious one; the annihilation of Israel.

There was an electric silence of disbelief in the room as Sir Charles continued. He could only advance a further theory that its membership consisted of power hungry young men from the less wealthy Gulf States who had been western educated and only now coming into their own, in their own countries. With the return of many states to more fundamentalist Moslem ways, they had perhaps felt robbed of power. Combined with a strong anti-American feeling, generated by the inward looking Nixon administration, they had turned to the Russians for support in the conception of creating a much wider Islamic world of which, jointly with the Russians, they would have substantial control. A combination of Soviet military might and Arab financial clout, linked to guaranteed oil supplies and backup manpower of millions of religious 'soldiers' is a tempting situation with which to get involved if someone wants to take over the world. However, to do that successfully, the Zionists would have to go. Charles therefore had a distinct feeling that as part of any kind of military confrontation, Israel would be in the front line. Heinrich felt the time was right to ask another question.

'OK, I've listened to all this verbiage and I'm basically convinced, so what do you want me to do?' Sir Charles took up the query.

'*If* the Soviets are really in on this deal; *if* Iraq has managed to persuade Kuwait to join forces in withdrawing its European and American deposits, and finally, *if* there is a plan for this declaration to be made anytime soon, then we would forecast some very hectic movement in Soviet financial circles. You are an expert on Russian financial affairs, the best we have in fact; your contacts are widespread and intimate. You will be aware of most currency or metal transactions at least twenty-four hours before those transactions become common knowledge. To us, that foreknowledge is vital in putting together a minute by minute action brief to ensure that if the Americans do take the decision to withdraw financial support from Europe, that this decision will have been taken with all of the up to date facts that we can muster made available to them. Once that decision is finally taken, it cannot, under any circumstances, be reversed.'

'What I simply do not understand,' insisted Heinrich, 'is what the Americans stand to gain by such an action. The US dollar would loop the loop as well as European currencies. I mean, how can they possibly think of doing such a thing?'

Joe spoke again, rubbing damp palms together to the accompaniment of nervous perspiration breaking out on an already glazed forehead.

'You have got to understand, all of you, that the United States does not want to enter World War Three. Public opinion will live with a medium term financial crisis, but not a nuclear holocaust. You must face the fact that America is a totally self sustaining economy and with the alliance of South Africa and Japan can weather out any storms in Europe. We will not confront the Russians on foreign soil. The American people are convinced that they have been kicked in the teeth over the past five years with a near trade war going on between the US and Europe'. He paused to ensure he chose his words carefully.

'Fellas, let me again confirm that we will co-operate with you on all matters concerning this present situation, but if we decide to return to a gold standard at the beginning of next month, I can assure you, that with the full support of South

Africa, we are able to do it. There is nothing more to be said, except that you guys have a problem and the onus is on you to convince the President of the United States not to do something, rather than do it, and his mind is already made up.'

'If that is the case,' screamed an over excited Willard P. Morgan,

'why the fuck didn't you people tell *me* about it? As far as I can see you must regard me as a complete idiot. You can also tell me why the hell you bastards flew me over here...... to a foreign country, just to tell me that my own damn government is going to pull the plug on all its promises and commitments to half the free world; *and*, I might add, most of those commitments, one way or another, guaranteed by my own fucking bank!'

There was a slight wince from Sir Charles at the language and tone of Willard's comments and he interrupted with a restraining hand on the shoulder as the American rose from his seat, looking likely to initiate physical violence on the man from the CIA.

'Mr. Morgan, please calm yourself. We are all here attempting to try and *control* a situation, not to create new ones and we all have a particular role to play in the coming days that will result, in the worst case, some ordered command of events, and in the best possible case a delay and even retraction of your country's decision and therefore it's disagreeably drastic consequences.'

Willard sat down, but continued to glare across the table at Starkley, relieving the tension a little by loosening his tie and removing his jacket, placing it fussily on his chair back. Hamish finished jotting down more notes and took another swift look at his watch. It was a few seconds off midnight and the date flicked over to the twenty fourth. Christ, not many days left, he thought, and already one of them is slowly disappearing. He looked up. Fotheringale was speaking.

'….. and so how long will we have if our American cousins,' he intoned sarcastically, 'declare their financial support for the European monetary system as defunct on say the fifth, before we see some reaction from the east? That is, of course, assuming that they themselves haven't made a move by that time.'

Sir Charles replied that they still did not have a date for any kind of combined move by Iraq and Kuwait, working on the still active theory that in fact it would be Kuwait that turned out to be Iraq's partner in the conspiracy; but it made sense to assume any declaration by the Americans would confirm to the conspirators that their plan had been tumbled and they would then immediately request the return of their investments. Fotheringale continued

'Well then, to me it appears that if the American declaration is made before the repatriation request is received from Iraq and or Kuwait, then we would all be playing straight into their hands by giving them a legitimate reason to ask for the return of investments presently in our custody. The simple fact that the value of their paper holdings would drop dramatically in the first few months of the reorganization of the European monetary system, would be enough reason for them to ask for the paper to be liquidated at the pre-declaration 'price-to-value' level or reimbursed in gold. This is a very risky business we are engaged in and as far as I can see, it's rather ridiculous of the American President to start fixing the date of this declaration when we have no firm evidence to suggest that the event will take place this year at all.'

There were more nods and further murmurings of agreement from around the table.

'I can only reply,' said Sir Charles, 'by telling you that we will have a man heading in the direction of Iraq by tomorrow' he glanced at his watch. 'correction ... *today* ... and he is one of our most experienced agents. With the co-operation of certain concerned ministers of the AGCC, we expect him to meet with Sulayman bin Abdullah. I can assure you that although he is an operative of the SIS, he is also one of the few people in the world who, in this present predicament, stands any chance of getting to the man. He will be given minimal information regarding the depth of the problem and has only been told that the AGCC are concerned with Sulayman's present state of mind and they wish to avoid another Libyan Qaddafi Situation. This way, whatever he finds out will be relative fact and hopefully accompanied by unbiased opinion. He is a good man, Sulayman trusts him, and it's our only chance.' He looked towards Hamish.

'Please don't make a note of that particular point, Mister McWilliam; just in case.'

Hamish didn't know what 'just in case' meant, but he hadn't made a note of it anyway. Sir Charles looked at a blinking digital clock on the control console next to him and asked the assemblage if any more coffee was required. A pouting Willard replied in the positive and shortly after was heard the familiar buzz and click accompanied by the gyrating posterior that signaled the arrival of two more white plastic insulated coffee jugs and a set of fresh cups and saucers. Sir Charles took up the conversation again.

'I don't want to keep you any longer than necessary, gentlemen, so before I give you details of the specific services that we request of you, can I ask if there are any further questions?'

He looked around the room but no-one indicated they had any more to say, so, to the renewed background orchestrations of clinking china, he continued,

'Those of you who do not already have electronic scramblers fitted to your telephones will have them by the time you reach your various residences. He reached inside the console and produced six sheets of paper which he handed around the table; one to each man.

'These are the telephone numbers which have been made secure and only these numbers are to be used for communication between yourselves and my office. I will be available to speak with you around the clock and I must stress, yet again, the utmost secrecy of this operation. You may take the files with you, but their contents are for your eyes only, and should be kept in a totally secure place in your homes. Although it hopefully will not be too noticeable, your residences will be guarded and protected twenty four hours a day whilst this operation is in progress and you should not leave your accommodation under any circumstances unless you check with me first and even then use your official cars and drivers. For those of you without residences in England, such as Willard and Joe, we have made arrangements for you to be accommodated in two of our safe houses on the outskirts of London, where you will be well looked after and provided with everything you need.' He turned in the direction of Heinrich.

'We have assumed, Her Smitt that you will be staying at your Mayfair flat and have made all the necessary arrangements there.'

Heinrich confirmed that that would be the case, as he neatly tucked the telephone list into the folder and replaced it squarely and correctly in front of him. Like all good Germans, Heinrich was a neat and disciplined person, who hated disorder and was having a hard time digesting how the resulting chaos would be handled if 'the event' took place. But handled it would be, he told himself comfortingly; shit to the Yanks, the French and the British . . . the Germans would handle it and on their own if need be, like they'd had to handle just about everything else since 1946. He turned back towards the head of the table. He was confident, he looked confident and he felt confident. Whatever they wanted him to do, he would do and do it well . . . the German way. Sir Charles now spoke to each man at the conference table in turn, starting with Lord Fotheringale.

'Peter, we would like you to use your incomparable connections to monitor the currency exchange markets, especially in Bahrain and Hong Kong; also give us a complete breakdown of the present financial situation in the Pacific economic block, including the truest and most accurate assessment of Australian and New Zealand gold reserves. If the event takes place, we have to know exactly how long they can last and what political decisions would be made if they were totally isolated from the other world blocks and trading partners for a period, of say, eighteen months; also accurate information on strategic food and raw material reserves, including, of course crude and refined oil stocks. It does not need to be said that you will have to find a way of obtaining this information without arousing any suspicions whatsoever. One of the main reasons we have asked for your co-operation on this committee is that you are one of the few people in the world who has direct access to most of this information; but once again I must stress caution and ask you to spread your sources of data around as much as possible.' Lord Fotheringale nodded his head and tapped his ballpoint again, presumably as a confirmed sign of agreement.

'Now, Heinrich, I want you to make contact discreetly with your Russian friends. I need the most accurate information you can give me on the present state of the Russian economy, with a stress on military and civil vehicle production, grain reserves, money washing operations, gold reserves; in fact, just about anything you can come up with. You can imagine that if our theories are correct, and the Soviets have been planning this for a long time, then you can bet your bottom Deutschmark that they have been fooling us for years with the officially published Soviet economic figures and even the ones allowed to sneak through unofficial channels.' He paused thoughtfully.

'We've got to find out how strong or weak they really are, and how economically well prepared they may be for a possible lengthy European war. We need your independent opinion, and fast if we are going to be able to erect any economic trip wires or throw suitably designed financial bricks in their path, forcing them to think again or even delay any action they plan to take within the next few days. Can I leave that with you?'

'Of course you can,' retorted the German banker. 'I will get you everything you need'. The chairman of the meeting turned his attention to a now somewhat brightened Willard.

'Mister Morgan, I have to ask you to break certain banking confidences and betray certain trusts but I hope you agree that the situation is critical!'

Willard leaned forward to lend emphasis to his words, as he informed Sir Charles that he would do whatever was necessary to avoid the kind of world disaster that had been discussed during the past hours and all he needed was to be pointed in the right direction.

'Good,' Sir Charles said in a tone of encouragement.

'Now, we need the fullest possible details of all your central bank arrangements with South Africa and Japan, in the event of a national crisis. These are obviously not available in complete form to the CIA or any other agency as far as we know. This will require a lot of detective work coupled with a fair amount of logical thought and fortunately you are somewhat famous for possessing both these attributes. We need to know at what level the gold standard would be put in to effect, what support to that level will be guaranteed by South Africa during the critical first six months and what arrangements have been made to support the industrial base of Japan. If we know this in detail we may possibly be able to come up with an alternative to total withdrawal by the US from European monetary support. No-one in the administration or any of the government agencies knows of your involvement in this operation, except Joe Starkley. If you are caught you are on your own. Will you help us?'

'Yes,' was the simple, tense reply, and for one short moment Sir Charles thought he detected the beginning of a smile in the depths of the American's dark and serious countenance. Willard obviously loved a challenge. Attention now focused on Hamish.

'From you, Hamish, we require basically the same job done on the Arabs as Heinrich is doing on the Russians, but with special emphasis on personalities. See if anyone jumps out of the pot that could be a member of this Unicorn group. Go back mentally through the personnel files on some of the young, educated, privileged class types that you've indoctrinated into the money business over the years and see if any of them fit the picture of the angry young man'. After a pause for breath, Sir Charles turned his attention in the direction of the General.

'James, I want you to work with one or two of our people on possible military strategy that could be employed by a joint Soviet, Arab force to possibly knock out Israel and then be capable of carrying on to invade Europe. You will work with our Russian and Arab analysts separately and come to your own conclusions as to what moves will be made and, hopefully, when we get some dates from our undercover source, you will be able to provide us with some approximate timings as to military movements and initial strengths. We will tomorrow be setting up a direct data link in your residence connected to SIS and one that will compliment the dedicated lines you already have to the foreign office and Central European military command, so that the results of your studies can be passed directly through to me. I hope these arrangements will not cause you too much inconvenience but it was the best we could do at short notice. If there is any paper or archive material you need, then phone in and we'll send a runner with it.'

The SIS director was not looking for a sign of acceptance or approval from the General, obviously working on the principal that it was pretty pointless asking a man who had been trained all his life to take orders, to now accept requests.

'Now, a word to you all,' he continued, 'I appreciate that most of you have families and probably contradictory in terms, I would ask you to try and maintain your daily life in as normal a manner as possible. Keep everything in low key and use the 'pressure of work' excuse to keep out of the family's way. All phone calls to all residences will be monitored and recorded and all movements of your immediate family, children, grandchildren, will be covered. The protection teams will be working in your interests gentlemen, so please co-operate with them and they will ensure you some peace of mind whilst you concentrate on the job in hand.'

Sir Charles stood up for effect and checked his watch.

'It is now just turned one thirty, let's all get some sleep for what's left of the dawning hours and get at it bright and early. Everything you have, no matter how small, please communicate to me immediately, and once we have enough raw material to work on I will call another meeting, here at this office. Good luck, gentlemen, and good hunting. The other six members of the gathering raised themselves; some yawned, some stretched, some rubbed tired, red-rimmed eyes as they muttered various words of departure, thanks and goodbyes.

# Chapter Seven

*September 24th 1973 – London – UK*

Hamish gathered his file together and was the first away. The conference room door buzzed and clicked its way open as he approached and with overcoat in one hand and pink file in the other he wished the blonde person good morning and made his way out of the building. He spotted his driver waiting patiently in the entrance lobby, sitting with four other similar looking types. As he approached, his man briefly touched his grey, peaked cap, and directed Hamish to the underground car park, where the metallic, green Jaguar was waiting in a reserved bay. After settling into the soft leather hide of the rear seat, he replied to his driver's question with,

'Home, please John, and as there's not much traffic about I think it's probably quicker up the A40.'

'Right you are, sir,' confirmed the driver, accompanied by another quick touch of his cap. The powerful Jaguar XJ12 purred along the edge of Hyde Park, turned left up Park Lane and left again at Marble Arch to get on route for the A40 dual carriageway that would take them directly to Oxford, after which it would only be a twenty odd mile run towards Banbury and Sutton Manor; home. He thought fleetingly of ringing his wife and telling her he would be home within the hour but, much as he longed to hear her voice again, he thought better of it, placed the file on the seat beside him and settled back to try and relax. His brain though was still working overtime. He leaned forward and pulled open the door of the walnut drinks cabinet fitted between the front seats, pouring himself a small Ballantines Scotch into a hand-cut, lead crystal glass. The whole bloody thing was too fantastic for words, he thought wearily. There was no doubt that once a move was made by either side, and for whatever reasons, the net result would be total disaster for the free world. How the Soviets stood he didn't know, but one thing was certain, there was going to be a lot of subterranean dealing in the money markets during the next few days, probably starting with movements out of dollars, sterling and Deutschmarks and buying forward into gold. A few billion dollars registered on the gold market in a period of, say, twenty-four hours, would send the free market price rocketing and within a week could push it from the present fairly stable seventy seven dollar level to well into three figures. The way he saw it, the Arabs couldn't really lose, because as the dollar fell their gold stocks would increase in value against other European currencies, and if the Yanks pulled out from support of the European currency control system, then sterling and the deutschmark would go for a ball of chalk, bringing the dollar back up again. The only parties to all this intrigue taking a significant risk were the Russians. If for any reason they were unable to persuade the Moslem block to go to war, or if Europe and the United

States came up with some sort of compromise plan to either the White House decision to withdraw from Europe or the Arab request for redemption of western funds, then they would be in the proverbial shit. Once the western money markets settled down and reorganized after the initial shock to the system, there was no doubt that a recovery could and would be made and the free world market price for gold would settle down to a sensible level again. Comecon would be left in a nearly impossible situation, holding high levels of devalued gold stocks, coupled with low levels of foreign currency and still having to trade in great measure with the west.

The dark green car sped past High Wycombe at well over the obligatory seventy, with John, the driver, relaxed and comfortable at the wheel and held firmly in his seat by the two part lap and shoulder belt restraint. The rain had stopped momentarily, but in the early morning hours the road ahead was pitch black, broken only by the twin stabs of searching halogen light carving a way ahead for the fleet footed Jaguar. Hamish reached down and refilled his glass with the warming, golden liquid and pondered further on some of the subject problems that would consume all his time and energies over the coming days.

As the car cruised quietly through the outskirts of Oxford and approached the Banbury Road roundabout, black and yellow road signs could just be distinguished in the distance, illuminated every two seconds by flashing portable strobe lights. Signs displaying 'Road Works' and 'Diversion' confirmed to John that the only sensible route to take now, without some amount of backtracking, was through Bicester to join the main road again at Adderbury. Hamish agreed and his driver swung the nose of the car to the right and headed down a narrow, unlit, side road towards Bicester.

The big car took most of the road width as John carefully maneuvered his charge through the winding bends, passed gated tracks and towering oak trees painted with white reflective stripes, warning late night drivers of their closeness to a roadway that was rapidly turning into a narrow lane. Another five miles and they would be in the old Roman town of Bicester and from there the way would be a lot better. At that moment a blinding light appeared, right in front of the car, creating dazzling, crazed spectrums of luminescence that cascaded through the windscreen. Both occupants of the car instinctively put their arms up to shield blinded eyes and John, in an instantaneous reaction, hit the brakes. The lane, covered with wet leaves, loosened the grip of the all weather footpad tread on the HR Michelins and despite the desperate workings of the anti-skid braking system, the back of the heavy car began to break away.

In horror, Hamish digested the scene as if through the wide angle lens of a slow motion movie camera, frame by frame, millisecond by racing millisecond. In one careless sweep of the windscreen wipers the dazzling light changed dramatically to a horizontal beam, attached to which, and now picked out vividly by the Jaguar's headlights, was the looming deadly shape of an oncoming motorcycle. The rear nearside wheel of the seemingly helpless car slipped over the edge of a narrow drainage ditch as John swung the wheel to the left. The corrective action was too severe and in reply the car's rear scudded back across treacherous leaf mould and the shape of the motor cycle and its leather clad rider disappeared beneath the bonnet line. Hamish was thrown back across the seat, unable to register the band of white luminous tree bark absorbing the car's swaying headlight beam in cloud-like ghostliness.

The radiator made first contact as careering emerald coated steel struggled to bury itself into the depths of the two hundred year old oak tree. In his last seconds of consciousness, Hamish felt himself being dragged from his seat by the deathly unseen forces of momentum, squeezed helplessly through the narrow gap between front seats and the roof of the car and hurled carelessly through the windscreen to the accompaniment of shattering glass and his own screams of agony.

By the time his body made contact with the great oak he was already dead and his crushed and battered human remains sank back in a collapsing, crumpled heap on the twisted car bonnet. A minute later, except for the light patter of rain on the Jaguar roof and the subsiding hiss of steam from the demolished radiator, all returned to quietness in the dark, damp confines of the country lane. A motorcycle lay on its side in the middle of the slippery black tarmac road surface and after a few seconds its rider appeared from the temporary captivity of a ditch on the opposite side of the roadway to where the mangled remains of the vehicle rested. He stood up and quickly checked himself for cuts or small fractures. There were none, as expected; he was a professional and professionals didn't get hurt in his business.

'You don't last long as an amateur' he thought determinedly to himself, his pulse normal and a barely perceptible sign of perspiration breaking out on a hard, square forehead buried within the padded interior of the dull, black, fiberglass crash helmet. The dark figure stood for a few seconds, listening, checking the air for any unusual or unwelcome sounds. Satisfied, it moved swiftly over to the wreckage, wrenched the driver's door open and bent inside, switching off the ignition and checking the driver for signs of life. The body was still strapped securely in the right hand seat and except for faintly protruding eyes fixed in a hypnotic, dilated stare and a head lolling sideways at an unusual angle, the grey uniformed occupant seemed to have escaped without obvious injury. The dark figure knew otherwise. He had broken enough necks in his time to recognize the angle at which heads fell afterwards; this man was definitely dead and probably killed by the unrestrained movement of the rear passenger's body as it was thrown through the car. He was satisfied. The first part of his job was done. There were one or two papers scattered on the carpeted, front passenger side floor well which he gathered together; then he leant back out of the wreck and moved to open the rear door. Valuable seconds were consumed as he freed the jammed lock by forcing it with a compact tool steel jemmy extracted from a thigh pocket in the leather riding suit. He pulled down a long zipper drawn diagonally across the suit jacket and produced a miniature, high intensity video light which he plugged into an alkaline battery set taken from another leg pocket along with a miniature eight millimeter Minox automatic camera. With all the documents in the file now gathered up, he carefully photographed each one in turn, including all the notes and scribbles on the back of two or three of the foolscap sheets. He glanced at the luminous dial of his wrist watch. Nearly three minutes had passed since he had checked the driver; there was still plenty of time.

With steady hand and holding the camera about a foot away from the papers laid out carefully on the rear seat, he clicked away until he was sure nothing had been overlooked. He replaced the photographic equipment in his suit pockets and closed both the front and rear doors, leaving the pink folder and its contents in the back of the car. Strapped to the motorcyclist's left wrist with black linen adhesive tape was a small aluminum cylinder which he now released and proceeded to extract a small steel pin from the squat narrow neck. He listened for the faint click that told him that the timer contactor had released and carefully placed the device underneath the fuel tank of the car. He then ran back to the motorcycle, pressed the electric starter and the machine roared into life. With a quick flick of a right foot, gears were engaged and the motorcycle and rider sped off into the night. Two minutes later, there was a small explosion beneath the wreck, followed by a much bigger detonation as the fuel tank erupted in bouts of searing orange and yellow flame. The job was now thoroughly completed and the motorcycle rider smiled confidently to himself as he listened to the echo of the explosion in the distance, whilst leaning the powerful four cylinder BMW into the roundabout and heading back towards London.

\*\*\*\*\*\*

At twelve hours local time that same day an unusually long message, in one time code, was being received at the communications centre buried deep in the heart of a nine storey building, located at Number 2, Dzerzhinsky Square, Moscow. After making its way through the cipher department of the Komitet Gosudarstvdnnoi Bezopasnosti, the complete decoded message was dispatched with some haste to the ninth floor office of Victor Chebrekovski, head of the Russian KGB. He studied its contents carefully for over an hour and then reached for the handset of his internal telephone, placed to the left of a massive brown leather desk. Except for the decoded message, four telephones and one thick red cardboard file, the desk top was clear. In response to the call a tall, young, uniformed lieutenant, wearing a guarded expression, entered the expansive but sparsely furnished room and progressed with practiced haste towards the big desk, looking questioningly at the Russian spymaster.

'Take this down personally to General Lubikov on the second floor and tell him the date has been set; then find the whereabouts of the First Secretary and tell him I need to see him immediately.'

The young lieutenant, with a well rehearsed click of his heels, left the room. From that moment, the financial sinew and military muscle of the great Russian bear was to shake from years of slumber and rise up to cast a lengthening shadow of fear over Europe and the rest of the free world.

# Chapter Eight

*September 24th 1973 – Ras Al Khaimah – United Arab Emirates*

Maxwell stepped off the Learjet to be greeted by a still, cold, morning air and a dark, grey half light which signaled his arrival somewhere in the lower Arabian Gulf. He had been told little on the flight from Kenya, except his final destination which was to be the airport at Ras Al Khaimah in the United Arab Emirates. They would land sometime before six o'clock in the morning and upon disembarkation he would have the benefit of further discussion and consultation with unnamed senior members of the Arab Gulf Co-operation Council. The trip had been uneventful and mostly conducted in polite silence, punctuated by long, examining and only partially hostile glares from the two Arab guards on board, who, in-between their studies of Maxwell, passed the time in close examination of well oiled AK 47 automatic rifles, their constant companions. Complementing the fact that from the outset Maxwell felt venturing out on the whole trip had been a mistake, was the worrying discovery of the Unicorn footprint, including all the possible conclusions that somehow his host was involved in organized and barbarically executed poaching on the Weismuller farm and nearby game reserves. During his first hour on the plane the possible results of all kinds of verbal confrontations with Mohammed had been simmering in Maxwell's mind. Maxwell had been unable to sleep on the flight to the United Arab Emirates and as he strolled purposefully across the coal black, dew dampened airport apron, the evidence was reflected in sore and watering, red rimmed eyes. He rubbed them for the twentieth time with the back of his left hand and this made them water even more, increasing his overall feeling of uncomfortable shabbiness, coupled with a disarming sensation of isolation.

It was very cold and the damp, humid atmosphere penetrated his short sleeved shirt, adding to a growing sentiment of exhaustion. He followed one of the guards towards the rarely used arrivals building, illuminated in the early morning gloom by two wall mounted flood lights fixed above a door, proudly marked in Arabic and English with the words, International Arrivals. Maxwell looked up to his right just before entering the terminal building, his gaze directed towards the control tower. Through the mist a figure was motionlessly watching, backlit by diffused, fluorescent light filtering through soundproofed, tower survey windows. He was aware of other unseen but guarding eyes watching his progress as the terminal doors closed quietly behind him, but he was here now and there was no going back.

He blinked and rubbed weary eyes yet again in reaction to the sharply invading luminescence inside the terminal. He was ushered by smartly dressed guards through the empty lounge and into a lavish, but garishly furnished room that bore the title, VIP ONLY.

Sheikh Saif bin Fahkaroo Al Tamimi, chairman of the Arab Gulf Co-operation Council, President of the United Arab Emirates and ruler of Abu Dhabi, sat at the far end of the room, conversing in hushed tones with an aide seated on his left. On his right sat Sheikh Khalifa bin Warqra Al Rashid, UAE prime minister and ruler of the bustling entrepreneurial state of Dubai. Both men appeared bright and in good health despite the early hour of the morning and, as Maxwell approached, Sheikh Khalifa extended both hands in greeting. The ensuing hand shaking and back slapping felt warm and sincere as the three old friends greeted one another. The aide and the guards discreetly left the room, leaving only Maxwell, Saif, Khalifa and Mohammed. The four men made themselves comfortable, pulling the heavy chairs around a low, brass coffee table, with Mohammed lifting a push button telephone to order refreshments of Arabic sweet tea for all, and a breakfast of steak and eggs for Max. The two rulers looked alert but relaxed in crisp, freshly laundered thobes and fine woven cotton gujras, framing deep, copper tanned and ageless faces, reflecting a rare depth of character and strength. Both men wore small, manicured beards much favored by the Gulf Arabs and, except for the appreciably lengthier face of Saif and the wider set eyes, they would have been taken for brothers. Sheikh Khalifa, was in fact estimated to be much younger but both were filled with a controlled nervous energy that shrugged off the obviously passing years.

Maxwell began to feel immediately more relaxed and some of the strain of the past hours was washed away with the first cup of boiling, thick, sweet tea that had been poured carefully by Mohammed. The first half hour of conversation was consumed by questions concerning Maxwell's activities since leaving the Gulf, interspersed with occasional rings of laughter as the three men recollected minor, amusing episodes of their past time together in the New York headquarters of the UN, London, Paris and most of the other capitals of Europe. Although those times were very often tense and sometimes stretched tempers to breaking point in their joint efforts to resolve the situation with the Imam of Awabi, the hours and hours of meetings did not lead to a final solution but were regularly lightened and at many times only made bearable by the magnificent sense of humor of these two great men. Maxwell's favorite breakfast of steak and eggs came and went and with a full stomach his head began to clear, assisted by further cups of the rejuvenating Arabic tea. Until now, Khalifa's hooded eyes had sparkled with the pleasurable memories of old times and his undisguised joy at seeing the Englishman again, but as he gave Maxwell's shoulder a friendly pat, the sparkle gradually disappeared and was replaced with a deepening glint of serious thought and obvious concentration. He looked towards Mohammed enquiringly.

'What have you told our friend, so far, about the circumstances we find ourselves in and the mission we would like him to undertake for us'?'

Mohammed's face reflected the new mood of conversation and he replied that he had followed his brief to the letter, telling Maxwell only those facts which were necessary to achieve the prime object, which was to arrange this very meeting. Sheikh Saif nodded in silent approval and indicated he would take up the dialogue. He produced from his thobe a small, wooden, copper lined pipe, which he proceeded to fill with a fine stranded aromatic tobacco and light with a match taken from an etched, brass matchbox, resting on the coffee table. He spoke carefully and painstakingly, reverting to the Arabic tongue. Saif was decidedly more comfortable with Arabic than the English language which had been spoken throughout the preliminaries.

He opened by apologizing to Maxwell for carrying on the conversation in Arabic as he knew Maxwell's command of the idiom was considerably better than Saif's command of the Englishman's native parlance, and he wished not to prolong the meeting by having to struggle for correctly expressive words. Max listened intently.

'We have what some people regard as a serious problem in the Gulf at present and if handled incorrectly could turn out to be a major disaster for the AGCC'. He looked up to make sure Maxwell was paying attention.

'That problem is Moslem unity. It has taken us many years of painstaking effort to build up to the level of international Islamic co-operation which exists at this moment in time, but there is a possibility that one Gulf leader is attempting to take advantage of this new found harmony for personal glory. This would result in the destruction of the AGCC and its principles of operation as we know it today.' Saif relit the little pipe and, after a couple of short puffs, tapped the bowl on the table. He continued,

'Since what he conceives as the diplomatic world has turned its back on him, Imam Sulayman bin Abdulla has become a bitter, reclusive individual as a result of moving to Iraq; building a personality cult around him over the past few years that is quite frankly frightening and if we believe his published rhetoric, it is his intention to encourage Middle Eastern leaders to embark on some sort of campaign in the near future, either militarily, or in some other manner, against the American and European economic blocks.' The room was silent.

'He has so much influence over Iraq's Ahmed Hassan al-Bakr, that the President has more or less refused to co-operate with members of the AGCC which, as you know, he has declined to join, and he refuses also to work with other Gulf countries regarding the joining of common economic policy or OAPEC agreed oil production levels. We are finding it nearly impossible to communicate with him or the Imam and for the past year or so, little or no reliable information has come out of Iraq to indicate the state of current political thinking. The Imam's propaganda machine though is enormous and effective, preaching revolution and preparation for some sort of Holy War.'

At this point he paused and Khalifa took up the conversation.

'He has become a virtual recluse, except for various excursions into Kuwait, details of which are kept tightly secret. We have spoken in depth to Sheikh Hamad of Kuwait but he denies that he has had any regular contact with Sulayman bin Abdullah and states they are certainly not meeting in secret. The other worrying factor is that the Russians are now operating inside Iraq in some force and, although we have managed to control their activities in Iran, Saudi Arabia and the rest of the lower Gulf, we are seeing ominous build-ups of military support inside Iraq.'

'What if any,' said Maxwell, 'is the most serious action you believe President al-Bakr could be planning to take and why do you think my talking to the Imam will make any difference to al-Bakr? From what you say, he's already kicking the traces by isolating Iraq from the rest of the Gulf; so now is the time for you to slap his wrist, so to speak.'

Saif spoke in reply.

'This we are prepared to do as a last resort and we know he has made alternative plans of involvement with other economic blocks. If we cut Iraq off from our economic and joint trading agreements, there would be a great deal of disruption to our own growth and stability for a while, and our bargaining strength with Europe would be considerably reduced; but we are able to live with it if we are all convinced that the problem ends there. The danger is in the process, and a unanimous decision from all AGCC members to isolate Iraq might not be obtained. The Russians might see their way clear to move against all the weaker Gulf states and then we would be back to where we were forty years ago, with total Arab disunity and the big industrial powers trying to move in and pick the bones clean of a finally rotting Arab carcass.' He paused, grim faced.

'We have fought too long and too hard to allow ourselves to be driven back to the desert whilst the Americans or the Russians sit happily on our oil wells, exploiting an asset that we claim as our birthright. We have even considered the possibility of al Bakr joining forces with the Russians to make a move down the Gulf in force, but only a madman would consider such action. However, al-Bakr's deputy, Saddam Hussein is another matter altogether. He is an unknown piece in this current game of chess. Whatever the motive, everyone involved needs to see that such action would start World War Three and possibly trigger a nuclear holocaust! No, Mister Armstrong, we need to know what and who we are dealing with, and quickly. Are we looking in the face of a lunatic, or a committed and respected Moslem leader who truly believes in what can only be described now as some form of Jihad against western interests? We feel passionately, that only you can tell us that. We trust your judgment. Will you help us?'

The Minister without Portfolio fidgeted nervously with a set of silver prayer beads and, although he had said very little so far, Maxwell was fairly well convinced there was more to the story than had been presented to date. He targeted his question towards Mohammed. It all seemed a bit murky. Whatever their problems were, they were Arab problems and not ones that a foreigner should be involved in. What the hell was actually going on? Why was he really here? Mohammed, sensing that maybe some awkward questions were coming his way, got up from his seat to order some more tea and coffee. Maxwell interrupted him.

'Tell me, Mohammed, what of Sulayman's brother Tammam. How does he figure in all of this?'

The Arab diplomat remained on his feet as he calmly but pointedly explained to Maxwell that he knew the two brothers were in regular contact by telephone and Tammam had made irregular visits to Iraq from his exile home in Qatar. However, he seemed to have distanced himself from the politics of the situation and is still pushing at every level to have Britain hauled up in front of the UN over the still stinging exile of fourteen years ago. He spoke without emotion.

'He knows it's useless, we all know it's useless and as a result he, like his brother is a very bitter man. He continues to promote the Imam and his cause but we know nothing else untoward about the man'.

'No one so far had mentioned Israel in all this bloody intrigue' Maxwell thought reflectively ; now would be about the right time.

'So the big question really is gentlemen, what happens with Israel. Any planned military movement west by Iraq, Egypt or Syria would have to consider the actions or reactions of Israel. You must all be aware that Israel has a nuclear capability. We don't know in detail what that is but you can bet your bottom dollar, that in the face of the Biblical Arab hoards bearing down on them, from any direction, they would not be afraid to use what they've got'

He paused for a second his eyes resting momentarily on Mohammed who purposely avoided Maxwell's gaze and continued fidgeting with his prayer beads, back and forth between soft hands and manicured finger nails. Maxwell purposely finished his sentence.

'……. and they wouldn't ask permission either!'

The room remained silent and suddenly, without excuse or reason, Mohammed got up and left. A few seconds later, the thoughtful President of the United Arab Emirates spoke.

'Without doubt a limited nuclear confrontation in the Gulf region could be contemplated only as a last resort, neither side gaining any worthwhile advantage in the final accounting'. It was a bleak statement. The Englishman continued.

'Well, gentlemen, if the Iraqi President is about to call for any kind of confrontation, legitimized by some form of holy Jihad, it has to be either military or economic. But …. and it's a big *But* …. for either to be effective, he needs a reason gentlemen ….. *he needs a reason*! So, where do we stand now? What could he possibly do to create a plausible scenario for some kind of economic war against the west, and one that would weld together a strong enough support among Islamic ranks to follow the path of Jihad? If he tried once and failed, then he would be finished and so would the powers that were backing him. The whole theory could be described as Generally risky and at the moment all the cards seem to be stacked against him'.

Khalifa leant forward and affectionately placed his hand on Maxwell's shoulder, speaking once again in English.

'That's why we need you; go to the Imam and find out what is in his mind. Without the approval and backing of such a highly respected religious leader, living literally within the walls of his own house, President al-Bakr will not make any move outside of his own borders. We are convinced of that. That's all we are asking you to do, the rest we can handle ourselves. Whatever you may need in terms of intelligence, assistance and ongoing information, we will provide; and to this end by eight o'clock local time today, you will have half a million dollars in your Jersey bank account as a sign of our appreciation of your co-operation, even up to the point of coming this far to meet with us. If you decide to continue, you can name your own price for your efforts and inconvenience and be assured that, whatever happens, we will honor our agreements to have you back in Kenya within ten days.'

Regardless of the overgenerous offers of money, Maxwell began to see the exercise as having some form of merit. When it came to out and out war, these guys knew what it was all about and even in a straightforward political situation, if a few heads had to roll to save some face, then so be it; but money and its power, they still did not totally understand. Although they had manipulated a lot of finance over the past four decades, they really still did not comprehend in detail how the whole world monetary system worked. He had made up his mind. If they could get him to Iraq, he would talk to the Imam Sulayman bin Abdulla and try and find out what was going on. But something which still niggled at the back of his mind was why London had not briefed him on the military aspect of the situation, especially the extent of the moves the Russians were obviously making within Iraq. A confrontation in the Gulf was therefore more than a distinct likelihood. Time appeared to be short. He'd better get on with it.

Maxwell stood up to stretch his legs a little and spoke to Sheikh Saif again.

'What arrangements can you make to get me in front of the Imam within the next couple of days?'

'Those arrangements are already made,' replied Saif, his words accompanied by a wry smile.

'You will be able to leave the UAE at twelve o'clock, midday tomorrow and in about three hours you should be at the Iraqi air base of Kirkuk, where the Imam has agreed to meet with you early tomorrow evening. For obvious reasons of security, as you have arrived, you will leave, from this rather quieter airport at Ras Al Khaimah and we have made arrangements for you at the Airport Hotel until your departure. Sulayman bin Abdulla has requested that you come alone and therefore, if you agree to these arrangements, we will have the Falcon 10 flown over from Dubai and you may use the aero plane to go wherever you please.'

Maxwell registered the connotation of the smile. The crafty old devil had known he would go along with the trip all the time. Before he could reply, Mohammed re-entered the room, plain faced, but seemingly more relaxed than he had been when they arrived. He spoke directly to Maxwell in English,

'Do I take it from the look of you gentlemen that we are all agreed and Mr. Armstrong will be going to Iraq?'

'You are correct, Mohammed,' stated the Englishman, 'and I think if I am flying tomorrow I'd better get some sleep, but only after a damn good meal, a long hot shower and a quick phone call to London.'

'Certainly,' said Mohammed, 'I will contact the director of civil aviation immediately and get the plane over here today. If you will permit…..I will now take you to the crew room where you will hopefully find everything you require, including a complete change of clothing and a flight bag with all the up-to-date route information you will need for your flight.

The two Arab leaders now stood. Saif moved forward, shook him by the hand, and lightly kissed him on the cheek.

'Maa'a salam, Maxwell, may God go with you.' Sheikh Khalifa approached and repeated the farewell formality, shaking his hand encouragingly. The four men left the room together, with Maxwell and Mohammed turning left in the direction of the crew room and the other two Arabs heading toward the lounge, through to the exit, and out on to the airport apron. Bright daylight filtered through cream net curtains which covered the green tinted glass walling, making up one side of the terminal facility. He turned to enter a door marked, No Admittance - Crew Only. Inside the room Mohammed, who had walked ahead, was waiting to show him a collection of suits, shirts and other clothes, all obviously purchased and probably very discreetly from a well known Jewish tailoring house somewhere in London. Maxwell checked the flight bag for maps, aircraft check lists, navigation and communication frequencies and the essential pair of Ray Ban pilot's sunglasses. Everything he needed was there and Maxwell thanked Mohammed, who told him the aircraft would be on the ground later that day and he would be back before Maxwell's departure time to ensure that all arrangements in Iraq had been confirmed and flight clearances obtained. As Mohammed left the room Max looked around for a phone and spotted a red push-button model on the crew counter. It was an open line, but now that didn't really matter. He walked over to it, dialed a London number, and waited for a few seconds until he was connected. A female voice answered and after a short delay put him through to the person he wanted, the connection being acknowledged with a gruff

'Hello.'

Maxwell explained briefly what he was doing, including his possible travel schedule and confirmed he would make contact again on his return to the UAE after further conversations with the AGCC chairman, Sheikh Saif. The conversation was necessarily brief and terminated by the male voice at the other end in an equally gruff,

'Thank you,' followed by a distant piping noise as an indication that the trans-continental conference was over.

\*\*\*\*\*\*

Sitting in the back of a metallic silver Mercedes on the outskirts of the airport, Mohammed al Shukri replaced the handset to the car radiophone. Within a few seconds he picked it up again, to dial a number which connected him with the airport engineering department. He spoke in Arabic to the chief engineer.

'You may now remove the tap on the crew room telephone and patch my radiophone back to the normal dialing net system …… and make sure that Armstrong receives no other calls before I return or contact you again.'

He pressed the 'Nett' button on his handset and waited for the familiar dial tone. A red transmit light glowed steadily as he dialed another number in distant Iraq. The number answered immediately.

\*\*\*\*\*\*

Unaware of the fact that his communication with London had been overheard, Maxwell, now comfortably settled in to his hotel suite, showered under an abundance of piping hot water and then turned the mixer control over to full cold. He toweled his body dry, slipped on fresh underclothing and threw himself on to the welcome upholstery of a king size bed. He ate an excellent meal in his room accompanied by a very reasonable Chardonnay and immediately fell into a deep, well deserved, sleep. As the evening light began to fade, outside the terminal building, on the tarmac of the loading apron, a plain white colored Falcon 10 coasted to a stop and the pilot switched off the whining jet engines. A maintenance crew, followed by a fuel bowser, made its way down the yellow lined service road towards the aircraft and began re-fuelling operations and ground checks.

Hamza, a Pakistani crew chief, checked the maintenance schedule and carried out a quick start check on the Falcon's twin rear mounted engines before clearing the men and ground support machinery back to the maintenance base, leaving the aircraft in the care of eight watchful armed guards. His instructions were that the whole area was to be cleared by ten thirty of all ground staff and no-one was to enter the terminal building for any reason whatsoever before the Falcon had taken off. Having worked in the Gulf for over twenty years he was used to secret comings and goings at all hours of the day and night and was long past being curious as to what might possibly be going on.

He shuffled his men off the apron and took a quick look around to make sure any fuel spillage had been properly cleaned up and that there were no bits of rag lying around to be ingested by the compressors of the jet engines. Satisfied that all was correct he too returned to the maintenance base for a welcome cup of coffee and a bite to eat.

******

It was gone ten thirty on that hot and stifling September morning, when the silver Mercedes appeared through the shimmering heat haze which now hung over a baking runway. The car made its way slowly towards the terminal building. In the back, Mohammed was still talking on the telephone and when the vehicle eventually stopped outside the arrivals lounge, it was a further ten minutes before he finished his call and emerged into the mid morning heat. Some short time later the tinkling sound of his watch alarm woke Maxwell, informing him it was time to hit the shower again. He sat up quickly and for a few seconds experienced complete disorientation. He rubbed his eyes vigorously; they were less painful now; his senses re-animating details of the activities of the past twenty four hours which now came flooding back. In bare feet he padded his way to the shower, shedding his underwear on the way, and five long minutes under the soothing outpour made him feel completely revived and wide awake. After donning a pale blue, lightweight silk suit and cream cotton shirt, chosen from the small wardrobe provided by Mohammed, he finished his dressing with a dark blue tie and navy socks, set off with a pair of soft hide moccasin style matching shoes. The fit of everything he wore was perfect and the shoes were especially comfortable providing a more than acceptable level of confidence as Maxwell booked out of the Airport Hotel and walked quickly over to the Terminal.

Now in the crew room, a white faced analogue clock above the Met table revealed it was nearly half past eleven and therefore he should hurry if he was to submit a flight plan and get away by twelve. At that moment Mohammed entered the crew room to inform Maxwell all was on schedule. Max took ten minutes to write up a brief, on-board flight plan. He bade Mohammed farewell and headed out towards the apron to inspect the gleaming white aero plane. On completing his outside visual checks, he noticed that the aircraft had no markings, except for a barely readable registration number, written in black letters on the tail fin. Maxwell called Mohammed over from the terminal building where he had stood patiently watching. He agreed with Maxwell; the tail markings were actually illegal for identification purposes, but that was how the Iraqis had requested the plane to be equipped, along with a special on-board radar identity coder and transmitter, which was to be switched on after confirmation of entering Iraqi airspace or at the specific instruction of Basra control.

'Jesus Christ', Max muttered to himself, 'we're back in the bloody cloak and dagger brigade again. I hope this untrustworthy bastard is telling me the truth, or I'm a sitting duck for all kinds of manufactured international incidents.'

Mohammed sauntered away without further word as Max entered the aircraft, tight-lipped and alert. 'If for some reason I'm being set up here, I've got probably two chances once I leave UAE airspace, and that's little and fuck all'. The thought gave small comfort, as he worked his way through the pre-flight check detail with a mechanical professionalism that only hundreds of hours of flight deck experience were able to bring.

With the two turbines running and throttled back, checks complete, doors closed and controls free, he was ready to go. The lift-off was comfortably uneventful and the climb out rapid, with the assistance of the two Garret Turbofan engines throwing out over 6,000 pounds of thrust, pushing the little Falcon up to its cruising altitude of 25,000 feet in a matter of minutes. On the turn, Max checked with Sharjah and then Dubai radar before settling down on a north westerly course up the Gulf towards Basra. Finally he switched over to auto pilot and locked in the area navigation system. He noted his take off time and calculated he would be over Basra on schedule and as long as he had no problems from then on, it would be about another half an hour plus to Kirkuk.

# Chapter Nine

*September 25th 1973 – Hawar – Qatar – Arabian Gulf*

The sprawling, two storey, Islamic style, beach palace complex on Hawar Island would have seemed deserted, viewed through the swirling depths of a midday sandstorm and except for the motionless Arab guards placed every hundred meters around the perimeter wall, there would have appeared to the casual observer to be no other sign of life. The brother of the exiled Imam of Awabi, Tammam bin Abdulla was in residence but receiving no-one that day and therefore the three gated entrances to the palace were closed and all telephone lines had been switched off, except for one private line through to quarters in the east wing which were used by Tammam as an office. The beach residence, situated on an island to the north west of the tiny Gulf state, was purposely isolated from the main town of Doha and had been built on reclaimed land, exposed after dredging works for the extensive private harbor forming part of the total palace construction. The whole area was sealed off and guarded on the land side by units of the Qatar rulers paramilitary police and on the seaward side by a contingent of Qatar's Navy, which consisted of two constantly patrolling Vosper fast attack gun boats.

Tammam bin Abdulla possessed neither the intellect nor the personal charisma of his brother, the Imam. His frighteningly powerful driving force was ambition, coupled with a certain amount of cunning, making him often difficult to deal with and at other times downright dangerous. He was still young at fifty seven, having received the benefit of a top line education in Europe and the United States and travelling extensively before his exile as a member of his brother's entourage. He wanted, and he knew he deserved, much greater things. He paced the cool marble floor of the vaulted inner office reception room, waiting for a call. The telephone was defiantly silent as he strode in frustration mode through into his office, sat down at an immense rosewood desk and lit yet another cigarette, which he poked into a solid gold holder and puffed at impatiently. Events were moving apace and the plan had gained momentum and substance during the past few weeks. The seven members of Unicorn had worked long and hard for some years to bring about the present firmly orchestrated situation and the finale was now only a matter of days away from being enacted. Once the machinery they had painstakingly created started to move, literally nothing could stop it and although the terminal scenario was still to be planned in fine detail, events were moving quickly in that direction. Tammam lounged restlessly in the molded, dark brown leather chair, pushing himself away from the desk now and again and then reaching out with one hand to pull himself back, gliding on noiseless nylon Castors. He smiled quietly to himself as he recalled the stroke of luck that had enabled him to involve Maxwell Armstrong in the workings of his plot; the Englishman that half the Arab world trusted and the one man he hated with a vengeance. With the help of his Russian friends and the diligent maneuvering and manipulating of Unicorn, his brother, the Imam, had been pushed nearer and nearer the edge of sanity. They had managed to isolate him completely from all other friends, family and advisors; sowing the seeds of distrust which had blossomed over the years into a near neurotic hatred of the Gulf Arab leaders in General and the British in particular.

The Imam had been gaining followers by the day as his frustration at the injustice showered upon him increased. The devious involvement of the British and eventually the Americans in stifling his rightful voice at the United Nations, had been underscored to the Imam Sulayman with the help of cleverly forged documents and the administration, over an extended period of time, of certain drugs, recognized as 'state of the art' in Soviet chemical therapy. But still there were stumbling blocks scattered on the cunningly contrived path to glory and power that members of the Unicorn craved for. Even within the manipulated, chemically damaged and drugged depths of Sulayman's mind, there was something holding him back from the final decision. The conspirators had not yet managed to control him completely. He still talked of his friend Armstrong, but now a little less than he used to as the message became more powerful in his mind; how he could make the non believers understand; how he, himself, was Allah's chosen leader here on earth and how the world must look to Islam for its future. Other Moslem leaders must follow *him*, they must be made to comprehend the consequences of not acknowledging him as the unchallenged leader of a greatly expanded Islamic world. The Imam was in danger of developing a split personality, with one side attempting desperately to reason with the other in a tortured consciousness, which, if allowed to continue, would blow the whole plan. Things had to start moving quickly but, do as they may, members of the Unicorn could not finally push the Imam and therefore the Iraqi President into some sort of action. The problem was that Sulayman was not inherently unstable and really did believe he was the chosen one; the one to embark Moslems all over the world on a holy war in support of international Islamic rights. The only difference between the war Sulayman *called* for and the one Tammam *planned* for was that his brother's Jihad would be one of words and psychological pressure, whereas Tammam and the Unicorn wanted force of arms; they wanted to literally take over the world. Somehow the Imam had to be sparked into violence but years of careful mind management had, in effect, created a self defeating situation. By isolating him from anyone or anything that could exercise an unwanted influence on the outcome of the joint Unicorn,

Soviet plan, they had removed him from close relationships with just about everyone.

The answer had come several months ago, when one of the Unicorn members had discovered a diary in which Sulayman was recording rambling secret thoughts that were obviously a private analysis of his growing schizophrenia. The diary contained pages of dark and light and captured mood and counter mood but there, time and again, the name of Armstrong was mentioned, a man for whom he held a consuming secret affection and respect. It was the perfect opportunity to push him over the edge and so the Unicorn had gradually worked on the Imam over the ensuing weeks until he was talking openly of his old European friend and declaring that this was the one man above all non believers who could understand the true meaning of the world eventuality and take his message into the unheeding corridors of western political power. He, alone, could convince the other leaders of the Moslem movement to put aside their tribal and territorial differences and follow him on the great Islamic march.

Tammam glanced at the Longines desk clock, set in a block of crystal, occupying space on the far left corner of his desk and then looked back to the still silent telephone. It was time now. Why hadn't he received a phone call confirming the Englishman was on his way? This was the final stroke. Within forty-eight hours the waiting would be over. Whatever the revered Mr. Armstrong said now could not affect the outcome of a carefully conspired scheme. He would be dead. His death would be just the required lever the Unicorn had been cunningly fabricating during the past frustrating weeks of inaction and procrastination. The scene was already set to blame the happening on his employers, the British SIS. Evidence had been manufactured, people bribed, documents forged and motives concocted to such an extent that whatever moves were made by the SIS or CIA, they would all be too late. The murder, by clandestine western agencies, of his last and only European friend would push the Imam over the edge. The bond would be sealed with the faltering Kuwaiti Amir and then the declaration could be made. A confused AGCC would collapse in disarray as the request for repatriation of Iraqi and Kuwaiti assets in Europe and the United States was rejected and then, like a Phoenix, from the ashes of Arab dissent, would rise a new Gulf leader to urge and commit support for the visionary Moslem prophet Imam Sulayman bin Abdulla.

'Yes that would be it,' Tammam muttered confidently to himself. He lit another cigarette whilst continuing to stare sightlessly at the inanimate telephone receiver. Once they had persuaded President al-Bakr of Iraq to make the declaration on behalf of Iraq and Kuwait, there could be no turning back and from then on events would be under the control of the Unicorn. Even before the first tank track had turned, they would be in command and the great Moslem visionary, merely a puppet dragged along a path of escalating violence, until all before them were taken up and swallowed within the entrails of a holy war that would not stop until they had reached the eastern shores of the Atlantic. Even thinking about the terrifying consequences of his plan excited Tammam to such an extent that he began to break out in a cold sweat and his pulse raced in contemplation of so much power, power to do anything he wanted, anything a mind could possibly conceive.

The telephone rang suddenly and shattered his climaxing dreams to such an extent that the conspirator nearly screamed out loud in an enveloping neurotic response. He pulled the dead cigarette filter from the holder and carefully placed it in a green onyx ashtray next to the desk clock and after the eighth ring, leaned towards the telephone handset and picked it up. It was Mohammed from Ras Al Khaimah, his voice distorted by the atmospheric transmission of the radio telephone link.

'Salam al'ekum, greetings, my brother, in the name of Allah. I am now able to inform you that our friend of European origin is committed and is on his way to Iraq. I have delayed calling you until I was sure he had cleared UAE airspace and passed through to Bahrain, which is now confirmed. He could be in Kirkuk in about an hour and from there on we have our plan primed for action; everything is working well. I am now returning to Dubai, to wait as agreed'.

Tammam, with handset crunched between cheek and shoulder, reached for the gold holder and lit another cigarette. He slowly exhaled the first draw of pale blue smoke and replied,

'Alekum salam, my brother in arms, all arrangements are made in Iraq for his safe passage and proper reception in Kirkuk. Our man will have transmitted to me a full and detailed account of Mr. Armstrong's meeting with my brother as soon as the discussions are concluded. Contact me again, after Isha prayers, so that I may update you with any information concerning the movements of our European emissary. Afterwards, I will confirm with General Lubikov the timing and extent of assistance we may require from thereon in, but stay within reach of your car phone in case I need you during the next few hours. Ma'asalam Mohammed.'

Tammam replaced the telephone handset and rose up from his chair to pace the room, again clearing his mind and searching for any last minute alternatives to the already formulated and minimal risk scheme. It would be put in to effect on the Englishman's departure from Iraq. There really were no alternatives; the infidel envoy would die quickly and painlessly and with the help of General Lubikov's specialists, there would be no link back to the Russians, the Unicorn or its members. It was time to ring Rasheed al Sheikh in Kirkuk and make sure there were no last minute hiccoughs in the preparation for the Imam's meeting and to double check that their Russian friend had come up with the right equipment to fulfill his side of the bargain. Although Tammam was assured of an ally in the Russian military machine, he did not particularly like dealing with them and didn't trust General Lubikov completely. All in the game were playing for big stakes. It was well recognized that the two main players needed one another but the chips were not finally laid out on the table. The next move they made together would be an indication of total commitment and it had to go right, there was no margin for error; Mister Maxwell Armstrong had to be eliminated before his return to Dubai. It was essential he did not report back to the AGC Council members and it was even more essential that his death was contrived in such a manner that there existed no hard evidence to point a qualified finger in any direction, other than the one fabricated by the members of the Unicorn. Then it could begin. The unstoppable tide would be on the turn.

He returned to his desk and picked up the telephone again. He made two calls, the first to Iraq; a long, deeply intoned conversation with Rasheed al Sheikh and the second to Moscow, a shorter, crisper discussion with General Andrea Lubikov, the officer commanding an operation coded in Dzerzhinsky Square as Crescent Moon. As he replaced the handset, the phone rang immediately. It was General Saleh Haji, a senior member of the powerful Egyptian Armed Forces Central Committee.

'Salam Ale'kum my brother' The voice was deep and controlled.

'After our discussions yesterday and a meeting I had last night in Cyprus with Mustafa Ibrahim of Syria, we are agreed on a date to make our moves on Israel. It is to be at dawn on October sixth, the day of the Jewish festival of Yom Kippur' Tammam smiled knowing well that such a strategy could well take the Israelis by surprise. Not only was it the most important festival of the year for Jews, it was also Rammadan, the most holy fasting festival of Islam. No one would be expecting a hungry Arab to be sitting in a tank, driving across the Suez Canal and fighting for his life...in Rammadan!

'And what about the bomb my friend'

'We inspected it in Cyprus yesterday and it leaves by boat for its detonation point on the seventh, during the initial confusion created by our first attacks. Transporting a stolen nuclear device across water is not an easy task but we have a trusted contractor on the job, in fact it is the expert team that removed the device from the Ukraine in the first place'.

'Is the plan still to explode the bomb at sea level in the Mediterranean..... just north of Port Said?'

'It is my brother. This Egyptian city will be evacuated as soon as the first troops cross the Suez Canal. The boat carrying the bomb will be attached to a prepared sea mooring and set off on a timer'

'Are we still fixed on a time?

'We are. It is as we have discussed before, to be on day two of the invasion, the morning of the eighth of October. We have everything in place to effectively accuse the Israelis of using a nuclear bomb in the conflict and we will be able to comfortably confirm that the explosion was as a result of our forces bringing down an unmarked aircraft, heading for Cairo and refusing to answer radio calls to identify itself. We have prepared audio tapes to play on the VHF frequencies that will be our evidence.'

'The job has been well done General.' replied a satisfied Tammam bin Abdulla.

'It has indeed my friend. Myself and the Defense Minister of Syria, Mustafa Ibrahim, have worked hard. The date is fixed…..and now it is time for you to keep your promise. You must ensure that the declaration of economic war on the west is made by Iraq and Kuwait by no later than Thursday October fourth. That will give you two days, before the military plan is put in to action, to rally as many Islamic nations to the repatriation policy as possible'.

'We are of course relying on the west to say no' interrupted Tammam bin Abdullah. He spoke in a bitter tone. '…. and our inside information from within the new European Community is that even if they wanted to, they could not look at putting together even ten percent of the amount required in gold within two days, let alone all of it. This is simply the lever we need. You get Israel out of the way and the Russian backed Iraqi forces will move through Syria and in to Turkey within twenty four hours.'

'You do your part my friend and we will do ours. If there is no declaration, there will be no invasion of Israel…..and with all the planning undertaken so far…some heads will have to roll. One of them will be mine!'

The line was abruptly disconnected, the conversation over. The leader of the Unicorn conspirators turned to quickly study a desk calendar. Not long to go. All was now in the hands of others; nothing should go wrong and if it did, those responsible would answer to him, possibly with their lives. He was in total control of the brilliantly conceived plan. The brother of the religious leader, with a world-wide following of several million Muslims, raised his body finally from the chair. He would be up late tonight and probably tomorrow night. As soon as the news broke of Armstrong's demise, the telephone lines between the Gulf states would be red hot and that was the time when he must rise from the shadows of disaster and begin to exercise some kind of political control.

He would need all his wits about him, especially when dealing with Khalif bin Warqra al Rashid, the ruler of Dubai. He was a crafty one and not easily bluffed or pushed into any course of action that he didn't totally believe in. He was the most unpredictable and independent of all the Gulf rulers and although not sitting directly on the main AGC Council, was very influential in his own right. He would be reluctant to take a simple line and if not carefully controlled, could delay or even upset completely the timing of the final push into military action. Food appeared and a hungry, self satisfied Tammam bin Abdulla sat down to eat.

## Chapter Ten

*September 25th 1973 – KGB Centre – Moscow – Russia*

On the second floor of the centre, Colonel General Lubikov replaced the telephone handset after terminating the oblate conversation with Tammam bin Abdulla in Qatar. He was less interested at the present time in the movements of the supposedly secret British agent than the contents of a lengthy decoded message that lay on his desk. He stroked his chin reflectively as he continued to absorb the pages of dense, Cyrillic script. The message had been delivered to him without comment, except for a date scrawled on the top of the front page in the recognizable hand of his lord and master, Victor Chebrekovski. He finished the last paragraph of the twenty-six page document and flicked through it once again, to refresh his memory on certain points. It was quite astounding how the mind of Sir Charles Hawthorn worked, and in fact how accurate he had been in terms of attempting to fill in all the theoretical blanks with guesswork. The old man had gone up a few notches in Lubikov's estimation but so had the leader of the new European Section C, whose men had obtained the documents and information making up the meat of the report.

There was no accompanying detail on how the information had been obtained, except the time and place of the top secret meeting and the time of document transmission from the cipher room of the Soviet Embassy in London. It was interesting to receive yet another, further, confirmation that the Americans would not want to become embroiled in a prolonged military action in Europe; but a little disconcerting to find out that Heinrich Smitt was involved in the secret games the SIS were now trying to play; disconcerting to such an extent that a certain amount of consideration would have to be given to perhaps eliminating Herr Smitt altogether. He spoke to his secretary on the intercom and requested his car to be available in half an hour and his plane made ready at Bronnitsyo Airfield for a return journey to Kirkuk. He turned back to study the document further and moved again to page eight, which described the SIS view of Russian involvement and activities to date in the northern Gulf territories. He was pleased and reassured that western intelligence agencies were still unaware of the code name, Crescent Moon, although they had managed to root out some basic information on Unicorn, and had accurately counted the number of its members, even though they remained, at present, anonymous. Being in possession of an accurate and up to date report on what western intelligence agencies knew of his plans at that time was extremely important and gave him an advantage which was a highly welcome bonus just now. His counterparts in the financial directorate, who's plan was to create chaos in the western currency markets, would have to be even more circumspect in their future dealings on the foreign exchange and doubly cautious in buying gold through their existing and limited sources. The moves in world financial markets had already begun and would not be increased in intensity for another few days. However, the General made a note to communicate with the head of the financial directorate and issue instructions to increase their spread of buying agents and also to activate, immediately, all Soviet controlled shelf companies in the Far East and southern Europe. He made a disapproving face as he sipped at the cold coffee resting accusingly in the bottom of a chipped stone mug, discovered half buried under piles of paper and files cluttering the grey enameled steel desk. After finishing the stale cold liquid, he laboriously collected all the files from his desk and placed them in the fireproof security cabinets lining one wall of the drab office. He paused and looked around.

'Perhaps, after all this bloody lot is over, the powers that be will condescend to put a lick of paint on the walls of this mausoleum of a place,' he muttered despairingly to himself.

The General hated his office in the overcrowded and decaying building, still used by the KGB as its headquarters and despite all requests to the contrary, the chief had refused to move out. The rat like existence that nearly all permanent staff had to suffer there made for bad tempered inmates and low levels of co-operation between departments. Still, 'thank God he could get out of it more than most', he thought to himself as he finally locked away all the remaining loose papers and documents, leaving the desk top bare except for a telephone, intercom and the ancient coffee mug. The grey haired Russian officer took down a heavy fur collared over-coat, fur hat and leather gloves from a wall hook and proceeded to dress against the chilling early autumn winds. Afterwards he called his secretary to confirm his car was ready.

On the way to the airfield he turned the latest series of events over in his mind concerning operation Crescent Moon. He had been working on the military aspect of the operation for nearly two years now; all the final preparations were complete and the whole, complex plan seemed to be working well. Of course, there had been problems and there would no doubt be a few more but, in General terms, the troop movements and equipment build up in Iraq had not caused too much of a public outcry and Soviet politicians had done an admirable job, for once, in directing world attention away from the Gulf. The only difficult area to control had been the unpredictable demands of that fucking lunatic despot in Qatar. Lubikov did not enjoy being treated like shit by anybody. The man had ideas of grandeur well above his station and would get a well deserved reward when his individual usefulness to the operation was over. The time would not be long coming and the General looked forward to taking care of that little detail personally.

Meetings between himself and the leader of Unicorn had become more and more strained recently. His number one confidant and head backscratcher, Mohammed al Shukri, was not much better, but at least, on the surface, he was easier to deal with, although he was as cunning as a snake and had to be watched carefully. The plan to put the Englishman in front of the Imam Sulayman bin Abdulla was verging on brilliant; the plan to kill him afterwards, was not. The point had been argued with the traitorous Tammam, hour after hour, backed by reams of documented expert psychiatric opinion which clearly indicated that in the Imam's current state of mind, the result could go either way. Lubikov's opinion and also that of his masters, was that the result of any meeting between the Imam and Armstrong would leave the Englishman having to admit he was unable to help his friend in his visionary mission to convert the world to Islam; that it was misplaced ambition and he should advise the Iraqi President al-Bakr to start talking to the AGCC again. Armstrong would walk away from the whole problem maintaining an acceptable level of respect and then the final screw would be tightened within Sulayman's schizophrenic mental deliberations, creating a determination in the man to prove Armstrong wrong.

On the other hand, killing the religious leader's 'Fidus Achates' could possibly push him right over the edge into uncontrollable insanity and might result in him becoming a mental vegetable, or even worse. No, a more cautious approach was required and this had been confirmed by medical opinion which could not be ignored. It was the

General's job to make sure events were programmed in favor of the Russian's and not that of some half-baked megalomaniac, who wanted to muscle in on the outcome of a Soviet plan which had taken many years and billions of hard earned dollars to prepare and execute. He would tackle the problem as soon as he arrived in Kirkuk. He would make sure the visitor to Kirkuk had a healthy stay in Iraq and that he also lived to tell the tale in Dubai, Kenya, or wherever he wanted to go afterwards. It was Lubikov's job to ensure his vast military machine was well oiled and moved into action at the right time with the least possible resistance, and that he would do. Dates were fixed now. The Egyptians and Syrians were ready to move. Once the plan moved to the military phase, he would be in charge …. and one or two politicians may be 'lost' along the way.

\*\*\*\*\*\*

The stretched, black limousine cruised to a gentle halt in the brightly floodlit inspection area of the main entrance to Bronnitsyo. Two smartly uniformed guards extracted themselves from the comfort of the concrete gatehouse and marched quickly over to the dark vehicle displaying three red stars above front and rear number plates. Both shouldered their 7.62 mm Kalashnikov assault rifles and saluted as the General slid down his window a few inches to hand out a red plastic security pass. After returning the plastic card to its owner and offering a courteous salute, the guard stood back and steel gates slid silently aside to allow the vehicle into the main air base complex. Lubikov ordered the driver to go straight to the flight briefing room, situated at the far side of the main administration block. His crew were waiting patiently, had filed their flight plan and were all kitted up and ready to go. At first sight of the General, the four airmen stood up and with a wave of the officer's hand, moved outside to board the waiting crew wagon which would take them to the Antonov light transport airplane, sitting duck like on one of the nearby dispersal pans. After quickly filling out a crew form and ensuring it was stamped by the crew room orderly, Lubikov followed the men to dispersal and boarded the plane.

Fifteen minutes later they were airborne and climbing steadily through the thick layer of low level grey cloud surrounding the airfield. The General consulted his watch. In three or four hours they would be at Kirkuk. He smiled in quiet satisfaction; at least then he would be able to have a decent cup of coffee. He settled back in his seat in search of comfort. Although the sixty-three year old General was fit and looked remarkably younger than his true years, the strain of the past few months had begun to take its toll. Organizing the logistics and support for a near secret army of over three quarters of a million men on one side and satisfying the needs of his political masters on the other was a nearly impossible task, but one that he had originally undertaken with gusto and a certain flourish that was unique to the man. He had no family distractions, his wife having died over fifteen years ago from a sudden and uncontrollable bout of viral hepatitis, and both his sons being fatal casualties of a series of covert actions along the Sino-Mongolian border in the 60's. His life, his family, was the army. He was a dedicated officer and could take whatever they threw at him. The General pushed himself further down into the grey nylon covered cushions of the narrow sling seat, massaged weary eyes for a second or two with his fingers, laid his head back on the minimal head rest and let himself be lulled into a shallow sleep by the synchronized rhythm of droning turboprop engines.

\*\*\*\*\*\*

Sir Charles Hawthorn had been in his London office for nearly three hours and was in the process of finishing his fourth cup of over-sweetened tea. The report on his desk was the result of initial investigations by Thames Valley Police units and the pathology section of SIS. The death of Hamish McWilliam was a bitter blow to his plans, and the most disturbing aspect was that his death was no accident. It was a highly professional job, well planned and well executed. The SIS man banged his fist on the desk top, setting the teacup shaking in the saucer and releasing a telephone handset from its cradle. He was angry and frustrated; angry with himself for not tightening up security on the operation early enough, and frustrated with his inability to grab the whole thing by the balls and give it a damn good shake

The Jaguar car had been nearly burnt out by the time local police forces arrived on the scene and initial investigations led to the belief that it was a simple but fatal accident. The pathologist reports on the remains of the two bodies were unable to identify any physical abnormalities, although more detailed work was now being carried out and a further account from his men would be available later. The local forensic guys, however, had pinpointed two important details confirming that the accident had been carefully contrived and carried out with the use of some highly sophisticated explosive device; the remnants of which were totally untraceable.

Firstly the car ignition was established in the off position as the key had been welded into the lock by the fierce heat of the explosion. It was clearly evident then that spilt fuel had not been accidentally ignited by a live electrical circuit. Therefore, the conclusion was that someone had switched off the ignition system after the crash.

Secondly, from examining fragments of metal known to be part of the fuel tank, it was obvious that an initial explosion had been generated externally and by a device that left no trace of itself whatsoever.

This was a most worrying feature, as in most explosive devices, with timing and fuse mechanisms, parts of the timer or the fuse casing were nearly always found at or near the heart of the explosion itself. In this instance, there was nothing; not a trace of anything, only evidence that the fuel tank had been ruptured from the outside over a tiny area with tremendous force. Charles considered it was fairly safe now to assume that whoever had engineered the death of McWilliam had also photographed the documents he was carrying and there was also little doubt that in some darkened room somewhere, the KGB were analyzing them in detail. The whole bloody operation had now been exposed, including the results of months and months of SIS investigations. If someone didn't do some smart thinking and pretty damn quickly, the whole of the intelligence services of the free world would be forced into a position where they would be able to do little other than sit back helplessly and watch as the accepted enemy of democracy rolled its way effortlessly towards the Atlantic.

He put the report down and called for another cup of tea and some whole-meal biscuits in a continuing, but vain, attempt to settle a discomfortingly nervous stomach. He then picked up the telephone and called Joe Starkley, asking him to drop what he was doing and get over to Bowater House as quickly as possible. There would have to be some action and Starkley would *definitely* have to get his backside back to the States to keep a tight lid on everything over there, until some decisions could be made.

He wasn't looking forward to the meeting. The SIS were in control of security and there had been a slip up of major proportions resulting in the unquestionable fact that there had to be a leak *inside* 'The Company' or else how could such a professional assassination job be arranged and executed at such short notice. Christ almighty, he had only put the meeting together himself, twenty-four hours previously and he'd estimated that all those present would be safe, at least, for a few hours, or until they could get to their own homes or safe houses. Wherever the leak was, it could be narrowed down to a few people, all of whom were in a position of extreme trust and tested loyalty. How the hell did the Russians find out?

By now he was convinced it was the Russians, purely by considering the sophistication of the explosive device and the speed with which the assassins had reacted. It took time to process intelligence information from a foreign country; it took time to pick a target and plan an operation; it took time to gather together the right people and equip them. It all took time, yet these bastards had sorted out the complete bloody operation in less than twenty four hours and got clean away. Every known Communist agitator, KGB contact or hit man had been carefully monitored for months now and, during the time the hit took place, they were all accounted for, so it had to be someone not on their radar and probably an imported asset. Whoever he, or she, was, they were bloody good and more than likely still around, waiting to be given the go ahead for the next hit. The head of the British SIS was beginning to feel the strain. There was a mole in his organization and there was also a highly skilled assassin on the loose. He had to find both of them quickly or else they might as well all give up now and start packing bags for sunny Australia.

The intercom buzzed, breaking his train of thought and the familiar female voice announced the arrival of the CIA man, who seconds later, entered the director's office.

'Sit down, Joe,' said Sir Charles. 'We have a lot to talk about.'

Joe's face paled visibly as he listened to the director and then read the report of McWilliam's death. Much was going on in his mind. This kind of security leak was an absolute disaster and would do nothing to ease the already tense situation which existed between Europe and America. The event could prompt all kinds of unwanted reactions from the guys back home. What a fuck up…. and what was even worse was the resulting loss in personal credibility he would now suffer with his political masters in Washington. There were forces at work within his Government who wanted to declare a new gold standard now and balls to the consequences; who wanted to kick the Arabs up the arse, dump the Europeans now and fuck the rest of the world. It was a very fine line they were all walking and he had to agree with Sir Charles that his best bet was to get back over the pond and try to keep the lid on it all; try to buy a little more time, but time for what?

# Chapter Eleven

*September 25th 1973 – Kirkuk Air Base – Northern Iraq*

The gleaming white Falcon inched its way forward under the direction of a baton waving, boiler suited, ground technician. The aero plane came to a halt as batons were raised vertically and then drawn across the technician's chest in a sharp, cutting movement, indicating that engines could now be shut down and parking brakes applied.

He had arrived at Kirkuk Airbase on time and in good spirits. The flight had gone smoothly. The little Falcon had performed faultlessly on the trip up the Gulf and he was quietly relieved to discover that all arrangements made for his safe journey had been adhered to by flight controllers. The fans on the Garrett jet engines turned their final, sluggish, revolutions as the pilot stepped down from the aircraft to be greeted by a slim figure, dressed in olive combat uniform, bearing no markings or badges of rank. The four Arab guards, waiting at the bottom of the stairs, were saluting and standing rigidly to attention. Maxwell was unsure as to whether the salutes were for him or the unranked military figure, who now moved forward to introduce himself to the visitor.

'Welcome, Mister Armstrong, welcome to Iraq. My name is Rasheed al Sheikh and I am the private secretary to the President, Ahmed Hassan al-Bakr. I bring you the greetings and very best personal wishes from the President and I am instructed to be at your disposal continuously during your stay in our country.'

The man who spoke was shorter than Maxwell by about an inch or two lean faced and strikingly good looking with finely chiseled features and dark brown, penetrating eyes of magnetic quality. He grabbed the Englishman's hand and shook it warmly as he turned to one of the guards still standing stiffly to attention and barked instructions in Arabic to bring his car to the plane. The guard saluted once again and rushed off towards a large Volvo limousine waiting about a hundred yards away from the parking apron.

'I am very pleased to be here, Rasheed,' replied Maxwell disengaging himself from the firm grip of the Arab's handshake and altogether feeling a mite surprised at the warmth and obvious sincerity of the greeting.

'As you are aware, I am here to meet with the Imam Sulayman bin Abdulla and it would be most helpful if I could have a short discussion with your President before I leave. Are you able to tell me at what time I'll be able to meet with Sulayman?'

The President's secretary informed him it would be about six o'clock that evening and the Imam was on his way to Kirkuk from Baghdad right now by helicopter.

'Unfortunately, I am not able to confirm any arrangement to meet with our President, but I will gladly pass on your request. What would you like to do until then Mister Armstrong?' the uniformed emissary continued.

'If you would care to see over the air base, I will be only too pleased to arrange a tour for you.'

Maxwell was quite taken aback at this suggestion. Military activity at Kirkuk was intense, with aircraft taking off and landing every five minutes and huge Antonov AN-22 Antheus transports loading and unloading all over the place. The markings were mostly Russian, intermixed with a few East German and Polish insignia, indicating that whatever was going on was more than simply a limited Soviet movement but one involving many of the Warsaw pact forces as well. He looked back towards his smiling escort and said,

'I would have thought the last thing you would want, was for me to view what is going on here, especially with the obvious, close involvement of the Soviets and their friends. Whatever is happening it's clearly a massive and obviously tight security operation and I suppose, from certain points of view, I could be regarded as the enemy!'

'On the contrary, Mister Armstrong,' Rasheed beamed, 'if we did not want you to see what we're doing here, why would we invite you to meet with the Imam at Kirkuk, rather than in Basra or Baghdad? No sir, you are not the enemy. The President trusts you and our vice President, Saddam Hussein trusts you ….. because the Imam trusts you and although I have only been close to him as the secretary to the President for the past couple of years, I have heard much about you through the Imam and I'm happy to carry out my instructions to let you see whatever you want and answer all your questions to the best of my ability. The discussions you have with the Imam will be crucial concerning the potential outcome of any actions we take as a nation in the coming weeks and it is the President's wish that you are as fully informed as possible regarding our intent and our support for that intent.'

The secretary remained smiling blandly as the matt green staff car pulled up behind him. Maxwell shrugged his shoulders in acquiescence and said,

'OK, let's go'

The two men climbed into the rear of the Volvo and after a short instruction to the driver from Rasheed, the car moved off, picking its way through the parked transports and piles of offloaded equipment.

The airbase covered a massive area and military police were everywhere, directing traffic and checking personnel moving from one security zone to another. It was an incredible sight and at one cargo terminal alone, Maxwell counted over a dozen Antonov's discharging cargo ranging from light tanks of the Soviet PT-76 series to compact SA-6 missile control radars. The unloading program had obviously been carefully organized and well managed with hundreds of men moving purposefully and efficiently from one consolidation bay to another. It took nearly half an hour for the staff car to negotiate and maneuver its way through the several cargo depots and parking aprons on the western side of the military base. They continued heading north, through two security gates and on to the service and maintenance facilities of the Iraqi Air Force.

Lined up on the aprons were seventy of the very latest Mig 21 fighter aircraft and twenty Mig 25 Foxbat interceptors. They had evidently only arrived during the last couple of days and ground tugs were busy pulling the airplanes, one by one, off the line and shuttling them out to blast proof dispersal areas spread around the northern perimeter of the airfield. The under-wing and belly pods of each aircraft were full, with some carrying electronic counter measure equipment; some, air to air missiles and others, air to ground anti-tank rockets. Although the high technology machinery spread out before him was not actually the very latest in Soviet military aviation hardware, Maxwell knew it was pretty damn near, and was astonished at the efficiency and confidence with which the mainly Iraqi ground-crew were handling their delicate charges. That could only mean good training and lots of it; a training program that must have been going on for a period of time and somehow camouflaged from inquiring western eyes. What was equally amazing was the discovery that all of this present movement was happening out in the open. It would be impossible to cover up a military build-up of this complexity and from satellite pictures alone, the Americans must have known for ages what was going on.

This was no Military Assistance Programme. This was preparation for an all-out war.

The tour continued, down through the east side of the base where could be seen hundreds of T-72 tanks, SCUD missile carriers and lethal Mi-24 helicopter gunships. The English visitor was gloomily impressed and his Arab host took great pleasure in the fact. There were still many questions crowding Maxwell's mind which the Arab secretary was eager to answer; so both men retired to a briefing room in the main headquarters building of the base and continued talking detail.

They sat together for a further half an hour, until Maxwell had run out of questions except for the obvious and most puzzling one.

'Surely my friend, the western intelligence agencies must have more than a faint idea of what you're doing and making at least some kind of diplomatic approach to assess the motives for such an astounding upgrade in Iraqi military strength.'

Rasheed leaned forward from the grey leather sofa in which both men were sitting and, without looking directly at his visitor, stated firmly that this question could only be answered completely by the President himself. Although the long term build-up of forces and equipment had been well disguised and obviously in-evident or of no interest to western powers, the increase in activity during the past forty-eight hours could not be hidden, and therefore no attempt had been made to do so. At this point, Rasheed got up from the sofa and excused himself on the basis he should now seek the whereabouts of the Imam. He added that he should also arrange for sandwiches and coffee, if Maxwell cared for some refreshment.

'Sandwiches and American coffee would go down a treat, right now,' he replied and with another one of those infectious, ear to ear, smiles Rasheed left the room, giving an assurance he would not be long. Ten minutes later the single door to the briefing room opened.

The steward approached Maxwell and addressed him in perfect English, to take his order for coffee. The visitor accepted his coffee with a generous dollop of cream and sweetened with half a dozen lumps of brown crystalline sugar. It was excellent; hot and refreshing; the caffeine kicking in. The steward fiddled a selection of the sandwiches onto a bone china plate edged in gold leaf and with a respectful bow, retired solemnly.

He was on his second cup when the door of the briefing room re-opened and Maxwell stood up to greet the Imam Sulayman bin Abdulla. The man stood framed in the doorway for a second or two, dwarfed by the figure of Rasheed, who waited directly behind him. Maxwell was unable to move. Sight of the man he had not been in contact with for several years gendered feelings of extreme warmth, which were instantly overshadowed by sensations of complete horror. This could not possibly be the man he had shared so many memorable and happy hours with in the past, a man who had always seemed much taller than his five feet eight inches. A man with a brain as sharp as a sewing needle, bright, sparkling eyes, a quick humorous wit able to be expressed perfectly in several languages; a man full of energy and composed of a personality and style which had charmed and gained the respect of Muslim leaders all over the world. This shadow of the man he had once known so well, stood in the open doorway, stooped and bent, leaning heavily on a plain varnished walking cane, seeming slightly out of breath and working very hard at shouting a greeting in Arabic to Maxwell which, from even such a short distance away, was barely audible.

The Imam began to move hesitantly towards his friend, refusing all support nervously offered by an over attentive Presidential secretary. Having successfully negotiated the brief space between the door and sofa, the Imam slumped down and threw his cane onto the floor. Maxwell remained standing in undisguised astonishment as Sulayman waved a bony, liver spotted hand in his direction, indicating he should be seated. Maxwell, left totally speechless, looked questioningly at Rasheed, who simply shook his head and mutely left the room on a final sharp instruction from the Imam.

'Stop sitting there gawping, Max, and get me a beef sandwich. You *know* how much I like them, especially as it was you who forced me into a near addiction to the horrible things, during all those hours of never-ending meetings so many years ago.'

'It's only just over two, my old friend,' Maxwell stated.

'Well, it seems a lot longer than that to me,' the religious leader muttered, '……and it had no need to be, you know. Why have you not visited me in these recent years? You could have had anything you wanted from me, you know that. Not even a letter, in all this time, *not even a letter.*'

Maxwell could not believe his eyes. The man sitting beside him weighed no more than fifty kilos and was looking as if he was still losing weight as evidenced by the loose and ill fitting thobe he was wearing. His slender hands were shaking violently as he concentrated on attempts to feed half of a beef sandwich into a thin, pale lipped mouth, which involuntarily gave out small amounts of saliva each time he made the attempt to chew. His features were taut and canopied with prematurely ageing skin which took on a disconcertingly opaque appearance in the examining, artificial light of the briefing room. A once crowning mop of naturally waved thick black hair had turned to limp strands of sparse grey and the memorable, steel cutting flash of ebony eyes, reduced to a limpid stare, holding little expression and projecting nothing of a once great personality that had, in the past, been associated with the workings of an even greater mind. This was a disaster. Maxwell had not expected such a change and he didn't know quite what to say or do at this precise moment. Sulayman saved him the trouble of trying, and having finished his beef and onion sandwich, leaned back into the warm leather of the sofa and continued the conversation, his voice raised higher in tone and sounding a little stronger.

'I welcome you, in the name of the great prophet Mohammed, peace be upon him; we all welcome you, my old friend. You are a wise but cautious man, respected by many and I need your ear and your counsel in these troubled and anxious times'.

He moved closer up the sofa towards Maxwell and feebly clutched his hand, waiting hesitatingly for a reaction,

'Tell me, how have you been and what are you doing now?'

Maxwell sighed inwardly, a symbol of remembrance and regret for what had been. With misty eyes he clasped the old man's palm in his and began to tell Sulayman just about all that had happened to him since they last met. The Imam listened attentively, occasionally letting out little chuckles as his long awaited visitor recounted tales of meetings or small adventures with people who were common to them, both as past friends, or sometimes enemies. The following hour passed quickly as Maxwell spoke almost continuously and was encouraged by the visible improvement in the Imam, both physically and mentally. The person in the man was coming alive, his back became a little straighter, his short periods of speech were clearer, firmer and more animated, with much clenching of fists or slapping of thighs, as his mood changed with the ebb and flow of conversation. Simply sitting and talking was a rejuvenating tonic no doctor could have ordered or pharmacist concocted; the dark glassy stare was replaced with a simmering light, a light of new probindity that flashed now and again to disperse the subterranean grey shadows, trapped in deeply etched lines of premature ageing. The two men devoured the sandwiches and coffee in a pervading mood of restrained excitement and Sulayman asked if they should order some more refreshment before they got down to discussing the real reasons for their meeting that day.

'Perhaps you would like some tea, my friend, instead of all this coffee; I read somewhere that too much of the stuff can be bad for your health.'

For the first time that day, that week, that year, Sulayman laughed out loud. It was a cackling, strained sound that reverberated round the bare concrete structure as the Imam carefully raised himself and paced slowly towards a wall mounted bell push, without the aid of his walking stick. Seconds later, the steward appeared and Sulayman ordered tea and fresh samousas for both, and a bottle of whisky for Maxwell. He was still beaming childishly as he returned to his seat.

'You see, my old comrade, I am not the terrible ogre they all make me out to be and I have even remembered the disgusting way you like to drink your tea'. He patted Maxwell's knee affectionately.

'Relax young man, relax and enjoy yourself a little. You will not give any offence by drinking alcohol in my company; my religious beliefs do not necessarily have to be yours and although I am chosen by the great prophet Mohammed, peace be upon him, to lead the world's Moslems to a greater unity and higher place in this earthly existence, this does not mean I am unable to accept and respect other theologies and ways of life. This is something, you above all, must understand.'

Maxwell pondered thoughtfully for a few seconds and then spoke.

'I want to understand and I want to believe that all the non-complimentary statements being made about you are untrue. I desperately want to believe that everything you are doing now is by your own volition; that you are being motivated by careful consideration and good counsel rather than manipulated by other, less honorable forces….. who will lead you to a crossroads of violence from which there will be no return.'

The frail figure issued a long contentious sigh, a grey shadow falling gradually across his craggy face, as he mentally paused and focused undiscerning eyes on some point in the far distance, some point beyond this room or this time. The next minute passed in complete silence, and would probably have gone on longer if it were not for the interruption of the steward, bearing a silver tray containing further refreshment. After he had left the room, the eyes of the Imam refocused on the teacup Maxwell was handing to him. He accepted the fervid liquid without comment and deciding it was far too hot to drink immediately, replaced the cup and saucer on the table in front of him. He calmly crossed his arms and began to speak.

'Perhaps, we should start at the beginning, and the beginning started for me the day I was placed in this firmament. There is now no doubt in my mind that I am placed on this earth for more than earthly reasons. I am here to carry out God's will. I am the chosen one, and whatever has happened in the past, or happens in the future, of this I am sure. The path has only been revealed to me in recent years, but I now know the road I have to take. It is written, it is prophesied and I can do nothing to change that. This knowledge is a great but inspiring responsibility which I am prepared to bear, whatever the consequences to myself or my followers and you should understand that my course is set, I cannot go back, only forward and I am being guided only by God .'

He paused momentarily to catch a labored breath

'It is impossible to explain why I know this to be true, even to a man such as yourself, and therefore you must accept that I am being solely motivated, not by my will or any other human direction, but the will of the great prophet, Mohammed, may peace be upon him. If you accept this fact completely and unquestionably then there are many things we can discuss; if not, I will be left with no other alternative than to gladly shake you by the hand and leave you. We will still hopefully be good friends and companions, but you will be unable to help in sharing the tremendous burden of responsibilities I now have to face.' The Imam took both of Maxwell's hands in his, looking him directly in the eye.

'Responsibilities to my people are only part of that burden and although I regard *all* Moslems as my people, wherever they are and of whatever nation, I answer only to God and God will require much more than benevolence and the execution of merciful acts. He will demand justice as well; justice for over one and a half thousand years of injustice conferred upon his true followers and their children and their children's children. As you can see, I do not believe I am the mindless fanatic that most would make me out to be, but the willing servant of a God who has become impatient with the imperfect people he has created. It is now time for the reckoning.'

He spoke with a calmness and conviction which touched Maxwell deeply. Although he still looked unbelievably tired, drawn and aged, there was a passion entrained in Sulayman's words, crying the truth of his belief, a belief which obviously haunted and gnawed away at his intellect like a feeding lion. It had also undoubtedly taken its toll physically and as if in confirmation of the fact the President took a small bottle of pink capsules from a pocket in his thobe and slipped two into his mouth. He swallowed them both and looked up at Maxwell guiltily.

'These are only iron and vitamin pills, given to me by my doctor to help me through the day. I am working very long hours and eating irregular meals, so I take a couple of these now and again, just to beef me up a little.'

Maxwell returned the comment with a concerned frown.

'Do not worry, my friend. I assure you these are harmless little vitamin pills,' said the Imam, but he quickly replaced them in his pocket and reached for more tea before any criticism could be voiced. The boney, fleshless hand was still a little shaky, the grip a little loose and Maxwell's host needed both hands to grasp the brimming teacup without spilling any of its contents.

Maxwell continued to weigh the situation in his mind, knowing the consequences of continuing the present line of conversation could be far reaching and totally unpredictable. He had thought that up until now, he knew this man well; knew what basically made him tick. Today he was not so sure. He needed a lot more time with Sulayman bin Abdulla before he made any decision as to whether or not he should become involved further, but he was obviously not going to get it. A firm resolution needed to be made and all he could promise to do was to listen and perhaps play the Devil's Advocate, where necessary; but without any other commitment than the one he had made to the chairman of the AGCC, which was simply to report on the subject of his meetings and any conclusions reached as a result. Sulayman waited patiently for a reply to his earlier request for an agreement of trust between the two of them. Maxwell spoke;

'You must understand, my dear friend that I come here at your personal invitation and by petition of the AGCC. You are well aware that this meeting carries no official recognition and if you will permit, I must tell you that the only reason this kind of discussion is necessary is because *you* refuse and therefore, through his belief in you, the *President of Iraq* refuses to talk to anyone in an official political capacity. You have isolated yourself from people who want to understand, who need to communicate, and more importantly, who do have a strong and genuine concern for your personal welfare. You and the President of Iraq must sit around a table with other world leaders and sort out your differences with them.'

Sulayman's reaction was totally unexpected. His hands began to vibrate, blood fused to his cheeks, turning his face a dark crimson as he attempted to rise. He found it impossible without the use of his walking stick. He grabbed the stick in clumsy frustration and leant heavily with both hands to raise himself from the sofa and lurch unsteadily away from Maxwell, knocking the coffee table as he went and spilling tea from his half filled cup. After managing one or two steps, he turned sharply to face Maxwell, replying with controlled emotion thickening his voice.

'You above all people must know what I have been through in the past years since being exiled from my true place as the Imam of Awabi. I was sold out by the damned British and the fawning dogs of the Trucial States. Do not talk to me, my friend, of the AGCC or the principles by which it stands. The AGCC serves only the interests of the rich and as a reluctant alms house for the poor. This great country of Iraq and its people did not suffer the years of humiliating British rule after the first world war, the installation of political puppets and the horrific and murderous campaign, again carried out by the British in May 1941, to now be dictated to by the semi literate leader of some deceivingly corrupt form of Arab Common Market. *No* my friend. *No*. The Iraqi nation has survived in its own way and we have made our own alliance, a Moslem alliance, that does not involve us in any compromise of our beliefs or our strengths. True believers, will follow the will of God and I have been chosen as his instrument, not some 'hotch-potch' of insignificant, posturing Gulf Sheikhs who in no way represent the majority of Islamic thinking in the Middle East or anywhere else for that matter.'

The exiled Imam of Awabi still stood, his face even more flushed with the effort of added emphasis and intensity to his accompanying words. The trembling had worsened. Maxwell was unsure of his ground. He didn't know whether to say something suitable in reply or say nothing; stay where he was, or go immediately to his dear old friend and offer a firm hand and more sympathetic ear. He decided on the latter. Maxwell left the comfort of the sofa and approached Sulayman, taking his still quivering arm and leading him towards the door.

'Come, let's go outside and walk a little in the night air, as we used to. I find this room very claustrophobic and it's not doing my nerves any good. Come, my old friend, let's go and smell the flowers, feel the grass beneath our feet, let's step back to some semblance of reality.'

The old man, now light of breath, replied with raised eyebrows and a despairing, apprehensive look and then allowed himself to be gently ushered outside of the single storey building, until they were both strolling along a wide grassed verge leading to a small, well maintained garden area, dotted with steel ventilator covers, which Max supposed fed fresh air to the many underground levels of the headquarters building they had just left. Two Arab armed guards trailed about fifty yards behind; they looked alert and efficient. The early evening air was cooling and even a little chilly. Still arm in arm, the two men perched on a flat, table-like rock which had been carefully placed in the miniature garden as the centre-piece to a landscaper's floral montage. Although there was continuous and sometimes noisy activity all around them, with trucks and staff cars moving hurriedly about their business up and down the roads which circuited the headquarters building, Maxwell seemed to take on board very little. He was first to break the private silence. He felt awkward and spoke with a noticeable amount of hesitation in his voice.

'Sulayman my friend, you know why I am here.....but I am only able to listen. I cannot possibly give you advice in any way whatsoever.......' he paused searching for words of meaning.

'From what I hear, you are treading a stony and bloody path, the effects of which may not simply be confined to the Gulf region. I can listen, I can struggle to comprehend and I can promise to try and make others understand. But you must realize that I haven't got a clue what is going on here. Just look around you; all this military hardware and manpower, it looks like preparations for the start of World War Three and how the Yanks aren't on to it by now, beats me completely. Whatever the

Iraqi plans are, they appear to be pretty far down the road; just tell me what the hell is going on' he paused, still searching. '…….. and if there are any alternatives to embarking on a plan which will lead to greater pain and more bloodshed, then I implore you to let me know in plain and simple terms'.

Sulayman's breathing returned to a revealing shallowness, his head raised at an odd angle as he stared into the middle distance wearing a near hypnotic expression, accentuated by the subordinate garden lighting; his skin clammy and chilled even further by the cool evening air. The reply came in spasmodic bursts as if he were reading with difficulty from an in-concise visionary script.

'It is the way. It is written. The Islamic world must rise up. Justice must be done. I am the instrument of God and you have been chosen as God's courier. You have no choice, and no other duty than to make the enemies of God realize the dire consequences of ignoring his word.'

The weary looking Imam paused for long seconds, then turned to his companion, looking him full in the face; a pleading, haunting look that Maxwell knew he would remember for the rest of his life.

'This is how it will be. Our nation has for years been cheated by the western powers, both politically and financially. The northern Gulf States have billions of dollars invested in Europe and the United States; those investments have been manipulated for the good of their managers, not their owners. We want them back. We have an agreement with Kuwait to make a joint request to all overseas investment organizations, and all companies in which our joint stockholding is greater than twelve per cent, to immediately liquidate such investments and stockholdings and repatriate them to us at the full dollar value on the day of request'. He paused again, his eyes distant focused.

'That value is to be paid in gold bullion and from the time of presentation of our request, all oil contracts will be cancelled and payment for new future contracts will be based on a free market gold value calculated on the day of uplift in Gulf waters. Shipment out of the Gulf will only be allowed in our own tankers, at a price not referenced to a European manipulated world scale but calculated on the basis of supply and demand. The object of this action is to return to ourselves that which is rightfully ours. We are aware there will be a certain amount of distress in the Americas and Europe, but we feel that with a little belt tightening and good management, in a few years, they will recover'. Maxwell remained in thoughtful silence. The words failed to immediately distress him.... the delivery did.

'In this time, we will use our own money to re-invest in our economy, to increase the spread of our basic industries and increase the ability of our own people to manage their own affairs. This will mean that in ten years time, we should be totally self-sufficient in manufactured goods, basic foodstuffs and energy. We shall then be happy to compete with the western world on an equal footing. The movement of finance and creation of reinvestment programmes will be guided by Sharia Law which, as you know, forbids the payment of interest, and will be open to all countries in the world embracing Islam and following the teachings of the great prophet, Mohammed, may peace be upon him. This is how it will be, this is how God demands it and this is the task I must undertake'.

Maxwell was struggling to put it all together. It was an incredulous undertaking and one which stood to break the economies of many countries outside of the Islamic block and definitely destroy the industrial muscle of many countries in Europe.

'Well Sulayman, I must admit, at first hearing you seem to have a show-stopper but let us suppose for one moment, that your request is to be granted. What will happen to the lower Gulf States? Surely if they maintained their deposits in Europe and America and were prepared to take an initial loss, they would provide Europe especially, with enough clout to weather the storm and therefore knock a rather big hole in your plan. Without some co-operation from at least Saudi Arabia, and possibly the newly formed Emirates, I would think the amount of hard cash you were able to pull out of the system, in one big hit, would only be enough to rock the boat, not sink it.' The Moslem leader's face was now so close, that Maxwell could feel the heat of irregular breath on his cheek.

'You are probably not aware, young Maxwell,' he replied confidently, 'that since the coming to power of the new President, the Iraqis have been living as a frugal nation and along with our brothers in Kuwait we now jointly hold title to investments and overseas holdings just short of one trillion dollars.' Maxwell's jaw dropped as the Imam continued '..... and let me assure you that a sum such as this is more than enough for our direct and singular purpose. As for Saudi Arabia and to a lesser extent, the lower Gulf, they have concentrated during the last ten years on stimulating and providing for an industrial economy which, with the help of their friends in the west, has cost them a small fortune. The west has been the only beneficiary in such forward looking programs. From the time a smelter, for example, is placed on the drawing board, to the time it is handed over to its proud Arab owners, the project has trebled or quadrupled in cost as the value of European currencies shifts during the construction and commissioning phase. But ask this question at the end of the day ....... who are the *customers* for this fine Arabian product? The western nations of course! They then jointly manipulate the world market price for the required commodity so that the Arab smelting industry can never make sufficient profit to show any capital return. The net result is that our great Arab benefactors have put the whole value of the project, costing billions, in the back pocket of European industrialists who are now buying smelted metal cheaper than ever before in real terms'. The Imam moved uneasily on his hard stone seat.

'They also know the workings of the Arab mind well enough to be assured that for the sake of saving face, not one plant will close, even if it's losing millions operationally. No, my friend, do not be deceived by the brash exterior workings of the AGCC; they are hurting and hurting hard at the moment and within forty eight hours of our request being made public, they will have two choices; stick with their so called western allies or join a new, greater Islamic economic community. Be assured they will take the second course. The people of the Gulf will not have it any other way. We have nothing to say to them; they will quickly see the error of their ways and rotate in our direction. Then it will be the turn of the Islamic movement to control the world price for aluminum, refined oil product, iron, rolled steel, copper, nickel, potash and fertilizer; all the base materials the industrialized nations of the west need ….. *to survive.* We will require their assistance no longer; we have not been standing idly by during the past decade; we have been learning from them and training our engineers, our designers, our managers and our marketing men. We can do what we have to do on our own, except for a shortage of basic manpower in some areas and even that is freely available in third world countries containing large Moslem populations in Asia and Africa. Have no fear Maxwell; this plan has been neither ill conceived, nor have I been ill advised. It has been revealed to me in every detail.

It will go the way that God has willed it. I am merely here to communicate this will to the Moslem people of the world. They will know that this is the work of God; they shall be given the sign and you will know also, Maxwell, you will know.'

Sulayman now spoke steadily and confidently, his voice strong and vibrant, a voice full of conviction and an assurance of tone that reminded Maxwell of the time Sulayman had stood at Jebel Ahkdar. Talking like this, he was still a very persuasive man, and at that moment he seemed to have lost little of his old charisma. His words burnt the crisp night air and hung heavily with the consuming passion of his views. Maxwell knew he would have to be careful.

'OK Sulayman, let us now assume another situation. What if America and Europe refuse point blank to grant your request for repatriation of funds and simply tell you to go stick your head up your backside. What then?' …..a Hollywood pause.

'Then, my friend, we shall simply have to go and take it from them'.

Maxwell looked up sharply and indicated all before him by moving an upturned hand in a horizontal, spreading motion.

'What, with all this?'

'No, no, no,' Khalid quickly replied.

'This…. as you call it……all this military preparation is for self defense, the defense of ourselves and our allies. No my friend, we do not need military might. We only need to weld all our

Moslem brothers together under one banner and bring about the political collapse of Europe. We are in a position to cut off all oil supplies to those countries who do not support us in our claim. Within one month, Europe, as a whole, would be hard pressed, even relying on reserves and war stockpiles. Japan, New Zealand and Australia, South Africa and most of South America would definitely not be able to last out longer than six weeks. Whichever way......governments will fall. Civil riots, prompted by Moslem reaction in those and other countries, would have to be contained. We will not need to use weaponry of any kind other than that required to ensure our own protection, considering a possible over-zealous reaction by those rather hasty and immature Americans. But this matter they would have to consider very carefully. Nearly one third of the Soviet nation now embraces Islam and truly is allowed to live by its laws; they are my people, and if a holy war is declared they will follow my direction. The time has come for us all to stop fooling either ourselves or one another; we have rights, we have needs and now, thanks be to God, we have strength.' The Imam raised a hand to deter Maxwell from interrupting.

'The support we enjoy from the Soviets is not motivated by some outmoded colonial philosophy but by political necessity. When Brezhnev came to power, he knew it would be impossible to continue maintaining control of a federal nation of such mixed ethnic origins, amounting to some two hundred and fifty million people spread over nearly nine million square miles, without some sort of political reform and a severe review of human rights. He is a man of much vision and we have talked, at length, together over the past few years. He understands the problems involved in trying to take a horse to water and then forcing it to drink. It is a time-consuming undertaking and eats up valuable resources, manpower and money. At the same time a tremendously gross and unmanageable secret policing operation has to be carried out to ensure that the people leading the horses are in fact leading them to the right river. The USSR, although still maintaining an iron curtain pose with the west, is today, unrecognizable in terms of human rights and religious freedom, the net result of which is that horses don't have to be led anymore and they drink freely from the river. The only control necessary today is the flow, direction and quality of the water in the river and that is far less time consuming, delivers much better results and requires a much smaller and more manageable secret police force to do it. You must know Maxwell, that presently in Soviet Russia the Jews, the Moslems, the Christians and even the Buddhists are able to practice their religious beliefs with General impunity. Don't be deceived, my friend, by American propaganda. The Americans are a nation running scared and no longer regarded as the saviours of the free world. They are presently reaping the harvest of years of political ineptitude and double-sided aid policies alienating them from most of the third world and straining relations with Europe to nearly breaking point. I have not turned to the Soviets for help or guidance at any time; they have turned to me .... and the millions of Moslems who today live inside the borders of the Soviet block, look to me for a pathway back to respect, a respect for themselves and for God.'

Maxwell pondered long and hard. Certainly, most of what Sulayman had said was true but he still found it hard to accept that in less than ten years, the great shoulder bruising Russian bear had turned into an enlightened, politically philanthropic pussycat, without territorial ambitions or colonial aspirations. If most of the hardware he had seen today, on his short trip around the base at Kirkuk, was defensive, then it was a pretty bloody sophisticated defense! Perhaps the forces assembled here were not for moving down the Gulf at all; perhaps there was a much wider ranging plan afoot and therefore would explain, in some measure, why he had been allowed to see so much.

He made a mental note not to jump to any early conclusions and although it was obvious that Sulayman had been fairly well convinced of the genuineness of the arm of brotherly love reaching out to him from Iraq's northern neighbor, the overall policy as described by the Imam contained one or two loopholes. They were dangerous loopholes which, combined with a sprinkling of conspiracy and dressed with a little greed, could turn the whole event into a frightening new world war.

It was getting colder and, although the light breeze had dropped almost completely, Maxwell shivered involuntarily, perhaps partly with the continuing drop in temperature and partly with a foreboding awareness of what was to come if his friend's calculations and detailed forward planning proved to be wrong. Sulayman had obviously noticed the small shudder and suggested they go back to the briefing room, to which Maxwell readily agreed.

Neither spoke on the short walk back. As they arrived in the entrance of the administration building, the attentive steward hurried away for more refreshments; the two following guards took up new positions just inside the door, their faces expressionless, indicating a lassitude able to deceive most assassins. The two men felt much more relaxed with one another now and disturbed by no-one, other than the steward and a short telephone message from Rasheed to the Imam, informing him of the arrival of General Lubikov, who was now in his quarters, should he be needed.

Sulayman explained to Maxwell, after putting down the phone, that General Lubikov was the General officer commanding the Soviet Assistance Force, who liaised directly with the President through normal staffing routes and was the only non-Moslem staff officer in the force. Maxwell expressed a wish to meet with the General if possible, a request which was willingly granted, and the Imam agreed to make arrangements for the following day.

'Tomorrow,' Max replied, 'I had hoped it would be possible to fly over to Kuwait to meet with the Emir, Sheikh Hamed Al Shab, with your and the President's permission, of course, and preferably your blessing'

Sulayman gave Maxwell's knee another one of his affectionate little caresses.

'Mafi mish-kellah, my friend, no problem. I will make arrangements for you to meet with Lubikov in the morning and, depending on what else you wish to do, you should be able to get away before midday. I have already spoken to the Emir and once I can confirm the time of your arrival, he will make himself available to meet with you.'

It was getting late and Khalid suddenly looked tired and drawn again. He had been unable to walk back to the administration building without the use of his stick. During the course of their meal, he had again popped two or three more pills into his mouth, returning Maxwell's questioning looks with an embarrassed, half hearted smile. His skin still reflected an unhealthy pallor and as much as he tried to keep them under control, his hands trembled involuntarily. They had talked and talked for hours and although Maxwell felt he had grasped the overall meaning to Sulayman's struggle or 'Jihad', as he called it, he was not convinced of the sincerity behind the parts some others might be playing, or to the extent to which the Emir of Kuwait was prepared to co-operate. Still, by tomorrow he would hopefully have a better idea of key figure involvement after his meetings with Lubikov and Sheikh Hamed. It was obvious that the Imam wished to prolong their talks, but both men had had a long day and dark shadows framed drooping eyelids as Max let out an involuntary, semi-stifled yawn. Sulayman stood up, leaned with one straight arm on his walking stick and shuffled towards the door. The meeting was over.

'Come, my tired young comrade. Time has beaten us yet again. Let us both get some badly needed sleep and I will see you tomorrow before you leave.'

He pressed the wall bell push and the steward immediately appeared.

'Ali here, will look after your needs and show you to your quarters and if you decide to leave the complex for any reason, one of the guards will go with you, purely for your own protection, of course. Goodnight, my dear Maxwell, may your God be with you and may the great prophet, peace be upon him, smile upon you '.

With a half wave of his hand, the Imam of Awabi departed. The steward stood by, expectantly, waiting for Maxwell to move.

\*\*\*\*\*\*

At the third underground level, the lift stopped; olive enameled doors slid open to reveal a dimly lit corridor, lined in un-plastered concrete and stretching for some three hundred feet in an unbending line. The steward walked ahead and stopped at a steel door on his right, which he opened with a magnetic key. He gave the key to

Maxwell and waited deferentially for him to pass by and enter. The windowless quarters consisted of four rooms divided into a large well furnished lounge, an adequate and separate kitchen area, a bedroom combined with a small alcove study and a fully tiled modern bathroom. His clothes had been laid out on the bed and Ali now hurried to hang them in a spacious, built-in wardrobe. Upon further inspection, Maxwell was pleased to discover in the bathroom, a complete selection of toiletries and fresh towels. He spoke to the steward,

'Thank you Ali, I think I have everything I need here. I would appreciate it if you'd wake me at about six in the morning and try and scout up some steak and eggs for breakfast. If the General calls, please tell him I'll be free any time after seven fifteen.'

Maxwell had noted that the only useful item missing in the well appointed little underground apartment was a telephone and he therefore assumed the steward would be contacting him regarding his meeting with the Russian commander the following day. Ali silently nodded an indication of understanding and with a flat subordinate expression, quietly left the company of his foreign visitor. Despite the continuous hum of the air conditioning and the initially disturbing intermittent clicking of a poorly maintained thermostat, Maxwell slept well that night.

# Chapter Twelve

*September 26th 1973 – Kirkuk Air Base – Northern Iraq*

Next morning, after a long and invigorating shower and a piping hot plate of steak and eggs, washed down with heavy black coffee, Maxwell felt fit and rested. He dressed in a light brown, cotton safari suit and prepared himself to face the day, mentally sifting through all that had been said the previous evening. He was disturbed from silent deliberation by the steward, who brought news that the General would be pleased to meet with him at his convenience. The two men set off for the lift and upon arriving back in the foyer of the building, Maxwell was handed over to the care of two new guards, who led him courteously towards a waiting staff car. When loaded with all three men, the car moved off in the direction of the Military Air Wing Headquarters. During the short journey across the south side of the base, Max noted an increase in activity compared to the previous day. The car sped forward, through two raised security barriers and after a short detour around a giant ground handling tug, they pulled up smoothly outside the headquarters building. Inside there was feverish activity, as army and air force personnel purposefully shifted multi-colored files from here to there, collars open, ties slack and vivid shoulder flashes indicating the presence of a multitude of military units; Russian, Iraqi, Polish and even some East German and Czechoslovak. Maxwell confidently followed his two Arab guards as they led him through to the back of the building, flashing security passes every few seconds in their progress from corridor to corridor, until eventually they came to a large teak paneled double door. The two Arabs stopped and told the English visitor to go on through.

He entered into a spacious office suite, paneled throughout in teak relief boarding. The General was seated at the far end of the room behind a large, black leather trimmed desk. He raised himself as Maxwell approached, extending a hand of welcome and smiling a genuine looking greeting. The General spoke perfect English and after the usual introductions, made a few flattering comments concerning his visitor and the high regard in which he was held by the Iraqi President and the Imam. He re-seated himself at his desk after pulling up a chair for the Englishman and offering some coffee or tea which was politely refused.

'Now, Mister Armstrong, I am completely at your disposal. Please feel free to ask any questions you wish and I shall do my best to answer them,' said Lubikov. He paused for a moment.

'You will hopefully appreciate I am only able to speak to you in my capacity as a liaison officer but I am asked to give you full co-operation and within the bounds of my knowledge, I will be as truthful and accurate as I can.'

Maxwell warmed immediately to the man in front of him. He possessed an outgoing personality and a vibrant quality to his voice, matched by twinkling eyes, engendering an unexpected feeling of trust and honesty. He had had the experience of meeting with several senior Russian military men and politicians in the past and to his overall recollection, had not been overly impressed. This man had obviously been chosen carefully for his assignment, with charm and personality as high on the list of required attributes as organizational ability and a probable sprinkling of complete ruthlessness. No one looked as if they were here on holiday, especially the Russians, and putting in a man of some quality, such as the General appeared to be, did not belie the fact. Maxwell chose his words prudently in opening the verbal sparring.

'Well, General, I think it's better to start at the beginning and offer you my view of how I came to be here in the first place, so there is no misunderstanding between us concerning my motives and my interests in what is patently your business and that of your friends and allies.' The General relaxed back in his chair a little.

'That would be excellent, Mr. Armstrong. I would appreciate your frankness.'

Maxwell proceeded to recount as much of the detail of the past few days as he reasoned was necessary in explaining the background to the undertaking of his 'mission', as the Dubai ruler had called it. He left out nothing in terms of the content of discussions with the Arab Gulf Co-operation Council members, but decided to be cautious in wording his impressions of his talks with the Imam Sulayman bin Abdulla. The General listened attentively and without interruption, occasionally leaning forward in his chair to make short notes on a small desk pad. He attended to his guest for nearly an hour and when Maxwell finally fell silent, the General again offered coffee, which this time was gratefully accepted. Pausing now and again between sips from a delicate bone china cup, the Russian filled Maxwell in on the background to his presence at Kirkuk and went into some detail with reference to his responsibilities, not only to his own government, but also to the Iraqi President.

General Lubikov spoke calmly and authoritatively on the delicate position in which he found himself, especially relating to the sometimes tricky politics he often had to become enmeshed in. However, the man omitted to reveal his connections with the KGB but told Maxwell the half truth, in that he was a General officer in the artillery. This was supported by the military shoulder boards he was wearing as part of an immaculately tailored, grey field officers' uniform; shoulder boards which Maxwell recognized and noted, as he had with most of the uniform insignia he had seen since arriving at Kirkuk. Lubikov continued for a further ten to fifteen minutes, with his visitor asking the odd question and clarifying various points of particular interest. Maxwell continued the conversation.

'Tell me, General, as a broad question, what do you know about the medical treatment the Imam informs me he's receiving from your doctors?

Although I haven't seen him for several years, he has deteriorated physically beyond recognition since we last met and this is of personal concern to me, as well as it must be to you'.

Lubikov paused to carefully select the right words.

'It is true, Mr. Armstrong, that Sulayman is not the man he once was and some of our medical specialists are treating him. You must understand this is not my particular field of experience and to complicate matters still further, there are two viewpoints on the subject; one official and the other unofficial. The official view is he suffered a minor stroke about two years ago, is Generally fit but is under treatment for a continuing but controllable heart problem. The truth of the matter is, he is suffering from a psychosomatic condition which expresses itself in deteriorating motor functions from time to time.' Maxwell was paying full attention.

'From what I know of the problem, I understand he is being treated with General therapy and given harmless drugs and he believes the doctors are treating a defined physical condition, such as the hand trembling, loss of weight and a pronounced limp which comes and goes, depending on his particular mood. Other than that, I have personally always found his mind active, his speech lucid and his General grasp of what is going on around him to be more than acceptable. The President's private secretary, Rasheed al Sheikh, probably writes most of his speeches for him and does tend to rather isolate him from visitors. There again, I understand he reads all speeches and statements, before they are made and he, himself, directs Rasheed to keep him away from the public and visiting dignitaries; so you must form your own opinions as to his General health and competence, especially as you are one of only four foreigners who have managed to obtain a private audience with him during the past two years'. The General's visitor nodded in silent agreement.

'He holds you in very high regard and I think his doctors would agree with me when I say that he needs something deeply personal to hang on to. He is a very dedicated man to the cause of Islam and although both you and I may not exactly accept his finite religious ideals, we must make every effort to understand them. From what you have told me, this seems to be your job now, as well as mine.'

As Lubikov spoke, he drummed thick, stubby fingers on the desk top constantly. He didn't appear nervous or put out by the question, but simply concentrating hard on trying to précis a deeply complicated subject into a few understandable words. Maxwell spoke again.

'Are you really sure the diagnosis of his physical and mental state is correct? Aren't you at all worried that a man with so much power is unacceptably isolated from actual reality and that someone could be manipulating him into embarking upon all sorts of adventures which, if they fail, would result in some fairly dramatic consequences?'

The Russian officer drained his second cup of coffee and leaned forward across the desk. He spoke in a lower and more guarded tone.

'Look, my friend, I personally, and my country in General, have much at stake here, I am being as truthful with you as I possibly can when I say neither I, nor my government, would back this man or the President of Iraq, by going this far down the road with either of them, if we felt we were not working in a controlled situation. As far as we are concerned, the Imam commands the will of nearly one third of the population of the Soviet Union and possibly four times that number in the Middle East and Asia. We simply cannot ignore him. He believes he is the new Islamic prophet and so do nearly four hundred million others. He believes the Islamic nations have got and have had for many years, a raw deal from the west and we believe that also. He believes that Arab money should be used for the good of the Arabs and that other Moslems in the world should also benefit from that money; and so do we. He believes, if he does take the needed step to retrieve Arab assets from America and Europe, the rest of the Gulf States will follow him; and again, so do *we*. How then, can we say someone is manipulating him, or if they are, should we really care? He wants what *we* want, it's as plain and as simple as that.'

The General leant back away from the closeness of the situation and continued.

'I have a brief to support this man in any way I can and if I thought for one moment that the President or the Imam was incapable of making a clear-cut decision on any subject or was being manipulated by a third party, who didn't appear to understand and recognize our joint interests, then I would pull my men and equipment out of here tomorrow. The Imam isolates himself because he is frightened of assassination before his vision of putting the Moslems back into their rightful place in the world can come to fruition. The President of Iraq has had to accept our military assistance because he has no one else to turn to. In my book, both these men know what they are doing. You may like it or not like it and that goes for the people who sent you here, but the fact remains that the Imam is committed to carrying out his divine plan to the bitter end and as I see it, through you, he is giving all who don't wish to bow to that will, one last chance to swim with him up the river or be drowned in the rush when the flood gates open'.

The General's fingers were drumming constantly now, emphasizing literally every syllable. Maxwell knew the truth of the matter. Sulayman had told him and now the Russian was telling him. Christ, what a bloody mess ! He had been right in his first assessment of Lubikov; he was charming and polite but the way he had just been speaking displayed something of a ruthless streak that one would be wise to be wary of. He was not simply playing soldiers or soldiers' politics; he was convinced of the correctness of his position and assessment of his country's exposure in a tricky political maneuver, which, if it came off, would be the greatest coup of all time and if it didn't, would stoke the fires for the start of a major military confrontation.

Everyone needed to be right in this situation but, inevitably, someone had to be wrong; and Lubikov's appraisal of the real meaning behind all the international camouflage associated with such an unbelievable scheme would be essential in deciding who the wrong party would turn out to be. Maxwell finished collecting his thoughts and moved onto a new subject.

'OK General, I suppose, reluctantly, I have to accept all you've just said. What interests me, is how this rather delicately balanced 'defense force' will work in actual reality. I am not a trained military observer, but I have been able to tour the base here at Kirkuk and estimate there is an awful lot of very high-tech hardware out there, which couldn't conceivably be construed as for *'defensive purposes'* only.'

Lubikov leaned back in his chair, slapped his knees violently with both hands and head back, laughed out loud. When the laughter subsided and his visitor's engaging look of curiosity had returned to a patiently blank expression, the General replied,

'Tell me, Mister Armstrong, I thought we were trying to be frank with one another here. I am well aware of your activities within the British Secret Intelligence Service and most of your undercover movements with them over the years; also the fact that you are still in communication with that organization. Not a trained observer indeed. You are probably more conversant with manufacturing marks, firepower and capabilities of military hardware in the eastern block and Soviet Russia than most of my own men!' He smiled patronizingly as he spoke.

'*You* above all must realize there is no such thing as a defensive capability unless it is backed up by an offensive capability. That is military strategy in its crudest form and I'm even surprised you asked the question.'

'Does that require the deployment of Mig-25s outside of your borders with only Russian pilots trained to fly them in a combat role?' questioned Maxwell.

'Ah! said Lubikov, I fear you have not understood my meaning when I say we have a total commitment to support this venture to its extreme and final conclusion. The forces presently installed in Iraq and to a lesser extent, Kuwait are all, and I mean all, of Moslem origin. They are units from places inside Soviet Russia, such as Georgia, Tadzhik and Uzbek. They have Moslem commanders and live a Moslem way of life and since the advent of the Brezhnev era, have become some of the most trusted and well trained fighting units we have in the Soviet military. There has, of course, been certain resistance in our Army and Air Force High Command to this rather sharp about-face in turning the Islamic element of our military machine from what was regarded as 'limonshchik' cannon fodder, into front line squadrons equipped with the best weaponry. At first, even I was against it, but time has proven us wrong. These units are some of the best we have.

The only legacy of hawkishness left over from this period of traumatic change was the insistence by the Air Force hierarchy that all high technology development aircraft be flown only by what are regarded as white Russians. You are correct in stating the Mig-25 has not to date been seen outside our borders and they are available at present in limited numbers only. Unfortunately, Mr. Armstrong, if I am to carry out my job efficiently, I need them'.

'If you do start to move west, militarily, what do you think Israel is going to do....simply let you walk straight through Jerusalem?.

Let us not beat around the bush Mr. Armstrong. We know the Israelis have nuclear weapons ....... and the means to deliver them. So now you know why I need my squadrons of Mig 25's. They are the means to neutralize the Israeli nuclear deterrent. Hopefully the very threat of such a possibility will engender serious thought by the Israelis before this kind of move is made; prompted either by their own concern, or that of their American allies. I repeat to you; we have a joint Arab, Soviet Army under our control which will only move outside of our common borders at the request of the governments who follow the Islamic movement and require greater security than they enjoy at present.' Maxwell interjected,

'Something like *Czechoslovakia* in 1968, you mean!'

'*No*,' the General continued, '.... *not* like *Czechoslovakia,* and you are well aware that this is not what I meant'.

'…… and Egypt … Syria .. for example … are they essential to the military master-plan?' Lubikov denied his visitor a reply, remaining stone faced.

There followed a short pause of re-entrenchment as both men took stock; neither too sure about what to say next. Maxwell captured the running and re-adjusting his position in his seat, asked for some more coffee. Lubikov knew he would have to be careful. Armstrong was not going to be easy to convince. The General's visitor spoke again,

'Let us move on for a moment to the economic question. If the President and the Imam succeed in recovering some, or all, of the assets and cash they request, then even to a layman it's obvious there will be a horrific fiscal imbalance between east and west and this will precipitate an economic landslide which will cripple most of Europe; the American economy could be pushed to the edge of bankruptcy. I can understand the Soviet's keenness to get their hands on some of the repatriated Arab cash, but you still have to trade to a great degree with the west. You only get what you pay for and with a part gutted economy and limited export markets, the Yanks will make you pay dearly for it. The accepted world currency unit is still the US dollar and remains the platform for all oil trade. If the dollar devalues by sixty per cent, then all exports will simply revalue by two hundred per cent, and Soviet governments will have to find the money from somewhere ….. and find it in foreign currency.' He paused; the General was listening intently.

'It doesn't make too much sense to me............ and from a quick first appraisal, I would estimate your initial gains as low, and long term gains as minimal.'

Maxwell had ignored the earlier reference to his links with the SIS and although he had managed to maintain an even expression and calmness of tone during the ensuing conversation, he was not happy, in fact, he was bloody angry. He had worked hard at maintaining an unbreakable cover for years and there it was in one swift moment ripped up in shreds and thrown on the bare boarded floor in front of him. Somebody in London had a lot of explaining to do.

He drank more coffee and attempted to concentrate on what General Lubikov was saying.

'......so you see, Mr. Armstrong,' intoned the Russian, 'we are prepared to take the gamble. If all I have been told by our great and respected leaders is correct, the whole world will be forced back to basic bartering again and probably the re-introduction of a new gold standard. Next to South Africa, Russia is still the largest gold producer in the world. We are also the largest producers of iron ore, pig iron, crude steel, copper, zinc, nickel and platinum among others.' He allowed himself a smile.

'Tell me, Mr. Armstrong, in a world of *real* barter, as opposed to falsely valued and manipulated currency exchange rates, who do you think has the ability to survive longest and who is in the best position to take immediate advantage of any return to a new, floating gold standard? The only hope in hell the Americans will have is to do some kind of deal with South Africa and tighten the screws on Canada. Who will be seen to be dictators then, my friend? You should note in your report back to the SIS, that I am not fully acquainted with the will or plans of my masters as far as economics are concerned, especially relating to this particular subject, but I'll bet you a jack boot to a dumdum bullet that this estimate of my government's thinking is fairly accurate.' Lubikov confidently leant forward again

'Let's put it this way,' Lubikov grinned. 'I would much rather be on my side than yours.'

The General leaned back again, crossed his hands and rocked gently in the narrow office chair.

He was satisfied. He could tell from the expression of undisguised gloom on the face in front of him that he had done it all right; told him enough to sow most of the selected seeds but not enough to give the details of the game away. The General had taken a surprisingly quick liking to Mr. Armstrong and suddenly wondered if he played chess.

Maxwell glanced at his watch, partly as an excuse to avert his eyes from the General's piercing gaze for a few seconds and partly to extend time for thought. The clock face told him the morning was passing by rapidly. He was further annoyed by yet another reference to the SIS, but he was becoming more and more convinced the man was telling the truth. He knew that in many ways he was being read a script of sorts, but even then he was able to gain a fair idea of how prepared the Soviets were and how much thought and planning had been put behind the operation; rather more in fact by what had not been said, as opposed to the 'analysis of the official word.'

The grey haired, distinguished looking Russian host busied himself at the percolator; grinding fresh coffee and filling a clean jug with bottled mineral water ready to place on the blackened hot plate. He shouted a few words across to the Englishman.

'Don't ever come to Russia for coffee, Mr. Armstrong, its absolute crap.'

When a remote buzzing sound told the General that fresh coffee was ready and with the agreement of his visitor, he poured two more cups. Maxwell obtained the distinct impression that coffee was perhaps the only thing Lubikov was addicted to, as both men sipped and savored the excellent, freshly brewed Mocha. A satisfied and respectful silence passed between them. Maxwell wondered if the General played chess.

# Chapter Thirteen

*September 26th 1973 – Farm Street – London – UK*

It was some several minutes before six o'clock on a blustery, damp weekday morning in London. There was little traffic about but odd people could be spotted wrapped up against the dreary wetness and gusting winds; rushing for the first bus or diving into dark, subterranean railway stations to start the day opening up offices or taking up an early morning shift in some West End garment factory; underpaid, undernourished and underprivileged.

The man from C section drove the black Ford panel van with care, his passenger sitting contentedly beside him listening to the early morning news on the car radio, barely heard above the noise of the rumbling heater fan. The driver turned the van cautiously off Curzon Street and into South Audley Street, where he braked gently and slowed to a halt beneath the dim light from a street lamp. He kept the engine running as both men checked their watches, confirming for the last time they were both synchronized. The tall passenger pushed back the woolen glove on his left hand, turned up the collar of his knee length, black leather coat, and with a nod to the driver moved out into the chilled street air, pulling a grey knitted hat hard down over his head as he went.

The van moved off without fuss, indicators blinking religiously. The leather coated figure walked briskly north along the pavement until he came to a junction which would lead him into Farm Street. He continued along Farm Street and on into Hays Mews, where he stopped and quietly faded into the shadows of a basement stairway belonging to one of the ponderous Victorian mansions which lined three sides of the small square, made up of Farm Street and Waverton Street on the one side, and Charles Street and Hays Mews on the other. His hands thrust deep into overcoat pockets to keep them warm, he looked toward an impressive four storey building situated nearly halfway along Farm Street. The structure had been recently renovated and boasted a large private garage on the ground floor, a real London luxury, for the sole use of the owners of the two large apartments situated above. The leather coated observer knew the numbers of the apartments; he knew them very well. The lower one was number 34 and belonged to a Herr Heinrich Smitt; the upper one was number 34A and was presently empty, although there was no For Sale sign outside to indicate the owner wished to dispose of his investment. The sign had been taken down three days previously by a confused estate agent. Seemingly Herr Smitt did not want anyone moving in above him, just yet. He checked his watch, it was just gone six, they would all be up and about soon. At that moment, a light burst from the curtain-less window of 34A. Right on time, reflected the watchful stranger and turned his gaze in the direction of Waverton Street, focusing on the very end house at the junction with Charles Street.

The signal he was waiting for was to be a light on the top floor for ten seconds, followed ten seconds later by a light permanently switched on in the left hand room of the middle floor. He heard a car door slam somewhere on his left, then a stamping of feet and muttered oaths.

The signal came and the seconds were counted as two men moved hurriedly towards the house on Farm Street. The leather coated observer suppressed a smile; the English must have their bloody tea. The two men entered the house on Farm Street as a light was switched on in the lower apartment. Everyone was up and about now; the security men in 34A; the ever patient, but ever obvious Special Branch guards from the parked car on Charles Street, and now the 'mark' himself, Herr Heinrich Smitt.

The man from C section felt in the inside pockets of the leather trench coat, checking the equipment he would need during the operation. He took a long look around, practiced eyes working hard to pierce the early morning darkness, broken in varying patterns of glimmering light issuing from scattered street lamps and odd house lights. He would have to be quick. This was the only chance, the only break in the tight security net wrapped permanently around Herr Smitt. The tenebrous shadow moved quickly from the protection of the stairwell and in seconds, had reached the garage door of the Farm Street house.

With gloves removed sensitive fingers felt carefully down each side of the aluminum up and over door and in the top right hand coping, he found what he was looking for; a small raised line in the cement finish next to the door frame. The Russian agent removed a miniature, thumbnail sized, electronic device from his pocket, and, peeling off the cover to a layer of double sided tape attached to the bottom of the device, pushed it hard against the garage door frame, parallel with the beginning of the raised line in the cement. Two seconds later a miniature light emitting diode glowed red, then green.

The magnetic alarm on the door was now neutralized with the permanently coded magnetic field being generated by the device, and the leather coated intruder could safely work on the lock of the garage door. He checked his watch again and noted he had exactly nine minutes to complete his task and get back to the van which would be waiting for him on the junction at South Audley Street. The lock was uncomplicated, turning at the first attempt, and the door moved easily on well oiled, overhead runners; the intruder moved soundlessly inside and closed the door. A single car was parked in the middle of the garage, with the boot nearest the door. He paused and listened for sounds, satisfied with hearing only the rattle of the wastepipe as shower water dropped through to the sewers below. From his inside breast pocket, the man from C section extracted a miniature battery light attached to a long strip of Velcro tape, a new set of keys and a small rechargeable cordless electric drill. He strapped the light around the woolen cap and switched on the pencil thin beam. He manipulated several keys in the boot lock of the silver Daimler Sovereign, until, with a muffled click, the lid sprang open. He checked the time; only six minutes left. The car boot was clean and empty. The agent jumped in, squeezing himself down sideways and, measuring two hand widths from the side of the rear seat pressed steel support; he marked a spot and started to drill a small hole. It took exactly thirty seconds to break through with the tungsten twist drill and in one quick movement he changed his position and repeated the exercise on the other side of the seat support. With two holes now drilled through to the sponge and spring filling of the rear seat, the intruder felt inside a small pocket in the sleeve of his coat and extracted two thin blue steel nail-like objects with a white plastic cap pushed over one end. He carefully removed the caps and inserted each object through the freshly drilled holes until he felt the front tips pushed firmly into the sponge rubber filling of the seat. When he was sure the spring loaded needles were placed correctly, he tapped the short end still sticking through the steel pressing and three slender gun metal springs popped out to secure each structure in the holes.

Nearly done!

Finally, with great care, he pulled a wad of black putty from a strip of plaster which had been used to attach it to the inside of his right wrist. The putty was carefully molded over the protruding spring clips to disguise the instruments from a cursory glance and finally satisfied the Russian jumped out of the boot and checked the time yet again. Three minutes left. He removed the torch and scanned the boot lining for tell-tale signs of metal swarf and spotting several pieces he patiently ran the magnetized rear of the drill over the boot pan until the floor was clean of metal fragments. With the boot closed and after a final, careful, look around, the shadowy figure switched off the miniature lamp, replaced all the tools of his murky trade in his pockets, and slipped out through the garage door which he shut firmly and soundlessly behind him.

With the electronic alarm short circuit device back in his pocket and signs of any presence of sticky tape removed from the door frame with impregnated cleaning cloth, the man from C section strolled casually away from the house in Farm Street, towards his rendezvous with the Ford van. He wore the satisfied smile of the professional who knew when a job had been done well, and took personal pride in the fact that he was still thirty or more seconds ahead of the game as he pulled open the van door and nodded to the driver, indicating that all was well. Now they could move off to claim a well deserved breakfast in one of the north circular transport cafes his companion frequented so much.

Back in the house at the end of Waverton Street the KGB man sitting in the darkness of an attic window put down the field glasses, having confirmed the departure of the assassin from the garage of the Farm Street house. He felt tired but relaxed and was pleased with the way the operation had gone so far. He hadn't worked with members of the recently formed C section before, but he was impressed with their technique. He didn't know what had gone on in the garage. They wouldn't tell him. That was their way, total secrecy; total anonymity. His orders were to watch and wait until Herr Smitt left and report all events including the movements of the Special Branch provided protection squad. He waited, chewing absent mindedly on his twentieth mint since starting his shift at three o'clock that morning.

There was new activity at the house which was immediately the focus of his attention; the garage door had opened and a thin, dark haired, rain-coated SIS man was looking around the area in front of the garage entrance. The silver Daimler backed out into the street with a stocky, grey haired individual at the wheel. The KGB man checked his rubber banded digital watch. He made a short note and studied both men through the field glasses.

Paul Lewis backed the official car out onto the short driveway whilst his partner, Roger Simpson, cleared the police no parking signs from in front of number 34 Farm Street, to enable the car to be parked and await the arrival of its passenger, the German banker they had been 'minding' for the past few days. Both men had been with the Special Branch many years and were thorough in their work. Although 'baby-sitting,' as it was called in the trade, was not really their cup of tea, they asked no questions when detailed for the job and simply saw it as all part of a day's work. This didn't mean they were any the less diligent and before moving the car, they checked it completely with electronic 'sniffers' for explosives or hidden gas canisters, or in fact, any sign of tampering. As far as they were concerned, the vehicle was clean. The banker would be down in a minute; just time for the first cigarette of the day. Both men lit up and were puffing away happily, leaning against the car, as the German appeared on the short steps leading down to the pavement from the portalled entrance of the Farm Street house. Lewis and Simpson respectfully stamped out the half consumed cigarettes and instinctively felt for their shoulder holstered Browning M1922 pistols; door to car, car to door; this was the most dangerous time. Simpson glanced up to the window of 34A and two pale looking but alert faces signaled the all clear.

'Good morning, gentlemen,' hailed Heinrich, 'and what a terrible morning it is, at that,' to which both men muttered agreement as Lewis walked round to the driver's door and Simpson opened the rear passenger door for Herr Smitt.

The banker threw his full briefcase ahead of him and climbed in, pulling together his open rain coat.

He settled back in his seat just as the engine was started and felt a sharp prick in the middle of his back. It was the very last thing Herr Smitt would ever feel. He died instantly and as the pathology report would later confirm, from a lethal power injected dose of pure refined nicotine. The KGB man in Waverton Street noted the time of death to the second and put down the field glasses which would not be required any more that day; he wondered how the hell they had done it.

# Chapter Fourteen

*September 26th 1973 – Kirkuk Air Base – Northern Iraq*

It was getting on for eleven o'clock at the Kirkuk airbase as Rasheed al Sheikh strolled over to parking bay six, where the white Falcon jet was being serviced and fuelled up for Mr. Armstrong, special envoy of the AGCC. The area was a hive of activity, with two men working a fuel tanker, three others completing a line service on the engines and a couple more carrying out battery instrument checks. The crew chief was an Iraqi sergeant, who could be seen wandering around the neat little aero plane, making notations on a clipboard full of documents and stopping now and again to have words with the instrument technicians or the electricians, confirming pre-flight states of navigation gear and battery packs.

Rasheed called the chief over and, out of earshot of other members of the line crew, talked animatedly for several minutes before dismissing the sergeant and striding off in the direction of the Air Wing Headquarters. A service ladder was drawn up beneath the port engine nacelle and an engine mechanic was finishing a lube oil refill and grease inspection before closing up the lower inspection cover and preparing to sign off the pink flight form. The sergeant motioned to the mechanic to come down from the ladder and leave what he was doing; his crew chief would finish the engine pre-flight and sign the check list and flight form. The mechanic obediently packed up his red boxed tool kit and marched off in the direction of the nearby maintenance hangar to grab a short break in the crew room. The pump on the tanker whined down to a stop as the re-fuelling element of the pre-flight service was completed and one by one each member of the crew presented pink forms to the chief for signing out, until the service was finished. The fuel tanker, with hoses neatly stowed in the side storage panniers, trundled off in search of other thirsty customers and the last of the ground crew disappeared from sight within the depths of the nearby maintenance hangar. When he was satisfied no-one was paying him any particular attention, the chief pulled an oiled paper package from the knee pocket of his fatigue overalls. It weighed about half a kilo and carried the dimensions of a small box of chocolates. He carefully pulled the wrapping from one end of the package to expose the top of a red switch and a small inset dial marked from one to sixty in even increments. Taking an instrument screwdriver from his top pocket, the sergeant turned the setting on the dial until it lined up on twenty-five. After covering up the tear in the outer wrapping with black plastic electrician's tape, he carefully placed the package inside the inspection hatch in the engine nacelle and pushed it tight against the fuel monitoring valve. This was the coolest part of the engine and relatively vibration free. Satisfied that the package would not move or drop out if the hatch cover was opened again before take-off, he locked the panel back up into position and twisted the six spring loaded fasteners half a turn to complete the operation. Still standing on top of the aluminum steps, he signed off the engine inspection form with a left-handed undecipherable scrawl, checked his overall pockets for all his tools and pens, and then cleared the ladder away to the edge of the parking bay to be picked up later by a tractor tug. The whole process had taken a little more than two minutes and as far as the crew chief knew, everyone in close proximity to the aircraft had been too engaged in their own busy work schedule to notice the placement of the plastic explosive. The fuse to the bomb was a sophisticated incendiary type, triggered by a barometric pressure switch which the chief had set for twenty five thousand feet above sea level and from the information given him by the President's secretary the aircraft would be well out of Kirkuk airspace before the switch activated and the bomb exploded. The sergeant knew what he was doing and also knew he was in no position to question his orders, but as a naturally cautious person he estimated it would be prudent to make his signature unreadable on the flight form and as a double precaution, he would ensure the duty ground crew officer countersigned the pink slip before the aircraft took off. Sergeant Mustaffa did not relish the thought of ending up as a scapegoat for anyone; he did as he was told and if the President's secretary told him to put a bomb on board a plane, he would do it. After all, a word from the secretary was as good as the word of the President himself; nevertheless, Mustaffa concluded that a little arse covering exercise would do no harm. That's what officers were for anyway.

He strolled unhurriedly back to the hangar and sought out the duty officer, to whom he presented the pink slip, which the officer obligingly signed without second thought. The sergeant placed one copy of the flight form in the aircraft service register and the original in the flight pouch that would go with the aircraft. He was quietly relieved, and now went off in search of Rasheed.

The President's secretary was a busy man that morning as he made sure he always was. But today, there was such a lot to do; so many preparations to make, so many meetings to schedule and on this particular day, the welfare and requirements of Mister Armstrong to consider. The Imam wished to see the Englishman before he left, which could be any time now and so he'd better get cracking. He checked his schedule for the tenth time that day and wondered if he had time to go out to his car and phone or use the instrument in the air-wing office. He decided to use the office phone and, although there was no scrambler fitted to this particular unit, he knew the line was clean and he didn't have time for any protracted conversation. He picked up the handset and dialed a number in Qatar. The call was answered immediately and Rasheed told the connected party that all was well and his foreign charge would be leaving Iraq, possibly within the hour. With that small task complete, Rasheed spoke to General Lubikov on the internal communications system to inform the Russian that Armstrong's plane was available and ready for take-off. Next, he sent a car for the Imam and humming happily to himself he departed the office and moved to wait outside for Sulayman's arrival.

The morning meeting had been a long one but both men felt individually assured that it had also been fruitful. On the one hand, the General believed he had told all and said nothing; and on the other, Maxwell was confident he had said all and told nothing. The bishops and pawns were well entrenched in defensive maneuvers on both sides and so far in the game, neither thought they had lost a piece. Max wore a slightly bloated expression from drinking endless cups of coffee, which Lubikov was still manufacturing in one liter jugs at a time; the General looking relaxed and unjaded even though he had been doing most of the morning's talking. They were both left chuckling at the cryptic punch line of an amusing Polish joke the General loved to tell whenever he had the opportunity, when the lofty double doors to the General's office swung open and the Imam Sulayman bin Abdulla entered, closely followed by Rasheed. The two men stood as Sulayman approached, waving a limp hand as he went, indicating they should remain seated. Rasheed popped in front of the President to pull up a chair and get him settled in front of Lubikov's desk.

'Well, gentlemen' said Sulayman, 'you two look as though you're enjoying yourselves. I would have thought you'd have been at one another's throats by now, but here you are laughing and joking like two misbehaving schoolboys.'

The General put on his well trained but nevertheless highly infectious grin again and spoke with quick apology.

'Please excuse us Sulayman, but I was just telling Mr. Armstrong one of my old well used Polish jokes, which I'm afraid would not stand repeating in your presence'. The Imam replied with a mock frown and turned the conversation towards Maxwell.

'I hope then, my friend, you have found everything here you came in search of and that I can rely on your assistance with those bull headed sheikhs down the road. What is even more important to me is your conviction that I am a man of sincerity and not a sick lunatic out to drag the world into the depths of a nuclear holocaust.'

There was a certain amount of humor in his words at which all smiled, except Rasheed, who remained impassive to the sentiment.

'I see things from a much clearer point of view now, sir, but as I said before, I cannot guarantee to generate any favorable reaction to your plans with either the AGCC or, indeed, the leaders of the European community' replied Maxwell.

'I am more than willing to be your messenger and I promise to offer to deliver a fair assessment of your aims and capabilities, if asked, but there it ends. I'll go from here to Kuwait and speak with

Sheikh Hamed, then back to Dubai or Abu Dhabi and if necessary on to Europe, but you must promise me you will make no moves to endanger my talks in what we all appreciate is an already tense situation.' He posed a question to Rasheed.

'Will it be possible to have a short meeting with President al-Bakr …. or Saddam Hussein before I leave?' The President's secretary replied with practiced speed.

'Unfortunately not Mister Armstrong! My President expresses his very best wishes to you but affairs of state keep himself and the vice-President extremely busy' Eyes did not meet and the manicured fingers played even more intently with the ever present prayer beads. He looked uncomfortable, and he was. Maxwell turned his attention back to the Imam without comment.

'I will keep you up to date with what is happening as much as possible, but I have a limited time scale. What can't be achieved during the next week, cannot be achieved at all in my opinion; either the will to compromise is there or not. I must therefore have a commitment from you not to make any declaration before then and to keep a tight rein on your forces in Kuwait.' He looked in the direction of the Russian General.

'The Saudis are already nervous to an unhealthy degree and we don't want the whole thing to blow up in our faces over some unfortunate border incident, do we?'

The General linked his hands together in a compressed, slightly nervous gesture and considered the problem for a few seconds.

'You have my word, Mr. Armstrong,' said Lubikov, 'there will be no embarrassing border incidents; our men are well commanded and very much aware of the consequences of letting any border situation get out of control. General Bishara is in charge of the border forces from Wafra to Umm Qasr. He is a good man and his troops are well disciplined. I feel confident in offering assurances on his behalf.' Sulayman spoke again,

'I am also prepared to give my word that Iraq will not make any move politically until we have heard directly from you and under no circumstances before the end of this month.' He looked toward the President's secretary for confirmation and received a barely perceptible nod of the head.

'I believe Rasheed has provided you with ways to get in touch with any of us at any time of day during the coming week.' He glanced enquiringly to Rasheed who stated that a complete list of contact telephone numbers and radio frequencies had been placed in Mr. Armstrong's flight bag. The Imam continued,

'So now, Maxwell, we leave the problem in your capable hands. May God go with you.'

He stood up awkwardly, brushing off attempts of assistance from Rasheed, grasped Maxwell's hand in a prolonged, heartwarming, handshake and with clouded eyes, moved to leave the room.

'……and don't make it so long next time, my friend.'

The words reverberated back through the closing doorway. Maxwell and Lubikov were alone once again.

'Come, Mr. Armstrong, I will see you to your aero plane.' The two mental adversaries gathered themselves together and negotiated their way through the still busy command building accompanied by much saluting, the odd inquisitive stare, and the two implacably silent Arab guards.

The gleaming white Falcon rested majestically on the parking bay with a ground power unit connected and humming away confidently. Maxwell bade the General farewell and climbed up into the aircraft. He checked his luggage, which was neatly stowed in a floor locker, and his flight bag resting on the right hand co-pilot's seat. A neatly typed flight plan lay on top of the bag which he studied for a few minutes. He would have to taxi north along the perimeter track and line up for take-off on runway one six left, and after take-off, was cleared to fifteen thousand feet as far as Tuz Khurmatu. From there he could climb to twenty eight thousand feet and turn southwest to Al Khalis, down to Basra and then on a final direct track to Kuwait. With engines run up and 'comm.' jacks disconnected, Maxwell received the all clear from the marshaller, released the brakes and persuaded the little jet to move forward under the watchful eyes of alert ground controllers. All other traffic was hastily trying to nudge its way off the perimeter. The clear for take-off signal came immediately over the headphones and the pilot answered back with confirmation of altimeter settings and climb out procedures, finally adding his estimated time of arrival at Basra control. The compass swung onto a heading of one six zero and Maxwell released the brakes, at the same time pushing the twin throttle levers forward.

On reaching fifteen thousand feet, he pulled the power off and trimmed the aero plane before setting the autopilot at the correct cruise level and airspeed. Overhead Tuz he checked with Basra for a route level change according to the flight plan but was told that due to the activities of other maneuvering military traffic in the area, he could only be cleared to twenty thousand feet. He took up his new height and heading to put him on route to Basra and settled down to enjoy the flight.

******

In the control tower at Kirkuk, General Lubikov watched the milky streamlined shape of the executive jet disappear into the distance as he picked up the telephone and called Basra control to inform the duty officer of unscheduled Russian military traffic operating about twenty two thousand feet near the Iranian border at Khanaqin. The officer, who was Polish and an experienced air traffic control technician, gratefully acknowledged the information. The General replaced the receiver with a satisfied expression on his face and, from his vantage point high in the main tower, watched contentedly as Rasheed al

Sheikh strode out to his car and busied himself on his car phone.

'Now let's see you work your way out of that one, you fucked up little fart,' Lubikov murmured quietly to himself. He watched the car as it pulled away in the direction of the outer perimeter road and headed for the main administration building on the far side of the base. The General had work to do, leaving the tower to return to his office and tackle the ever increasing mounds of paper that seemed to pile up on his desk daily. This could turn out to be a better Wednesday than most and for once, General Lubikov looked forward to lunch.

# Chapter Fifteen

*September 26th 1973 – Kuwait – Northern Arabian Gulf*

The unmarked Falcon executive jet landed at Kuwait International Airport two or three minutes behind schedule. Maxwell was met by Hamdan bin Sultan, the Emir's personal assistant. Both men knew one another well and Maxwell was pleased to see that Hamdan hadn't changed a bit over the years. He was an unimpressive character, short and clean shaven with pudgy little hands and a neglected middle age spread, but he had a lively personality and an optimistic viewpoint on life which expressed itself in a more than passing affection for the eye of a pretty girl and the bottom of a Johnny Walker Black Label bottle. They were not easy to come by in Kuwait, but Hamdan made the effort and was rarely disappointed in his ability to pursue and capture both in satisfactory quantities. After noisy greetings and a measured amount of banter accompanied by the odd explanatory wink and nod, the Emir's assistant rapidly led the Englishman through the usually tedious airport formalities and made arrangements for his aircraft to be tended by ground staff and re-fuelled. An official car waited directly outside the airport building and once they were inside, with

Maxwell's light luggage thrown hurriedly in the boot, the car and its VIP passengers took off for Safat and the Kuwait Hilton. The suite reserved for his visitor was extremely spacious and well appointed. Hamdan took great pleasure in showing Maxwell around, pointing out the air conditioning controls, the facilities in both bedrooms and bathrooms, the sunken Jacuzzi and finally the miniature bar kitted out with a more than adequate supply of Teachers and Black Label.

Maxwell 'tut tutted' as Hamdan broke open a bottle of each and poured goodly measures into two glasses chilled with several lumps of spherically shaped ice cubes dispatched from an automatic ice machine. 'Cheers,' and 'Skol,' were dutifully voiced as glasses clinked and both friends settled down to enjoy their illegal drinks in a merry mood. Hamdan opened the conversation.

'Tell me you old son of a gun, how's that absolutely gorgeous little girl you've got tucked away down on the old farm? The last time I saw her was over four years ago in Mombasa; I hope you're looking after her or else I'll be on the first plane out to offer some comforting assistance.' Maxwell grinned sheepishly,

'Helga is fine Hamdan, and being well cared for, so you needn't worry about having to make any unscheduled travel plans in the near future, unless it's to come to a wedding of course. It looks as if I've been caught at last and later in the year we're planning to get married in Kenya. You are definitely invited, as long as you don't bring half the bloody air hostesses in the Middle East with you!'

'Ah!' said the Arab hesitantly, 'that reminds me; I hope you don't mind, but I've arranged a little party up here tonight, just you and me and a few friends'

'Firstly,' replied Maxwell with mock somberness, 'if they're female, you can forget it, and secondly, I may not be here tonight. I hope to be on my way by this evening. You are nevertheless welcome to use the room but don't count on me being here.' His Arab host looked hurt at the rejection, but his eyes twinkled mischievously as he spoke, further.

'There, my friend, we have a small problem. The Emir is unable to see you until tomorrow and much as I've tried, he will not budge. You know what he's like and, although I can only apologize, I'm afraid you must resign yourself to spending the night here with us and sample some real Kuwaiti hospitality'

'You bastard,' Maxwell retorted, 'you set this up on purpose, didn't you? I haven't got twelve hours, or any hours to waste right now. Please see what you can do to get me in front of him today. I need to get all this over with and I'm really short of time.' Hamdan chortled away, slapping his flat palm repeatedly on the bar.

'No, my friend, I'm afraid that this time you are stuck with me as your close companion for the next twenty four hours, like it or not. Come on, don't look so bloody gloomy, let's send down for a good lunch and have a nice long chat.

The waiter served lunch with an exaggerated flourish and left the room. Both hungry souls sat down to eat. In the ensuing General conversation, Maxwell questioned Hamdan about several people he had met in the Gulf during the past few days, picking his brains for more in depth knowledge of characters such as Rasheed al Sheikh, the Iraqi President's secretary, Mohammed bin Abdulla from the Oman and General Andrea Lubikov, top drawer Russian military strategist. Hamdan was as forthcoming as he possibly could be and in most instances, confirmed Maxwell's initial impressions, with both men eventually agreeing that they held a grudging respect for the General and a wary distrust of Mohammed Abdulla. The Englishman decided to tell his host about the worrying incident in Kenya and went into a fair amount of detail concerning the merciless poaching that had taken place there recently. He got to the point where he was describing the strange footprint discovered near the area where an elephant had been brutally slaughtered, and its re-appearance at the bottom of the aero plane steps, before he boarded the Learjet. A sudden change in Hamdan's normally mild expression made him stop short. It was a look of anger and fear. There was a brief but strained silence as he waited for Hamdan to speak.

'I must tell you something Maxwell, but please, please do not repeat this to anybody, not a living soul. If anyone found out who told you this, I'm dead.' He looked nervously at the Englishman begging for a sign of agreement. Maxwell was curious and concerned; he had never known Hamdan to be afraid of anything. He was a boisterous, energetic and good humored man but not without influence or power in his own right and Max couldn't imagine what could be so frightening as to make his friend this serious and uneasy. The promise was made and Hamdan continued.

'I know little about the subject in question, but what I do know is there is some form of secret alliance operating at a very high level within the loose arrangement known as the AGCC and people who cross its members suddenly find life very short indeed. They operate outside of any normal laws and no-one seems to know who they are, but it looks as if you have inadvertently stumbled across the identity of at least one and that is dangerous information.'

Hamdan appeared visibly shaken as he laid down his knife and fork, nudging a half consumed lobster away from him. Maxwell was now fascinated and pushed for Hamdan to continue. All I am able to repeat are rumors generated by uncoordinated bits of information coming from all kinds of sources here in the Gulf and no-one is really sure that half the rumors aren't being created by the alliance itself. We only know its name for certain ….. Unicorn. There have been murders and assassination attempts; three against senior members of cabinets and all kinds of strange goings on since the discussion first started relating to the Co-operation Council. Our security and intelligence services have been trying for some time now to find out about the Unicorn movement, the name of which came to light during the interrogation of certain criminal elements responsible for many sabotage operations in Kuwait during the late sixties and early seventies. We know about as much today as we did then; just the name Unicorn; and that's little enough to go on if one is unable to link the movement with any solid evidence of its membership' Maxwell asked an important question.

'Do you know if western intelligence agencies know about this so called Unicorn movement?'

'Yes, very much so,' replied Hamdan. 'We have requested the help of all major intelligence networks in trying to pin down the origins and aspirations of these bloody animals, but to no avail.'

'Well,' said Max, 'give me a quick rundown on exactly what you do know and try not to leave anything out; you have a fairly clear idea of what I'm about right now and I must have all the facts if I'm to do this present situation any good at all.' Hamdan folded his arms and sat thoughtfully for a few seconds before carrying on.

'I can only tell you this. Firstly, as I've just said, the name Unicorn has been linked with several sabotage and assassination attempts in Kuwait and our first indication of the existence of such an organization came through the interrogation of a sabotage group suspect in 1970. The person concerned was held under the strictest security but was discovered dead in his cell within twenty-four hours of the interrogation report being passed to the cabinet.' He paused, now looking very uneasy.

'He died from a massive dose of cyanide and try as we may we were unable to find out who did it or how he was got at. The Unicorn was not heard of again until early last year and then only loosely linked with preparations for a coup in Qatar. Whether the movement had anything to do with that we shall probably never know, but the coup did take place and Sheikh Khalifa is still very much there.' He leant forward and spoke in a lowered tone.

'Secondly, we have been able to ascertain with a fair amount of certainty, that the hard core leadership of the movement must consist of several well placed people sitting at high levels in Arab politics. Their sources of information are excellent, their communications and access to one another are immediate and their ability to maintain secrecy, incredible. Apart from that, there is absolutely nothing available on file or known further about them except that they possess extreme political ambition and are ruthless in silencing their enemies. We can't pin the Unicorn down to being behind any particular event, murder or act of sabotage, but, because they are *so* indiscernible as a whole and unidentifiable as individuals, they could be behind every piece of nasty work carried out in the Middle East during the past few years.'

Hamdan paused for breath. He was still agitated, and moved constantly in his seat as he spoke further on the subject of the secret society. Here again, reflected Maxwell, his own security services had let him down. He had been badly briefed by SIS, but on further deliberation he supposed he hadn't really been briefed at all. Even Hamdan had admitted that western intelligence knew of the existence of this group called Unicorn, and therefore one would assume the SIS would know about it also; the whole confusing scenario was getting worse, not better.

'Do you think,' asked Maxwell, 'that the mysterious footprint really offers up proof that Mohammed is a member? He's a senior minister in the Gulf Council, for Christ's sake. If he's implicated, even with some sort of fringe element, let alone being a member himself, then the repercussions in political terms are unbelievable; not only here in the Gulf, but all over the world.'

'I have told you my friend, these people are powerful, and no-one knows who they are or how far their influence stretches,' breathed Hamdan. 'The reason they can get things done in such anonymity, is that they are each a force in their own right and anyone carrying out their orders for murder and assassination are unaware that they're perpetuating the existence and executing the wishes, of the Unicorn. This is big, high level stuff Maxwell, and if I were to tell the head of our security forces our suspicions concerning Mohammed, how do l know he is not one of them? I'd probably be dead in an hour and then you would be back to square one. No, no, my friend, please tell me you will keep this information to yourself, do not discuss the subject of the Unicorn with anyone, especially any suspicions about Mohammed. Just stay armed and alert with what you know and maybe we will all remain alive to witness the satisfactory conclusion to whatever it is you're doing.'

Hamdan got up and walked to the bar, poured two long whiskies on the rocks and brought them back to the table. There followed a meditative silence for several minutes as each man took stock: Maxwell, of the fact that he now knew of the existence of something called Unicorn, and Hamdan of the possibility that he now knew the identity of one of its members. They pulled on their drinks until half melted ice cubes rattled around the bottom of empty glasses. Maxwell looked up decidedly.

'Come on old buddy, let's forget all this secret society stuff and have another drink; and if you're really good I might even come to your party tonight.' Hamdan beamed once again, shook off his morbid mood and jumped up to race his friend to the bar. Maxwell laughed out loud. All gone but not forgotten.

\*\*\*\*\*\*

The muted tones of an electronic alarm awoke Maxwell at seven o'clock the following morning. He felt hung over. The party had been as expected; more women than men, more whisky than soda and more cigarette smoke than fresh air. With forced effort, Maxwell dragged himself from his bed, showered, and ordered breakfast. By eight o'clock he was feeling much better. The phone rang. It was Hamdan, letting his visitor know an appointment had been made for him with the Emir at twelve o'clock and a car would be sent to pick him up at eleven forty five. Someone had been up bright and early and completely cleaned the suite, removing all evidence of the previous evening's 'unlawful' activities; empty beer cans, booze bottles and brimming ashtrays. Maxwell called reception for the loan of a portable typewriter and some paper and filled the morning hours making notes on the activities of the past few days. They were sketchy and brief and would be used later simply as reminders, but even then he managed to fill several pages by ten fifteen. At twenty to eleven, reception phoned up to inform him that a car was waiting and inquired if he would be coming down. He replied in the affirmative and was strolling through the marble and coppered interior of the hotel lobby a few minutes later.

The car was a cream Bentley Musulane Turbo, jockeyed by a smart, navy blue uniformed local who settled Maxwell in the rear seat before pulling smoothly away from the hotel entrance and heading west along the corniche in the direction of the ruler's beach palace. It was an awkward sprawling affair of mixed architectural styles, reflecting something of the identity of the man who had built it. A bit of Hollywood, a taste of Malaga and a touch of Versailles; the only redeeming feature being large pleasing areas of landscaped greenery bordering each side of a long drive running up to the main entrance of the palace. Hamdan was there to greet him, dark circles beneath his eyes and a jaded smile upon his face. The two men shook hands as Maxwell left the cool comfort of the Bentley, and Hamdan sheepishly whispered a hoarse welcome.

'From what I remember, it was a good night, my friend. I hope your suite had been cleaned up properly before you woke this morning and that the staff didn't disturb you too much.' Maxwell replied that all was well and thanked him once again for his hospitality. They walked through the main reception area and on into a set of private rooms at the rear of the palace. The splendid rooms looked out onto a magnificent kidney shaped swimming pool, containing an elliptically contoured island in the middle, planted with palm trees and wildly running bougainvillea.

The Emir waited for his visitor beneath a broad, cream and gold umbrella, shading a seating area consisting of several levels of marbled benching strewn with cream, silk cushions. Knowing the Emir as he did, Maxwell thought that there was probably something like it in the back yard of a well known Los Angeles movie star, but nevertheless the setting was superb and instantly relaxing.

The Emir of Kuwait grunted half intelligible words of greeting to his guest in Arabic and returned to a lounging position on one of the cushioned benches. He was a short stocky individual, with bulbous eyes and thin, lank hair which looked as if it regularly received artificial coloring to match a clipped, jet black goatee beard, lending some length to an otherwise rounded, podgy face. Hamdan seated himself near to the Kuwaiti ruler and began chatting away in an attempt to relieve some of the tension in an obviously strained atmosphere. The Emir spoke little during the preliminaries and when he did, had the annoying habit of not looking directly at the person with whom he was having the conversation. He always seemed to be talking to someone or at something in the middle distance. It was a disconcerting trait and did nothing to endear the man, who Generally lacked personality, to the other Gulf leaders and heads of state. At twelve thirty, the Emir suggested that they eat lunch and pressed a button recessed into the side of his seat, summoning an army of waiters and stewards who began serving an Asian meal of substantial proportions. The Emir's languid expression changed perceptibly. Eating was one of his most favorite pastimes and generated his mild claim to fame as something of a gourmet; a reputation, he was happy with and took pains to preserve.

'I hope you enjoy Indian food, Mr. Armstrong,' intoned the Kuwaiti ruler.

'This is Kashmiri Pandit cuisine and a little on the spicy side, but nevertheless quite delicious if proportioned with the correct amounts of rotis and rice.' The meal was as expected, excellent. Over Arabic coffee, Maxwell moved to the point of his visit. The Kuwaiti ruler was obviously disinterested and unable to be forthcoming in depth on any individual subject.

'You must understand, Armstrong,' said Hamed finally, 'that as a member of the AGCC, I have their interests at heart, but I have the interests of my own country to consider also. With a total state population of just over two million people, I am not in a position to take political viewpoints harmful to any indigenous sections of the community. We have witnessed over the past decade many acts of sabotage in Kuwait and even attempts on my own life and this is a sign of restlessness among my people that I am unable to ignore. We are a small nation, surrounded by powerful countries that could have aims and ambitions beyond their own borders if I do not take up a stand with one of them.' He sipped further on his coffee.

'I have chosen to ally myself with the Iraqi President for two reasons. One is, that through the teachings and the continued blessing of the Imam of Awabi, he commands a tremendous, worldwide Islamic following, unchallenged by any other leader of a Moslem country and I hope you will note that even the Iranians are playing a back seat, 'wait and see' role in the situation of which we speak. Secondly, I will receive the benefit of high levels of military support from Iraq without political interference and this will enable me to rid myself of some of the fanatical elements bent on destroying this country and its present leadership. As far as I am concerned, the Council, as it stands now, is effectively a non-starter and in future each will have to look after its own. Between my country and Iraq we possess a potent economic weapon and if we don't exercise the right to use it soon, we will all be the losers as the western industrialist nation's gallop along a path of spiraling inflation and protectionist trading policies. No, your visit here is a waste of time, unless you wish to merely confirm my resolve to go along with Iraq in repatriating our joint investments in Europe and the United States.' The Emir spoke flatly without emotion and in tones bordering on verbal lethargy.

'But I was led to believe, your highness,' insisted Maxwell, 'that you hadn't actually made up your mind to move with Iraq just yet and the subject was still open for discussion.' The Emir offered his guest a stabbing, angry look and then quickly averted his eyes to trace some object of interest above and behind Maxwell's left shoulder.

'Then you are misinformed, my friend' he remarked. 'I am a man of my own will and I can assure you I intend to move in the same direction as President al-Bakr and support him in any request made to western financial institutions to recover that which is rightfully ours. Now, if you will excuse me, I have other business to attend to.'

With this ultimate dismissal, the ruler of Kuwait rose up dramatically from his seat and strode off. Maxwell was left speechless and Hamdan turned to look apologetically in his direction as the Emir finally disappeared inside the palace building.

'Well, what do you make of that?' asked Max despairingly, as he helped himself to another glass of mineral water.

'I'm afraid I don't really know,' replied a baffled Hamdan.

'Someone's got to him since we last spoke and that's for sure. The day before yesterday, he seemed totally uncommitted and I was hoping your meeting with him would slow down the decision making process, but it looks as if it's had the reverse effect. I can't think of anything to say; I am as surprised as you are. Hamdan raised himself resignedly,

'There's not much more we can do here. I suggest we go back to the hotel and unless I can do anything else for you personally, we'd better make arrangements for you to fly back to the UAE today. I don't like the mood he's in and the sooner you're out of here, the better. Maxwell agreed and both men made their way to the front of the palace building and the waiting Bentley.

Back in the hotel, Hamdan mixed himself a drink and offered Max one, which was sensibly refused, due to the fact that he would hopefully be flying later in the day. Hamdan put a call through to the Dubai Ruler's secretary to find out what Maxwell's next move should be. He was put through to the airport and eventually the director of civil aviation, Salem al Thani. Salem confirmed the Sheik's wish that he return to Dubai airport that very evening if his business in Kuwait was concluded and a meeting would be arranged with the ruler on the following morning. He would get flight clearance to leave Kuwait about six o'clock, getting him into Dubai before eight.

Hamdan transported his guest to the airport at just gone five and ushered Maxwell through the building with a flourish of authoritative commands, accompanied by much respectful saluting and offers to bear the burden of the respected visitor's minimum hand luggage by uniformed officers of the airport military guard. Hamdan walked him all the way to the aero plane, where at the bottom of the steps he made his final farewell to the British aviator and moved off into the airport complex, waving cheerily as he went.

Maxwell got down to the task of checking his flight plan and working through checks, whilst the ground crew waited patiently beneath the pointed nose of the executive jet, listening to the pilot's conversation with ground control through external headsets. It was a few minutes before six when Maxwell received permission to start engines, and ten minutes later he was pulling the eager little aircraft through a steep ascending turn, to head east over the Arabian Gulf, searching for his initial climb-out of twenty thousand feet.

# Chapter Sixteen

*September 27th 1973 – Dubai – United Arab Emirates*

An hour previously, the telephone lines had warmed somewhat as Salem al Thani, Head of Civil Aviation in Dubai spoke in rapid dialectic Arabic to Rasheed al Sheikh, the Iraqi President's secretary. Rasheed had explained in detail the reasons why the Falcon had not been allowed to clear to the height described in the original flight plan from Kirkuk to Kuwait. It was not his fault. The bomb had been set to detonate at twenty five thousand feet for a reason. At that height, an explosion would scatter wreckage over a massive area, which would make the piecing together of the cause much more difficult.

Tammam bin Abdulla, brother of the Imam of Awabi, sitting impatiently in Qatar, was not a happy man. In fact, he was after blood, and much of it. Salem would have to guarantee that the European envoy did not reach Dubai. To do that, he had to exercise more than a normal amount of skill in persuading his controllers to re-arrange civil air traffic in the area, accommodating a flight clearance from Bahrain which would enable the Falcon to climb above twenty five thousand feet. There were already questions being asked. All internal non commercial Gulf aviation traffic was normally kept to below flight level two zero south of Bahrain and to maneuver the private jet above that level meant diverting high flying, thirsty, intercontinental jets, which were less fuel efficient at lower altitudes. Questioning communications with airline pilots flying through the area, and even more questioning looks from his controllers, had made Salem extremely nervous. Still the deed had been done; when the Falcon received an instruction from Bahrain flight information region controllers to climb to thirty thousand feet for the south eastern leg down the Gulf to Dubai, success would more or less be guaranteed. The explosion would take place well south of Bahrain, in deep water. Nothing could possibly be recovered from the wreckage for days, and then it would be too late. The Unicorn would have made its move. Rasheed had been left to communicate directly with an enraged Tammam in Qatar; a duty he did not enjoy. The exiled brother of the exiled Imam had screamed down the phone at him like a lunatic, threatening all kinds of very unpleasant personal consequences if his ineptitude resulted in Armstrong reaching Dubai in one piece. It was a black day for Salem and would get blacker during the next few hours if his maneuvering and planning failed to show the required result.

\*\*\*\*\*\*

Climbing through eighteen thousand feet, Maxwell hit a problem. He was losing revolutions on the port engine and the aero plane was beginning to yaw erratically. He leveled the aircraft out and monitored fuel pressure on the port engine which was fluctuating wildly. He switched tanks but it made no difference. He made the final, crucial decision and cutting the fuel supply to the weak engine he went through an emergency shutdown procedure and radioed Bahrain to inform them of his situation. Although the loss of one engine over water was a delicate matter, it was not over serious and the Falcon would fly happily on one engine for the remaining fifty minutes or so of his flight time, but there was no way he could climb on the single engine to his cleared altitude of thirty thousand feet. Bahrain controllers acknowledged his condition and calmly asked if he needed immediate assistance or would like arrangements to be made to divert to another airfield. Maxwell quickly considered the problem. The starboard engine seemed to be running smoothly and was developing more than sufficient power to see him through to Dubai. He also had nearly full tanks, so, with grateful thanks for all their concern, he informed Bahrain he would carry on if he could be cleared to maintain his present flight level. Permission was granted and Dubai was instructed by radio to prepare for an emergency landing.

******

Salem al Thani was irritably pacing the floor of the control tower when the message came through from Bahrain. He went perceptibly white as blood drained from his cheeks and his heart began to race. Not only did the Englishman seem to have a charmed life, he also seemed to be a bloody good pilot as well. Anyone else in his present situation would have diverted to Bahrain, but no, not this lucky son-of-a-bitch; he was coming straight in with over half a kilo of plastique, high energy explosive stuck to his tail, oblivious of the fact that one slight mistake in attempting to land his aircraft on one engine, in a higher than average cross wind, could blow the whole place to shit. He spoke hurriedly to the chief controller, sweat breaking out on his forehead and twitching hands crossed behind his back in an attempt to conceal the level of his anxiety.

'Bring him in on runway one two; let's keep him as far away from the main terminal buildings as possible until we know he's down safely.'

The controller acknowledged the Director of Dubai Civil Aviation's instruction and a few seconds later confirmed the Falcon's clearance to begin finals. Both men watched as fire tenders and emergency support vehicles snaked their way across the airfield, yellow strobe lights flashing and sirens wailing, advertising the urgency of their task. Maxwell placed the compact jet on the runway without incident, to his relief and those around him watching agitatedly from beneath aluminum crash hats and cotton anti flash masks. Five tenders followed the wounded aircraft down the runway until it came to a gentle halt. The fire chief rushed out from his command vehicle and plugged in a combination headset to the ground communications jack, enabling him to talk directly to the pilot. After confirming everything on board was OK, he waved the emergency tenders away and gave Maxwell permission to taxi off the runway and over to a parking bay in front of the arrivals terminal. It was a fairly minor emergency but one which had held the interest and attention of passengers and staff alike for brief minutes. It was also a busy time of day for Dubai with three wide-bodied jets on the parking apron and several smaller, short haul aircraft, waiting to swallow up passengers outside the departure building and transport them to over forty destinations in the Gulf and neighboring countries. Maxwell edged the Falcon up to bay twelve on instructions from the marshal and, when satisfied he was lined up correctly, shut down the single operative engine and pulled all the electrical contact breakers to immobilize the aero plane completely. It took about three more minutes to complete all the flight paper work and a ground crew chief waited at the bottom of the steps for instructions concerning the engine problem. Maxwell told him about the fluctuating fuel pressure and loss of power on the port engine. The chief summoned one of his engineers, who began to search for a set of ladders which would enable him to pull the bottom engine cowling off and check a possible malfunctioning fuel monitoring valve; a complex little piece of machinery but normally very reliable.

Maxwell pulled all his belongings together and, with a last quick look around the Falcon, descended the air-stairs and began to walk in the direction of the arrivals terminal. Two of the three wide-bodied jets on the ground were beginning to disgorge travel stained passengers. The Air France Boeing 747, it's huge wing mounted fan engines still revolving lazily, was surrounded by ground staff and great low ground clearance, air conditioned, passenger buses, as the aircrew worked desperately to usher ever chattering customers down the gangways and away to the terminal building, so that as many dollars as possible could be spent within the superb airport duty free shopping facilities.

A team of frustrated stewardesses were suffering from an age old problem as they toured the departure terminal, attempting to herd their imbibed charges through to the departure gate and thereby top up the human cargo being loaded onto the waiting British Caledonian Tri-Star. The aircraft was already five minutes late off the ramp and ground staff were busy attempting to disconnect an armored, flexible hose from an underground re-fuelling line with the minimum of spillage. That particular connection to the fuel line had always been troublesome and leaked almost permanently. The airline's ground engineering officer made a note to report the problem, yet again, before there was some sort of major accident.

Several bays away from the Tri-Star, a shirt-sleeved mechanic pulled the last two fasteners on the Falcon's engine cover. He looked frustrated as he shouted for some assistance to lift off the aluminum panel and expose the underside of the port turbine. The mechanic would then be able to check the fuel delivery system and the monitoring valve. By this time Maxwell had reached the terminal building and was being directed to the VIP reception area, where the Director of Civil Aviation was waiting to receive him.

He walked up to the smoked glass doors and pushed one open. Standing right in the doorway was Salem al Thani; he looked strange, lacking color and composure. Maxwell paused, the door still open.

Down on the parking apron, two mechanics now struggled with the engine cowling; it was caught up somewhere and both men were gently trying to pry it loose. One of the laboring, perspiring figures working on the jet lost his grip on the polished surface of the alloy cowling; the weight and awkward angle of purchase were too much for one man to hold on his own.

The cowling slipped.

Then it happened.

The first explosion killed the two mechanics instantly and took the tail completely off the Falcon, spreading it in millions of searing red hot pieces of shrapnel, cutting through the air with a velocity greater than the speed of sound. Maxwell felt the shock of the initial detonation and hit the floor seconds before a confused Salem, the plate glass door beginning to close automatically behind him as the second eruption flung the remains of the Falcon executive jet into a thousand fragments, travelling in a wide, rising arc through the still evening air, straight at the arrivals terminal. The doors, half closed behind Maxwell, were ripped from their hinges and whilst still airborne, shattered into a myriad of toughened glass shards cutting through the VIP lounge and carving down anyone and anything in their path. The horror continued. With the second more violent explosion, a partly melted piece of turbine blade had been thrown with lightning force beneath the B-Cal jetliner and imbedded itself in the outer covering of the armored re-fuelling hose. In microseconds it had burned through the rubber lining and made contact with pressurized aviation fuel, trapped within the hose. The initial realization of what was happening had taken time to sink home and a passenger bus still moved on the apron with the last of the duty free shoppers, semi-inebriated ships' engineers and able bodied seamen.

The fuelling hose ripped apart in a bout of dazzling orange and blue flame, spreading sheets of burning aviation spirit over an area of half a square mile; the ground valve, attached to the subterranean pipeline shattered in an instant and the two foot thick concrete and tarmac hard standing, ripped up, with a deafening crack, flinging huge chunks of condensed aggregate and steel reinforcing bar high into the air. A blazing fire immediately filled the exposed trench, engulfing the passenger bus which carried relentlessly on, plowing through the inferno, until it crashed, at a drunken angle, into the starboard undercarriage of the 747. Maxwell struggled to bury himself deep within the carpeted floor of the VIP lounge as explosion after explosion shattered the air, followed by waves of breath-taking heat, ripping his shirt from his back and dragging the last remnants of life-giving air from over compressed lungs. A full five minutes went by before the sounds of the last detonation gave way to a roaring cadence of hundred foot high fire columns, fighting for every available ounce of oxygen on which to feed, pushing volumes of acrid black smoke into a spiraling murky cloud nearly a mile above the airport.

Then the screaming started; a sickening, pungent smell of burning flesh filled the lounge as Maxwell retched and retched until he thought he would choke to death on his own stomach fluid. He rolled over, out of his own pool of vomit, and attempted to stand. It was impossible. His back was lacerated by flying glass and his legs, torn clean of all protective clothing, were swollen in large patches of blistered skin that looked as if they were verging on third degree burns. He managed to sit up, trying hard to gather his senses before making the severe effort to absorb the mind numbing scene of carnage all around him. He was the only one left alive in the lounge; with shredded and confused emotions, he screamed out loud in part pain and part anger; a prolonged high pitch scream which made his whole body shudder in near convulsion. Sounds of sirens echoed in the distance. The effort of sitting up was too much; he dropped back to the floor, unconscious.

# Chapter Seventeen

*September 28th 1973 – Dubai – United Arab Emirates*

When Maxwell awoke, he had difficulty in seeing properly and shadows swam dreamily in front of his eyes, merging pale colors with indistinct shapes attached to murmuring voices, seeming far, far away. He worked to raise himself from the crisp white bed linen, his senses recovering gradually as he realized he was in a hospital bed, propped on his side and supported with a bank of bloodstained pillows. By keeping his arm outstretched, he managed to swing his legs over one side of the bed; his vision clearing to such an extent, that he was able to take in with reasonable clarity the scene around him. Someone in a white coat moved swiftly in his direction and grabbed his shoulder, preventing him from slumping forward onto the floor.

'Come, Mr. Armstrong,' a voice from somewhere within the white coat said. 'You've been very lucky, but no sitting up just yet.'

The voice was female and spoke with a Scottish accent. He stared up into a round, bespectacled face as the voice continued.

'I'm Doctor Browne and at the moment I'm very busy; please lie quietly there for a while and I'll send someone over to talk to you in a few minutes.'

Doctor Browne gently pushed her patient back onto the bed and rearranged the pillows to keep his body wedged on its side. Maxwell's memory was recovering from the initially scattered, flashing visions of blood, flying glass and billowing smoke as he lay uncomfortably on his side, the smell of burning flesh still clinging to singed hair and cracked and bleeding lips. He was surprised to feel little sensation of pain. His legs ached and his back stung where it touched the pillows but, apart from that, he felt in amazingly good shape. A new face came into view. The visitor pulled up a chair near the head of the bed-space and Maxwell recognized the man immediately as Tom Hardmain, financial advisor to the ruler of Dubai. The welcome Englishman spoke concernedly.

'Well, old son, you've had a very, and I mean *very*, lucky escape. I'm afraid others have not got off so lightly and every hospital in the state is full to overflowing.'

'What's the score, so far, Tom'?' asked a still shocked Maxwell.

'Well, at first count we have a hundred and twenty dead, over three hundred severely injured and another two hundred or so with relatively minor injuries of your category. The airport is an absolute mess and we have several hundred men still there fighting fires. The final toll will not be known for days, until we have the ability to search through the mounds of wreckage inside and outside the terminal buildings. It's a disaster of gigantic proportions and we're still piecing the facts together. The only reason you're still alive, is you were lying so close to the lounge door that when it shattered, nearly all the debris went over your head. Everyone else in the room is dead, I'm afraid, including Salem Al Thani, the director of civil aviation, and some of his senior staff who were there to meet you. The whole bloody thing is absolutely unbelievable and at the moment, we're all living in a state of semi shock.'

Maxwell asked Tom to help him up. He held him until he was steady. His voice was still croaky and throat sore from smoke ingestion, but with a level of determined concentration, he was managing to communicate.

'Tell me,' said Max. 'What the hell happened out there; it was sheer fucking carnage; explosion after bloody explosion. I thought it would never stop. I've honestly not witnessed anything like it in my life.'

The face of the sixty three year old man with a reputation of being a financial wizard, took on a pained and grim expression.

'I'm afraid to have to tell you that all initial information leads us to understand there was a bomb planted on board your aero plane. It must have been in the port engine cowling and when the mechanics removed covers to inspect the fuel feed lines, they somehow set the bloody thing off. We're 'fulltime' searching the particular area around bay twelve right now to see if we can come up with something and we might know more tomorrow morning.'

'What time is it, now?' Maxwell asked again.

'It's just gone ten fifteen in the evening. You'll have to stay here for the night but probably by lunchtime on Sunday they'll let you leave and then we would very much appreciate your help in the investigation. I know it's a bit of a bugger to talk about things like this, right now, but we have an American federal aviation investigation team arriving tomorrow afternoon and it's essential that we are able to present as many of the facts as possible.'

Maxwell felt suddenly tired and was manifestly suffering from some of the after effects of pain killing drugs but he wanted to get out of the hospital right now and he told Tom that. However, there was no way he would be allowed to leave until the doctors were happy with his mental and physical condition, the white coated Scots lady informed him by way of admonishment. Then, upon his insistence, Doctor Browne gave her patient a brief rundown on the state of his injuries.

The burns on his legs and lacerations on his back were fairly minor. The back wounds had been cleaned of all glass fragments and one or two had required a few stitches. As long as he was able to keep everything clean, he should be all right, with very little scarring to show for it afterwards. Tom smiled down at him.

'Now be a good boy and follow doctor's orders. I'll come and pick you up on Sunday morning....settle you in one of the ruler's guest houses for a few days and get you kitted out with some fresh clothes. The gear you arrived with is something of a mess but I've sorted out your personal bits and pieces and I think you know by now, we have your shoe size and inside leg measurements fairly well taped?'

Tom grinned reassuringly, extracting a half smile from Maxwell's previously somber face and then with a shake of the hand, picked his way with difficulty down the congested ward to attend to other equally important business.

\*\*\*\*\*\*

The scene inside the private office of Tammam bin Abdulla resembled a football pitch after the playing of a well fought derby game. The floor was littered with various bits of half torn paper; side tables were turned over, drapes ripped and the Longines crystal table clock lay shattered in a myriad of pieces up against the wall behind his desk. The exiled Omani paced the room, kicking a turned over table here and heeling scattered sheets of handmade velum into the carpet there. He had lost his delicately controlled temper completely upon hearing of the arrival of Maxwell Armstrong in Dubai and was even more distressed to find the Englishman was still alive and relatively well after surviving the indescribable events at Dubai Airport. There was no doubt now that whatever material evidence existed proving the planting of a bomb on board the Falcon, it would all shortly be in the hands of a professional investigating team from the United States. He had to be sure now, that any such evidence pointed decidedly away from the possible exposure of Unicorn and was waiting for Rasheed al Sheikh to phone him back from Iraq. He definitely did not trust that slimy Russian toad Lubikov; in fact, he really didn't trust anyone with a name ending in 'ov', but this one was trickier than any he had come across and Tammam sensed that somewhere along the line, the General had played more than a passing role in conjuring up the recipe of ingredients that had conspired to produce his present misfortune. By now, the interfering Englishman's body should have been spread halfway across the banks of the River Euphrates or swallowed up permanently in the depths of the Arabian Gulf, not lying back in some damnable hospitable bed, receiving some of the best medical treatment the Middle East had to offer.

Every bloody thing was going wrong. He was surrounded by incompetent idiots and if he didn't regard the services of Rasheed as essential to the satisfactory conclusion of his immediate plans then he would have been a dead man by now. Somewhere could be heard the shrill sound of a distantly ringing telephone. Tammam launched himself in the direction of his desk, kicking over a waste paper basket as he went. The telephone was resting upside down on the floor; he picked up the whole unit and slammed it on the desk top. He grabbed the receiver and acknowledged the call by shouting down it. The caller was not Rasheed from Iraq but Mohammed, calling on his way back to Muscat from Dubai. Tammam vented his not insignificant wrath verbally for several seconds, before asking what the hell Mohammed was doing by leaving Dubai. Someone had to take care of Armstrong. Salem was dead and so he was now relying on Mohammed to be his eyes and ears in the Emirates. It took more than a few minutes for Mohammed to calm down in response to Tammam's opening invective and begin to reveal his thinking on the problem. The conversation continued for nearly twenty minutes, until finally Tammam said,

'Do you really think this will work, Mohammed?, frustration and anger still heavily present in his voice.

'I assure you, my dear brother, this is the only way to get the required result. It's no use me staying in Dubai; they've got him bolted up like a trapped rat, with guards around the clock at the hospital, and we don't have the right kind of influence there since we lost Salem. Mounting a successful operation in Dubai is a tough nut to crack. I'm better off going back to the Oman where I can guarantee getting things properly organized. I can put together this venture within twenty four hours, if I can contact and assemble the right people by tomorrow morning. If we can't kill the cat, at least let's take his cream away and make him come looking for it. There is still time; only a few days I admit, but still enough to force Armstrong into our way of thinking. Before the coming week is over, he'll loathe the very sound of the initials SIS and that factor alone will tip him over the brink. He'll bend with us, his true and proven friends, and within hours I guarantee he will be simply begging your brother, the Imam and the Iraqi President to press the damned button. Then we can stop all this undercover crap and get into action. Just leave it all to me and when I have some news I'll contact you again.'

Mohammed ended the conversation abruptly and Tammam stood still and silent for a few moments before replacing the handset. Mohammed's plan was risky but admittedly well conceived. The only problem that loomed immediately to mind was the necessary involvement of other countries, countries outside the normal influential sphere of Unicorn members.

'But still,' pondered the leader of the Unicorn, 'I suppose what Mohammed says is true; you can buy anything and anyone with enough money. Every government and every individual has a price, be it for high profile assistance or complete diplomatic silence.

'Yes,' he pondered, 'given a bit of luck and careful timing, the plan could work!'

The telephone rang again. This time it *was* Rasheed, calling from Iraq. Tammam was somewhat calmer now as he listened to the distant, shaky voice, describing the lengths he had been to in order to confirm the structure of the explosive device placed aboard the Falcon. The plastique was definitely the same type used by the British Special Air Services Regiment and had been acquired from a certain armory in the Duke of York's Barracks, London, only two weeks previously. The fuse and timer had been confirmed as manufactured by Nico Pyrotechnick of West

Germany and were of a new type being tested by the British Ministry of Defense research establishment at Boscombe Down. Finally, Rasheed informed Tammam that the barometric switch was of a type well used by the British Meteorological Office in automatic weather information transmitters. The whole device could be proven to be *British* to the core. The Russians had done a good job. There was no need for concern. Tammam rang off without comment, sat himself at his desk, and began pushing himself backward and forward in his chair as he had done hundreds of times before during the passage of that long, exhausting day.

# Chapter Eighteen

*September 30th 1973 – Dubai – United Arab Emirates*

By noon on Sunday, Maxwell had been discharged from the hospital by a reluctant Doctor Browne and was settling into one of the Dubai Ruler's vast guest houses on Dubai's Jumeirah beach. Indian servants rushed around and fussed over him, whilst Thomas Hardmain, in a sanguine mood, showed him the qualities and extent of his temporary home. The extensive patio gave view to a deserted, golden beach, lapped by warm, azure Gulf waters and as he stood, contemplating moodily for a few moments, drinking in the crisp sea air, Maxwell found it hard to believe he had been embroiled in so much death and suffering, less than forty eight hours previously. Tom was talking on the telephone in Arabic, a language he had mastered with ease during his thirty odd years spent in Middle East. The man was regarded as a highly intelligent and skilled financial manipulator, who commanded considerable respect from within the Dubai royal family. The tremendous growth and prosperity generated during these halcyon days had been overseen and directed by this singularly pleasant and amiable character and Dubai had shown its thanks by giving Tom a permanent home in the Emirate; a fact Her Britannic Majesty's Government had chosen to ignore completely. With knighthoods and distinguished orders being handed out left, right and centre over the years to pop singers and captains of industry, a man who had given most of his life to maintaining good relations with the most entrepreneurial and wealthy Emirate in Arabia, to the particular benefit of British industry, had been forgotten. Tom put down the phone and walked briskly out on to the patio to join Maxwell, pausing on the way to inspect the barbeque pit being laid with fresh coals by a dutiful Indian house cook. Tom walked up to Max, rubbing his hands together as an indication of his satisfaction with the way preparations were going for lunch.

'Sheikh Khalifa will be with us in an hour and I thought it would be a good idea to have a barbeque out here, especially as the weather is so nice.' Maxwell agreed. Although his legs still ached and he would have to wear shorts for a day or two, he felt well rested and little the worse for wear, considering the frightening ordeal of the previous evening. One of the stewards approached, dressed in a well tailored pale blue uniform and requested orders for lunchtime drinks. No matter how fundamentalist the peninsula had become during the past few years, Dubai was still a place where one could drink alcohol in public without greatly offending the local constabulary and this had been of great benefit to the town itself, as more and more foreigners chose to make Dubai their base for doing business rather than less socially agreeable Gulf countries.

Maxwell broke away from secondary thought and ordered a beer, joining Tom with his gin and tonic. The two old friends settled down on cane patio chairs to enjoy their drink and have a quiet chat whilst waiting for the ruler. Tom gave out more news concerning the airport disaster and the sabotage of the Falcon. The whole area of the initial explosion had been scoured for evidence to support the bomb theory and certain items had been found, indicating the presence of an explosive device of some sort in either the tail section or engines of the Falcon. Professional American investigators would be arriving shortly and it was hoped that from the sifted wreckage recovered so far, the team of experts would be able to draw some sensible conclusions before tomorrow morning. A steward arrived with fresh drinks and announced the arrival of Sheikh Khalifa, the Dubai Ruler, who strolled out on to the tiled patio seconds after the steward disappeared. He was accompanied by a dark faced, unsmiling guard who quickly checked the area and then loped off to join a string of similarly employed local military patrolling the perimeter of the walled guest house development.

Security throughout Jumeirah was high that day, with the town beach palace and its adjacent guest houses completely sealed off from normal traffic. The ruler of Dubai would be taking no chances after what had happened the airport and he was confident that his British SAS trained palace guard would not allow the repetition of a similar attempt on the life of his guest. The Ruler looked fatigued but fit, and had enjoyed barely any sleep during the past twenty four hours. He greeted Maxwell and enquired concernedly after his health, adding his personal apologies for the horrific ordeal he had endured on his arrival and vowed that nothing like it would be allowed to happen again. Maxwell thanked the ruler for his concern and offered counter apologies for being the carrier of such misfortune to his beloved country. Cook hovered in the background, waiting for a sign from Khalifa enabling lunch to be served. With the usual wave of a hand, the presentation began. The lunch occupied a leisurely hour and it was past two thirty by the time the last plate was cleared and house staff retreated into the confines of the beach villa. Khalifa extracted his pipe from a pocket in his white cotton 'dish dash' and puffed away contentedly, waiting for someone to reopen the conversation. Maxwell sipped his third beer and began.

'Well, sir, I have much to tell you relating to my talks with the Imam Sulayman bin Abdulla. I have also had the opportunity to meet with a certain General Lubikov at some length and carried on a less productive and much shorter discussion with Sheikh Hamed in Kuwait.'

The Englishman paused, putting his recollections together in some sort of chronological order. Unfortunately his notes made in Kuwait, had been mostly destroyed in the airport incident, along with the rest of his baggage and therefore it was important that events, as they happened, were correctly related with regard to time and background, if the conclusions he would draw were to be understood without long and involved explanation.

Firstly, he explained his surprise at being given free run of the facilities at Kirkuk and the eagerness with which Rasheed al Sheikh had shown him the quantity and quality of military hardware being distributed from the base. Then he moved on to his meeting with the Imam and his impressions concerning the religious leader's health, finishing the first part of his summary with details of his morning spent with Lubikov. Neither of the two men in the private audience seemed over interested in the military aspect of his revelations; on the contrary, Khalifa questioned Maxwell closely regarding the Imam's health and Tom was more concerned with understanding Sulayman's viewpoint relating to the economic aspects of such an unbelievable plan. With the main questions answered, Maxwell moved on to his talks in Kuwait, purposely omitting any reference to his discoveries relating to the existence of a secret society called Unicorn. The General consensus was that the Kuwaiti Emir was a man running scared and for him to have jumped off the fence so quickly meant something had happened very recently to tip the scales.

All pondered on what that could be, but no mention was made of anything called Unicorn and Maxwell supposed his two listeners knew nothing of its existence or were camouflaging the extent of their knowledge extremely well. The ruler and his financial advisor discussed at length their country's preparedness and ability to handle the short term repercussions involved in coping with a nearly bankrupt Europe and the ability of the AGCC to go it alone, thereby isolating Iraq within the confines of its hair-brained scheme. Whichever angle the problem was viewed from, Kuwait and Iraq together would be a powerful combination economically and could well hold the western world to ransom the way things stood right now. The overall conception was admittedly nigh on brilliant and timing impeccable if the plan could be enacted before the end of the month. The time of year brought the beginning of a quarter of some of the highest oil consumption in the west and lowest reserve levels. By the time bankers, stockbrokers and oil traders got their acts together, got the money machinery going again and running in top gear, it could take days and by then it would all be too late. They would have to open a new month with new oil contracts, highly devalued currencies and inflated gold prices, waking up to the possibility of only being able to deal with one governmental agent for more than sixty per cent of the world's oil supplies. Knowing the Americans and having viewed the evolution of their vehemently protectionist policies over the years, all three regrettably agreed with Lubikov's view that America would do nothing at the end of the day and in reality, whatever action they were unable or unprepared to take militarily on the first day of any invasive action, would not take place at all. They could possibly force through a few useless United Nations motions of censure to keep the newspapers happy for a while, but, in essence, if the Yanks were unable to support Europe in a military action, then the Russians would have their own way in the Middle East and Western Europe as well.

Three glum faced figures sat on the patio, chilling to the early evening sea breeze as each mentally searched for a new angle on the subject, or for a sensible loophole in the Iraqi plan to shatter the world's monetary system and recreate trade by barter; a system where he who has, gets all, and he who has not, gets nothing. Finally Sheikh Khalifa spoke.

'Well, my friend, I cannot thank you enough for your help and efforts on our behalf. At least, now we know the truth of the matter and it is left with us to make our decision. I must obviously consult with Sheikh Saif in Abu Dhabi and should set off immediately; please don't leave Dubai until I get back and have had a chance to talk with you further. You are still the only person with direct access to the Imam and we could possibly need your services further tomorrow'.

The ruler got up, said his farewells and left the guest house to make the two hour road journey to Abu Dhabi. Tom and Maxwell retreated from the cool northern wind and went back into the spacious lounge area to order another drink and talk further.

The two men spent the next couple of hours discussing in more detail what would happen to the Gulf states in General, and the UAE in particular, if the Kuwaitis and Iraqis went ahead with their proposed demand for repatriation of overseas financial investments and resources. The mystery card-player would undoubtedly be Iran and its leader the Shah, estimated Tom. It was admitted that although he had not actively encouraged support for the following of the President of Iraq and the Imam on their visionary trail, he had not spoken out against it either. Maybe the Shah felt he had nothing to lose and everything to gain by keeping quiet and waiting to see how events materialized when the Iraqi declaration was made. They had substantial investments in the west, but a strong industrial base of their own which was being expanded at some pace using their own petro dollars and more importantly, had locked in customers for oil exports in the Far East, such as Japan and Korea. If an attempt at holding the west to economic ransom failed, they could quite comfortably turn round and say, 'I told you so;' revitalizing their diplomatic and trading links with the United States through Japan. If the Iraqi gamble came off, then Iran could sit back quietly and reap the accrued benefits in declaring support for a greater Islamic brotherhood. When Maxwell had discussed Iran's possible role with the Imam, he appeared supremely confident in his ability to count on support from the Shah. Tom confirmed the Dubai ruler's view that Iran was the dark horse in the race, but then, with them or without them, the Iraqi President's plan was more than workable. What everyone needed to avoid was the necessity to revert to force of arms in this particularly tricky situation; as inevitably, such action in the Gulf would escalate very quickly into World War Three and the Gulf States would be right in the middle of it. Without war, Tom could see the UAE, and Dubai in particular, not only surviving but prospering in the short term, although it would mean an end to the present system of government all along the western Gulf coast, terminating in all the present rulers paying homage to perhaps one political head of state, backed by a massive military machine. It seemed to be a catch twenty two situation, with the Russians having basically nothing to lose by putting their full weight behind Iraq, and the Americans nothing to gain, in the long term, by putting any weight at all behind a militarily weak and squabbling European community.

This, unfortunately then, was the net gain of centuries of economic rape of third world countries by the old colonial powers such as Great Britain, France, Spain, the Portuguese, Holland and Italy. Tom finally summed up the prevailing attitude.

'The natives are restless, my old friend, and now they have the wherewithal and the muscle to fight back. Hundreds of years of having Christianity shoved down their throats by slave trading missionaries and avaricious industrialists is remembered, and remembered as if it happened yesterday. It was the British who gave the Jews Jerusalem and the Russian Orthodox Church who desecrated mosques in Georgia: the Dutch and the Germans who trod carelessly on the Koran in East

Africa and the Spanish and Portuguese who forcefully tried to create a Jesuit Society in the Far East. No old son, I'm afraid we all now have a problem and the best and sincerest negotiating in the world will fail to diminish the enormity of it. Even if we manage to prevent the enactment of the Imam's present little bombshell, we are only putting off the day when something else will happen; twice as big and twice as difficult to deal with.'

Both men sat in silent contemplation for a few minutes. Tom looked at his watch; he was getting ready to leave.

'One last question before you go' Maxwell asked. 'Do you think I should go to Europe, if requested? Sulayman wants me to, and I promised to give the subject serious consideration.' Tom paused before answering.

'If you want my advice, old chap, I would get yourself on the first plane out of here, put everything you've got into gold and lock yourself away on Weismuller's farm in Kenya. You'll have a beautiful, loving wife, a nice home and loyal staff who will work their butts off for you. You'll be able to eat well and live to a better standard than any of those supercilious buggers in the UK whilst all this lot comes to a head and has time to settle down. This won't be the end of the world, and you could sit there and breed kids, knowing that when they grow up, at least they'll be living in a society much better off for having cleaned out all the festering cupboard bound skeletons and cobwebs.'

'What will you do, Tom?' Maxwell asked wonderingly.

'I, my friend, shall sit back in sunny Dubai and try to enjoy my thirteenth year here hoping upon hope that I'm able to see another one; that's what I will do, and if it does all finally come to out and out war, then I will make efforts to ensure my children and grandchildren end up on the winning side; whichever that may be.'

Tom finished his final gin and tonic in one swallow.

'And now Maxwell, my dear friend, I will leave and see you again tomorrow morning, when hopefully the ruler will have some news for us.'

With that, and a final word of goodbye, the old man left the guest house and drove off into the night, leaving Maxwell standing on the entrance steps, consumed in quiet meditation as he watched the tail lights of the silver Mercedes disappear from sight at the end of the darkened driveway.

Next morning, he woke early and had breakfast put away by seven fifteen. The wind had dropped and the sea was laid a flat, glasslike calm; an iridescent orange sun hanging low on the eastern horizon, and Maxwell decided this was the time for a long and leisurely swim.

He swam a round circuit of about three miles and felt much better for it. His legs had stopped aching and the muscles in his back had loosened up considerably. He walked cautiously up the beach, making sure the minimum amount of sand was thrown up on to his scarred and bruised legs and then jogged around the patio area for a few minutes to generate a bit of internal heat. After a long shower and careful drying of his body, he inspected the patches on his calves and thighs, deciding to give a pair of slacks a try. He hated wearing shorts at the best of times and the sooner he could get back into trousers, the better. A steward entered the first floor bedroom and gave the news that Mr. Hardmain was waiting downstairs.

Maxwell finished dressing, by carefully covering his torso with a pastel yellow, short sleeved shirt and slipped on a pair of tan leather shoes. Tom spoke up, hoping he'd had a good night's sleep and was fit and ready for action; whatever action that might be! Maxwell ordered some coffee and the two men ran over his itinerary for the day as it had been organized so far. At eight thirty, a meeting with Sheikh Khalifa in the creek-side Majalis; at eleven thirty a meeting with the American investigation team and one thirty, lunch at the Dubai golf course, with time to knock a ball about if he felt like it. Any time after six, a plane would be available to take him anywhere he wanted. The British Consul would like to see him, if he could spare a few minutes, an offer which Maxwell politely declined, and the vice President of Atlantic Richfield Company would be happy to join him for lunch, if he would so desire. Maxwell nodded at that one. It had been a long time since he had seen his old friend Alan Woodly, the only European to make it to the top in the massive American oil exploration and development company; a great character and a good friend, who had helped and advised him in all kinds of tricky situations over the years.

'Right then,' said Maxwell brightly, 'let's be on our way and see what this new day brings.'

A cavalcade of motor vehicles left the guest house complex at eight twenty, consisting of the car Maxwell and Tom were travelling in, two police cars front and rear and the whole convoy flanked by police outriders, complete with sirens blaring and blue lights flashing. At eight thirty, exactly, Maxwell was again sitting with the ruler, but this time in the Majalis building overlooking Dubai creek, a narrow inlet of water dividing the town into its two distinct parts; Deira side and Bur Dubai. Through the Majalis windows, tiny overloaded abraa taxi boats could be seen plying back and forth across the murky water; a still popular form of transport despite the availability to most traffic of one tunnel and three bridges across the creek. Large bulbous Arabic dhows were loading and offloading a miscellany of cargoes on the Deira quayside and freshly painted oilfield workboats picked their way ponderously through dense marine traffic, as they headed towards the creek loading points of Oilfields Supply Centre and Dubai Petroleum Company.

It was altogether a colorful and busy scene and an attraction to tourists and residents alike. This was where it had all started; with the widening and dredging of the creek some years ago by a far sighted and highly commercial ruling family. Dubai had leapt into the oil business and trebled its trading and commercial capability in two short years. The jewel of the Gulf, they had called it and they were right; the scene that Maxwell was presently witnessing proved it. Khalifa was busy signing sheaves of paper, and talking to some of his top aides, as the first round of over sweetened Arabic tea arrived. Maxwell and Tom sipped away unobtrusively as the ruler put down his papers and waved a hand in a short sharp dismissing motion, thereby clearing the room in seconds. Armed guards closed the door firmly behind the final, exiting visitor, leaving the three men completely alone.

Khalifa sighed deeply as the doors closed, either with frustration or exhaustion. Maxwell didn't know which, but one thing he knew for sure was that the ruler had been up and at it since five thirty that morning and had probably not had sight of his bed until the early hours. The ruling family were all hard workers. Each one had a job to do, and was required to do it well, putting whatever hours were necessary into the working week, managing day to day the inestimable wealth of the one single economy called respectfully in banking circles, Dubai Limited. Sheikh Khalifa tasted his tea and then motioned Maxwell to move up closer to him. The ruler spoke.

'Well, my old friend, we are all a bit undecided as to what to do, and now all the AGCC ministers are in possession of the facts, we have had immediate reactions from some, ranging from total surprise and confusion to outright anger. The present score on a basis of, 'Shall we support the

Iraqi move or not,' is as follows; Qatar and Bahrain, yes: Oman and the UAE, no and Saudi Arabia, angry and undecided. As for other opinion in the Moslem block, Iran is uncommitted one way or the other, both Yemen Republics in favor and Pakistan still considering its options. The only agreement Sheikh Saif and I have been able to extract from all the heads of state we talked with, was not to do anything foolish in the money markets by taking up large forward gold options, until the Middle Eastern close of business at lunchtime on Thursday, October fourth.' He paused.

'But, I'm afraid the rot has already started with this morning's London gold fixing expecting to be up several points, which means the Russians must be buying gold through varied and diversified sources and in fairly large quantities. It will be interesting to see what the Hong Kong bullion exchange closes at later on in the day. What we are trying to avoid here, is any form of panic which could light the financial blue touch paper, before we have had time to make a unanimous decision on where we stand. A panic move would play right into the hands of our Iraqi cousin and even force him to break his promise to you and make his declaration early'. Maxwell listened carefully.

'I hope he wouldn't do that, sir,' said Maxwell,

'I put great store by the promises made to me by the Imam and he by mine.'

'I agree,' replied the ruler, 'but if the gold price rises much higher tomorrow, then we may be forced into a situation where he has no other choice.'

A grim faced Hardmain told Maxwell he was monitoring the international money markets closely and although there had been no single large deal reported during the past couple of days, there was a steady movement out of dollars, sterling and deutschmarks and into gold. Dubai's forward situation, as one of the biggest gold traders in the world, was fairly good, Tom explained.

'We have a forward buying situation normally one or two months ahead and at this time of year, in particular, we are usually looking for large deliveries. Our total contract, to cover ourselves for the next month, is about one hundred and seventy tons, of which ninety tons has just been delivered and the balance will arrive in two further consignments next week. Our contract price on most of the gold averaged about sixty dollars an ounce. This price could double within the next week and although we do not wish to drive the price up too sharply, we are presently negotiating in Switzerland for a further thirty to forty tons, which is a little more than we would normally be looking for right now, but hopefully not so much as to cause the raising of enquiring eyebrows. If we are really lucky, we may be able to close the deal this morning at something between eighty two and eighty three dollars an ounce. If we freeze all Dubai trading, for which contracts are not already agreed, we may be able to retain half of the total quantity. This will see us through any immediate crisis and unless everything else goes down the tube, then we could batten down the hatches and sit tight for a year and see what happens.'

The ruler and Tom had obviously been busy during the early hours and had staked their claim no matter what happened at the weekend. Tom went into a lot more detail during the following couple of hours and Maxwell was impressed with the calmness of action and depth of thought that had gone into securing their own position in such a short space of time. There was a twinkle in Khalifa's eye as he listened to Tom explaining the financial maneuvering taking place right at this moment, with the dealing room staff of the National Bank of Dubai locked behind closed and guarded doors as they wheeled and dealed by telephone and telex on all the major precious metal and foreign exchanges of the free world.

'….. and you have no need to worry either, my young friend ,' interjected the ruler, 'we have made suitable arrangements for you as well and have opened a bullion account for you here which will more than cover your requirements during the next few years.'

Max and Tom both smiled, knowing it would be impossible to refuse Khalifa's generosity, and therefore Maxwell simply echoed his thanks and gratefully accepted the small white envelope Tom slipped to him with an account number neatly typed in the top left hand corner. No more needed to be said on the subject and Maxwell thought it was time he established what more might be required of him.

Sheikh Khalifa ruminated on the matter for a while and then decided there was little else he could accomplish in the Middle East immediately, except to communicate to the Imam the final decision of the AGCC ministers and other Gulf Heads of State. This duty he could perform as well from Kenya as he could from Dubai and no final decision would be arrived at before Tuesday. Even then the Dubai ruler did not expect a unanimous vote in favor of supporting the Iraqi President and the Imam in their volatile maneuvers. A non-unanimous decision would mean a guaranteed collapse of the AGCC as it stood right now and would therefore overshadow any further discussions Sheikh Saif might get involved in as chairman of the AGCC, purely because he would be unable to speak on behalf of the whole council. The ruler gave Maxwell's shoulder a friendly little tap.

'This is the time to "dig in," my friend which, as from today, is what we will all be doing and I would suggest you do the same thing. There seems little point in you going to meet with the EEC President to tell him by now what he already knows.' He paused for a second. 'If we in the Gulf, were all united against the Iraqis and Kuwaitis, then that would be a different matter, but we are not and unlikely to ever be. Therefore, they must do as we are doing and that is to prepare to fend for themselves. Between Saudi Arabia, Oman and the UAE, we might have been able to put a sufficiently large and effective spanner in the financial works if we were all resolute, but the simple fact is, we are not; therefore, we are unable to help the Europeans and between us exists little or no will at all to help the Americans, so there be it.' Maxwell replied in a surrendering tone,

'Well thank you for your confidence and honesty, your highness. I will finish my schedule here today and then return to Kenya tonight, if transport can be arranged?'

Tom informed him that arrangements were being made to have him flown back to Archers Post that evening on the council's Learjet and he would be able to leave as originally planned by six o'clock. The ruler agreed to start talking to European heads of state that afternoon, giving them an appraisal of where they stood and Sheikh Saif would probably already be talking to Senor Bantellas in Madrid. There was really nothing else to discuss and as the time was approaching eleven o'clock, Maxwell said his farewell to Sheikh Khalifa and accompanied by Tom Hardmain, left the Majalis for his next appointment with the American accident investigation team.

# Chapter Nineteen

*October 1st 1973 – Dubai – United Arab Emirates*

Four men were waiting on the ground floor of the Majalis building, in one of the large airy conference rooms. As Maxwell and Tom walked in, the team got up from a table in the centre of the room, one end of which was littered with charred fragments of metal, all neatly tagged and labeled with a mystifying assortment of numbers and letters. The leader of the team, a well built broad shouldered man of about fifty, walked over, shook Maxwell's hand and introduced himself and his three compatriots. The leader's name was George Maitland and his ruddy complexion gave away possibilities that he made most of his living out of doors. He was in fact a qualified commercial pilot and aeronautical engineer who had headed up the American Federal Aviation Air Investigation Board for several years and wandered more or less permanently around the globe carrying out the board's business. Another member of the team was introduced as a specialist engineer from Dassault Aviation who had worked extensively on the design of the latest Falcon 10. Preliminaries over with, the six men settled themselves at the single, cloth covered table. George opened the meeting with a General appraisal of the routing of their investigation so far, gradually working up to the questions they wished answered concerning the port engine failure Maxwell experienced north of Bahrain. He could add very little detail to the information given so far; only that the engine suddenly lost power, and fuel pressure fluctuated to such an extent that he thought it wise to shut the engine down. It was noted that during the sixteen hundred hours both engines had been running in that particular airframe, there had never been a problem, if the maintenance logs were to be believed, and there didn't seem to be any reason not to believe them. The airplane had been serviced regularly by qualified engineers attached to Dubai's GA Facility, Aerogulf, who had a faultless record to date in fulfilling correct and approved maintenance procedures. One of the other members of the team took up the conversation and explained that he was an expert in the science of explosives, attached to the enquiry by the Federal Bureau of Investigation.

'I have to tell you, Mr. Armstrong, that at this early stage,' the professional looking gentleman paused, glancing in George's direction, looking for a sign to continue,

'….. we suspect sabotage.' George interrupted.

'Let's be totally honest with you, Mr. Armstrong. We more than suspect, we know it was sabotage and the evidence is before us on this table right now. Someone wanted you very much dead and we are fairly sure the only reason you are alive today, is because a quirk of fate did not allow you to fulfill your original flight plan from Kuwait to Dubai'.

Maxwell remained unmoved and silent, taking in everything being said. The explosive expert continued after another hesitating look at Maitland. He picked up a minute piece of brass looking material, encapsulated in a self-sealing plastic bag.

'I won't bore you with a lot of technicalities sir, but I will explain that under normal circumstances, in any explosive device, the impact of a secondary, terminal explosion is thrust outwards and that the secondary explosion is triggered by a much smaller one, caused by the pyrotechnic action of a detonator. The detonator is clearly at the seat of the terminal explosion and the detonator casing obviously fragments, but does not necessarily disintegrate and can often be recovered along with any other timing or switching devices used to set off the detonator. Are you with me, so far'?' Maxwell nodded.

'Well, in this bag are the remains of a detonator used in a very sophisticated bomb which had been planted in the port engine cowling of your aircraft. From the items recovered so far and the initial analysis, with the assistance of some fairly modern laboratory equipment available here in Dubai, we are able to make some reasonably accurate judgments as to the type of explosive and triggering device used in the bomb.' Maxwell fidgeted restlessly on his seat.

'The components used to manufacture this particular explosive device, are, I'm afraid, of European origin and their distribution so well controlled that, in fact, we believe one or two items are only at a testing stage in the United Kingdom.'

The American paused for effect, or the opportunity for querying looks to be converted into words. No words came and so he continued.

'The bomb itself consisted of about half a kilo of dense plastique used almost exclusively by the British Special Air Services. The reason we can pin its use down so well is that this particular mix is of an extremely high yield but very difficult to set off and requires the application of highly trained men and very special chemical detonators to guarantee ignition. Its force per pound is treble that of standard C-5 material which is used widely in demolition operations, but this particular plastique is unique in that we only know of the SAS training with it at the moment. To guarantee a successful detonation of a device using this kind of explosive, one would require two chemical detonators linked by a micro second delay timer; the first detonation puts the plastique into a momentarily unstable condition and the second actually sets the thing off. The detonators and timer are manufactured in Germany and are still under test by the British Ministry of Defense, under a Nato contract. They are half the weight and size of equivalent systems presently being used in fragmentary grenades and are considered the latest advance in this particular technology'.

Maxwell was paying full attention.

'Finally we have discovered the remains of a very reliable and accurate barometric pressure switch of a type used in transmitting weather data back to a ground receiving point. They can be set to trigger at just about any height as the air pressure changes and although this type of switch is used extensively by meteorological offices around the world, they are also used and manufactured in Great Britain. The conclusions arrived at so far all point to the fact that this particular device was more than likely manufactured from materials originating from within the UK and only officially accessible with clearance from some pretty high levels within the British Government, or military. These are our thoughts so far, painful as they are to relate'.

Maxwell asked if the FBI man had come across anything like it before and the answer was a blank, 'No.' The whole thing was worrying indeed, and whichever way Maxwell looked at it, he was convinced the only agency who could put such a complex little bomb together and have under their control the contacts to plant the bloody thing on his aero plane, presumably in Kuwait, were those clandestine, scheming assholes in the SIS.

His face remained impassive as his mind searched desperately for a reason. Firstly, SIS were putting him back on a job when they knew he had packed it in for good; then they were not prepared to brief him properly with facts they must have known before he left Kenya and now, for whatever reason, they were trying to kill him before he reached Dubai and had a chance to talk with the Dubai ruler. It didn't make sense, but so little made sense within the closed and secretive society of Her Majesty's Secret Intelligence

Service, that he wondered why he was even asking himself the question. Those bastards; once in, never out! Eh! But he would get out and quickly, making sure he trod on a few balls and brains on the way. Tom had not spoken once during the meeting but finally had to ask the question preying on everyone's mind.

'Is it possible, Maxwell, that someone in the British Government wants you dead?'

Tom was partly aware of Maxwell's other activities besides the official positions he had held over the years from Embassy attaché to FAO advisor, but wanted the question asked in front of the Americans for the purposes of record. Maxwell replied,

'As you are well aware, Tom, I have been engaged in work for the British Government for many years now, but nothing of a sensitive nature and if all the evidence points to this device being manufactured and planted by British sources, then all I can say is that I'm completely bewildered'.

He glanced at his watch and made an excuse to leave the gathering saying he had an important lunch meeting.

'Will you be around tomorrow, sir?' Maitland asked.

'Yes,' Maxwell lied, 'I'll get in touch with you tomorrow and give you all the time you need to make your report.'

With that, Maxwell and Tom left in search of their car and waiting lunch appointment at the golf club. The blaring cavalcade wound its way through a bustling Al Faheedi Street, picking the most rapid route towards the Zabeel roundabout and then out onto the Abu Dhabi road. The journey was short but pleasant and Tom proudly pointed out new developments and park areas that had risen up from the depths of a hostile desert environment since he had last been in the country. The golf course itself was something of a minor miracle, consisting of lush green areas and man-made lakes fed by processed sewage and desalinated ground water. Major international tournaments were programmed to be played here and would help put Dubai on the map as the leading sports and leisure centre in the Gulf. The convoy drew up to the club house entrance where the General manager, Christopher Davy, was waiting to greet his guests.

Chris had been around for many years and had visited the farm in Kenya on several occasions. He and the Weismullers got on well and so the man bubbled with questions about Helga and Kurt as the three of them walked through the pillared reception area to the restaurant. Alan was already sitting at a central, circular table and tucked well into his first drink as the three men approached; a small and pleasant reunion of old friends. Maxwell looked forward to his lunch, even though it was to take place under the watchful eye of the royal guards, trying hard not to look over conspicuous as they obligingly made half successful efforts to merge with the pastel background shades of the restaurant's well appointed decor.

The 'lunch' carried on to well past four o'clock, which was something of a habit in Dubai, and all four men thoroughly enjoyed themselves. Tom reminded Max that they should leave shortly and, glancing at his watch, he agreed. The time had swept by all too quickly and as Maxwell rose to leave, Alan and Chris rushed away to collect small bags of presents for him to take back to Kenya for Helga and Kurt. The question had never once been raised as to what he was doing in Dubai, especially surrounded by armed guards and seemingly getting the royal treatment. Both had known Maxwell Armstrong a long time, and knew better than to ask.

\*\*\*\*\*\*

The journey to Sharjah International Airport took less than an hour. Dubai remained closed to air traffic and Sharjah was struggling hard to manage with the massive inflow of diverted passengers and cargo. Fortunately, Maxwell and his escorts would not have to fight their way through the traffic piled up on the Dhaid road, battling for a way into the arrivals car park; their route took them into the military entrance on the south side of the airport through which they were quickly ushered by smart looking military policemen. The Learjet waited at the edge of the perimeter road and was ready to get away immediately. Max thanked a worried looking Tom for all his help as the grey haired old man pushed a small brightly wrapped parcel into his hand.

'Something for you and Helga from all of us here and especially a grateful ruler' Maxwell shook his hand firmly.

'You've done more than enough already Tom and remember if things get a bit rough here, you and the kids are more than welcome to come and stay with us on the farm'. Tom smiled encouragingly.

'It's you who has to watch out, my friend. This bomb business is difficult to fathom and I have a feeling that none of us have heard the last of it yet, by a long way. Remember, if you need any help whatsoever, we are all here and will do anything we can for you, even if it means putting two thick fingers up the arse of your playmates in Bowater House. Be careful and vigilant, for all our sakes.'

At that moment, Maxwell wondered if he really should tell Tom about the Unicorn. He gazed steadily into the old man's eyes and knew he couldn't load him down with any more worries or problems than he already had. But Tom sensed the meaning of the searching look.

'Is there anything you want to tell me, Max?' Both men paused for long seconds at the bottom of the aircraft steps; but eventually Maxwell said,

'No thanks Tom, you be on your way and I promise I'll take care.'

'You do that old chap.'

The air-stairs clamped back up into the fuselage as Tom Hardmain and the motor cavalcade drew away and Maxwell laid back in one of the wide lounger chairs and clipped his safety belt together. Except for the flight deck crew, he was alone and that suited him fine; in about five hours he would be back in Kenya and that suited him fine also. He hadn't realized exactly how tired he was and how many hours he'd been on the go during the last couple of days. His leg burns were healing well and he felt no discomfort at all in his back. The salt water had done them good although the mental scars of Saturday's experience would stay with him forever. He shuddered slightly at the thought of reliving the experience as the executive jet winged its way southwest on its journey to the East African continent. Within ten minutes the single passenger on the four million dollar aero plane was fast asleep.

\*\*\*\*\*\*

Maxwell awoke with a start three hours into the flight. He had been dreaming and was bathed in sweat, his mouth dry and chapped lips stinging. He pulled himself together and checked the time. Only a few more hours and he would be home. The drinks cabinet was located next to his armchair seat and with a press of a button he released the seat from its locked take-off position and swiveled round to open the cabinet and built-in refrigerator. There was an ample supply of Teachers and soda water inside. He poured a large one with trembling fingers into a wide bottomed, lead crystal glass, gulping it all down in one go. Sitting back in the chair and unclasping his safety belt, he reached for a refill. This one he topped up with ice and sipped gently, waiting for the panic of dream conjured visions to subside.

Who the hell was trying to kill him? Maxwell pondered. More importantly, having failed once, would they try again? Whoever it was had wished to prevent him talking to Sheikh Khalifa, but that had already been accomplished; so did it mean now he would be left alone, knowing that whatever damage the bombers thought would result to their cause by such discussions, had already been done?

There were possibilities of course, other than the SIS, but they were fairly remote and manufacturing the sort of evidence displayed at the meeting with the American investigators would be nearly impossible without the help and assistance of someone fairly powerful within the ranks of the British intelligence community. There was, of course, the so-called Unicorn, which seemed so bloody secret that even they didn't know what the right and left hand were doing. He scratched his brains for a few minutes and eventually concluded that, as well geared up for this kind of assassination attempt as they may be in the Middle East, they would have to be bloody good to get their hands on some of the equipment Maitland described, especially from a body as astute and careful as the Special Air Services Regiment. They were some of the world's toughest customers, as he well knew from personal experience and there was little chance anyone could 'nick' a quantity of highly potent explosive from them without paying dearly for it.

Nevertheless he decided to check up when he got back to the farm. He still had good contacts inside the 'regiment' and if any report had been made concerning missing explosive stocks, he would soon be able to find out about it.

The next possibility, of course, was some kind of unexplained move by the Russians. They, more than likely, had the ability to put such a bomb together with most of the original components, but, yet again, the actual plastique itself would be hard to come by and difficult to fake. There was little doubt in Maxwell's mind that if the British or the Yanks were experimenting with something worthwhile, then the highly efficient KGB had managed to get their hands on it ages ago by either stealing the finished product or making a perfect copy of their own. Yes, there was an outside chance the Soviets had made the bomb, but what interests of theirs would be served by blowing him up in mid-air, which was obviously the original plan, and using a bomb made of materials which could be directly connected back to the SIS or some other British agency? If the damn thing had gone off as apparently planned, over the Gulf, then there would be little recoverable evidence left to point a finger in any particular direction, so why go to the trouble of making the bloody bomb look British?

No, at the end of the day, it smelt more like a typically bungled operation by the Secret Intelligence Service and when he got back to the farm, he would damn well make sure he found out. They were no doubt up to something on their own, and for some reason they wanted Maxwell out of the way. That supercilious prat, Charles Hawthorn, would pay dearly for this if Maxwell managed to unearth one single scrap of evidence, other than the now highly obvious, that the SIS had had anything to do with the blood and tears spilt on that unforgettable September day in Dubai.

# Chapter Twenty

*October 1st 1973 – Archers Post – Kenya – East Africa*

The Learjet touched down at the Archers Post strip at ten thirty. Harry Jordan had received the pre-alert message from Nairobi over the radio and flares had been carefully laid out at ten meter intervals, enabling the pilot to make a first time, perfect landing. The aircraft stopped at the end of the runway, whilst Maxwell said his thanks and goodbyes to the British crew; and as he let the stairs down, there was Harry waiting for him accompanied by the beaten up old farm truck. Harry shouted words of greeting through the pallid smoke of dying flares and both men piled into the truck to complete the journey home.

Sitting in the dusty interior of the bouncing vehicle, Maxwell breathed a long sigh of relief and closed his eyes, wishing to kill all conversation until he could be with Helga again. Harry got the message and remained respectfully silent. As they drove up the extended drive toward the main residence, Maxwell re-opened rested eyes, seeing the whole house lit up before him. He smiled with quiet satisfaction at the thought of being home, this indescribably beautiful place in the middle of East Africa that no-one would ever drag him from again; whatever the reason, whatever the cost. Here he would stay, bar the gates, lock the doors and let the rest of the fucked up world do what it wanted.

Ralph hovered at the bottom of the veranda steps, looking immaculate as usual, beaming a flashing greeting as he eagerly grabbed Maxwell's bags from the back of the pick-up.

'Welcome home Mr. Max, and this time we hope it's for good,' growled the chuckling old retainer.

'It will be, Ralph. This time it will be . . . where's Helga and Kurt?' Maxwell asked.

'Mr. Kurt is holding dinner for you and Miss Helga is upstairs dressing, but I suspect if you went up straight away, you would be doing us all a favor.'

Harry shouted back that he would put the truck away and shot off into the dark. Maxwell took the stairs, two at a time, reached the bedroom door and paused to knock.

'Come in, you stupid bastard, Jesus Christ, anyone would think .... ' The muffled reply tailed off as he opened the door and drank in the view of his woman, her back to him and head half turned as she tried, in vain, to zip up the back of a flowing white cotton dress. Helga froze as he stood immobilized in the doorway. Hundreds of words tumbled around in his head as he stood there for those few short seconds, but the only one that would freely come out was,

'Hi!'

She deserted the half zipped dress, turned and rushed towards him and with her arms clinging to his neck, their lips met in a long and passionate embrace.

'Bloody hell,' she breathed, '....it's been less than a week, but I've missed you like anything; promise me you'll never go away again without me'.

Maxwell pulled backward and focused on those beguiling glistening, emerald eyes, gazing intently and bringing all the conviction to his voice that he could muster, said,

'Never again, darling, *never* again'. Tears welled up and began falling down her cheeks as Helga pulled away sharply.

'Shit, now I'm crying and I've just done my make-up. Get in that shower, while I finish getting ready, dinner will be served in five minutes'.

She moved back to the dressing table, sobbing quietly to herself, reaching for a box of pink paper tissues and dabbing her eyes as Maxwell walked towards the bathroom, shedding his clothes on the way. Minutes later he walked out of the bathroom, naked and wet, drying himself on a soft, bleached white bath towel as Helga turned round from the dresser mirror, her dress now zipped and her make-up thoroughly renewed. She was smiling to herself and preparing to share the joke with her man when she stopped short, her face changing from flushed pink to pale grey. She spoke in a hoarse whisper.

'What the hell happened to you?' She put her hands to her face in undisguised horror. Maxwell self consciously pulled the towel over his back as he realized what a stupid mistake he'd made. She was about to burst into tears again.

'Darling, honestly, it's really nothing; just a few minor scratches and burns, nothing to worry about at all.'

He'd forgotten that the several stitches still hooked in his back must look hideous and he cursed himself for not having them taken out before he left. His legs were still covered in ugly red blotches from the burns and he knew they must appear ten times worse than they really were; he should have prepared her and said something before getting in the shower. He could kick himself.

'You'll probably have heard by now of the catastrophe at Dubai Airport last week, and I'm afraid I caught some of the backwash. I really am perfectly well and these scars are simply superficial. In a few days you won't be able to see a thing'.

He put on his little boy look, hoping to decharge the electric atmosphere of the moment but Helga remained motionless, working hard at holding back further tears. There was nothing more he could really say and so stood there, foolishly, while she studied him from head to foot. He dropped the towel and eventually, she walked towards him, inspecting his back carefully for a while and then stating in a resolute tone that Doctor Johnson would be called for, first thing in the morning, to remove the stitches and make sure everything was as it should be. Her final word was,

'I do not trust those bloody Arab doctors and I want you looked after by Alf.'

'But darling' Maxwell protested, 'the doctor who attended me was a Scot, for Christ's sake, and she assures me everything will be all right.'

'That settles it, then,' Helga retorted, 'I trust women doctors even less than I trust Arab doctors, so Alf Johnson will have to come over and look at you in the morning. Now hurry up and get dressed,' she said, patting freshly dampened cheeks with the last of the pink tissues. She paused once more, then smiled, a gentle loving smile; the anger of the moment forgotten.

'Father is waiting downstairs and I would suspect, by now, he's very hungry.' Maxwell dressed hurriedly in fresh shirt and slacks and hand in hand the couple left the bedroom to eat. Sitting down at dinner the questions came thick and fast, especially from an over inquisitive Harry, who propelled himself verbally head first into every topic of conversation. Kurt remained a lot more subdued and looked in greater pain than usual. For the first time in his life, Maxwell felt free to tell most of what had happened to him during the course of his last mission, leaving an ebullient Harry asking for more, a pensive Helga prepared to simply listen and absorb, and a contemplative Kurt saying little, knowing that he and Maxwell would be talking in depth later.

With dinner over, they went to the lounge for coffee and liqueurs. Maxwell noted the time. It was past midnight and he had a phone call to make. He excused himself and walked through into the study to telephone London. The number rang and was answered straight away. The voice at the other end of the line refused his first request to speak directly with Sir Charles Hawthorn; but after expressing himself in more urgent, less polite tones, he was asked to wait while the connected party tried to put him through. Sir Charles came on the line a few seconds later, a detectable sign of agitation in his voice.

'Yes, Maxwell, what can I do for you? I'm in a rather important meeting at the moment and I was hoping that you would be able to make an initial verbal report to your handler.'

'Well Charles, before I make any kind of report,' said Maxwell, in a controlled effort to maintain an even temperament, '…..there are one or two questions I need to ask of you in particular. Firstly, why did you allow me to set off on this little caper without being properly briefed?'

Sir Charles replied in a matter of fact kind of voice that he didn't know what Maxwell was talking about.

'Then let me enlighten you,' said the caller, 'The build-up of Russian military support in Iraq and Kuwait is so vast and comprehensive that you must have known about it weeks ago. I have actually been to Kirkuk and been given the full run of the bloody place and I can tell you, it's frightening'.

The head of the SIS moved into a long series of why's and wherefore's, ending up with the explanation that he had wanted a completely fresh viewpoint of the whole military scenario and an independent but qualified opinion by a trained observer, before putting on record the information received from other western intelligence agencies, such as the CIA. He finished with

'You know how our friends across the Atlantic like to exaggerate, old man, and in these critical times, we need accurate confirmable information. Just get your report coded up and I'll send someone from Nairobi to collect it tomorrow? Maxwell was now at the point of losing his temper completely.

'There will be no need to code any further communications of mine Charles, because my cover is blown and has been for some time. A certain General Lubikov was able to tell me, more or less, the time, date and place of every fucking operation I've been involved in during the past five years, and there's only one place he could have got that information, Charles; from the Company.'

There was a strained silence from the other end. A voice came back.

'Do you think it could be a little knowledge colored with some fairly accurate guess work, perhaps'?'

'For crying out loud Charles, this Lubikov is a professional and although he sells himself as a General in the artillery, I'll bet you a pound to a pinch of shit that he's one hundred per cent KGB and probably in at his displayed rank to boot.'

Maxwell wiped his brow, now perspiring as a result of his pent-up anger and frustration. Sir Charles spoke again.

'We cannot talk too much over the line but I can tell you, I have lost two very essential men during the past few days, men who were being minded by our own people and at this moment I have nothing to show for it. Two highly professional jobs carried out with the utmost accuracy and all pointing to the work of our 'eastern' competition. The whole security aspect of the Company is now under close investigation and I expect a result shortly. More comfort than that I am unable to offer at this particular moment, but be assured we will get to the bottom of it'.

Maxwell waited for something further, but nothing came.

'You are aware, Sir Charles,' said Maxwell with unrestrained bitterness in his voice, '…..of the recent happenings at Dubai Airport?'

The man in London replied with a Curt,

'Yes.'

'Well then,' continued Maxwell, 'you may also be aware that the cause of such mindless carnage was the detonation of a very sophisticated bomb planted aboard the aero plane I was flying, and, although the whole matter is still being investigated in detail, the preliminary results make for some interesting reading, especially the source of the components used to manufacture the bomb. I would suggest you contact the investigation team right away and find out what the hell is going on, because at present the deadly finger of suspicion points at you .'

A further silence. Maxwell waited.

'I don't know quite what to say, all I can tell you is .... ' Maxwell cut him off.

'All you had better be able to say within the next twenty four hours is that you can prove categorically that you, the Company, Her Majesty's Government or any other smart ass UK agency, had nothing to do with that bomb and then you'd better work your butt into the ground trying to find out who did ...... or else I'm going to kill you. Not today and maybe not tomorrow, but you'd better be prepared to look over your shoulder for the rest of your short life because I'm definitely going to kill you.' The line was silent.

'One last thing: if you send anybody out here to get at me or any member of this family, I'm going to put them away as well. Think about it. Unlike most of the Eton and Cambridge frustrated gays and masochists you've historically employed, I have the ability, the resources, and the will to do it. Now get back to your fucking meeting and there'll be no need to contact me again unless you can come up with some answers.'

Maxwell slammed down the telephone and sat for several minutes composing himself. His hands were still shaking as he picked up the telephone once more and dialed another number in the UK, this time the Duke of York's barracks in London's Chelsea. The person he was looking for was not in the barracks but he was given the number of a club after confirming his 'need to contact' by delivering a coded password for use in emergencies only, by security cleared Government officials wishing to contact officers of the Special

Air Service. Within two or three minutes, Maxwell was speaking to the SAS captain he had been searching for and asked him pointedly about the plastique explosive. The captain confirmed his regiment was testing a new type called Cl2 but to his knowledge every gram was accounted for used during exercises and tests and there was no way anyone could have obtained such a large amount as half a kilo or more, without proper authority. Certainly, he would check quietly on Maxwell's behalf and let him know if any had been signed out of the armory other than on internal request. Maxwell thanked his friend and replaced the receiver. He was calmer now and needed a drink. A good long glass of port would go down a treat. Walking back into the lounge, Maxwell noticed Kurt had left for his bed but waiting for him on the low coffee table, rested a glowing glass of ruby colored liquid obviously spirited from some of Kurt's older and more coveted stock of vintage port.

He sat next to Helga and silently sipped away. Harry finished his coffee, made his excuses and quietly left, leaving all arrangements open for the following day's activities. Helga sat on the floor, leaning against Maxwell's knee, her face glowing in the reflected amber light of decaying coals in the open fireplace. For those few brief moments, all was at peace, but how long would it remain that way? Maxwell finished his port and the tired but relaxed couple climbed the stairs and made their way to bed. It had been a long day. They had made love. He had promised never to leave her again.

She had to believe that or else there was no point in living.

Snuggled between the sheets, Helga pressed her body closely against her man. The man by her side and her father were the two most precious things in her life and one was slowly, day by day, slipping away from her. She knew her father had very little time left to live and permanently steeled herself for the day when that deep gruff voice would no longer echo through the dining room. It would be the worst day of her life but as long as Maxwell was there, she would be able to live through it. She soon fell quietly asleep whilst Maxwell closed his eyes but was unable to settle immediately. He knew he had told a lie to Helga when he made a final promise never to leave her again; there might be one more job to do yet and not too far in the distant future if Sir Charles Hawthorn was unable to come up with a damn good reason why he shouldn't have his scheming brains blown out. Maxwell hoped upon hope that he would, so that this whole sordid and deceitful part of his life could be put behind him.

******

Hawthorn hung on to the telephone, the line disconnected, a single monotonous tone ringing in his ear. His knuckles were protruding and skeleton white, as he gripped the handset; finally he let it fall from his hands and crash onto the desk top. His face was drawn and his hands trembling as he reached down into the top drawer and pulled out a handgun and leather shoulder holster. He unclipped the safety strap on the holster and extracted the matt black, cold steel body of the Beretta nine millimeter automatic. Pressing the magazine release button on the side of the trigger guard, he checked the fifteen round staggered clip and pushed the magazine back home until it locked; finally working the safety blocking device before replacing the gun in its holster. He didn't wear a gun all that often and Generally felt uncomfortable around them but now the inevitable time had come. Two well protected men dead in London and now hundreds more in Dubai. Everyone was after his blood, the Russians, probably the CIA and now one of his own men; one of his very best men.

After fitting the holster under his jacket, he sat down and rested for a brief few seconds. The meeting he was supposed to be attending would have to wait. He checked his watch; ten past seven. It had been a long day so far and it had just gotten worse. Recovering his composure, he kicked the bottom desk drawer in a final act of pent up tension and got to work on the telephone again. He knew he had better come up with some answers and a good start would be a call to Dubai to find out about the bloody bomb.

******

Seated quietly at her desk in the reception area of the eighteenth floor offices of Research and Development Finance Corporation Limited, the imperturbable, blonde Louise Stone switched off a pocket Sony tape recorder, disconnected the earphone cable from the input jack, and removed the micro recording cassette. She returned the recorder to her middle drawer and slipped the cassette into her handbag, replacing the bag back in its normal resting place; the bottom left hand drawer, to join an uneaten, cellophane wrapped sandwich and an open packet of rye biscuits. Her face remained impassive, as always, as she calmly prepared herself for the impending onslaught from her director. There was not long to wait. The internal phone rang and Sir Charles Hawthorn immediately barked orders at her, ending with a list of priorities which she patiently noted down on a yellow desk pad. Two minutes later an ashen and visibly shaken Sir Charles stormed from his offices, slamming the door behind him and without a glance in Louise's direction, headed back down the corridor in the direction of the conference room to continue with his interrupted meeting. She smiled confidently to herself as she began the task of trying to raise the Company man in Dubai.

\*\*\*\*\*\*

In Kirkuk, General Lubikov had been marshaled from his bed in the early hours and was now studying a precise and detailed report on the happenings at Dubai Airport. Somewhere there had been a fatal error. When his men had set the bomb trigger mechanism, they had purposely not connected the secondary detonator and although the plastique material would have flashed into ignition when the primary detonator went off, there should not have been an explosion as such, and after questioning the artillery officer responsible for putting the whole device together, concerning the detonators, he was convinced his man wasn't lying. The only plausible explanation could be that somehow the explosive had momentarily fallen unstable, maybe due to engine heat or some kind of sudden pressure, and the wired detonator had gone off at exactly the right time.

What a fuck up. He now had everyone on his back. The bloody politicians in Moscow and Baghdad, the security forces in Kuwait and that asshole Tammam bin Abdulla in Qatar. The American investigation team had done their job well and even Lubikov was surprised at the speed with which they had reached a more than basic conclusion about the origins of the explosive. To date, he had avoided making any categorical statement concerning either the explosion or the evidence relating to the bomb itself, but he had to do so by eight o'clock that morning and it wouldn't be easy. Rasheed had screamed down the phone at him like a man possessed, followed closely by a raving Tammam. Victor Chebrekovski had sent long coded signals, wanting to know what the hell was going on and the Emir of Kuwait sent a message through the Iraqi President's office telling him to make sure that whatever answers he came up with, he'd better make sure the Kuwaiti security forces received a clean bill of health.

He viewed hopelessly all the different bits of paper littering his desk, with not a single useful thought in his head. A weary looking signals corporal walked into the office and laid yet another decoded signal in front of him, which Lubikov ignored momentarily in favor of another cup of coffee, freshly percolated. He returned to his desk and drew on the coffee pensively, hoping to Christ he could come up with something plausible in the next few hours. He glanced disconsolately at this latest signal brought in by the corporal, marked in longhand Cyrillic script, *Most Urgent* and underneath *Eyes Only. General Lubikov.*

Without picking it up he scanned the first few lines and then, with a start, put down the coffee cup, grabbing the signal flimsy and beginning to read again from the first decoded block. The source was identified as a London KGB agent, codename Satsivi. He laughed inwardly at the ridiculous choice of codename. The General read right through to the end. The information contained in the message was heaven sent and consisted of the bones of a conversation Maxwell Armstrong had had not less than hours ago with the infamous Sir Charles Hawthorn. Andrea Lubikov chuckled happily to himself.

'I'll bet Hawthorn is shitting his pants,' he muttered, 'Well, here we have it then, an answer to a maiden's prayer; za zdorovie satsiva.' With that mental word of thanks to Satsivi, he pushed all the papers on his desk to one side and began to write his much awaited reports. The first one was to 'The Centre', telling all, including the lunatic plan of the Unicorn to eliminate Armstrong and describing the General's efforts to foil any such plans without actually telling Rasheed or Tammam to go stick their heads up their rectum. This he justified by categorizing his unwillingness to see the Englishman murdered on the one hand but a similar unwillingness to refuse a direct request for assistance from their so called allies, in the shape of the Unicorn movement, on the other. This was known as diplomatic deviousness, a phrase well understood in the hallowed halls of 'The Centre' and the Kremlin. The second report was to Rasheed, and thereby the Unicorn, expressing his regret on the obvious malfunction of the carefully engineered bomb, manufactured by his explosive experts, but expressing that after a thorough investigation he was unable to assess why the bomb did not go off as programmed. He also noted that on the Falcon's departure from Kirkuk, certain air traffic problems had not allowed the aero plane to reach its planned flight level, thereby ensuring that Mr. Armstrong was unfortunately able to meet with the Emir of Kuwait. But, he continued, that was how those things sometimes happened and all reports from the air traffic control officers and technicians at Basra indicated it had not been possible to clear the aircraft to a greater height inside Iraqi airspace. The General went on to coyly suggest that Rasheed's men had planted and set the bomb and he, as the commander of the Soviet Assistance Forces, had only co-operated with a request to provide the specialist hardware and technical back-up, which he had duly done. He added a final sarcastic note to the report stating that at least the Imam and the Iraqi President were both pleased their English friend had been reported alive and well.

'That will make the bastards grind their teeth a bit,' Lubikov said out loud, as he pushed the report to one side and started another.

The note to the office of the Emir of Kuwait simply stated that, following intense investigations within Iraq, his staff could find no evidence connecting the planting of any kind of explosive device aboard the executive jet used by Mr. Armstrong on his brief tour of the Northern Gulf, and that the plane had been carefully inspected by Iraqi security staff before it left Kirkuk. He finished off by stating casually that he had heard some unconfirmed reports indicating that the bomb, or whatever device it finally turned out to be, had all the hallmarks of British involvement, and perhaps the Kuwaiti authorities would like to follow up the incident from their end, working on this assumption. The final report was penned to the Imam and the Iraqi President, denying all knowledge of just about everything except the fact that certain information had come to his attention, relating to a telephone conversation Mr. Armstrong had recently held with the head of the British Secret Intelligence Service. From the scant, but considerably reliable information received regarding this conversation, the General was under the impression that Mr. Armstrong himself was more than convinced that the director of SIS, Sir Charles Hawthorn, had played a major role in an obviously bungled assassination attempt. Lubikov went on to assure the Imam and the President that, if this were the case, his Government would do their utmost to ensure no similar attempts upon Armstrong's life were made in the future and he would personally be more than happy to offer to the Englishman any help or assistance he might require in resolving his present problem with the British Government.

The General put down the final piece of handwritten script and proceeded to re-read all the reports, checking content and phrasing to ensure that the readers would be able to decipher the intended meat of each individual message. There were no hidden conclusions to be drawn from any of them; just the plain facts as they were written, and as long as that lunatic Tammam, the Imam's bitter minded and totally deluded brother, kept his head and didn't go knocking people off right, left and centre, then the whole ongoing scheme would be seen to be working perfectly. If Tammam could limit himself to kicking a few backsides and the Kuwaitis went off chasing rainbows with the British, then the pressure would be off the Iraqi President and the Imam, and hopefully, as a result, the final seed would have been sown. With a bit of luck and some fine timing, Armstrong would vengefully put Hawthorn away; which even his own people in C section would find difficult to do and with an encouraging word from the obviously embittered Englishman, the President of Iraq at the insistence of Sulayman bin Abdulla, deposed, exiled and Internationally shamed Imam of Awabi, would press the required button, having given up all hope of trying to communicate with those bloody procrastinating Europeans. Then *finally*, it could all begin, and the greatest pleasure of all that the old General looked forward to, was getting his hands around the neck of a certain Arab gentleman destined to be the first casualty within the ranks of the whole fucking Unicorn movement. He savored the thought for a few more moments before tidying up his desk and ringing for the signals corporal.

# Chapter Twenty One

*October 2nd 1973 – Archers Post – Kenya – East Africa*

Maxwell woke at six; he'd had a restless night and his eyes were heavy lidded and dark ringed. He turned towards Helga, who was still sleeping contentedly next to him, curled up in a ball with the bed sheet pulled tightly over her head. He gently removed himself from the bed covers, taking care not to disturb Helga from her slumbers. When he'd showered and dressed he made his way downstairs to grab some coffee and toast before the labors of the day began. Kurt was already up. He looked deathly pale and had also suffered from lack of sleep, but due more to a continued night long battle to suppress rising waves of pain rather than efforts to anaesthetize an over-active thought process. Both men murmured barely audible words of morning greetings, sensibly omitting to question whether either had managed to achieve the sought after 'nirvana' state of true restfulness. After one cup of coffee and his first slice of crisp browned toast, Maxwell considered opening the conversation but Kurt beat him to it.

'Well, now we are by ourselves for a moment, perhaps you can tell me what is going on.'

Kurt gave out a stern and piercing look; viewed over the rim of a pale blue china coffee cup, his eyes locked on to Maxwell's in an unavoidable, penetrating gaze. Max put down the toast he was in the middle of buttering and waited purposely before answering. He knew there were lots of things he could say, many stories he could concoct and even lies to tell convincingly, but not to this man. Kurt knew him better, in some ways, than he knew himself, so he decided to come straight out with it.

'The plain and simple truth is that it looks very much as if those bastards in London tried to kill me. Unfortunately for them, but fortunately for me, someone made a fuck up and the bomb that was planted aboard my aero plane exploded at the airport, as opposed to in the air. I'm alive, but I think I've just about used up my nine and the next time this particular cat gets thrown from a high tree, will be the last. Someone wants me dead and I have two choices as of right now; one is to sit here and wait it out, and the other is to somehow take the battle to them. The only problem I have at present is establishing for sure, who 'they' really are, but I have some phone calls to make this morning which will hopefully shed more light on the matter.'

Max finished buttering another slice of toast whilst Kurt thoughtfully absorbed his words.

'Other than what you said at dinner last night, have you told Helga any more...... about the bomb, I mean?' The quick and simple reply to Kurt's question was,

'No.'

'Let me ask you something else, do you think Helga is safe here, whether or not you decide to carry on your private war in Kenya, or elsewhere?'

Maxwell answered reflectively,

'I don't think there is anything to worry about on that particular score; it's me they're after and not because of what I know but what I could do. It looks as if they simply want me removed as a negotiating point in all this bloody havoc and therefore, they would have nothing to gain by harming you or Helga, or anyone else come to that. I've been dragging the thing backwards and forwards through my mind all night and if the party trying to put me away really is the SIS, then I'm confident it's only me they're after. If I didn't believe that, you know I would tell you.'

Kurt put down the coffee cup and sank back in the chair, a look of complete despair shrouding his craggy features. He spoke again.

'Are you going to tell Helga about this bomb business at all?'

'Not yet,' Maxwell replied, '….. and maybe never. Let's just wait and see what today brings. I'm taking everything one step at a time so far, making sure my brain is fully engaged at each step. I cannot afford to make a wrong decision, or view anything with clouded judgment at the moment; but mark my words someone will pay for what happened in Dubai.'

'So whilst you're running around on your trail of vengeance or justice or whatever you like to appease your conscience by calling it,' said Kurt in a strained and bitter voice, 'who will be looking after my daughter and this farm, its workers, its stock, its crops? For Christ's sake, Maxwell, give all this up. Haven't you had enough? Leave it alone, let those imbeciles play their childish cloak and dagger games, but for our sakes, get out of it and do it now.'

The old man was trembling with emotion and spilling coffee down a clean shirt front which he suddenly noticed and exclaimed,

'Oh shit!' as he dragged himself from his chair and made his way out of the breakfast room to go and change.

'It's gone too far, Kurt,' Maxwell muttered to himself. 'It's gone too bloody far and I have to clear this matter up once and for all.'

He was disturbed from further thought by the clatter of high heel shoes in the hallway. Helga strode in, looking refreshed and radiant, dressed in a pink, light summer frock and matching shoes. She bounced over to where Maxwell was sitting and kissed him on the cheek affectionately and taking in the used place setting, said,

'Good morning, darling .... has father had breakfast already?' Maxwell forced himself to brighten up and replied that Kurt had spilt some coffee and gone upstairs to change his shirt. She gave him one of her matronly looks, saying,

'He seems to be doing a lot of that lately; you really must help me persuade him to get down to Nairobi for a complete check up, I'm very worried about him.' Maxwell agreed to talk to Kurt later and then asked what Helga planned to do that day.

'It really depends on you darling. What have you got organized, or is that still top secret?' She gave out a coy little smile, at the same time refilling Maxwell's cup with fresh coffee. He explained he had lots of things to clear up that morning, mostly by telephone and he hoped to be free by lunchtime.

'Good then,' said a bright and sparkling Helga, 'it's such a really lovely day I think I'll take Gypsy for a thoroughly good run up on the south strip and then get back for say . . . twelve thirty' Her eyes glinted mischievously, 'and then after lunch, maybe we could have a little siesta before doing the evening rounds?'

Maxwell smiled back convincingly and took her hand, squeezing it tightly.

'That sounds about right, but make sure you take one of the boys with you when you're riding, just in case.'

'Just in case of what'?' Helga queried. Max paused, careful to try and suppress a worried look.

'Just in case you have a fall or the horse goes lame or something. You know I don't really like you going out so far on your own, especially with these bloody poachers about.'

There ensued a small argument whilst Maxwell insisted someone go with her and Helga maintaining she was perfectly capable of looking after herself. Maxwell lost, as always, and tried to console himself with the thought that he really didn't believe she would be in any danger right now. Sir Charles had twenty four hours to come up with something on the bomb business and even if he was responsible, he wouldn't dare do anything to jeopardize the possibility of talking his way out of the problem first. Further violent action would be a last resort; especially in Kenya, Maxwell's back yard, so to speak. He grinned widely.

'OK, off you go then but don't be later than half past twelve or else I shall come looking for you.' Helga got up from the breakfast table and kissed his cheek again.

'Don't you worry about me being late, you just worry about being available for our siesta …… and by the way, I shall phone the doctor before I go and get him to come and have a look at those stitches. If you want he could stay for lunch; you know how much you enjoy listening to all his gory stories.'

Maxwell agreed resignedly and, after finishing the last of her coffee, Helga rushed away to get changed into her riding habit, shouting to Ralph on the way to tell the boys to prepare her favorite grey mare for the morning's exercise. Maxwell checked his watch. It had gone seven. He deserted breakfast and walked through to the study to begin his round of morning phone calls to Iraq, Dubai and other global points north. Once in the study, he closed the door and locked it, then looked through the flight bag which Ralph had thoughtfully placed there until he found the list of telephone numbers Rasheed had given him in Kirkuk.

He got through straight away to the religious leaders office in Baghdad and after a few preliminary words of conversation with a secretary, was switched directly to the Imam. The ensuing conversation was long and involved with Sulayman going off at tangents now and again, from which Maxwell had to gently pull him back, until they were both talking sensibly about relatively similar subjects. He informed the Imam about the content of his discussions in Dubai, giving a vote by vote account of how each member of the AGCC stood on the subject of Sulayman and the President of Iraq's proposed declaration. He also passed on Sheikh Khalifa's view that he would be unable to force through an AGCC agreement by the deadline put forward. Therefore, it seemed the only conclusion to be reasonably drawn was the one the Imam had expected, which was every man for himself and that included Saudi Arabia and Pakistan.

'You will have noticed, my friend that the price of gold is steadily creeping up and is expected to hit the ninety dollar mark by close of business today. This is putting pressure on both President al-Bakr and me to act. What is to happen with the European governments? Will you be talking to them directly or do we assume they are still trying to work out some kind of compromise amongst themselves?'

Maxwell assured the President that everything possible was being done through diplomatic channels to put the chairman of the AGCC and the President of the European Community together and he expected to hear something later that day. The Saudis were talking directly to the Americans, but the General opinion in the lower Gulf was that the Saudis would have to go eventually with the Islamic cause and it seemed the Americans knew and had planned for such an eventuality. The problem would peak out when and if, the Yanks decided to cover their backsides as much as possible by declaring a gold standard of their own. If that happened, it would be tantamount to telling the rest of the world, including Europe, that they were no longer interested in anything but their own survival, and on their own terms. The Imam agreed: he had intelligence indicating that a final date had been set by the Americans as close of business on Friday the twelfth, which still looked likely to be the date all final cards were to be played. The Imam drifted off verbally again for a few moments, going into all the background of his exile from the Oman, the righteousness of his cause and the predicted destiny of his one Islamic nation. Maxwell listened patiently without interruption. A long silence followed. Suddenly, Sulayman said,

'Well, goodbye, Maxwell, my old friend. I'll speak to you later.' The line was immediately disconnected; his conversation with probably the greatest Moslem leader of this century had ended. It was going to happen. Of that he was now sure. Maxwell made several more calls. One to Sheikh Khalifa in Dubai and a further one to Tom Hardmain; both informing him there was little or no change in the political situation, with Tom adding a small postscript concerning four pissed off Americans on the accident investigating team, who would appreciate a full written report on the airport incident or his immediate return to Dubai. Maxwell voted for the former and Tom agreed to calm the agitated Americans until the report arrived. Maxwell promised to keep in touch and Tom agreed to phone through the results of a full emergency council meeting scheduled for later that day.

At eleven o'clock he managed to get his broker out of bed in London, making arrangements to liquidate all his European shareholding stock and buy gold at anything up to ninety five dollars an ounce. He followed that up with a call to his Jersey bankers, giving instructions for certain short term money movements and authorizing forward buying contracts against supplies and fresh livestock for the farm. After making a few short notes on the morning's conversations, and entering the transactions relating to the farm in one of the accounts ledgers, he checked the time at just before twelve noon and called for Ralph to get ready and start lunch. He hesitated before picking up the phone for the last time, but after only a few seconds decided he had to work on the 'shit or bust' principal and dialed a number in Kirkuk.

He spoke to General Lubikov for ten minutes, explaining his problem and asking for the General's help. Lubikov told him that the answers to his questions were the same ones he needed himself and voiced concern over the deteriorating mental state of the Imam, who had retreated into a complete shell since hearing of the attempted assassination. As far as Sulayman was concerned, that one foul act had convinced him the Europeans were simply playing for time and the rather startling evidence pointing to the bomb being made and planted by the British had just about finally driven the point home. Lubikov said he had been requested by the Imam and the President, and had therefore passed on an instruction to the Soviet security services, to find out who the perpetrators were. He spoke confidently as he informed Maxwell that the full and efficient might of the KGB was behind this investigation and as soon as the General had something he would let him know. Lubikov went on to offer various levels of personal protection for himself and the Weismullers, but Maxwell refused.

'Just you find out who did it, that's all. The name of an agency or an individual, either will do, then leave the rest to me. You and I know better than most, we might all go up in smoke in a few weeks time, but let me assure you, whoever planted that bomb will not see another summer basking on the beaches of the South of France.'

The conversation ended and Maxwell put the phone down, grim faced and feeling inwardly sick. As he left the study a voice called out from the drawing room. Alf Johnson had arrived and was obviously eager to get at his favorite patient with a pair of sharp scissors.

\*\*\*\*\*\*

Helga jumped down from the saddle to stretch her legs and give Gypsy the chance of a drink in the shallows of the Ewaso Nyiro river. She headed for a spot shaded by a clump of thorn trees and on a trailing rein, the lean Irish mare ambled up to the water's edge and bent her neck to lap contentedly from a half silted rocky pool. This was one of the most peaceful spots on the farm and Helga came here often; sometimes to reflect in private tranquility and other times to cry out loud in a vacuum of seclusion unavailable to her within the confines of the sprawling farm house.

She must have dozed off for a few minutes, as the next thing she felt was a gentle nudging in the face from an anxious Gypsy. She reached up and patted the mare's face, shaking herself loose from the cool, comfortable spot beneath the towering thorns. Gypsy raised her foreleg in a delicate hovering movement as an indication that she was eager to be away again. Helga brushed her hair back once more and retied it in a ponytail; dusted herself down and made ready to mount. She checked the time and calculated that a gentle trot along the river bank for a mile or so would bring her out onto the east track and from there she could head directly back to the house and be just in time for lunch.

As she mounted the restless mare, much scurrying could be heard in the bushes lining the opposite side of the river bank, followed by the screams of a family of marauding baboons as they attempted to beat away the attention of half a dozen waterbuck heading for the river's edge. Suddenly Gypsy pricked up her ears; she had heard something above the natural wildlife noises emanating from the river bank and then, after a short while, Helga heard it too. It sounded like a helicopter, but very far away to the north east. She hoped it wasn't those damn poachers again and for the second time that morning she checked the saddle clipped Purdy shotgun. The gun was fitted with two, three inch magnum shells and she had a further ten, loose in her jacket pocket; enough to stop just about anything on two legs. The sound of the helicopter dimmed in the distance and although she strained up in the saddle to obtain a clearer view over the low lying scrub and veldt grass, she could see nothing. Helga and Gypsy moved off up the river bank in the direction of the game reserve and the eastern track leading back home.

******

The single rotor of the dusted, dull black Hughes 500D helicopter juddered slowly to a halt as the two occupants released their safety belts and climbed out of the door-less airframe. The two men were tall and heavily built, wearing army bush combat jackets and webbing belts over sweatshirts and khaki, narrow bottomed fatigue trousers. Camouflaged beanie hats shaded their eyes and as the pilot began to unload two canvas satchels from the rear seat of the helicopter, the second man scanned the surrounding terrain with a pair of powerful field glasses. The man with the glasses was an old hand at this business and had spent most of the past fifteen years in Africa as a mercenary soldier. He was fair haired and suntanned, standing over six feet in his thick, rubber soled, combat boots. As a matter of politeness, he preferred the title, 'soldier of fortune' rather than 'mercenary.' Things had changed somewhat since the days of Mad Mike Hoare, and now mercenary soldiers were highly skilled technicians fighting well planned guerilla campaigns with sophisticated equipment and properly trained men. Gone was the time when you simply got together a crowd of mentally unbalanced ex-marines and issued them with a Bren gun and five hundred rounds of ammunition, with the intention of removing the King of Bonga Bonga before his next birthday. No, Major Sutton was a dedicated professional, and had been all his life, even though the British Army in General and number five commando in particular, had not thought so when they had dishonorably discharged him seventeen years previously.

His partner in today's little adventure had been with him for five years and had worked for the past two of those within the military wing of the Central African National Congress. The CANC had little choice in the matter of his employment; it was either him or the Cubans and after the rather embarrassing political fiasco in Angola some years back, it was felt throughout most of the numerous African liberation movements that although Castro's money was more than welcome, his advisors were not. They were simply outdated. One couldn't go round raping the local populace any more whenever one felt like it and the horrible habit of sticking babies on the end of bayonets was definitely out as a disciplinary tactic.

Business for the well trained and well drilled British soldier of fortune had become brisk lately and although Major Sutton was not used to doing quick, one-off jobs such as this one, the money was good and it would only take a week of his time. Notwithstanding all that, Major Sutton and his partner, Michaels, had agreed that a short, paid holiday in sunny Spain would do them both good anyway. The major put down the field glasses after satisfying himself that no-one had noticed their covert intrusion of Kenyan air space, or if they had, they weren't immediately following them by ground or by air.

Sergeant Michaels dropped the satchels down on the ground in front of the major and began to unpack a series of components that would quickly be made up into a pair of lightweight, Beretta BM59 automatic rifles. Two minutes was all it took for a deftly fingered sergeant to assemble the weaponry, test the action and fit a twenty round ammunition clip to each. This little operation didn't require heavy fire power and the four and a half kilo BM59 was the ideal weapon for both accuracy and reliability. The two hard faced mercenaries checked all remaining contents of the satchels; then hoisted them on to broad shoulders and set off to climb the small hillock, hiding the helicopter from the river bank and place themselves in readiness for the arrival of their target.

They didn't have long to wait, their intelligence information had been accurate. Michaels, with his ear pressed closely to the ground, heard the vibrating thump of steel shod hooves, minutes before Sutton saw horse and rider jump into view, cantering up along the river bank to their left. The major hesitated for a moment before taking careful aim and letting loose the first bullet. It would be a crying shame to kill such a beautiful mount, but those were the fortunes of his kind of war; he pulled back gently on the trigger and the great grey mare bucked up on her hind quarters as the first two high velocity bullets hit her square on the rump. Both horse and rider fell to the ground and as they did so, Major Sutton placed a further spread of six more rounds into the mare's head. She was dead instantly and before the echo of the last shot had faded, the sergeant was moving from behind his cover in a rapid, stooping run towards both horse and rider, pulling the dazed and trapped female from underneath the dead animal. The major joined his partner at the double. Covering the scene on bended knees, he scanned the surrounding bushes for signs of retaliation. All was quiet except for the sound of fluttering plovers and chattering hammerkops, disturbed by the unexpected violence of the moment.

The major continued to scan all points of the compass whilst both men waited for the noise of the agitated local wildlife to die down. One of the rules of this game was ..... no witnesses. After a minute, all returned to acceptable quietness. The major nodded to his sergeant. Michaels extracted a small medical kit from his satchel and filled a hypodermic syringe with a clear liquid from a smoked glass phial. The woman was still out cold and the major hoped to hell she was all right. There was no time to give her a detailed examination and although her face was pale, and breathing shallow, Sutton decided to risk it. He gave a murmured word of permission to Michaels, who injected the contents of the syringe into her arm, and then with the medical kit re-stowed in the satchel, the two mercenaries picked up their target in a chair and shoulder carry and loped back over the low rise in the direction of the helicopter.

So far, so good, thought the major, as he strapped the woman across the back seat and Michaels wound up the struggling turbine to get the helicopter away from the scene of the crime and over the border to Tanzania as quickly as possible. With a bit of luck and some damn good piloting they could be clear of the border in an hour and a half and with a quick re-fuel from barrels stashed at a location just inside Tanzania, could be safely down to Arusha in two. If the private jet was waiting, as promised, at Arusha airfield and all the correct paperwork had been arranged, they should be able to take off again straight away. With air ambulance emergency clearance over North Africa, the whole team could be nicely tucked away in Spain by midnight. This could turn out to be the easiest twenty thousand quid they had ever made, or the hardest.

So far everything had gone well, but being of a Generally suspicious nature, Major Sutton was wary of the fact, especially knowing the identity of his present employers. The helicopter took off, hovered for a few seconds, and then swung once on the rotor, pointing steadily south before heading for the border at tree top level and disappearing into the distance, swallowed up by the shimmering late morning heat haze.

# Chapter Twenty Two

*October 2nd 1973 – Archers Post – Kenya*

Maxwell re-buttoned his shirt before leaving the bedroom, hot on the heels of a constantly chattering Doctor Johnson who could be heard calling for Ralph as he made his way down the stairs; demanding his first glass of chilled wine immediately, whether lunch was ready or not. How the hell Alf Johnson could fly an aero plane and treat so many patients as well as he did, during any hour after midday, amazed not only Maxwell but half the population of Kenya. He was a tremendous character who should have retired years ago but no-one really wanted his job, so he carried on, jockeying his little Cessna around all over the place, drunk or sober and managing to save quite a few lives in the process. He had neatly removed all the stitches in Maxwell's back and inspected his burns and scars carefully. All he could offer to improve the situation was a small tube of ointment containing some sort of cortisone base which would speed up the healing process and hopefully reduce the level of permanent scarring. But apart from that, he was happy with the way the wounds were progressing and would now like his free lunch please, starting with the wine and moving on to actual solids if it became absolutely necessary.

Ralph and the staff buzzed about on the veranda laying lunch for four. Kurt was already seated in one of the loungers when Maxwell eventually caught up with Alf; both 'bwana's' were chatting happily away. Kurt appeared significantly improved since the morning; his eyes had cleared and a certain amount of color had returned to his face. Alf noted the time was nearly a quarter to one and enquired as to the whereabouts of Helga. Maxwell replied that she had gone riding that morning and would be back shortly. Alf quickly took up the subject of absent females and used it as an excuse to tell one of his often fascinating, and normally ribald, stories about his medical adventures since they had last met and within seconds had Kurt giggling like a schoolboy. This was going to be a great lunch. He hoped the bloody phone wouldn't ring to spoil it all and that Helga would hurry up and get here to perfect everything. He poured more chilled white Frascati for Alf. Over an hour passed by before everyone began to visibly show their concern. Conversation had become forced and Kurt was passing concerned glances in Maxwell's direction. Eventually Alf stopped in mid sentence and said to no-one in particular,

'It's Helga, isn't it?'

'Yes,' said Maxwell tightly, 'it's not like her to be this late; she knew you were coming, of course and was looking forward to us all having lunch together.' He moved about restlessly on the veranda, constantly staring up towards the run in from the east trail where he expected her to initially appear.

'Well then,' the ebullient Alf replied, 'let's not all sit here looking morose and pissed off, let's get on our way and look for her. My Cessna's at the strip, it's much better for spotting than your old tank; we can be up on the south run in fifteen minutes. She's probably had a hard morning's exercise, stopping by the river on her way back, and dropped off to sleep or something. Come on, Max, get your jacket and some specs and let's get at it.' Maxwell walked over and touched Kurt's hand reassuringly,

'We won't be long, Kurt. Alf's probably right. She's just stopped off somewhere. We'll find her, don't worry.'

Kurt remained silent as Max ran upstairs and grabbed his jacket and a pair of binoculars. When he arrived out the back of the house, Alf was already waiting for him in the Land Rover and they shot off towards the airstrip in a swirling cloud.

When they were up in the air and Maxwell had his large scale ordinance map stretched out on his knees, Alf looked for some kind of instruction before settling the single engined, high wing monoplane down into a low level cruise. Max decided the best thing to do was fly down to Archers Gate, a little further south and pick up the river, sweeping either side until they reached in to the Buffalo Springs game reserve. If they had not spotted her by then, Max decided he would ask for the help of the rangers, but he didn't want a load of men and vehicles wandering around the area, confusing all the tracks and destroying any possible evidence if something had really happened. He hoped to God nothing had, but already he was acquiring a familiar and dreaded sinking feeling in the pit of his stomach. His hands vibrated faintly as he picked up the binoculars and concentrated on sweeping the ground below. Within minutes they were approaching the river and Alf began to bank the Cessna round in a lazy left hand turn and lock onto a westerly heading; the magnificent backdrop of Mount Kenya now filling the window lights. Alf held the aero plane steady at three hundred feet which was enough height to clear most of the taller trees and yet low enough to obtain a clear view of the ground. After ten minutes flying they reached the main river bend and turned more southerly in the direction of the reserve.

Suddenly Max spotted a dark shape on his right, about eighty yards from the river bank and just before the junction of the east trail leading directly back to the farm. Maxwell tapped Alf's shoulder and he responded by putting the aircraft into a tight banking turn above the trail. It was unmistakably Gypsy and through the glasses he could make out the streaks of dried blood on her forehead and nostrils. Maxwell smacked the instrument coaming with a clenched fist and forced clipped words through gritted teeth.

'Alf, can you put down somewhere here?' He knew it was a senseless question; there was no way anyone in their right mind would attempt to land an aircraft of any description in this area, dotted with trees, anthills and potholes.

'No way, Maxwell,' the doctor replied, 'we'll have to carry on up to the game reserve compound where we can get a clear run in; five minutes and we'll be there. Just hang on.'

Alf Johnson pulled the wings level again and opened up the throttle, heading directly for the ranger camp. As the little aero plane came to a halt from its short bumpy landing roll, a striped Land Rover appeared, rushing out from the stockade to meet them; Joe Mogambo was at the wheel. Maxwell jumped out and quickly explained what was wrong; a second vehicle was already bringing up the rear loaded with four armed rangers. Alf turned the Cessna round and took off for the farm airstrip again, leaving Maxwell and the rangers to head off to the spot where Helga's grey mare had been seen. In twenty minutes they were at the trail junction and Max gave instructions to stop the vehicles about one hundred and fifty yards short of the motionless, stiff legged carcass. The rangers spread out in a wide circle looking for any evidence, clues to what had happened, or tracks which might indicate who had been in the area that day. Maxwell and Joe walked carefully up to the dead animal and checked its wounds. Joe said,

'Well, whoever did this was a good shot and knew what he was about, Mister Maxwell. I would say the first shot in the rear brought her down and probably whilst she was falling, the gunman put a good spread in her head, killing her more or less instantly. The gun looks as if it was a high velocity, low caliber, type and unless the animal has been moved, the shots must have come from somewhere over there.'

He turned and pointed in the direction of a rise in the ground, about sixty or seventy yards away. There were tears in his eyes as Maxwell asked Joe to help him take the saddle and equipment off the horse. Everything was there, including the Purdy and the saddle roll. He checked the shotgun; it was still loaded and hadn't been fired. Joe helped him back to the Land Rover with the gear.

'What the hell's happened here, Mister Max? There's no sign of Miss Helga and not a sight of vehicle tracks or anything. Who would want to harm such a lovely lady? How did they get away?'

Maxwell was tense with anger and grim faced, tears trickling down each cheek. Just then, one of the boys shouted from the top of the rise. They dumped the gear in the Land Rover and ran up towards the shouting ranger. He was bent down over some shining cartridge cases, there were eight in all. Joe pulled a pencil from his top pocket and picked up one of the shell cases. It was a 7.62 by 51 millimeter centre fire case, manufactured by Beretta and a current NATO standard It could have come from a variety of weapons but had more than likely been used in a late model BM59 semi-automatic rifle, the favorite tool of many agencies, including the Secret Intelligence Service. Maxwell took the pencil from Joe and gingerly picked up each shell case, wrapping them in his handkerchief. There were several footprints around and Joe estimated two men had been here for a short time; there was no other evidence, no cigarette butts or used matches, sweet papers or any other clues as to the identity of the gunmen. Two more rangers were searching behind the low hill and found signs of a helicopter having landed; the impressions of the belly skids could be clearly seen. Maxwell studiously measured the skid markings and noted the dimensions down on a slip of paper, hoping for a clue as to the type of helicopter used. There didn't seem to be any sign of a struggle around the landing area and Maxwell supposed that Helga had either been drugged or knocked unconscious as there was no way she would have boarded the helicopter willingly; especially if she had been in full control of her faculties.

There was nothing more anyone could do at the kidnap site, so Max agreed that Joe should take him back to the farm and the rest of the boys ought to get back to the ranger compound and put out a General radio alert, just in case there was an outside chance the abductors were still in Kenya. Maxwell was silent all the way back to the farm and sat in the passenger seat of the Land Rover gripping the Purdy so tight that his knuckles turned white. Joe didn't speak either. There was little he could say to help or console his friend and neighbor at this time. When they got back to the farm house, Alf was waiting for them on the veranda, an anxious Ralph hovering in the background.

'Where's Kurt?' Maxwell said sharply.

'I've told him the worst and put him to bed with a light sedative,' replied the doctor, 'and I think you could use a drink, young man. Ralph dashed into the house and fetched a large whisky and soda, which Max took without comment. He played with the drink somberly, glazed eyes glinting with pent-up anger in the fading afternoon sunlight.

'Do you want me to stay over for a while?' asked Alf.

'I'd appreciate it, if you would,' said Maxwell, 'as you know Kurt is far from well and something like this could kill him.'

'But tell me Max,' growled the doctor, 'who on earth would want to kidnap Helga; there's no guerilla activity around here and even poachers wouldn't do anything to harm a European. It doesn't make any sense?'

'That, my old friend,' came the resolute reply, 'is what I'm about to find out.' He turned to Ralph.

'Let's have something hot to eat Ralph, I've a suspicion it's going to be a long night and I don't quite know yet where my next meal could come from, once I get started on this thing.'

Ralph hurried away, a sob in his voice, as he said,

'Yes, Mister Max, right away.'

Without another word, Maxwell left the veranda and went up to the bedroom to be alone with his grief and his anger.

It was exactly seven o'clock when he reappeared and joined the others downstairs. Kurt remained in his room and the last time Alf had checked him, he was still sleeping soundly. Joe had been on the radio most of the afternoon as reports came in from all the ranger stations and border patrols. Parts of the puzzle were being slowly pieced together, as it was established that earlier that morning there had been reports of illegal helicopter activity on the Tanzania border and in fact a black, unregistered Hughes 500 had been spotted by a border patrol at about one o'clock, moving south at tree top height at high speed. The army had sent up one of its own machines to try and intercept but they were unable to catch the Hughes before it crossed into Tanzanian territory. The Tanzanian police and the military had been asked for assistance on the basis that the infiltrators were poachers; something which fired up a positive response on both sides of the border and generated some immediate action. The Kenyan authorities were now waiting for the Tanzanians to report back; nothing more could be done at present.

Maxwell joined the doctor and the game warden in getting stuck into a large plate of veal and potatoes. Half-way through the meal Harry Jordan called up on the VHF radio and informed Maxwell his plane was ready with full tanks, should he need it, and he would stay at the strip overnight to monitor the aircraft radio frequencies in case something came up. Maxwell thanked him and finished his meal off with several cups of strong coffee. Minutes later a report came in from the Tanzanian military at Arusha. An abandoned helicopter had been found in the bush surrounding the civilian airfield there and it had been assumed the occupants had probably left the area by aircraft. All flight movements were being checked for that day and it was hoped to have further news in an hour. Maxwell looked despairingly at Joe.

'It seems as if the bastards have got away, they could be anywhere by now. Get back on the radio, Joe, and get me all you can on that fucking helicopter; any painted out registration numbers, engine serial numbers and any details on paperwork they may have found that will give us an idea of where it came from, or better still, who owns it.'

Joe retired back to the radio room to set about his task. By nine o'clock most of the pieces were falling into shape and Maxwell sat down with Joe and Alf to review what they had learnt so far.

'OK gentlemen, let's see what we have to date and try to work out our next move. First, we have a clear indication that this was a well planned and executed kidnap operation and, what is more to the point, extremely well financed. Whoever is behind this caper has money and influence. We know there were only two men involved in the actual physical kidnap, one of which was a damned good helicopter pilot and perhaps the other, a trained sniper. Next, we now know the helicopter had been purchased, and paid for in cash, from Eastern Geophysical who are presently working on a seismic survey in Rwanda. This happened only yesterday and they took off from Kigali Airport perfectly legally at nine o'clock in the morning with a flight plan filed for Entebbe. After that, the bloody thing disappeared and between then and when it was found this afternoon, it had been nearly stripped of all unnecessary trimming to increase range and had also been repainted. All of that takes a lot of organization and facilities and money. This has been a highly professional operation from the beginning. Now, we find that at two thirty local time, an American registered Canadair air ambulance left Arusha on emergency clearance, taking a direct route to Europe with a flight plan filed for Heathrow, London. We know the ambulance followed its planned route as far as Tripoli but has now, to all intents and purposes, faded from the face of the earth. We also know, the aircraft is legally registered to Arab Wings airline and was booked on a mission to pick up a female patient suffering from severe kidney failure. The aircraft was boarded in Arusha by the so-called patient in a coma, along with two doctors producing British passports and medical documentation. Now, where do we go from here?'

All three sat in quiet contemplation. Doc Johnson spoke first,

'Tell me, Maxwell, maybe I shouldn't be saying this but your father used to work for the British SIS, didn't he? I would have thought there were people in that organization who could help you. Surely a phone call to London would get you some answers in a very short time.' Maxwell looked across sharply,

'That isn't quite what I had in mind, Alf.'

'Oh!' said the sour faced doctor, 'excuse me, I just thought .... ' There Maxwell cut him off.

'Look Alf, just accept the fact that I am not in a position to discuss this problem with any British intelligence agency at the moment and on that particular point you will just have to trust me.'

Maxwell's face had turned dark, his voice bitter as he got up from the table and strode out into the hall. Ralph shouted at him from the study,

'Mister Max, Mister Max, there's a telephone call for you from a place called Kirkuk and someone who won't give his name says it's urgent that he speak with you.'

Maxwell turned and raced into the study, taking the phone from a confused Ralph. It was Lubikov.

'Good evening, Mr. Armstrong, this is your favorite Russian General here.' There was little sign of humor in his voice. 'I know of your very sad situation down there and as I promised yesterday our men from 'the office' have been working on it.'

Maxwell asked breathlessly, if the General had any news.

'Well, I do have news though whether it be good or bad I don't really know. As you are aware we have some good connections in Tanzania and I would say we are about an hour ahead of yourself in receiving information on the kidnapping. This has given us time to spread our net wide and from our radar bases in Libya and with some unexpected co-operation from our Mediterranean naval forces, we have managed to trace the final destination of the air ambulance, which you must already know about. It landed at Valencia airport about twenty minutes ago and our men are following the situation closely. What do you want us to do?'

Maxwell's mind raced.

'Are the Spanish authorities aware of what is going on?' he asked quickly.

'Not at this moment, no. I would advise against getting them involved just now, until we are definitely sure who is behind it all. Do not worry my friend; our men will not lose sight of them whatever they do. I will ring you back when I have more news, but I think you ought to prepare yourself to accept the fact that your people in Bowater House may have had more than a passing interest in what is going on and therefore we should be most circumspect in our actions. Trust me, my friend, we will help you on this one and please make sure you don't contact President al-Bakr, the Imam or any of the other Gulf rulers. There are some serious leaks of information in that area and until we decide what to do, I want this kept strictly between you and me. Do I have your word on that?'

'You have it,' whispered a tight lipped Maxwell.

Lubikov disconnected without further comment and Maxwell returned to the dining room to rejoin the others. Ralph, Joe and the doctor were waiting for him. They all looked up expectantly. He told them he now had reliable information as to the whereabouts of the air ambulance and he was expecting more news soon. No one wished to question Maxwell in his current state of mind as to where the information had come from and Ralph went to pour some coffee, but Maxwell put his hand over his cup and asked for a large whisky. Another three quarters of an hour went by before the telephone rang again and, having left all the doors open leading to the study, Maxwell could hear the ring well. At the first long tone, he leapt up to answer it. Lubikov spoke straight away.

'Listen to me carefully. The *air* ambulance has taken off again with one of the so-called doctors on board and a *road* ambulance has left Valencia Airport moving in the direction of Alicante with two heavy looking male nurses inside, as well as your young lady and the other doctor. Our men are now following them. There is no way they will be able to leave Spain now and we have them well covered; do you want to have some personal involvement from here on in or leave it to our people?' Maxwell replied without hesitation.

'I want to be there; I want those bastards fried and I want to know who is behind this. I'll need some help though and at this moment it seems your guys are the only people I can trust.'

'You have nothing to fear from us, Armstrong; how quickly can you get to Spain? Once you are there, we will be able to provide you with everything you require as far as men and materials are concerned.'

Maxwell thought for a moment. 'Let me check on flights out of here and ring you back . . . say, in half an hour.'

'Good,' said the General, 'I'll be here waiting for your call and, remember, not a word about our involvement to anyone, for all our sakes.' Maxwell reassured Lubikov once more and put down the phone, instantly picking it up again to dial Nairobi Airport in an attempt to locate a friend of his in Kenya Airways.

Within fifteen minutes he'd established the departure of a flight to London Heathrow at 02.30 the following morning and with a little maneuvering, his friend assured him he could get him on the ten o'clock flight from Heathrow to Valencia that same day, having him in Spain by lunchtime. Maxwell called Lubikov back and told him the news. The General assured him that someone would meet him at the airport and would have the means to communicate directly with Kirkuk base should that be needed. Lubikov wished him luck and rang off. Maxwell rushed upstairs and packed a bag, grabbed his wallet full of credit cards and searched through a drawer littered with different amounts of foreign currency, until he managed to put together a hundred pounds in sterling and over a thousand dollars. That would be enough for immediate use. He leapt downstairs again and called Harry up on the radio, telling him to get the Cherokee started and warmed up as they were off to Nairobi.

\*\*\*\*\*\*

Flight zero nine two to London was finishing loading its last passengers as Maxwell arrived at the aircraft steps. The deputy General manager of the airline had met him at the private aircraft park and rushed him through all the airport formalities. Maxwell thanked Peter Ngulu profusely for his help and apologized for getting him out of bed, as he rushed up the steps of the waiting 707. Peter's last words were that a ticket would be waiting for him at the Iberia desk in Heathrow's terminal two, covering his trip to Valencia, and if there were any problems he was to contact his own Kenya Airways staff in London. The two men shook hands; boarding steps were dragged away and the aircraft prepared to take off. During the seven hour flight, Maxwell managed to snatch some semblance of sleep with the assistance of a helpful flight attendant who managed to arrange for three empty seats in the business class section to be made available, allowing him to stretch out in some relative comfort during the whole of the direct non-stop journey.

# Chapter Twenty Three

*October 3rd 1973 – London – UK*

His arrival in London was uneventful, although his passport was checked thoroughly at the immigration desk and, no doubt, Sir Charles would know of his arrival in the capital within minutes if an alert had been issued, but that was one of the risks he would have to take. There were some hours to go before he could board the Iberian aircraft and with the help of a very efficient Kenyan Airways ground hostess, he was able to book on the flight with hand baggage only and rest in the Iberian executive lounge until nine thirty. Maxwell had not been bothered by anyone and was fairly sure he wasn't being watched, but he stayed mentally alert; lots of things could go wrong at this point, especially if he got careless. There was little need to worry, he was allowed to board the Iberian flight without questioning or hassle and by ten fifteen the short haul jet was winging it's way south, over the English Channel towards Spain.

Flight time was just over two hours and accounting for the local time difference, Maxwell checked through customs in Valencia airport at twenty past one. There to meet him, in the marble floored arrivals hall was a tall, clean shaven, angular faced man who had a Latin complexion and engaging smile. He recognized Maxwell immediately from a photograph he was holding and walked up boldly to greet him. The man spoke in English with a strong Spanish accent and was immaculately dressed in brown heavyweight trousers and red Spanish leather boots, topped by a well cut suede leather jacket and cream open necked shirt. After only a few minutes preliminary conversation with the gentleman, who introduced himself as Juan Pascall, Maxwell was impressed. He told him immediately who he was, what he was doing there and the latest information on what he referred to as the 'hit.' He explained he was a naturally born Spanish citizen and his father had fought with the Communista against Franco. He had been employed at an early age by the Soviet security forces and now worked within C Section of the KGB, which had recently replaced the old Department Five of the First Chief Directorate known then as the Mokrie Dela. Maxwell had not heard of a 'C' Section but knew the activities of Department Five well. These men were professional killers and worth an army of lesser trained individuals.

'Why are you telling me all this, Juan? All I need to know is where Helga is and how we're going to get her out of the clutches of those murdering bastards. I really am not interested in your background or why you're here, as long as you're able to help me.'

The Spanish communist flashed one of his reassuring smiles; which must be all part of the training, Maxwell thought humorously, as they all seem to have them; the really dangerous ones anyway.

'I tell you this, Mr. Armstrong,' replied the impressive Spaniard, 'because I want you to know I have orders from the highest authority to help you in any way I can and if we two professionals are going to work together, we must maintain a high level of trust in one another. I know nearly all there is to know about you, but you know nothing about me, so I am telling you; and if there is anything else you wish to ask, please do so.'

Maxwell absorbed the point of comment which he felt did not warrant a reply. He looked deeply and steadily into those twinkling Latin eyes for a few seconds, during which time all the necessarily unspoken words were said. Juan was the first to avert his gaze. He picked up Maxwell's couple of bags and said,

'Right then, let's go.'

Outside in the open car park, a white Citroen was waiting, complete with running engine and Spanish driver. The driver was introduced as Eduardo and nothing else, just Eduardo. Maxwell and Juan seated themselves in the back and Eduardo rallied the vehicle expertly through the late lunchtime traffic around Valencia until they were on the motorway heading south towards Alicante. On the way, Juan explained that the 'hit' had holed up in a villa about half way between Valencia and Alicante, just outside a little village called Benidoleig. The nearest reasonable sized town was Ondara and that was where they had set up a small headquarters to plan the rescue operation. The development where Helga was being held was itself guarded permanently by its own security staff. The villa property was completely walled and fitted with high technology security and anti-personnel devices, linked back to a central control room beneath the main house. There were two more guest houses on the one and a half acre estate but, to Juan's knowledge, these were not presently being used. It would be a tough nut to crack, but his men were working on it and would hopefully have come up with something by the time they reached Ondara, in about half an hour's time. Maxwell checked his watch.

'Have you been able to establish who owns the house?' he asked.

'Yes.' Juan reached into his jacket pocket and pulled out a small notepad.

'The house is owned by a London based Lebanese business man named Suhail Jaffery. He rarely uses the house and leaves it to be let by the development management company, located in the village. It's been taken on a one month let by a British company called Crowthorne Investments, for the stated purpose of accommodating a small, high level conference of some of that company's directors. We are having the company checked out now in London and will hopefully know something by tomorrow morning; but, on the face of it, the deal looks legitimate.'

'No doubt, it would,' commented Maxwell, 'if the SIS are involved.'

'Ah, there we have a minor point of confusion. We have checked out all our contacts in Spain and to date we are unable to identify any unusual movements of SIS operatives in the area and as of today, they consist of two agents operating out of the British Consulate in Alicante, four more working under the cover of an import and export company in Madrid, one in Denia watching the undercover British criminal element and one more in Benidorm, monitoring the 'drugs' trade. Very mundane work, I must admit, but obviously essential in terms of the great master plan laid down by your Sir Charles Hawthorn.' Juan laughed openly at the puzzled look on Maxwell's face.

'We have someone inside every SIS operation in Europe, Mr. Armstrong; do not fret, we will find out what is happening and we will also get your Miss Weismuller back for you; of this, you can be sure. When she is eventually released, we have made arrangements to get you both out by sea from Denia and down to Algeria. From there, you will be taken back to Kenya on one of our air cargo transports. Have patience and faith my friend; when we do a job, it is done properly.'

Eduardo pulled the car up outside a terraced building in the middle of the town of Ondara signposted as Plaza de Carro. The three men left the car and waited outside whilst Juan talked into a small two way radio he'd taken from his jacket. The black, iron grilled door to number forty seven opened, and the three travelers went inside. Maxwell was somewhat apprehensive at first, especially as the door closed with an ominous click behind him and he found himself sandwiched between the two Spaniards, Juan in front and the expressionless, silent, Eduardo behind. The narrow passageway opened out onto a small cobblestoned courtyard, dominated by a central, circular, stone fountain, around which sat two more men in their early thirties. They looked lean and fit as they sprang to their feet, upon seeing Juan. He introduced them to Maxwell as Nickolai and Alexis, the two Russian members of his team.

'Nickolai is one of our best alarms systems men,' Juan explained.

'He will get us into the villa and Alexis here is an expert combat technician; he will get us out.'

Maxwell studied the two Russians for a moment. They looked capable of anything and knowing the company they were keeping, Maxwell decided they probably were.

\*\*\*\*\*\*

Major Sutton stood on the balcony of the comfortable white painted villa and took in his surroundings. He had already been shown the communications and control room in the basement of the house by the two Spaniards who had met his plane at Valencia. They were both rough looking types and not very communicative in any language, but he had been convinced by his employer that both men were reliable and that was all that mattered. The major checked his watch. Michaels would be joining him at the villa later that evening after escorting the crew of the air ambulance to Tripoli. The aircraft and its crew would disappear there for a while and Michaels would shortly be on his way back to Spain on a scheduled Libyan Airlines flight to Alicante, hopefully having erased all traces of their exit from the African continent.

The whole project had gone well up to this point, and Sutton was pleased with the attention to detail his employers had shown in all the arrangements made for their journey to Spain. The job itself also seemed simple enough; just hold the girl for a while, or until orders were received regarding her disposal. He hoped she'd be sensible when she recovered from the drugs Michaels had been pumping into her during the flight. He hated having to get violent with women, but if he had to, he would. The view from the balcony was magnificent. On the horizon the Denia coastline fell back towards the Gerona valley floor, packed with fruit laden orange trees, providing a carpet of greenery right up to the foot of the mountain where the villa had been built as part of a quiet and exclusive development at Aldea De Las Cuevas.

Directly below, in full view from the balcony, the winding surfaced road led up to the estate; the only road and only access for vehicles. The house was well sited and could be held secure for a long time, if necessary, although the major didn't expect any trouble and he knew it would take an army to get him and Michaels out once they had established a basic defense line. He walked back into the house to check his hostage. She was still comatose although her pulse was steady and the major calculated about another hour before she fully regained her senses, enough time to have a really good look around the estate.

He called down to the two Spaniards in the control room, telling them he was going walkabout and to monitor his movements on the closed circuit television system. The whole estate was north facing, so he decided to start on the bottom north wall and work his way back up towards the main house; first checking out the two small guest houses, nestling in a clump of pine trees next to the lower, gated entrance. The whole reconnaissance consumed an hour and a half of time and the major took careful notes on his way round the walled villa complex. The only real weakness in the defenses was the location of some trees by the smaller of the two guest houses. The tall pines were situated close to the wall and with minimal athletic ability an intruder could grapple the lower branches and haul himself over, without setting off the pressure plate alarms set in the wall coping tiles. He ordered one of the Spaniards to set up an extra video camera on the roof of the guest house and link it in to the main surveillance system before it got too dark. He was then as satisfied as he could be and thought it time to check the woman again.

When he opened the main bedroom door he could see she was awake and the effect of the drugs was obviously starting to wear off. He switched on a light and approached the bed where she was laying. She tried to speak, her lips moving, but nothing came out. The major checked her pupil dilation and her pulse; both were returning to normal.

'Well, Miss Weismuller, how are you feeling?' said Major Sutton.

'Don't try to speak just yet, nod your head if you can hear me and understand what I am saying.'

Helga's eyes flickered and eventually she nodded her head, twice.

'Good,' continued her captor, 'now I will try to explain the situation you are in. Firstly, you were abducted early this morning from your farm in Kenya and are now in Spain.' He paused for a second.

'Whereabouts in Spain is of little consequence at this particular moment. You have been permanently drugged during your journey here and you are now suffering from the after effects of those drugs. I would advise you not to try and stand up for another half an hour or so but I assure you that you'll be completely recovered by later on this evening. The chemicals administered to you have no permanent effect and we do not mean you any physical harm. We will all, hopefully, be spending a few pleasant days together in this rather magnificent villa, and as long as you behave yourself and don't try to escape, we should get along fine. This is your bedroom and you will find a selection of clothes and underwear in the wardrobe. I should warn you, this house is protected by a very sophisticated intruder alarm system, that is as good at keeping people in as it is at keeping them out.' He looked for signs of comprehension.

'There are four of us here and one will be with you at all times, except of course, in here. The windows of this room are fitted with security grills and sonic alarms. If you as much as breathe on a window pane, we will know about it, so for your own comfort and the sake of an easy life, please stay away from them. If you do not co-operate with us, we will be forced to drug you again and continued use of the particular drug we would administer will eventually cause damage to your brain.'

Helga stared back glassily at her kidnapper. He smiled condescendingly.

'We wouldn't want such a beautiful young lady as yourself walking around with half a brain, now, would we? I suggest you get some more rest and when you're ready we'll rustle you up something to eat. Do not attempt to drink any liquids until you have eaten, as due to one of the side effects of the drugs you've been receiving, this will result in certain embarrassing bladder malfunctions. Don't ask me to tell you why you are here because, quite honestly, I don't know. I am a paid operator and I'm simply doing a job, so don't ask a load of useless questions when you get up and about because I really do not know the answers.'

With that, Major Sutton left the room and extinguished the light, leaving his prisoner in darkness. He checked the time again.

'Another hour or so and Michaels should be here,' he muttered to himself. He moved back on to the balcony after fixing himself a lean gin and tonic; partly to enjoy the cool evening air and partly to check out a dark green canvas bag containing an assortment of weaponry provided by his employers. He placed the bag on the floor and unzipped it, pulling out two Heckler and Kock MP5, nine millimeter submachine pistols, fitted with folding stocks and banana magazines. They were used but well oiled and well cared for. Resting in the bottom of the bag were killing machines he was more used to handling; three Colt M16 assault rifles. They were brand new and provided the stopping power he needed if any attempt were made to try and take this miniature Spanish fortress. The major was well satisfied and proceeded to caringly strip each weapon and clean it; just in case.

******

Maxwell slid back into the cover of some nearby bushes as the headlights of a car swept the tarmac road about fifty yards below him. He waited in the cover for a few minutes until he heard a scraping sound to his left. Releasing the safety catch, he swung his AK-47 rifle round sharply, nearly catching Juan in the face with the barrel sight as the man from 'C' section crawled forward through the undergrowth and joined him. Maxwell turned his attention back to the car, which had now pulled up outside the south entrance gate of the villa. The vehicle had a tiny green light stuck on the roof, indicating it was a taxi and the single occupant was now out of the car and paying off the driver. The Peugeot taxi cab backed into the driveway of the villa, nearly touching the closed iron gates with its rear bumper before completing a turn and moving off back down the hill. The lone passenger talked excitedly into a wall mounted security phone and the heavy gates swung open to let the visitor inside. They closed quickly behind him. Maxwell checked the time.

It had taken more than two hours climbing up the mountainside from the village of Benidoleig to reach the point where they now lay, concealed in a section of scrub bush and decaying almond trees on a small terraced plateau, a hundred feet or so above the villa where Helga was being held captive. Maxwell and Juan were waiting for a signal from Alexis and Nickolai telling them the intruder alarms ranged around the estate wall had been neutralized or circumvented. Maxwell didn't know how Nickolai was going to do it and didn't ask. Nickolai was confident he could and that was good enough. Juan knew there were at least four men inside, with the arrival of the man in the taxi, so hopefully it would be no more than one against one. The men from C section agreed that there was to be no shooting until Helga's whereabouts had been established and, although everything was quiet on the estate, Maxwell guessed by now the two Russians should be somewhere in the villa grounds.

Just at that moment a rope came snaking over the boundary wall about twenty yards from the gate. Juan tapped his shoulder and Maxwell leapt forward, down the slope from the plateau, in a crouching run. He reached the wall and pushed himself flat against it, listening for any other sounds of movement. There were none and he signaled Juan to follow him. With the help of the rope, both men scaled the four meter high wall with ease and dropped to the ground on the other side, linking up with Nickolai and Alexis. The terraced garden area they were now in was well lit and a pole mounted TV camera, about ten feet away, scanned backward and forward accompanied by the mechanical whirring of a remote controlled servo motor. Maxwell whispered to Nickolai,

'Christ almighty, that fucking camera covers all this area and the gate; surely they've seen us by now.'

Nickolai pulled a knitted black ski mask from his face and grabbed Maxwell's arm, pointing up to the camera,

'They have not seen us, my friend, look at the camera lens, at the box covering it.'

Maxwell studied the camera more carefully and noticed that where the lens should have been was a large black box attached to the camera body with linen tape. Nickolai spoke again.

'That box is an imaging unit, which is like a miniature video recorder in itself and before we threw the rope over, I recorded one sweep of the camera from the gate to back here and put the imager over the lens when it finished its last sweep of the gate. The picture they are seeing now is perfectly normal except for an imperceptible change of frame angle and we will be inside before they discover anything out of the ordinary. We have fixed the camera on the other gate as well and neutralized the wall alarms so, if I have done my job well, they should still be unaware of our presence.

There was no time for any more chatter, apologies included, and Maxwell ran silently over to the entrance porch of the whitewashed villa, signaling to the others to move out as soon as he was established in the grey shadows of the dimly lit stone porch. Nickolai and Alexis edged their way round the corner of the building to prepare ground for taking the control room. There was only one outside door to the windowless chamber and that was expected to be locked. Nickolai had planned to pick the lock and Alexis would silently contend with whoever was inside. A signal of their success would be the switching off of the garden lights and at that point, Maxwell was to break in through the front door, taking whoever was inside the lounge and balcony area, whilst Juan would come up from the back of the house. But nothing was to happen until Juan had checked all the other rooms from outside to try and pin down the location of Helga.

Several minutes passed before Juan appeared from around the east side of the house and told Maxwell he had found her. She was in the main bedroom, lying on the bed and apparently asleep. Although there were no lights on in the room, a door was open leading into a corridor and there was enough light coming through to make a positive identification.

'Does she look all right?' Maxwell breathed.

'Yes,' replied Juan, in a hushed whisper, 'but we've got to keep whoever's inside confined to the west section of the house, as the bedrooms on the other side all have security grills fitted to the windows and there's no way out other than through the main body of the villa.'

Maxwell mentally studied the situation for a few seconds and then said,

'OK Juan, tell Nickolai to start on the downstairs door and then move up to the best position you can find on the east side of the balcony. This front door is locked and as soon as the outside lights go out, I'll shoot off the lock. When you hear the shot, come in from the side of the balcony. If we set up a crossfire line between us, we should be able to keep everyone's head down on the balcony and in the lounge, cutting off any movement into the bedroom wing. With a bit of luck that should give Nickolai and Alexis time to finish downstairs and then under our cover they can do a sweep of the house.'

Juan was listening intently, his breathing calm and controlled.

'Right, but make sure you get well inside the hallway before you let loose. From the drawings we've seen of the interior layout, there's a pillared archway leading to the kitchen and that could restrict your line of fire unless you're up close to it.'

With those final whispered words of warning, Juan melted away into the night's shadows. In thirty seconds the assault would begin.

\*\*\*\*\*\*

Sergeant Michaels handled a frying pan like an expert. All four burners on the central gas hob were ablaze as he monitored the progress of a late evening meal consisting of Spanish omelet, mashed sweet potatoes, bacon and diced carrot. The omelet was just about done and would only need a few minutes under the grill to bake the cheese topping. Michaels was rather proud of his culinary expertise, a subject his partner, Major Sutton took no interest in whatsoever. He shouted to the major, informing him that 'grub would be up' in five minutes. He fiddled the omelet under the grill of the eye level oven and absently picked up the H&K machine pistol from its resting place near the sink draining board. There was no obvious sound of movement from the lounge, so he shouted louder.

'I'll just go and check the young lady, sir, and see if I can persuade her to try some of my cooking.'

The major replied with something unintelligible and Sergeant Michaels shrugged his shoulders, wiped his hands on a red and white patterned tea towel, and pushed his way through the kitchen door leading out into a well lit corridor. Major Sutton had finished cleaning the last of the M16 rifles and walked casually off the balcony and back into the lounge as he slammed a full clip home into the case hardened breech.

He was about to lay the rifle down on one of the lounge chairs and head for the kitchen, towards his long awaited supper, when something stopped him and made him turn. Through the open windows leading onto the balcony, he could see out into the bottom garden. Instinctively he knew all was not well. It took microseconds for his brain to correctly filter all the evidence, but those same microseconds turned out to be fatal for Major Sutton. He realized immediately that the garden lights had gone out; his back was to the main entrance hall. The first shots rang out behind him, accompanied by sounds of splintering and shattering wood. As he turned towards the front door and raised the M16 to waist level, his right thumb feeling for the safety catch, the door flew open and a bullet from Maxwell's second burst of fire caught him in the knee, shattering it instantly. The major had started to go down and managed to let off a three round salvo before two more bullets entered his right lung and a third passed through his cheek bone and up into his brain. Major Sutton was dead.

At the sound of the first shot, Sergeant Michaels was about to enter the main bedroom and wake his sleeping hostage. He froze in the doorway. The interior of the room was dark but he could clearly make out the prone outline of the woman who had remained undisturbed on the bed for several hours. He slipped the safety catch on the machine pistol and turned back towards the corridor. Too late; he heard a rustling behind him and turned his head back to see a dark shadow lunging towards him. It was an automatic reaction. He pulled the trigger, bringing the gun up in a narrow rising arc at the same time. Helga, disturbed by the first shots and now half standing, half crawling, took a full magazine of nine millimeter bullets with a force so powerful, it lifted her completely off her feet and threw her back across the bed in a tangled bloody heap. The micro-seconds ticked by as Michaels stood paralyzed in the doorway, dazed and confused. This was not supposed to happen. The woman had to be kept alive. He knew that; why had he killed her? The next sound Sergeant Michaels registered was a faint click behind his right ear. It was to be the last sound he ever heard. In those few terminally hesitant time bytes, Alexis had found his target. With the barrel of his AK-47 now resting on the sergeant's right shoulder, angled upwards towards his ear, Alexis pulled the trigger and blew the English mercenary's head off.

The house fell abruptly silent, pale blue smoke and the reeking smell of burnt cordite filled the air. Maxwell lay on the cold tiled floor of the arched space between the entrance hall and the lounge and facing him on bended knee, peering through wide open glazed doors leading to the balcony, crouched Juan. The heavy, eye stinging layer of cordite smoke hovered about two feet from the deck and peering through it, Maxwell watched Nickolai cautiously raise himself up from a horizontal position on the kitchen floor. He slapped a fresh magazine into the assault rifle and called out in Russian to Alexis. A reply echoed back which Maxwell did not understand, but Nickolai, in response, lifted himself from the floor in one sharp athletic movement and scrambled into the corridor leading to the bedroom wing, slamming the door shut behind him. Maxwell peered questioningly across at Juan through the evaporating smoke and Juan signaled silently that he should stay put. Half an anxious minute went by before Nickolai and Alexis appeared through the kitchen doorway. Juan took this as a sign that all was clear in the bedroom wing and stood up. Maxwell pulled himself into a kneeling position, a puzzled expression on his face. He had expected to see Helga, but without a word to the Englishman, Alexis walked over to Juan and the two men whispered together. Something had gone wrong, maybe Helga had been injured. Maxwell picked up his AK-47 and rushed towards the kitchen. Nickolai raised his rifle and stopped him going any further than the kitchen door. Juan shouted over,

'Please do not go into the bedroom wing, Mr. Armstrong, I'm afraid we have been unable to succeed in our original objective.'

He paused, vainly trying to find the right words. There weren't any. Juan came over and placed his hands gently on Maxwell's shoulders.

'I have to tell you, my friend, we were unable to save her. She is dead. Please don't go in there and see her in her present state, please, I beg of you.'

Maxwell stood rigidly still, glazed eyes focusing only on the black steel barrel of Nickolai's gun, now pointing directly at him. Seconds later, something snapped. He shook and shuddered uncontrollably, as he raised a trembling hand and gently pushed the barrel of the rifle aside, stepping hesitantly through the open doorway and into the corridor.

He stayed alone with her twisted, contorted and bloody body for several minutes before Juan entered the bedroom and told him it was time to go. Maxwell looked up vacantly at the tall lean Spaniard standing before him, a dark shadowy shape, backlit by the artificial light invading the room from the open doorway. His cheeks were streamed with damp tears of heartbreak as he spoke in halting, graveled tones.

'Did we get them all?'

Juan replied that they had counted only four men and they were all dead. He waited, not knowing quite what to do next. Maxwell searched for a handkerchief and studiously wiped his eyes and cheeks. He raised himself from the blood sodden bed covers and walked past the motionless Spaniard. Juan turned to follow him. When they arrived back in the lounge, Maxwell gave instructions in robotic tones to the grim faced Russians to search the house thoroughly for any sign of evidence or clues as to the identity of the kidnappers. He elected himself and Juan to the macabre task of searching all the bodies. They searched and ransacked for nearly half an hour but came up with little that they didn't know already, except confirmation of the nationalities of the kidnappers; two definitely English and two probably Spanish. Maxwell called the three KGB men together and spoke with a crisp, hard inflection they had not recognized before. The essential questions were asked and authoritative instructions given. Could the bodies be disposed of without creating any local problems? The answer was yes. 'Good,' said Maxwell, 'please make arrangements to do so and clean up the villa as much as possible before daybreak.' Juan queried which bodies were to be 'disposed of.' Maxwell answered,

'All of them.' He paused before adding, 'I will get back down the mountain the way we came, and if possible, I would like to take the car we left in the village.'

Juan agreed. Maxwell continued, steeling himself to think logically and speak in an even, controlled voice,

'If I can use the car I shall go back to Ondara, collect my things and drive up to Valencia Airport and see if I can get on an early flight to London.' Juan looked deeply concerned. He took Maxwell by the shoulder again. The two men stood face to face, eyes locked together in a bond of new-found respect born of their joint sanguinary experiences on that cool and still autumn evening.

'Look, why don't you wait here for a day or two, get some rest, think everything through before you go off on a hair brained scheme like this. You can't take on the whole of the British Government and their security services. Give me time to contact my people and maybe we can provide you with some help.'

Juan knew it was hopeless, but he had to try. Maxwell carefully but deliberately removed the Spaniard's warm hands from his trembling shoulders and pulled them down in front of him, clasping them tightly in his own. He turned towards Nickolai and Alexis, who looked on expectantly.

'My friends, no-one could have asked for a better team than you. The fact that Helga is dead is not your fault, you all did your best but it was simply not to be that she should live. Now I must finish this thing, by myself. I must get to London as quickly as possible. Surprise will be my biggest weapon. Have no fear, I am now convinced this has been planned and executed by my own people and the responsibility for that must rest on one man's shoulders. Too many people have died and too many tears shed during the past days because of him, and now he must pay the price. Believe me, my friends, I am one of the few people able to do it and he will die, not only for the murder of the only woman I ever loved in my life, but for all those others whose lives he has scarred with death and destruction over the years.'

He turned back to Juan, who was wearing a dejected but understanding expression.

'It's time for me to be on my way, Juan. Thank you once again for all your help and trust. Give my regards to General Lubikov if you should speak with him again and tell him from me, I hope he has more success with his cover in the artillery than I had with mine in the FAO.'

He forced a smile to each man in turn as they mournfully shook hands. Then, handing Juan his automatic rifle, he left the villa and made his way slowly down the mountain to begin what would probably be his final journey; a journey of hatred and revenge.

# Chapter Twenty Four

*October 4th 1973 – Bowater House – London – UK*

Lord Peter Fotheringale sat in the SIS director's office, patiently waiting for Sir Charles to appear. He looked and felt dog tired and had managed to call on very little sleep during the past week. He got up wearily from his uncomfortable, straight backed seat and paced the room, glancing at his watch every now and then, wondering what the hell was keeping Charles Hawthorn. Sir Charles had requested a meeting for eight o'clock that morning and already it was eight fifteen. Louise Stone poked her head round the door to solicit interest in a cup of tea, which Fotheringale quickly accepted. She smiled politely and left the room, complete with undulating posterior and looking as fresh as ever. Peter wondered how on earth she managed to appear like that, at this time of the day, when he knew with certainty that for the past seven or eight days she had been blessed with only marginally more sleep than her boss.

The tea arrived and close behind it came a bleary eyed and disheveled looking Charles Hawthorn. He entered the room without a word of greeting or apology to Fotheringale and slammed a black leather briefcase on his desk; he was in an ugly mood. He opened up the briefcase and extracted some papers, relocked the case and placed it on the floor behind him. He flicked through one or two sheets of closely typed reports, then looked up and finally spoke to his visitor.

'Well, Peter, the whole damn situation looks hopeless. I've been receiving reports and updates all night, including your own of course, and I wish to give you a first-hand account of where I think we stand today.' He peered up at a distant digital wall clock cum calendar and said,

'Today is Thursday the fourth; we've now just about been a full week at it and the best news we still have is that the Yanks will now go ahead and do their thing in a week's time. That gives us an unexpected time break. The worst news is that we have indications that the Iraqi President, pushed of course by our disgruntled friend the Imam, will make a move, maybe today, possibly tomorrow. In a nutshell, the EEC President is quietly shitting himself and the Americans have begun the final evacuation of their remaining military forces on the Rhine. They are prepared to leave a token force in Europe of about forty thousand men; mainly communications and Special Forces personnel, but as for conventional ground and air forces they have in fact mostly disappeared. There is little we can do to stop them, Peter, and that's a reality! What's it like on the financial front?; don't go into a lot of detail, I haven't got the time. Just give me the bare facts.'

Fotheringale pulled a folded notebook from his inside pocket, filled with his own particular brand of banker's shorthand and began.

'Well, as you already know, gold is now trading above ninety dollars an ounce and short term futures are being negotiated at well over ninety five. Thirty-six major international manufacturing companies, based mainly in the USA, West Germany, Great Britain and Japan are preparing to file under various suspension of share trading laws as the whisper is now out. Just about everybody in multi-national manufacturing and banking has a better than good idea of what is going to happen before the weekend, but the biggest problem of all, for most of them, is they don't really know how much of their various companies and affiliates are actually owned by Iraqi and Kuwaiti interests. There has been so much buying of shares on the open market, through hundreds of paper offshore companies over the past ten years, it is nearly impossible to find out who owns what. Of course, losing the input from McWilliam and Smitt hasn't helped matters.'

He gave out a long questioning gaze but Sir Charles remained inscrutable and declined to comment. His arse had been on the rack enough already without having to explain himself to a banker. Fotheringale continued.

'South Africa have suspended all gold shipments as of midnight last night but are, of course, denying it on instructions from the States. Australia will have signed the biggest ever oil supply contract by lunchtime today with Indonesia and Papua New Guinea, in part cash and part manufactured goods. The rot is already starting. From other estimates coming in; the Brazilians and Argentineans seem blissfully unaware of what could turn out to be their fate and the Indians are screaming down the phone at anyone who can give them a clue as to what's going on. The Japanese are playing it tight lipped, the Chinese are buying agricultural machinery as if it's going out of fashion and the Canadian stock exchange will probably collapse tomorrow.' At this disturbing statement, Sir Charles face took on an even gloomier expression.

'In a General sense, there are licensed companies on all the major currency, metal, bullion and stock exchanges trading with resources no-one believed such companies had before and although we are still trying to find out whose interests they represent, we simply do not have enough time or manpower; and by the time we do, it will be all too late anyway.' He paused for a second.

'Basically the financial world is in one bloody great mess. Even in my own bank, we can come up with nothing conclusive; but latest estimates state that as much as thirty per cent of our equity shareholding could be in Arab hands through third party nominees. Our friends in Zurich, who could shed more light on the subject than they have done to date, simply refuse to communicate. You asked for the 'nutshell' version and there it is.'

Charles Hawthorn reached into his jacket pocket and pulled out a packet of cigarettes, accompanied by a box of matches. He had started smoking again three days ago, and it showed. As he drew the lighted cigarette to his lips, Peter noticed the nicotine stained index finger and the remains of carelessly brushed cigarette ash on his suit lapels. Charles inhaled long and hard, several times, before he spoke again.

'Look Peter, I need a favor. I have a meeting with the Prime Minister this afternoon. As you know, he has been aware of the gory details for three days now and although he is most pleased we are being seen to carry much of the weight of this thing on our shoulders, and all that, he is now more concerned about the survival of himself as Prime Minister, Her Majesty's Government, the people of Great Britain and then the rest of the world; in that order. He wants us to break away from EEC policy and go it alone; do our own deals whilst we still have a chance. If perhaps you could come up with me and explain the finer points of the problem to both him and the Chancellor of the Exchequer, I feel it may help matters somewhat and give us at least another twenty-four hours to continue our dialogue with the Arabs and the Russians'

Fotheringale stared uncomprehendingly at Charles and spoke through a bitter half smile.

'And where, may I ask, is the great and efficient agent you had right up the armpit of the troublesome Imam; the one man who would be able to delay the final decision declaring the international bill of Arab rights? What input has he provided so far?..... if that's not too pointed a question?'

Charles Hawthorn purposely avoided his visitor's penetrating gaze, looked back down at his papers and busied himself with stubbing out the half smoked cigarette. He mumbled more to himself than to Fotheringale,

'I've lost him.'

Peter jumped up from his seat.

'You've what?' he shouted incredulously.

Hawthorn stood up rubbing his hands agitatedly down the front of his jacket.

'Well, not lost, actually . . . just sort of lost contact with him rather than lost him entirely. But don't worry, I feel sure I'll be able to pin him down again by later today. He needs careful handling, at the moment. He thinks I tried to kill him.'

There was a long pause.

'And did you?' asked a pale faced Sir Peter.

'Of *course* not, and now it's even worse. Yesterday his fiancée was kidnapped, for which he also probably blames me and is on the loose, somewhere in Europe.'

Fotheringale slumped back down again. He didn't like this at all. Sir Charles lit another cigarette and spoke rapidly between puffs,

'You haven't heard the really bad news yet . . . we think he's gone over to the Russians, or at least, they seem to be backing him in some way.'

Peter Fotheringale could not believe his ears.

'You mean to tell me, Charles, that your inside man has gone over to the other side; he has failed to stop, or even delay the beginning of what could turn out to be Armageddon and you want me to come and tell the Prime Minister everything is all right and all we need is another twenty-four hours? You must be totally off your head my dear friend.'

He raised himself up with one swift movement and leant forward on the desk, eyeball to eyeball, with the director of SIS.

'I don't know if anyone has told you this, Charles, but you are an incompetent asshole and as far as I am concerned, from here on in, you must paddle your own bloody boat, as I will surely paddle mine. I came in here, knowing the situation was fairly hopeless, but prepared to do what I could up until the eleventh hour. After what you tell me, I perceive that very hour is here, and I will, therefore, be leaving you immediately to make good my arrangements to vacate England's fair shores as soon as possible; complete with worldly goods, intact bank account, wife and contactable offspring.' In his frustration, he spat the words rather than spoke them.

'You, Charles, are a shit, not only to me but to all those other poor bastards you've been leading along all week, convinced that you have a man inside who will put everything right as long as they all come up with the required information. Now, you want me to join your feckless little conspiracy. No way, old son; if our great Prime Minister wishes to save his personal arse and you along with him, then you two see to it on your own. Call me in Australia.'

With that, Lord Peter Fotheringale stamped out of the room slamming the door behind him. He passed the infamous Louise on the way out without a word, anger and exhaustion suppressing his humor and raising his blood pressure. He reached the smoked glass panel of the reception doorway and faltered, then stopped completely and looked back. Louise, sitting passively at her desk, stared back at him

'I don't think we shall be seeing one another again for some while Miss Stone, so I want to take this opportunity to thank you for all you've done for me whilst I've been scurrying in and out of these morbid offices at all times of the day and night. I shall miss you. Goodbye!'

He didn't wait for a reply, but maneuvered his way through the heavy plate glass doors and was away. Louise Stone sat for a quiet moment thinking calmly to herself; time for them to get her out of here. She called Sir Charles on the intercom system and explained that since she had been in the office from seven that morning, could she just pop out and do half an hour's worth of personal shopping? Hawthorn snapped back,

'What bloody kind of personal shopping?'

'You know, sir, a *ladies* kind of personal shopping,' came the tempered reply. It dawned on him seconds later what '*ladies*' personal shopping meant and so he grudgingly agreed to the half an hour as requested.

Miss Stone hummed soundlessly to herself as she gathered her personal possessions from desk drawers and stuffed them in a spacious, white vinyl handbag. She then made her way happily down to the ground floor reception and signed out of the building; pausing to pass the time of day with the security guard who was on book duty that day, and then left Bowater House.

Louise left the public phone box outside the south entrance to Knightsbridge underground station after making a short local call. She waited outside the station entrance for several minutes and eventually a black London taxi pulled up beside her with its hire flag down. The taxi driver didn't require directions; he knew where his passenger was going. As the vehicle pulled away from the curb, she took a final lengthy look up at the eighteenth floor, knowing she would never have to go back there again. She was going home at long, long last.

# Chapter Twenty Five

*October 4th 1973 – Kirkuk Air Base – Northern Iraq*

Back in Kirkuk, General Lubikov was spending time weighing all the evidence laid before him concerning the messy situation with his new friend, Mr. Armstrong. Again, it was report time, and he was in the unenviable position of having to sift through all the information that only he was cognisant to and make a decision as to who was to be aware of what. Firstly, there was the completely fucked up rescue attempt of Armstrong's woman, for which some 'C' section heads would roll, if he was not careful. Secondly, there was the disturbing thought that the Englishman was on his own in Europe somewhere and headed for trouble. What could be done about that, he didn't know. Thirdly there was that stupid ass Tammam bin Abdulla to contend with, who had organized the whole fucking kidnap in the first place; for what gain, other than some perverted feelings of revenge, he also didn't know. Lastly, the political element. He was on the rack from Moscow to give an activation date for operation Crescent Moon and jammed in a corner by the Imam, who by rights should have pressed the button hours ago with the Iraqi President.

Lubikov was stalling at present, not daring to tell anyone he was unable to contact the elusive Englishman. This was not going to be a good day, but the General was prepared for it and working methodically on the various problems. A small amount of extra caffeine circulating in the system would help in resolving the morning's matters, he decided, so he squeezed another cup of black coffee from the percolator and returned to his desk to start formulating some acceptable plan of action that would save as many heads as possible, including his own. Lubikov downed the coffee quickly and spoke aloud to the empty cup,

'Right, first things first'

The major problem, the one that had to be sorted out quickly, was what to do about Armstrong. He checked the time. Kirkuk was three hours ahead of the UK and if he was quick he could manufacture some information that would hopefully land in the right hands before the avenging Englishman hit Great Britain's shores. It would mean losing an unplanned bonus in getting rid of Charles Hawthorn, but keeping the Englishman alive was still a top priority. He thought for a moment and then started to scratch out a message on a signal pad. Maybe with one simple, sensibly worded and easily decodable radio transmission to Moscow he could kill several birds with one proverbial stone. He smiled inwardly as he wrote. The General was fond of the old English saying relating to birds and stones. Today he was in possession of a bloody big stone and if he could fling it far enough, quite a few birds would suffer as a result.

The message, he decided, would be in report form to the centre, giving them and his political masters in the Kremlin a carefully worded account of what had happened during the last couple of days and who he knew to be responsible. With judicious wording he should be able to work round to dove tailing in the main reason why the Imam still refused to push the required button, leading to the main conclusion that the Englishman should somehow be kept alive; at least in the short term. If he didn't go into too much detail on the activities of the 'C' section operatives in Spain, he may well be able to cover their backsides until Crescent Moon got underway and after that everyone in the Kremlin and KGB alike would be too busy to run around on a witch hunt. The only possible problem he foresaw, would be if the British radio 'ears' in Cyprus were somehow not with it and missed the message; but every plan had its associated problems and the Royal Air Force guys stuck up there on Troodos, were normally pretty alert.

The General finished writing the message and started to encode it. The code would be 'standard military' and the transmission sent at normal speed. This would probably raise some eyebrows in 'The Centre' but also create a certain amount of interest in Cyprus. If the RAF boys were on the ball the message would be decoded within fifteen minutes; recoded and retransmitted to the UK through Cheltenham within the hour. With a fair amount of luck, it could be on the SIS director's desk by nine thirty, UK time. If the English

Special Branch were doing their job properly, they would pick Armstrong up off the incoming nine thirty flight from Valencia and take him straight to Bowater House. That would save the life, for the time being, of Charles Hawthorn and hopefully save the life of the central character in today's little plot, Maxwell Armstrong. Lubikov accepted it was far from being the most perfect plan in the world and relied a lot on many mute players, acting their part as expected. The first bit; the Cyprus pick-up and retransmission, could be monitored by his own people in Bulgaria. The second bit would rely on the efficiency of the British Special Branch or C5, in getting their hands on Armstrong, or perhaps his ability at getting into the country and avoiding them. A quick phone call to his men in the London based Soviet Embassy should comfortably nudge things along a little there. The reaction of Hawthorn was the only phase of the deception plan he was unable to control, but if the man had half a brain he would let Armstrong go and guide him into wreaking his vengeance out on someone else.

General Lubikov leaned back in his chair and considered all the options for the moment. The only area not totally covered in the plan, was what to tell the Imam Sulayman bin Abdulla, unless he could speak to him personally. He knew he would be unable to get a message to him unless it went through Rasheed al Sheikh and that was tantamount to telling all to the Imam's asshole brother, Tammam bin Abdulla, someone who needed to be kept in the dark as much as possible.

It was quite feasible that those Unicorn bastards were not yet aware their little kidnap plot had gone disastrously wrong and they more than likely wouldn't know until Mohammed from the Oman had been able to establish just that. He was in London at present and would not be able to get his act together for another three or four hours to find out finally what was happening in Spain.

To the General's knowledge, his men in Spain had done a good job so far in disposing of bodies and cleaning up the mess at the villa. The outside phone line had been cut before they left and that would keep Mohammed guessing for a while. Lubikov was confident Mohammed would not communicate with Tammam in Qatar or Rasheed in Iraq until he had something positive to report. With no direct phone contact and very few friends in Spain, the only way he could guarantee obtaining accurate information was to get his arse over to Spain himself. With a little hope, an amount of prayer and a fucking great deal of luck, Mohammed would be unable to make a move out of the UK until at least early evening, which would give Armstrong, provided he was pointed in the right direction, enough time to get at him.

The General sat back and admired his handiwork. He felt pleased with himself, but there still remained the worrying problem of what to do about giving something to the Imam and due for even more consideration, was how to actually give it to him; through Rasheed? Or try to go direct? The second route involved a trip to Baghdad for which he didn't have time and the first required giving minimal hint to the Unicorn as to what was really going on. Lubikov poured some more coffee and ruminated on the subject for lengthy minutes. Finally, he decided; when in doubt, lie.

He got to work composing another signal to the Imam, declaring boldly that he expected his men to contact Maxwell Armstrong by the afternoon of that day and he could be assured that the Englishman would communicate with him directly. He counted on Rasheed being somewhat confused, but passing the communication along anyway and that would keep the problem of the Unicorn and the Imam on the back burner for long enough, enabling him to judge if his plan would work or not. If it did, then fuck Rasheed and Tammam; if it didn't then he was in the shit anyway and would be recalled to Moscow to be asked some very pointed and painful questions. The General stamped the two radio messages with origination, time and date and called for the signals corporal. All he could do now, was sit and wait.

\*\*\*\*\*\*

Maxwell left the Iberia jet at bay thirty-four, terminal two, Heathrow Airport and followed the other passengers along the covered walkway of the boarding finger, his soft hand baggage slung loosely over his right shoulder. He waited until he came level with one of the two service exits placed on either side of the pier and let the travel bag loose from his fingers. Someone bumped into him from behind as he bent to pick up the canvas bag and there followed a series of mutual but frustrated muttered apologies. He knelt down out of direct sight of a watchful ground crew positioned at either end of the adjustable floating pier. He unobtrusively tried the service door by leaning gently against it and the door gave; it was unlocked as he had hoped. As more disinterested passengers pushed past the hunched, kneeling figure, the door opened a foot or so and Maxwell was through. The door closed behind him as he took in the scene on the tarmac below. There was lots of activity but no-one had noticed him so far. He was on the blind side of the aero plane he had just evacuated, which meant he was out of the flight crew's direct line of vision. Stood on top of a set of aluminum steps leading down to the aircraft parking bay, he quickly pulled a set of dirty orange overalls from his bag and put them on. Still he went unnoticed. He tipped the rest of the bag's contents out on to the steel grating and turned the canvas bag inside out, then stuffed everything back inside except for a pair of blue ear defenders which he slipped round his neck to complete his disguise. The bag was now a dirty yellow on the outside and green on the inside. The faded orange overalls had a darker patch on the back where normally there would have been a sign saying, British Airports Authority, but the area around the patch was surrounded by broken cotton links, indicating to the casual observer that the sign had been ripped off over the years of consistent laundering. The bag and the overalls, in fact, belonged to Harry Jordan. They were leftover reminders from his days with the authority some ten years previously and were normally carried in his own aircraft in case he needed to do some remote maintenance or repairs. Before leaving the farm, Maxwell had pulled them out of the luggage compartment of his Cherokee on an impulse; what that impulse was triggered by, he didn't know but he had never travelled far without his bag and overalls and probably at the back of his mind he considered the overalls some kind of good luck symbol; today they certainly were.

He jogged down the steps and donned the ear defenders. Three bays away, a British Airways 747 was unloading and two baggage handlers were struggling to back up a chain of flat bed cargo dollies to the aircraft with the aid of a light tug tractor. Maxwell walked casually up and began to help the two men unhitch the dollies and load a mixture of suitcases and broken cardboard boxes. One of the men shouted over to ask what he was doing.

'I've just finished on thirty-three and four,' Maxwell replied, waving an arm in the direction from which he had just come,

'….. and I'm off shift in a few minutes and need a ride back to the terminal, so I thought I'd give you a hand and then take a ride back with you.'

The older man, similarly attired as Maxwell, sat on his tractor with a slightly bewildered look on his face. He shouted back,

'That's a bloody first; you go ahead mate, more hands, longer tea break.'

The man on the tractor turned back to the dollies. He paused for a second, then shouted out something else which Maxwell failed to understand immediately and when he only received a puzzled grin in response, the tractor man pointed to his green and white airport security pass displayed on a top left overall pocket flap. Maxwell pulled down the plastic ear muffs and shouted back over the noise of a starting jet engine that the crocodile clip had broken on his pass, and he therefore had it in his pocket. The driver nodded understandingly; Maxwell replaced the ear defenders and carried on loading the luggage trucks.

Five minutes later the first six were ready to go and the tractor driver signaled to Maxwell to hop onto one of them. A further ten minutes later the dollies were parked up outside the baggage reclaim area and Maxwell shouted to the tractor driver that he would have to go off and have a pee. The driver waved cheerfully as Maxwell headed for a signed door marked, Male Toilets and Locker Room. The toilets were empty so he waited inside one of the sit down cubicles until he heard someone entering and take up a stance at one of the urinals. Maxwell flushed the toilet and left the booth. The crewman standing in the urinal only gave him a casual glance as he strolled up to the sink and began to wash his hands. He picked the moment, moving back from the sink, quickly and silently, bringing the leaking individual down with one sharp blow to the jugular vein. Before he fell,

Maxwell grabbed the overall suited mechanic and dragged him effortlessly into one of the cubicles.

He sat the unconscious crewman on the toilet seat and removed his green and white security pass. With the door dragged closed and jammed with a wad of rolled up toilet paper, Maxwell calmly left the toilet facilities and made his way through to the security entrance leading into terminal two baggage reclaim hall. The door into the hall was constantly opening and closing as stewardesses and baggage controllers moved in and out, chasing up lost luggage, crew baggage and the odd something or other that had slipped out of a badly protected cardboard box.

He waited until the guard on the door had his hands full with two going in and three more trying to squeeze their way out. He joined the two baggage handlers going in with his thumb over the picture on the security pass and the metal, crocodile holding clip pulled off. He showed it briefly to the guard, who in all the confusion let him by with a minor admonishment calling for Maxwell to have the clip fixed as soon as possible. The guard's final words rang in his ears as he made his way confidently through the controller's office.

'You're supposed to be wearing the bloody thing, not carrying it in your bloody pocket!

Maxwell kept his head away from the door and replied with a mumbled and apologetic agreement as he walked out through the baggage controller's office door and on into the reclaim area.

'So far …. so good; …. only customs to get past now.'

Maxwell hoped the mechanic in the loo was a good sleeper. He aimed straight for the green section of the customs hall and walked boldly through. A young Pakistani customs officer jumped out at him.

'Hey, you know you're not supposed to come through here.'

Maxwell flashed the half covered pass at him and yelled back that he had to get away quickly, his wife was having a baby and the hospital had just called. He daren't stop moving. The Asian customs officer stood there, not knowing what to do. In the end, he distantly cried out words of grudging good luck and something like,

'Don't do it again, it's against the rules.'

'Fuck the rules', said Maxwell under his breath as he waved a final cheery farewell and disappeared round a corner, entering the greeting area half striding with purposeful step towards the nearest toilets. In went an airport baggage handler, and out came a normal, frowning, hassled passenger. He checked his watch. Whoever had been waiting for him, and he was certain somebody would be, was more than likely on the phone to half a dozen offices by now, explaining that the target had either not been on the Valencia flight as they expected, or else, somehow they had missed him. The last obstacle; get out of the airport premises as quickly as possible, but as always, there was never a taxi about when you wanted one.

He watched as an Avis bus pulled up outside the terminal collection point. Maxwell jumped on it. The driver politely asked, 'Do you have a car reservation, sir?' Maxwell replied in the positive and so the bus pulled away, taking the lone passenger to the Avis off airport car hire base on the A4. As the bus ploughed its way through the early morning traffic converging on the Heathrow access tunnel, Maxwell mentally ran through the next part of his improvised plan; in through the Avis reception one end and out the other; a quick walk to the nearby Heathrow Hotel and then with the slippery assistance of a generous tip to the head doorman, a locally placed airport taxi into London. He would be there in an hour.

# Chapter Twenty Six

*October 4th 1973 – Bowater House – London – UK*

Sir Charles Hawthorn was annoyed. In fact, he was more than annoyed, he was extremely angry. Every bloody thing was going wrong today and Louise had been missing for over an hour. The Special Branch team at Heathrow had somehow missed Armstrong and that was most worrying. He lit another cigarette, his tenth that day; the voluminous, frosted glass receptacle on his desk overflowing with ash and half smoked cigarettes. He glanced again at his watch.

Where the *hell* was Louise?

The grey phone on his desk burst into life and he let it ring several times before answering; was this more bad news? The senior signals officer at Bowater House spoke to the SIS director for half a minute and when Charles Hawthorn replaced the receiver, he was grinning from ear to ear.

'Got the bastard,' he shouted out loud. He threw all the papers on his desk into a bulging wire mesh filing tray and with a feeling of controlled elation, bounded out of the office and down an interior staircase to the radio room, all concern for the absent secretary momentarily forgotten in a newly triumphant mood. He nearly crashed headlong into a perplexed signals clerk, as he burst into the decoding section and grabbed the first part of a fresh signal relayed through GCHQ from the Cyprus listening station. Parts of it were still coming in but the first decoded flimsy contained enough information to make the director's pulse race. The Ruskies were having problems and they must be fairly serious ones for them to risk sending out such sensitive information at normal speed and in standard military code. Although the 'open air' military codes were changed daily for security, the SIS and British military intelligence had surreptitiously obtained all the key signatures from a very co-operative source in the GRU Russian military intelligence ages ago. The second part of the message popped out of the electronic decoder and Charles Hawthorn scanned it eagerly. It was all there, the kidnapping of the Weismuller woman, confirmation of the activities of Unicorn and a clear naming of one of its members; the disappearance of Armstrong and the Russian's concern over the attitude of a vacillating Iraqi. He grabbed the decoded paperwork and rushed back to his office. He picked up the telephone and called Madrid, issuing instructions to his office there to get moving on the kidnap information and find out what the hell had been going on.

Next he called Special Branch and told the inspector covering the Heathrow operation to forget about Armstrong and find the whereabouts of a certain Mohammed bin Abdulla, an Omani national and AGCC minister without portfolio, who was somewhere in the country and probably in the London area. The inspector seemed a bit confused.

'No George,' shouted an irritated Sir Charles,

'....don't go knocking on the bloody Omani Embassy door to enquire. If he was here on an official visit we would all fucking well *know* about it, wouldn't we? Just find him and be quick about it; and George, don't go giving him one of your little chats, just find him and watch him. I want to know where he is at every moment, do you hear? Every fucking moment George, and don't lose him; a lot of lives may depend on it and mine is one of them.'

He slammed down the telephone handset, muttering,

'Incompetent bastards,' under his breath. He picked up the phone again. Where the hell was Louise? Just at that moment one of the internal security officers charged into the room. He spoke breathlessly.

'Sorry to intrude, sir, but I'm afraid I have some bad news.'

He paused to get his breath back. Sir Charles waited expectantly.

'We have had word from the Soviet Embassy watch, sir, your secretary, Louise Stone, has just been seen entering the residency. They tried to sneak her in, dark colored wig and all that, but the photographs taken by the surveillance team have been developed and blown up. I'm afraid there is no doubting it.'

The security man nervously placed a large black and white photograph on the director's desk; it was still damp from processing. There was no question about it. Although the picture was hazy and showed a dark figure huddled in the back of an official diplomatic car, he knew that outline better than he knew his mother's. It was definitely Louise. Hawthorn was totally taken aback. Louise had been with the department for over ten years, her ancestry researched in depth back for more than three generations. It was impossible to believe she could have been a mole. But there was the irrefutable evidence before him. Sir Charles sat mesmerized by the photograph, cerebral activity at its height. The security officer spoke again hesitatingly.

'What do you want us to do, sir?' he asked.

'Nothing,' replied the director stonily. '….at this moment, absolutely nothing. We don't have time to sort this problem out now. Just get your backside in gear on security within this office, no-one is to leave; no-one for whatever reason and keep an eye out for Armstrong, he's on his way here. You are to let him get in, but not out, without my say so. Put one of your best girls behind the reception desk and make sure she's armed. Hopefully, you will be able to find one that is not on a bloody salary from Moscow as well as Her Majesty's Government.'

This final sarcastic comment dismissed the security officer who backed sheepishly out of the office to light some fire under his staff and kick a few exposed posteriors. The director slammed the desk top with a tightly clenched fist. Some heads would roll when all this was over; that is, if anyone was left when it was over.

\*\*\*\*\*\*

Maxwell directed the taxi to turn off the A4 motorway and into Hammersmith. Half a mile up the North Circular, the taxi took another turn and stopped in a back street outside a dilapidated shop front festooned with various items of ex-army and navy equipment. Here you could get just about anything in military and ex-government stocks, from a World War Two gas mask to a naval officer's greatcoat. The shop was empty of people except for a bristle chinned, slovenly looking man, bearing down heavily on a hand rolled cigarette. He coughed loudly and painfully as his first customer of the day entered the dingy shop interior. Maxwell brushed off the gruff,

'Can I help you, sir?' and began to poke around the stocks of overalls and loose pieces of equipment. He found what he was looking for, a large size set of overalls of the type used by British Telecom and a scuffed leather tool bag into which he shoveled a set of rusting screwdrivers, small spanners and a canvas sheathed twelve inch Commando stiletto knife. He agreed the purchase in exchange for a swiftly negotiated twenty quid and took off again in the taxi. Twenty minutes later he was walking down the steps to Knightsbridge underground station and heading for the toilets. He quickly changed into the blue grey overalls and emptied his canvas travelling bag of personal effects and money, placing everything except the yellow mechanic's suit into the leather tool bag. He stuffed the canvas bag and discarded overalls behind the toilet seat and reappeared on the station steps in his latest role as a telephone engineer.

Before moving off, he cautiously checked the area around him. The pavements were jammed with the normal array of west end shoppers, all crowding and jostling one another as they fought to cross through nose to tail road traffic, heads bowed against an unexpectedly chill wind. The sky was continuing grey and overcast. It would rain before the day was out and Maxwell hoped it would hold off long enough for him to do what he had to do and get away. Once it started raining in London, it was nearly impossible to get a free taxi or a seat on a bus and the underground would be packed. To get away, he needed space and maneuverability, something not easily come by in the centre of London on a wet and busy shopping day. He crossed the road from the station and turned left, past the front entrance to Bowater House and on towards the Wellington Club. Before he got to the club, he ducked into a driveway entrance leading down to the underground car park beneath the office building where he knew there was a lift leading up to the eighteenth floor and above. Maxwell managed to duck the view of a solitary parking attendant busily engrossed in the contents of page three of the Daily Mirror and slipped down to the first level of the car park. The two lifts were at the far end of level one; the doors lit by a single sixty watt bulb, shining through a broken, frosted glass diffuser cover. Maxwell reached up and unscrewed the bulb, dropping it to the floor where it shattered at his feet. He checked the lift security lock which could only be activated with a magnetic key card.

Maxwell scanned the lift indicator lights and waited patiently whilst the lift moved up and down between the various floors. Then he was in luck. One lift passed his level and continued down, stopping at the car park level below. Searching calmly in his bag of tools, he found what he thought would do the job, a heavy twenty inch, square shanked screwdriver. He jammed the screwdriver in the lift doors and levered them open enough to get both hands inside. With a final heave the doors sprang open and the lift shaft was exposed; the top of the lift itself, resting about four feet below. He jumped down onto the roof of the lift ceiling and allowed the sprung doors of lower level one to close silently behind him. He listened for signs of movement beneath his feet, but could hear nothing and carefully prized open the hinged ceiling inspection cover and lifted it an inch. The lift was empty; the outside doors had started to close. He dropped down to the floor of the lift, leaving the inspection cover to drop down behind him. Up to now it had all been relatively easy. The whole forced entry exercise had taken less than thirty seconds and whilst he knew the intrusion alarm would sound in the lobby, it would only have operated for about ten seconds and be hopefully ignored by the duty commissionaire. As normal, barely trained commercial building security staff, they were not renowned for their inquisitiveness or speed of reaction. Lights and alarms were going off on the lift indicator board all the time and as long as no-one phoned through that they were 'stuck', the venerable board at Bowater House was normally ignored.

The lift seemed to take an age to move, but eventually did so; a light glowed beneath the number four on the level indicator. Shit, someone was calling to go up. At the fourth floor, the doors opened and a young dark haired secretarial type female entered and pressed twelve. The lift started to move again, stopping a few seconds later; the young girl walked out without comment and Maxwell carried on up to the eighteenth floor, extracting the stiletto knife from his tool bag, on the way. When he got out of the lift, he breathed a short sigh of relief; the foyer was empty. He walked confidently up to the armored glass door separating him from the offices of the SIS cover company and his target. Through the glass, he could see a smartly dressed, ginger haired, middle aged female sitting at the reception desk. Maxwell pressed the buzzer button on a wall at the side of the door and the female looked up. She spoke into the microphone unit on top of the desk and through the two-way intercom asked what the stranger wanted. Maxwell explained he was from department six, communications, and he had been sent to install some extra telephone equipment. He pulled a scrap of paper from his pocket and quoted a fictitious work order number that obviously rang with a semblance of truth because the secretary released the electronic lock from a remote switch beneath her desk and Maxwell passed through. He knew he was now in for the difficult part. He sunk his right hand in a long overall side pocket and caressed the cold chrome steel of the knife blade. The secretary looked down at her desk as the telephone technician walked into the reception area, her hands beneath the desktop. As the visitor approached, she pulled a small frame Beretta pistol from her lap and said,

'Good morning, Mister Armstrong, we have been expecting you. Please put the bag down, take your hands from out of your pockets and lay flat on the floor, your hands behind your head.'

Maxwell had no choice. He did as he was told. Being discovered so early was a bit of a setback but all was not lost. At least he was on the eighteenth floor and that was the prime objective, the rest he would continue to take one calculated step at a time. From down a corridor to Maxwell's front appeared two heavily built men, who frisked him expertly, removing the knife and sitting him in one of the reception visitors chairs. The female went off in search of someone in higher authority. He was in luck. The figure who appeared in front of the returning secretary was none other than Charles Hawthorn himself. The eyes of the two men locked together glaringly. Hawthorn looked haggard but alert. He spoke curtly,

'Come with me, Armstrong,' and then turned on his heel. The two beefy, somber looking security men hustled Maxwell into the director's office and closed the door, leaving him and the director on their own. Sir Charles drew his handgun and laid it on top of his desk.

'You have caused me a lot of problems over the past week, Maxwell and before this day is out, you will want to apologize to me for your recent disgusting behavior!' Maxwell looked up at the director and stated calmly, without emotion.

'You killed Helga, and for that you must die. You tried to kill me and instead murdered hundreds of innocent people. For that alone, many others are after your blood and if, for any reason, I don't get you, then rest assured, they will.'

Charles Hawthorn slammed his fist onto the table and shouted,

'You hot headed bastard, it was neither me nor anyone else in the 'company' who did that and you'd better bloody well believe it.'

Maxwell was not listening; he was busy figuring out how he could get hold of Hawthorn's gun. The director slammed his white knuckled fist yet again into the desk in another outburst of rising anger and frustration.

'Read that, you cocky son of a bitch!' Sir Charles threw the communication flimsy at Maxwell who picked it up off the floor and began to read it disinterestedly. Slowly the expression on his face changed and changed dramatically. He was now totally confused and it showed. He carefully read the message a second time, as Hawthorn continued speaking.

'That was picked up this morning by one of our monitoring stations in the Mediterranean and unless you're totally stupid, you will see that the Russians have been doing their homework. We still don't know who planted the bomb on your bloody aero plane, but sure as hell we now know who planned the kidnapping of Helga and who is ultimately responsible for her death.'

Maxwell sat stiff, locked in his chair, dark ringed eyes glued to the document in front of him. He looked up bitterly at the director, speaking through gritted teeth.

'Is this another of your clever little concoctions of lies and deceit, Charles?'

Hawthorn rested his head despairingly in his hands.

'For Christ's sake, man, how the hell could I fabricate something like that? The original bloody signals tapes will be here by courier later today. You can see the de-codes yourself if you want to. That communication is genuine, Maxwell, totally genuine, and the time has come, old chum, for you to make up your mind whose side you're on and bloody quick too. The choices are these. You can go directly to our Berkshire house, where you know what will happen once those bloody psychopath interrogators get a hold of you, or you can stop all this shit; *finish* what you came here to do …… and that is to get the *killer* of your fiancée!'

He paused for a moment to add emphasis to his next words as he leant across the desk, pushing his red face as close to Maxwell's as he possibly could.

'Take your fucking pick Armstrong; you've as long as it takes me to finish a cup of tea to make your choice; after that no more discussion, no more arguing and no more favors. I can quite happily throw you to the bloody dogs and you'll end up spending the rest of your *fucking* life on a funny farm.'

The director grabbed his phone and grudgingly asked if Maxwell wanted some tea, the British antiphon to all life's major and minor problems. There was no answer. Maxwell was busily engaged in reading the signal yet again, looking for any clue which might indicate that the source and information it contained was somehow not genuine. Hawthorn ordered two cups anyway and past caring whether Maxwell was listening or not, continued to explain how his people had picked up the message and the puzzling way in which it had been sent.

'If that report had been transmitted at high speed, it would have been no more than a two second burst and could not possibly have been decoded until the recording tapes had been electronically processed and the constituent codes broken. Under normal circumstances that exercise would have taken nearly twenty-four hours, but this signal was sent in a code the Russians suspected military intelligence had cracked and, more mysteriously, at normal speed.' Maxwell was taking notice.

'The conclusion is, Maxwell,' added a now calmer Hawthorn, 'that your General Lubikov wanted you to receive that particular message and knew somehow we would catch up with you by today. Also, I would say, he's probably put his job on the line to do it. So where do we go from here?'

The tea arrived.

'Do you know where Mohammed bin Abdulla is, right now?'

Sir Charles shuffled through some papers on his desk and said,

'I certainly do. He's at a large and fairly well protected farm house just outside Henley and I have men covering the place. We've known his every move for the past hour or so.'

Maxwell threw the message flimsy back on to the director's desk and spoke angrily,

'I want him, Charles.'

'And you can have him,' retorted Hawthorn, 'but the only help you will get from me is the certain knowledge of where he is; apart from that, you're on your own, no weapons, no men, no other assistance at all. Is that clear?'

'Yes,' said Maxwell quietly. Sir Charles scribbled an address on a scrap of paper and pushed it across the desk.

'There you are. And now I've done something for you, you can do something for me. When this is all over, and if you manage to come out of it in one piece, I want the names of all the other members of this so-called Unicorn movement and a clear idea of their involvement in this bloody lunatic plan bringing us to brink of World War

Three. How you get the information out of that scheming pig, I really don't care, but get it you must. Then, you make sharp contact with the Imam in Iraq and tell him we want to talk…. and talk through you. I don't give a toss where or when, but this thing has got to be stopped before it goes any further. The rats are now deserting our sinking ship.' Maxwell got up from his seat.

'When you find out what you need to know from Mohammed, I shall expect you to tell the Imam and the Iraqi President all about Unicorn, and whatever they are up to. You have to convince the Imam he is being manipulated by his brother and this evil band of misfits. I can assure you, Maxwell, that every single European Government is scared shitless right now. Already half the EEC currencies are decimated and by this evening the Yanks will have pulled out, more or less completely, from West Germany. It's still not too late to talk; in fact, it's never too late to talk. Do you understand what I'm saying?'

Maxwell mumbled a suitable reply but his mind was blocked at this particular moment with the heart rending vision of horror that confronted him every time he relived those grief stricken moments in Spain, seated on a blood soaked bed, gazing down at the battered and destroyed body of Helga. Maxwell turned abruptly and glanced back impassively at the director.

'Can I go now?'

'Yes, you can. Make sure you get back here in one piece. I will be waiting.'

Sir Charles picked up the telephone and cleared Maxwell's path through security. Still carrying his tool bag and wearing his overalls, he left the building and caught a bus to Oxford Street, where he searched for, and eventually found, the Avis Central London office.

\*\*\*\*\*\*

Maxwell pushed the little Ford hire car along the A40 dual carriageway, the speedometer nudging ninety-five miles an hour; well over the speed limit. It had started to rain, making it more than usually difficult to keep a keen eye out for lurking police patrol cars; the last thing he needed right now was to be stopped for speeding. He turned the car off the main road just before High Wycombe and headed past Marlow and on towards Henley on Thames. He strained his eyes through the damp gloom and the constant swishing back and forth of busy windscreen wipers. There it was, on the right, Nuggets Lane.

He turned into the single track lane and managed to find a space to pull off, half hiding the car in behind the concealing trunks of several beech trees. He poked the slip of paper with the address into his top overall pocket and walked through the drizzle up the lane, his leather tool bag in one hand and the commando knife in the other. Ten minutes later the mud tiled roof of a substantial Eighteenth Century farmhouse came into view on a rise ahead. It was surrounded by a high brick wall, broken only by a single gated entrance. Several other farm buildings could just be made out in the distance, some way from the house, but there was no obvious sign of life; no lights on or parked cars to be observed indicating the presence of Mohammed or any of his inevitable bodyguards. Maxwell swore quietly to himself, hoping he hadn't been conned by Hawthorn. The director had said his men were watching the place, but if they were, they'd done a damn good job of concealment. He walked casually past the house, checking the faded name on the gate. This was it. When he reached the end of the boundary wall, he made a quick decision and pushed himself through a wringing wet hedgerow and forced his way laboriously across a clinging ploughed field until he came to the rear of one of the farm outbuildings. It was a large hay barn, built of brick to just above shoulder level and, from then on up, clad in wooden boarding.

He pulled the heavy screwdriver from his tool bag and began to prise one of the lower boards loose. It took some time and required a deal of patience, but eventually he succeeded and exposed a gap wide enough to climb through. The barn was half full with broken straw bales, and some high doors leading out onto the yard were open. The building was constructed on two levels and by climbing up to the higher one, he was able to obtain a respectable view of the rear of the farmhouse. Now he could see there were one or two lights on in the house itself and a black Mercedes parked in a driveway; somewhere in the distance pop music was playing and he could see shadows moving across a well lit but curtained ground floor window on the right. He was about to consider leaving the concealing protection of the barn when from out of a clump of trees to his left, Maxwell spotted a slow moving figure buried beneath a dark waterproof cape and carrying what looked like a shotgun. 'How many more are there?' he wondered as the huddled, shadowy shape disappeared back into the trees.

He climbed down from the mezzanine and crept back out into the rain. Miraculously, his presence had still gone undetected. He moved off among the trees and wet undergrowth in search of the armed guard. The rain had started to fall again, much heavier, assisting in covering the sound of Maxwell's squelching footsteps as he moved forward into the copse. Through the partial ground mist, about twenty-five yards away and sheltering under the broad boughs of an ancient oak, stood a silhouetted figure, cupping a cigarette with both hands, trying hard to draw smoke through damp tobacco and a disintegrating filter. The shotgun was left leaning carelessly against the tree trunk and half covered with the tail of a dark green waterproof cape. Maxwell took stock of the situation for a few seconds and when satisfied the guard was on his own, stepped carefully from tree to tree until he was right behind his prey. In one leap he rushed forward, kicking the shotgun to the ground and grabbing the sentry from behind. Moving his left hand deftly across his victim's face he pulled back sharply, thereby levering the body to one side. His right hand sprang up and dragged the razor sharp stiletto blade across the guard's neck. There followed a short, eerie, gargling sound until with a second sweep of the knife, Maxwell severed his prey's vocal chords. The struggling body went gradually limp in Maxwell's grasp and was allowed to drop gently to the sodden muddy earth, with Maxwell sinking down beside him and immediately checking the body for documents and weapons.

The dead man had a wallet stowed away in an inside jacket pocket containing a driver's license, two letters and one or two credit cards. The guard was Omani, and from the documents on him, he didn't seem to have diplomatic status, which Maxwell noted with quiet satisfaction. The only other items on the body were a cheap plastic lighter, a nearly full pack of damp cigarettes, and a half dozen magnum shells for the shotgun. Maxwell checked the gun. Both barrels were loaded. He took the gun, the shells and the lighter. He had hoped to find some keys, but there were none; he used the Omani's shirt to wipe off as much blood as he could from his slippery knife blade and then set off on a further reconnaissance of the copse boundary. The area appeared clear of other guards, and finally he completed a survey of all the other outbuildings, picking up on the way one or two items he thought might come in useful; a small bottle of concentrated liquid rat poison, discovered in a dilapidated greenhouse, and a miniature pack of superglue, found lying on a shelf of what appeared to be a maintenance garage. He concealed the rat poison and glue in the pockets of a now well soaked overall and edged along the rear of the house until he was crouched beneath the previously surveyed ground floor, lighted window. The music he had heard earlier was coming from inside and above that could be recognized the individual sounds of three distinct male voices speaking in Arabic. There was the accompanying clatter of cups and cutlery in the background and Maxwell assumed the room where the voices were coming from to be the kitchen or staff rest room of some description.

He moved, still crouched, past the window sill and up to a door spaced about eight feet from the window. He reached up and gingerly tried the handle. It was locked. Maxwell thought desperately for a moment. He had to take at least three men, possibly more, with as little disturbance and noise as possible. But before he could do that, he somehow had to gain access to the house. He checked the rear facade once again for signs of an unlocked door or an insecure window. There were none.

'Only one thing for it', he concluded, his brain, his pulse and adrenalin glands working overtime, '.... and that's to knock on the door and ask the nice kind gentlemen if they will let me in.'

He positioned himself to the side of the door nearest the lit window and still crouched down, knocked it with the butt of the shotgun. In response the radio was turned down a few decibels and a voice in Arabic shouted,

'Is that you, Abdullah?' Maxwell put his hand to his mouth and shouted back in a muffled tone,

'Of course it is, you prick, hurry up and let me in, I'm soaked to the skin out here. Someone else will have to come out and relieve me.'

There followed a short but disturbing silence. Maxwell hoped to Christ the guards, or whoever was inside, were not working to a strict patrol routine. But knowing the Arab bodyguard brigade as he did, he reckoned it would be highly unlikely. The radio raised itself a tone louder as in response, another voice shouted that someone was coming to open the door. He listened for the sound of weighted footsteps, in what could have been a stone flagged corridor, approaching the outside door.

'Good', he thought calmly, '... if this door doesn't open directly into the kitchen or room where the other two are, then I'm in luck.'

The next sound to be heard was the dry, scraping turn of a key in an ancient lever lock and the drawing of two steel bolts. The door swung open suddenly and after a second or two a head popped out in search of the lonely, cold and wet, complaining guard.

Maxwell lunged up from the floor and jammed the butt of the shotgun into the investigator's solar plexus, at the same time grabbing his hair and pulling him to the granite tiled paving of the door step. As the Arab's head hit the two inch thick stone, Maxwell rapidly reversed his grip on the shot gun and rammed the end of the twin barrels down hard, behind the guard's ear, feeling the fragile mastoid bone immediately give way with a sickening crunch. Even if the man wasn't dead, as he'd hoped, Maxwell knew he would be permanently paralyzed and didn't bother to check any further.

He was in.

The radio blared from along a short passage, illuminated only by a narrow shaft of light emanating from a half open door which looked as if it led directly to the kitchen. The two or more men inside would be expecting someone to return at any minute and Maxwell decided not to disappoint them. He withdrew the commando knife again and launched himself through the doorway. As the door crashed open, Maxwell took in the scene instantly. One man was sitting at a plain, deal kitchen table approximately three feet away and directly in front of him. The second, and only other person in the room, was in the act of turning away from a corner cooking hob carrying a tray filled with four glasses of dark brown tea. The tray carrier appeared intent on trying not to spill the steaming contents of the glasses and didn't look up straight away. The Arab guard at the table did and with an initially confused expression, began to rise, reaching at the same time for a shoulder holstered revolver. Maxwell was far too quick and had the full element of surprise on his side. He leapt forward and jammed the blade of the stiletto up to the hilt in the soft flesh of an ascending neck; it went straight through, severing the jugular vein on the way, causing the Arab to instinctively reach up and clench his throat as he fell backwards to the floor, leaving a fountain of crimson liquid pumping in a one meter high arc from the base of his neck. Maxwell carried on moving. Before the first guard hit the floor, he was on the second and with an outstretched hand arching forward and upward, pushed the tray of scalding hot tea into his opponent's face, following through with a leaping dive which brought both men crashing to the floor, the tray firmly trapped between Maxwell's hand and the guard's scalding features. He tried to scream out loud from the initial shock and pain inflicted by the scorching, skin searing tea but his cries were mostly muffled by the tray being pressed firmly to his face.

Maxwell rose up and put all his weight above the tray until the body beneath him gradually ceased struggling and wild clawing at his back had stopped completely. He slid the tray to the floor. The second guard was unconscious. Maxwell took precious seconds out to check the state of the first guard. The volume of violently pumping blood was decreasing as the dying man's heart beat became slower and slower. Taking pains to avoid the spreading sticky, red pool, silhouetting the bloated, agonized face against a sand tiled kitchen floor, Maxwell knelt down beside his dying victim and extracted the commando knife. He returned to the insensible guard; he was still out. Maxwell scanned the kitchen worktop and saw what he wanted, a two liter water jug. He filled it with water from the cold tap and threw in a few ice cubes from the fridge. He splashed some of the water in the face of the semi-comatose being at his feet and, waiting for a reaction, he quickly checked his watch. So far, the entrance phase of the operation had only taken two and a quarter minutes. The guard on the floor was still not reacting. Maxwell threw on some more water and the prone body stirred. Maxwell crouched down beside him, his right hand holding the water jug and his left pinching the Arab's nose. He bent closer and whispered in the tortured man's ear,

'How many more guards are there, and where is Mohammed? The guard's eyes were scalded shut and blistered from being soaked with the boiling tea. He gagged and attempted to scream again. Maxwell poured a good measure of water down his open throat until the Arab looked like choking to death. Maxwell turned the guard's head to one side for a second and let him cough some water out, but still pinching his nose shut. He pulled the face back upright, and spoke again in Arabic.

'How many more are there?'

No intelligible reply. Maxwell repeated the water treatment until the man was choking again. This was getting nobody anywhere. He stood up and taking careful aim stamped down hard on his testicles. The Arab's body arched upward in a paroxysm of unbearable pain but before he could scream out a second time, Maxwell had him by the nose again, pouring more water down his throat. When the gagging, gurgling and retching stopped, Maxwell asked once again in Arabic, adding that he didn't have time for any more delay. The man before him was now noticeably drifting into shock and Maxwell knew he didn't have any time to try more sophisticated methods; the water treatment was crude but normally effective. He let the guard's nose loose and bent forward in an attempt to make some sense of the spasmodic lip movements and hoarse whispers. The best information he could gather from the anguished uttering was that there was only one guard outside and Mohammed was resting upstairs. He endeavored to persuade the Omani Arab to repeat the information but he was too far gone and from his color and pulse looked to be falling into a state of severe shock. There was nothing more to be done with this man. Maxwell pressed down on the guard's forehead with his left hand and, releasing the water jug, picked up his knife and cut his throat. Standing up quickly, he wiped the blade on his sodden overalls and muttered,

'That's for some of the poor buggers at Dubai Airport. The next one will be for Helga.'

Maxwell walked determinedly back into the little passageway, switching off the lights and carefully closing the kitchen door behind him. At the other end of the passageway, and a few feet further on from where he had made his initial entrance, he came across another closed door that could be felt more than seen in the unlit space. He clutched his shotgun in one hand and his knife in the other, feeling for the door handle. He eventually found it, a lever type which he gently pressured with his left elbow until the latch sprung and the door creaked open. It led into a dimly lit, paneled entrance hall, dominated at one end by a wide stone winding staircase. He entered the hall cautiously and kicked off his wringing wet, blood stained and mud caked shoes. There was no immediate sign of life and with heart pounding he removed his socks and threw them over near the shoes. The measured words tripped through his brain as he approached the staircase.

'Now, Mohammed, my murdering little friend .... Where the fuck are you?'

Maxwell took the stone steps two at a time until he reached the first landing where the staircase turned at an oblique angle to the right. He paused and checked his path up to the next half landing and the clear way on up to the first floor. No movement, no noise; whoever was up there was either waiting for him, or totally oblivious of his presence.

He took a deep breath and continued on up the stairs until he came to the first floor level. The floor here was planked with pine and covered in the middle by a meter wide threadbare carpet. To left and right of the landing could be seen doors leading off into what were presumably bedrooms. Maxwell padded along the hall carpet and tried each one in turn. Most of them were locked but coming to the last one on the right hand side, the door handle turned easily and he pushed open the door a fraction until he was able to see in. This was it. The room was in semi darkness with only natural autumn light entering from two large mullioned windows, un-curtained and bare, giving out to the front of the house. A spacious four poster bed was pushed up against the wall between the two windows and a huddled shape could be clearly seen resting upon it.

Maxwell inched his way towards the bed until he was able to obtain a clearer and confirming view of the sleeping figure. It was Mohammed. He stood for a moment over the bed, expending a short nervous sigh of relief, thankful that he had got this far and then brought the butt of the shotgun down lightly but effectively on the skull of the slumbering quarry. He checked the room as carefully as he could in the suppressed light of the stormy afternoon, but quickly established that the four poster was properly equipped with a head and foot board made of solid old English oak, ideal for his purposes. He pulled the insensible body of the AGCC minister and member of the Unicorn conspiracy, over onto his back and stretched him out until bare hands and feet touched head board and foot board. Maxwell pulled down two sheet corners and methodically wiped the soles of Mohammed's feet and his fingertips clean of sweat and skin grease and then, searching for the superglue, dabbed a small amount onto the toes of the soft skinned feet and pressed them against the foot board. He waited for five seconds until they were stuck fast. He carried out a similar operation against the headboard, pulling the Arab's hands flat above his head and bending the fingers back until the tips made firm and direct contact with the oak. Maxwell finally shook the bed in an attempt to convince himself it was solid enough for his purpose. It was.

Now he had to cover his backside. First check the house from top to bottom and then telephone Hawthorn to tell him he was still up and running.

He gazed down unfeelingly at the still body of the Omani Arab, the ruthless killer of defenseless wild animals, the murderer of hundreds of innocent, unsuspecting people and the person responsible for the violent and bloody death of the most beautiful woman in the world; his woman.

Maxwell didn't relish the thought of the nature of work he might have to undertake during the next half hour or so, or however long it would take to make his captive talk; but talk he would and Maxwell would not back away from what he had to do. His life was now meaningless except for the one totally compelling thought which drove him on, revenge; he would extract his revenge and after that he didn't give a shit what happened to him. He began to tremble and sweat uncontrollably as the realization of what he had done already in the name of vengeance hit home; the blood, the pain and the cold calculation with which he had murdered and tortured other human beings on that inclement, wet and evil October afternoon. But it was still far from finished. He must steel himself for much more before this thing was finally over. He knew that afterwards he would never be the same again; and so, probably, did a man who knew his capacity for merciless revenge better than he knew himself, Charles Hawthorn. Even here, in this house, it would not be allowed to end. He was caught in a trap, a deadly, all consuming trap of programmed death and destruction.

Maxwell dropped the shotgun and the knife on the bed and hugged himself tightly until the shaking stopped. Fifteen minutes later, having thoroughly searched the whole house, recovered his shoes and socks, relocked all the doors and checked the windows, Maxwell made his way into the kitchen to search for items that would help bring Mohammed to his senses in the quickest possible time, and tell him what he needed to know. By checking all the cupboards he found a half used reel of black 'gaffa' tape He raided the fridge freezer for all the ice it contained and a jug of cooling water. He gathered the ice into an ice bucket conveniently found sitting near the sink, picked up the water jug with the tape and wearily climbed the stairs again; now the horrible sickening process would have to begin.

When he entered the bedroom, Mohammed had revived almost completely and raised his head in an attempt to identify his captor. He raised it too far and uttered a lip biting cry of pain as his fingers attempted to pull away from the head boarding. Maxwell placed the items he was carrying on the floor by the side of the bed and spoke quietly and calmly, looking directly at the perspiring and terror stricken face of the Arab minister.

'The only way you can find freedom from your present unusual, but high tech form of bondage, Mohammed, is to leave behind on the headboard, all the skin on the anterior of your fingers. Being well versed, I would imagine, in all forms of bondage, bestiality and sophisticated methods of torture, I should not have to tell you that the nerve endings in your fingers are extremely sensitive; a fact well proven by the Nazis during the Second World War when they extracted the fingernails of their victims with ordinary household pliers.' The face of the trapped conspirator was frozen white. Maxwell knew he had to sow the seeds of fear as quickly as possible.

'My method is a little less complicated and much more up to date. I have super-glued your fingers and the soles of your feet to some fairly solid and immovable objects and when I have finished with you, I would not be surprised to see at least one or two of those fingers ripped free from those objects, leaving behind a substantial amount of live tissue and nerve endings. So my advice at present would be to relax and save all your energy for the conversation yet to come.' The sheet white face attempted to utter a scream of fear, but fear itself would not allow it.

'You will need to concentrate if you are going to answer my questions accurately and depending on your level of co-operation, you may even live to tell the tale afterwards. As well as instilling fear….he had to give his prisoner hope. Through the gloom, two sharp darting eyes glinted with undisguised hatred above a wordless mouth, drawn in a stretched hard line across bared, gleaming teeth. A steady stream of saliva dribbled down from the corner of Mohammed's mouth.

The stage was set. Mohammed now knew he might live if he talked. Maxwell decided to let him chew on that for a while and went back downstairs to contact Hawthorn. In the hallway, stood a telephone table with a push button unit resting on it; Maxwell turned the hall lights full on and dialed a London number. He was put through to Sir Charles, who was waiting impatiently for his call.

'Well, Charles, I've got him. The house seems fairly secure but I'm afraid there's a bit of a mess in the kitchen and when I leave someone will have to get in and clear it up. Are your men still watching the house or am I completely on my own?'

The SIS director responded straight away.

'You know the deal Maxwell. Until I get the information I need, you are entirely on your own; after that we'll see. As for existing security arrangements, we have three men watching the house and they have already witnessed the results of your handiwork in the copse. The body will stay there until we agree on a clean-up operation. I hope you don't mind me asking but I would assume that your fingerprints are everywhere.' Maxwell replied bitterly,

'Of course they bloody well are. You can't do something like this with fucking gloves on.'

'OK, calm down old chap,' replied Hawthorn quickly,

'...... we'll do a full sweep for prints as part of the clean up, if you can get us what we need in the next hour; that's all the time I can give you. I have just had an extremely harassing meeting with the Prime Minister and the balloon is about to go up, so get at it and come back to me as quickly as you can.'

The line went dead. Charles Hawthorn had rung off. Maxwell replaced the receiver and climbed the stairs again.

Mohammed angled his head up sharply as Maxwell re-entered the bedroom. He had recovered some of his color but had also developed a slight twitching movement in his right eye; a sure sign that the central nervous system was working overtime. Maxwell approached the bed and took his pulse, speaking softly as he did so.

'Well, my murdering little friend, this is what I have in store for you. Firstly I shall ask you a series of questions to which I need accurate answers. You will be asked once and if you refuse to reply, or I get the slightest impression you are not telling me the exact truth, I will inflict upon your body various degrees of pain and permanent injury. I have no time to waste and if you tell me what I wish to know, I could be gone from here in half an hour. If you do not, I will definitely be gone within the hour, but you will be left crippled for life or dead, depending on my mood. But, let me assure you of one other thing, if I do leave you here alive, you will wish you were dead.' Mohammed glowered back and screamed haughtily,

'You would be better to kill me, Armstrong, because if I live, you will surely die.' Maxwell continued in an even tone,

'That matters little to me, Mohammed. You have destroyed the one thing in my life that was worth living for; you have murdered or caused to be murdered and maimed, countless hundreds of people with your mindless assassination attempt, not to mention the small aside of having brutally slaughtered some of Africa's finest animals. I can see a faint element of your twisted values of justice in the first two actions, but the third is beyond comprehension. The death of Helga could, I suppose, in your way of thinking be put down to a simple accident and even the airport disaster to bad planning; but the rampant and uncontrolled killing of helpless wild animals could only have been done for sheer, unadulterated and personal pleasure. Because of all that, you must now suffer'

The Arab's pulse rate rose a fraction as Maxwell picked up the gaffa tape, tore off two strips and placed them over the shivering Arab's eyes.

'Now, my friend, let's get on with it. I want to know all the names of the members of the Unicorn and their objectives with regard to your manipulation of the Imam of Awabi' Mohammed spat in reply. It was the wrong thing to do.

'Fine,' said Maxwell. 'From now on we can do it my way.' He bent down to the floor and picked up the bucket of ice and then leant over the bed to pick up the razor sharp stiletto knife. He ran the edge of the knife along the side of Mohammed's face, not quite cutting it, but letting him feel the coldness and the sharpness of it.

'This is a very sharp knife my friend. I have asked you what I want to know once. You have refused to answer me. So, now I am going to cut your body all over, slicing up your skin and your beautiful face like the crackling on a pig.' At the word pig, the body on the bed shifted and then a dry sounding voice cursed in Arabic. His torturer continued in an even emotionless voice.

'No matter how much you cry for me to stop….which of course you will, I will carry on until there is not a clean, unscarred piece of skin on your fucking body. When I have finished, I will finally cut your balls off….and if you are lucky, I may allow you to keep them….. by stuffing them in your ugly mouth'

Some low moaning noises were now coming from the squirming body on the bed. Maxwell took the knife and with one single upward movement from under the light cotton thobe the Arab was wearing, sliced it open to reveal the man's full nakedness. He then placed the flat of the knife on Mohammed's thigh and pulled it slowly up toward his crutch. The Arab was now convulsing with all sorts of strange high keyed sounds breaking loose from a dribbling, quivering mouth. Maxwell leant forward and taped the mouth. The scene was set, the fear of certainty implanted. Maxwell knew confidently that he would have all he required in a matter of minutes. Torture did not make a mind focus on how to stop it or the possible pain of it, but the *fear* of the torture and the pain itself did. He took the ice bucket and pulled out a square ice cube and quickly started to run the edge of the cube sharply down each side of Mohammed's face. His prisoner began to scream behind the captivity of the tape as the melted water track from each movement, warmed by the skin temperature, left the already programmed mind of the victim feeling that each movement was the slice of a sharp knife; the trickling of warmness to be his own blood seeping from the myriad of wounds being inflicted upon him. He began to shake violently as his torturer continued slashing his body relentlessly with fresh ice cubes to keep a sharp edge. Maxwell knew he would have to watch his victim carefully unless he went in to shock and possible heart failure. After some minutes, he had covered the Arab's body more or less completely. The body itself was shivering uncontrollably. This was it. Maxwell ripped the tape from Mohammed's mouth to release a suppressed, piercing, harrowing scream the like of which he had not heard before. He leant over and whispered in his ear.

'Now for your balls you asshole'

The writhing body suddenly became limp. The scream lowered and turned to a verbal babbling; words tumbling out in Arabic and English. The smell of fear, of involuntarily released urine and feces filled the darkened room.

Maxwell checked the fingers. One of them would break loose soon and as a result, the exposed nerve endings would add yet another dimension to the cocktail of self realized agony that Mohammed would have to suffer this day.

The crazed jabbering shell of the man before him had broken; now perhaps, this whole disgusting episode of his life could be ended. He wiped his forehead on a corner of the stained bed-sheet and sat quite still for a moment or two in a difficult attempt to compose himself. He stood back up beside the bed and leant over the human mess in front of him. Words were now becoming intelligible. Maxwell walked purposefully over to a dresser beneath the shaded window where some writing paper and a pen were visible. He picked them up, moved back to the bed and began writing down names; seven of them in all.

*Tammam bin Abdullah*, brother of the Imam Sulayman bin Abdulla and leader of the so called Unicorn Movement and resident in Qatar.

*Mohammed Al Shukri*, Arab Gulf Council Minister without Portfolio and the naked, shivering wreck laying before him.

*Rasheed al Sheik*, secretary to the President of Iraq and obvious minder for the Imam and currently in Iraq.

*Mustafa Ibrahim*, Deputy Defense Minister of Syria.

*General Saleh Haji*, Member of the Egyptian Armed Forces Central Committee.

*Prince Mansour*, Air Force Commander in Saudi Arabia and finally *Salem al Thani*, Head of Civil Aviation, Dubai, now deceased.

Twenty minutes later he knew all he thought he needed to about the Unicorn and Tammam bin Abdullah along with the unfortunate Imam's drug therapy, courtesy of the KGB, and their plans to finally put the Imam away once the invasion of Europe had started; it went on and on. Maxwell stood over the still babbling body for some time deciding what to do with the remnants of this man who had brought him so much personal agony and turned him into the cold blooded killer and torturer he had been today. He would never be able to look at himself in the mirror again. He would never enjoy a night of truly restful sleep or lay again in the warm secure arms of a lovely woman.

Maxwell sighed a long, grief stricken inward sigh and picked up the shotgun. Before the torture he had planned only two ways out for Mohammed; if he didn't talk, he got the long and painfully slow way out which was the full dose of rat poison. If he did, he got the short and more humane way out; both barrels at short range. He raised the gun, eyes glazed, pulse quickening and hands trembling. Would this be the last and final evil act in this whole fucked up life that someone, somewhere, had planned for him?

He doubted it and in that chilling realization, pulled both triggers. Maxwell trod the stone stairway for the last time and rang Hawthorn. There was little preamble, he wanted the information. No way would he get anything until the director confirmed his safe passage out of the house and out of the country. Sir Charles ranted and raved down the phone but Maxwell wasn't listening. He put the telephone down, unlocked the front door and walked out into the teeming rain.

'Fuck 'em, fuck 'em all.' He shouted to the blackened clouds as he walked openly down the lane back to the car. If they were going to get him, they could do it here; but somehow he knew they wouldn't, not without the information they desperately needed packed away in his cerebral filing cabinet; a cabinet impossible to open unless he was alive. He didn't care anyway. He needed a rest, a hot shower and time to reflect and recover from the day's ordeal before he had to face Hawthorn and his crew of bandits again. Maxwell reached his car and instinctively checked it for signs of tampering. The car looked as if it was clean. He got in and carefully drove down the lane and back on to the main road, checking brakes and steering on the way. All seemed as he had left it. There was only one item left to check and that was the radio, a favorite toy of the rat-arsed brigade of assassins from C5. He pulled the car into a lay-by, got out and I leant back in to switch on the car radio at arm's length. It burst into life. He waited for thirty or forty seconds to ensure there was no time delay fuse or long acting gas release mechanism lurking somewhere. Relieved, he flopped back into the driver's seat and listened dejectedly to the beginning of the news on Radio Two, the station the radio had obviously been tuned into by the last hire customer. He checked the time, it was nine thirty-three. The news reader continued with the main item ....

'. . . and so the confirmation at six o'clock this evening of the joint Iraq, Kuwait declaration concerning repatriation of assets held in the west has been accompanied by a statement from Ankara, offering political support for the Arab move by Turkey, and requesting military support from Iraq. We have unconfirmed reports that a substantial re-disposition of forces is taking place along Turkish, Iraqi borders and joint Soviet Iraqi armored divisions are already moving in to the border area of Van on the edge of lake Van Golu, well within Turkish territory.'

So, it had started.

'The White House has issued a statement to the effect that non-negotiable claims of this type cannot be entertained by the United States Government and has countered with a declaration of intent to fix a new gold standard for dollar exchange as of midnight, eastern standard time today, unless the request for unconditional surrender of western held Iraqi and Kuwaiti assets is immediately withdrawn. In Brussels, the EEC President, Senor Bantellas has stated he is in constant communication with the member countries of the Arab Gulf Co-operation Council and sees the move by Iraq and Kuwait as an empty threat to European stability unless backed by the AGCC. Meanwhile the free market price of gold continues to rise and at the London close this afternoon reached a staggering ninety eight dollars an ounce with share prices the world over expected to tumble to new record lows by tomorrow .... '

Maxwell switched off the radio, slammed the car door shut, and started off back toward Henley. It was too late now. The deed had been done. Whether the Imam himself or the Iraqi President al-Bakr had made the declaration or not, he didn't know? A much bigger question lingered in his mind, knowing what he now knew; was the Imam still alive? One way or another, the Unicorn appeared to have won; the only satisfaction left to Maxwell was that now there were only five left to deal with instead of seven. He checked his watch once again as he turned the car on to the A40 and the date sprang up at him from out of the luminous dial face; October fourth, nineteen seventy three. Maxwell wondered 'what to-morrow would bring', being a final thought as he headed at speed toward the rats nest that was the eighteenth floor of Bowater House.

# EPILOGUE

At dawn on Saturday October 6th, 1973 a coalition of Arab States led by Egypt and Syria invaded Israel. It was the holiest day of Judaism, Yom Kippur and Israel was taken by surprise. Egyptian and Syrian forces crossed previous ceasefire lines to occupy the Sinai Peninsula in the south and the Golan Heights in the north. Iraq stood poised on the Jordanian border in the east.

In the early hours of Friday, October 5th, three troops of SAS from the Oman parachuted in to Qatar, kidnapped the leader of the Unicorn Conspiracy, Tammam bin Abdulla and extracted him to Cyprus by air through Bahrain. He was 'interviewed' by British SIS special operatives on the morning of October 5th, without much resistance as he told his interrogators all he thought they should safely be aware of. He knew they would need time to check out this new intelligence. He had not however indicated any possible moves on Israel or the actual plan to explode a nuclear device, not more than 250 miles from where the very interrogation itself was taking place. As the first tank tracks rolled toward the Suez Canal the attitude of the Arab conspirator's interrogators changed and within two hours they had the full details.

The vessel carrying the Russian RDS-4 nuclear bomb was quickly identified in Limmasol Harbour. The nuclear device was disarmed and despatched to the UK on an unmarked C130 Hercules the very same day. The Prime Minister of Israel, Golda Meir was fully briefed on the known details of the conspiracy as were the Americans and Russians. This prompted a fierce fight-back by Israeli troops who launched a four day counter-offensive against the Arab invaders. The United Nations brokered a cease fire of sorts on October 22nd but Israel still had work to do encircling the Egyptian Third Army. Would the Russians step in? It was touch and go with the Americans hovering reluctantly on the brink of full blown military support for Israel. A second ceasefire was imposed on October 25th that finally brought an end to the war.

The Iraqis moved their forces back from the Jordanian border territory in no mood to take on a nation that was now only 40 kilometres from Damascus and 100 kilometres from Cairo. But what of the other conspirators involved in Unicorn.

*Rasheed al Sheik – Private Secretary to the President of Iraq*: He was involved in a car accident on his way to the command and control centre in Kirkuk in the early hours of Saturday, October 6th. He suffered head injuries and died on the operating table at 0700 Hrs as confirmed by his Russian surgeons.

*Prince Mansour – Saudi Air Force Commander:* He escaped in his own aeroplane from his base in Riyadh and flew to the Sudan during the evening of October 5th. He was found dead in the house of a Sudanese Air Force Captain with gunshot wounds to the head one week later.

*Mustafa Ibrahim*, the Syrian Deputy Defence Minister and *Lt General Saleh Haji*, member of the Egyptian Armed Forces Central Committee were present at the 'Kilometre 101' disengagement talks with Israel on October 28th. They both returned to their own countries on that day and were never heard of again.

*Tammam bin Abdullah*, brother of the Imam Sulayman bin Abdulla committed suicide, it was rumoured. However, no one from the British SIS could be definitive as to where and how.

*The Imam Sulayman bin Abdullah* himself was a very ill man and developed severe pneumonia at the end of October, dying peacefully in his bed on the morning of Sunday November 4th, 1973.

The Arab plan to extend the voice of Islam westward had failed as did the demand for repatriation of assets. America and the USSR moved back from the very brink of the start of World War Three and the money markets in Europe, the USA and the Far East now had a new problem to contend with. The 1973 oil crisis started in October 1973 as a result of OAPEC proclaiming an oil embargo on all countries seen to have supported Israel in the Yom Kippur war. It lasted until March 1974 when sense began to prevail in the world of International politics. It would take years and maybe a decade or two before the world financial situation improved and world stock markets bottomed out. Many lessons were learnt during this period of severe financial budgetary restrictions imposed by governments all over the world. They still serve as a yardstick to modern financial institutions to ensure that they could never get in to such a mess ever again. Unfortunately, this was very much wishful thinking.

# ABOUT THE AUTHOR

Quentin Cope was born in to a nearly bankrupt, struggling post war Britain in 1946 and spent a generally miserable youth amongst the beautiful rolling hills and dry stone walls of rural Oxfordshire. He swapped mediocrity and an unsatisfactory education for a life of absolute adventure by joining Her Majesties Royal Air Force as a boy of fifteen. He never looked back. The cold war was in full swing and nuclear war was a real and frightening threat. After serving time on 58Sqdn, Photo Reconnaissance playing about with Canberra PR9 spy planes, Quentin decided he needed to travel and see the world from the ground. He left the Air Force and working for a major UK Telecommunications company, voyaged extensively to strange places, working on strange projects for even stranger governments.

In 1973, he travelled to Dubai, a place on a map literally no one had heard of, blessed with a few tarmac roads, several mosques, infrequent electricity and even less frequent water supplies. For the next 25 years he became part of that hard living, hard drinking, frontier brigade that enabled a complete, antiseptic and self reflecting glass city to rise out of the parched and unforgiving desert; a place that is now the home of multi millionaires, the odd family of deposed royalty and a sprinkling of International scam merchants. Using his own aero-plane, Quentin travelled extensively throughout the Arabian Gulf and used Dubai as a base to see much of the Indian Sub Continent, East Africa and the Far East. He now leads a much more settled life at a substantially slower pace, mainly in Spain, where the weather is often good enough and the people likeable enough to inspire him to write full time.

Made in the USA
Charleston, SC
29 July 2012